Praise for

"Utterly unique, immersive an[...]
unputdownable entry into the [...]
Murder is a twisty, magical delight and I loved every second."
— Frances White, author of *Voyage of the Damned*

"Filled with conundrums, murder most foul, and more spells than you can shake a magic wand at, this original novel is a puzzler's delight."
— Nita Prose, #1 *New York Times* bestselling author of The Maid series

"*Knives Out*, but it's a family of sorcerers—an original and wildly entertaining mystery with a choose-your-own-adventure dimension that keeps you guessing until the very last page. Marais draws the reader in with a pantheon of layered, vicious characters and smart, interactive puzzles. Hats off!"
— Jenna Satterthwaite, author of *Made for You* and *The New Year's Party*

"*A Most Puzzling Murder* combines so many of my favorites—magic, family secrets, surprising twists, interactive puzzles, and a compelling mystery I'm still thinking about. This clever, unique book breaks all the rules in the most fun way. I loved taking part in solving the mystery!"
— Gloria Chao, author of *The Ex-Girlfriend Murder Club*

"How can so many delights be contained within one novel? A cracking mystery, a *Succession*-level feud in a magical family, talking animals, a brilliant heroine with a wounded heart that needs healing, and puzzles.... Bianca Marais's *A Most Puzzling Murder* is a treasure trove disguised as a book."
— Elizabeth Renzetti, author of *What She Said*

"*Buffy the Vampire Slayer* meets *Murder, She Wrote* in this fun, fresh and quirky take on a gothic mystery."
— Jessica Bull, author of the Miss Austen Investigates series

"*A Most Puzzling Murder* is a delightfully one-of-a-kind reading experience. Not just because the reader gets to solve a variety of clever puzzles alongside the characters (bring your pencil and notepad!). But also for a beguiling ensemble cast that are both wickedly fun and unexpectedly heartrending."
— Kirthana Ramisetti, author of *Dava Shastri's Last Day*

"*A Most Puzzling Murder* is a masterclass in multitasking. Puzzles and plot are brilliantly interwoven to fuel this turbo-charged concept. The most fun I've had reading a book in a long time. A truly outstanding accomplishment."
— Sue Hincenbergs, author of *The Retirement Plan*

Also by Bianca Marais

The Witches of Moonshyne Manor
Hum If You Don't Know the Words
If You Want to Make God Laugh

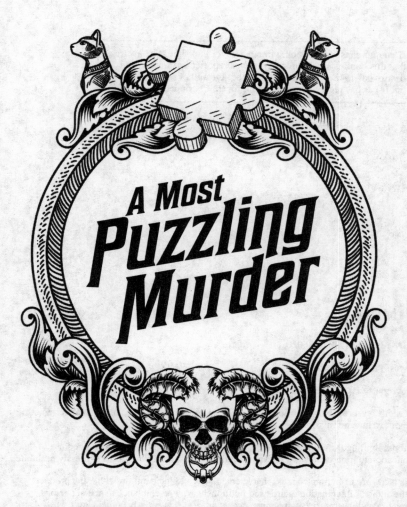

A Most Puzzling Murder

BIANCA MARAIS

MIRA

//IMIRA™

ISBN-13: 978-0-7783-6860-1

A Most Puzzling Murder

Recycling programs
for this product may
not exist in your area.

Mira
22 Adelaide St. West, 41st Floor
Toronto, Ontario M5H 4E3, Canada
MIRABooks.com

Printed in U.S.A.

For my awesome parents,
Lynda and Chris,
and my fabulous mother-in-law,
Barbara.
And for the rest of the reprobates in the family
who, while being dodgy AF,
are at least not as dodgy as the Scruffmores.

Dear Intrepid Reader,

Consider yourself warned; nothing in these pages is quite what it appears.

As our heroine, Destiny Whip, struggles to uncover the secrets of her past, which are somehow interwoven with the Scruffmore family's own dark machinations, she will be tasked with solving myriad cryptic clues, puzzles, and riddles.

You can do the same alongside her, perhaps even beating her in the race to figure it all out. After all, you'll have insider information that Destiny isn't privy to, and in some instances, you'll actually become different characters in the occasional Choose Your Own Conundrum chapters. Pick wisely in these sections, as your decisions will have consequences in terms of what new information gets revealed to you.

Pay close attention because almost everything is a clue, including the symbols at the top of each chapter, which are part of a greater puzzle. Only when you see ★★ will you be called upon to solve whichever puzzle is being presented to you. This may require going back to earlier chapters to make sense of information whose purpose wasn't clear at the time. You'll also have opportunities throughout the story to engage with Destiny herself, emailing her for clues and important bonus content.

As you're reading, if you spot something that might be important later on, go ahead and underline it or make a note in the text. If the thought of writing in these pages fills you with horror, let me assure you that this book is vastly different from other more prim and proper tomes. This most peculiar tale positively *demands* that you engage with it. Each time you bring pen to paper, imagine the pages purring in appreciation.

If this is a library book, or another format you can't mark up, don't fear. You'll find a downloadable booklet on my website that includes all the puzzles as well as various sections for note-taking.

Now, if getting down with your bad code-breaking self sounds nerve-racking, please don't panic. There's absolutely no need to chuck this book at the person who recommended it, especially not if that person is a bookseller. (*Never* chuck anything at a bookseller. Except wads of cash for more books. And maybe snacks!) You can skip each puzzle entirely by flipping to the relevant page at the back for the answer.

The puzzles all vary with regard to the degree of difficulty and the type of skill set required to solve them. Struggling with one doesn't mean you'll battle with all of them. At least give them a try because you just might surprise yourself. And isn't that one of the most incredible experiences of all in this puzzling adventure that we call life?

Signed,
Your Chief Exasperator,
Bianca

CHAPTER 1

Destiny

Sunday—9:57 a.m.

Destiny Whip warily eyes her bedside table which could easily be mistaken for a miniature graveyard, what with all the little pills neatly lined in staggered rows, positioned upright like tiny headstones. It certainly feels as though she's regarding the burial ground of her hopes and dreams, haunted by the specter of the enormous potential she's so dismally failed to live up to.

When you're declared a child prodigy, everyone expects you to go far in life, but all Destiny has managed today is a slow shuffle to and from the bathroom. Even that required Herculean reserves of energy.

Balancing her laptop on her knees, she reaches to the farthest side of the bed for her emotional-support urn, pulling it close and tucking it into her armpit as though cuddling a teddy bear. She kisses the top of the teardrop shape, the metal cold against her chapped lips.

Bex appears in Destiny's doorway, leaning her head against the frame. "Morning, sunshine."

Her best friend is still too scrawny, but not nearly as emaciated as she was a year ago when all she feasted on was beauty magazines and models' Instagram pages rather than anything resembling food. Bex looks mostly healthy again, her long chestnut hair gleaming, the hollows of her cheeks no longer reminiscent of sinkholes.

"You okay?" Bex asks, the corners of her mouth turned down.

It's the anniversary of the accident today, one year somehow crawling by on scraped knees.

Some people act like severe depression is a tarnish that can be polished off with the application of enough elbow grease. Luckily, Bex isn't one of them.

Destiny tries to speak, but a knot of regret is so tangled up in her throat that the words don't stand a chance.

Her laptop suddenly squawks with an incoming video call. In the months since Destiny has been seeing Dr. Shepherd, they've never had a virtual consultation over a weekend. But today is going to be a tough one, which is why the psychiatrist insisted on the appointment.

As the ringing continues, Destiny gently places the urn beside her and reaches for her notebook. She pages to the list of tasks the doctor suggested last month.

Bex sidles up, reading over her shoulder.

1. *Leave the apartment once a day to go for a walk or grab a coffee.*
2. *Reach out to an old friend or colleague to suggest a meetup.*
3. *Replace all the dead plants.*
4. *Keep a dream journal about the white-haired ghost woman.*
5. *Email the council expressing my wish to return.*
6. *Accept one of the consultancies I've been offered (one that doesn't require travel).*
7. *Work on forgiving Nate.*
8. *Limit my interactions with Bex.*

Bex side-eyes the last item on the list. "Rude," she huffs. "You'd think I was a bad influence or something."

Rather than answering Bex or the incoming call, Destiny thinks of how she's never flunked an assignment in her entire life. Always top of her class, and despite being admitted to university as a twelve-year-old, Destiny cannot fathom this degree of failure.

She's ticked nothing off the list, not even throwing away the plants whose shriveled corpses goad her, their untimely deaths undoubtedly due to the curtains constantly being drawn tight. That, and Destiny forgetting to water them.

The laptop's ringing grates on Destiny's nerves, but she can't force herself to answer and face Dr. Shepherd's disappointment. It will be carefully concealed, of course, with the psychiatrist gently pointing out there's always next week, or the week after that, to achieve these seemingly simple goals. But it doesn't matter how much of an extension Destiny is given.

It's no use.

For how can she possibly cut ties with Bex, who's her dearest, not to mention only, friend?

Plus, there's no way the Council of Enigmatologists will take her back after she's been AWOL for so long. Each time an envelope drops through the mail slot, Destiny fully expects it to be a letter informing her that they've revoked her membership. It hurts to remember how thrilled she was to be appointed president of the prestigious group just thirteen months ago, and how she, Bex, and Nate all splurged on a fancy dinner to celebrate.

When the call finally drops, Bex exhales, a long whoosh of defeat. "I know I shouldn't enable you with all the talking, but it's not like I can call anyone on your behalf."

They both look down at the image on the home screen of Destiny's laptop.

It's a photo that was taken thirteen years ago when Destiny was eight. In it, her mother's arm is flung across Annie's shoulders, happiness radiating from the two best friends in waves. Destiny's eyes fill with tears as she studies her mother's straight black hair and pale skin, and those enormous glasses obscuring most of her face.

Jutting her chin at Liz, Bex murmurs, "I wish I'd known her."

Destiny nods before turning her attention to Annie, with her striking Afro and beaded shoulder-duster earrings, and her smile as bright as the sun.

The image was captured two weeks before Liz died, and a year before the paperwork would go through to officially make Annie Destiny's second adoptive mother. Their deaths were wrenching losses, tearings in the fabric of Destiny's being that she never quite stitched back together.

There were times in the *before* when Destiny experienced the sting of loneliness, that awful yearning of the one forever stuck outside, nose and palms pressed against the cold glass, gazing in at what belonging looked like: foreheads bent together, raucous laughter elicited by inside jokes, sentences finished by those who knew you best.

But this is not loneliness, in the same way that a drop of water is not a deluge, the way a sigh is not a hurricane.

"I'm so sorry that you're having such a rough time of it," Bex says, reaching out to tuck a flaming red curl behind Destiny's ear. She freezes upon seeing Destiny's expression, her hand hovering like a ghost between them. "A year is a long time, though, and Dr. Shepherd is right despite the fact that she clearly has it in for me. You need to move on."

God, that Bex is apologizing to *her*, of all people, when everything that happened was Destiny's fault.

"No, *I'm* sorry," Destiny says, her voice pulled so taut that it snaps. Seeing the pills all standing to attention—no longer a cemetery full of headstones, but rather an army ready to fight the last battle—Destiny reaches for the urn again, stroking it like a security blanket. "If you stop talking to me, Bex, I don't know what I'll do."

"Not gonna happen," Bex replies breezily. And then more firmly she says, "Okay, it's tough love time. You seriously need to shower because you're stinking up the place. Plus, the kitchen needs cleaning. Those take-out containers have grown thumbs. I swear I caught them trying to hitch a ride to the nearest primordial swamp."

Destiny laughs at how incredibly bossy Bex is.

Especially for a dead person.

Still, it's reassuring that no matter how much has changed, some things stay exactly the same.

CHAPTER 2

Destiny

Sunday—10:15 a.m.

Destiny flinches at the unmistakable sound of the mail slot creaking open and a letter fluttering through. If she was waiting for a sign, then the arrival of a letter from the council would surely be it.

"Ignore it," Bex pleads as Destiny pushes her laptop aside to get out of bed. "Who needs those losers anyway?"

Bex has never understood Destiny's affinity for the council, but then why would she? Even before she died, Bex always managed to fit in. Near the end, when her eating disorder began devouring her whole, most people didn't even notice because she constantly surrounded herself with similarly emaciated women in an industry that normalized her illness.

But until the council, Destiny never knew what it was like to have peers.

When other children her age were being invited to birthday parties, or endlessly obsessing over their first crushes, Destiny was attending lectures at Yale, not only thoroughly annoying her professors—who felt they were above babysitting duties— but also the other students, who saw her as a precocious pain in the ass whose presence made them all look bad.

Nerd. Geek. Dork. Dweeb. Freak. Brownnose. Boffin. Propeller-Head. Prodigy. Wonk.

They called her everything but her name, making Destiny feel like a lone pelican in a flamboyance of flamingos, so bumbling and awkward that she'd never fit in even if she doused herself with pink paint and walked on stilts.

But the day she got the council's invitation, those hallowed hallways opening for her, Destiny found a squadron of other pelicans, with their shoulders hunched and giant beaks agape, devouring knowledge as hungrily and indiscriminately as she did. They welcomed her as a contemporary, someone to be consulted rather than avoided, allowing Destiny—for the very first time in her life—to embrace her very pelican-ness.

And now here she is, about to be booted out of the only club she's ever cared about.

Shuffling to the front door, she spots a dove gray envelope that's landed face up on the bamboo flooring, her name written across it in antiquated script. **Destiny Whip**. There's no address or stamp, which Destiny thinks is strange until she remembers that it's a Sunday, and that no postal workers will be delivering mail today.

She peers out through the peephole, spotting a cloak so black that it's almost blue. It disappears into the elevator with a swoosh, a matador challenging a bull, before the doors ding closed.

A heaviness gathers and settles in Destiny's stomach. Apparently, the council is so desperate to take her name off their letterheads that they've sent an emissary on the weekend. She wonders which one drew the short stick. Her money's on poor Dodkins, a delightfully eccentric little man whose area of specialty is nineteenth-century puzzle boxes from the Hakone region of Japan.

Sighing, Destiny trudges back to bed. Her laptop rings again, Dr. Shepherd calling once more, but Destiny slams it closed, not wanting any witnesses to this humiliation.

Bex sits next to Destiny, ineffectually trying to fluff the pillows. "The envelope doesn't have the pretentious wax seal, so it can't be from the council. Maybe you've been nominated for another award," she exclaims, ever the optimist.

But no, that can't be it. All of Destiny's work correspondence occurs over email. Her inbox full of hundreds of unread emails can attest to that.

After slicing the envelope open with the lone jagged fingernail she hasn't gnawed off yet, Destiny withdraws the page.

Dearest Ms. Whip,

I hereby acknowledge receipt of your application to replace Ms. Le Roux as the Scruffmore family historian. I'm sure you know how coveted the position is—it's no secret that ours is a most illustrious and mysterious lineage—and so I congratulate you on your compelling application and for making the short list of two approved applicants.

Our family history has been a rather fascinating one with most of the information required to unlocking it hidden within the Scruffmore vault, safe from prying eyes. Were you to be successful, you would be one of the rare outsiders granted access to those thousands of records that have come from all over the world, wherever a Scruffmore has lived in the past two thousand years.

Come via the last ferry on the 27th of February and then make your way to the Grimshaw Inn and Tavern for the night. Tell them arrangements have been made and all expenses will be taken care of. Be at the castle on the morning of the 28th ahead of your interview at 12 p.m. Should you be awarded the position, the secrets of the vault will be yours to be revealed.

Until then,

Mordecai Scruffmore

Scruffmore Castle
Eerie Island

P.S. Your ferry tickets have been purchased. The ticket number for the 27th is L2-3-3-4-5-7-7-8-8-9-12-12-14-14-14-16-13-4-7 and that of the return is W1-7-10-2-4-2-4-5-11-2-1-11-2-4-5-9-8-1-9.

The original read through is confusing.

"Told you it would be something interesting," Bex crows.

"But I'm not a historian," Destiny replies, brow furrowed. "And I never applied for this position."

"Hmm, weird," Bex says, tapping her French manicure against her chin. "Have you ever heard of the Scruffmore family?"

Destiny mulls it over. "No." The name is unusual enough that she'd remember it.

"Google them," Bex instructs, her answer to everything.

Destiny opens her laptop again with a pang of guilt over Dr. Shepherd's two missed calls. She makes a mental note to pay for the consultation and email an apology.

Googling the Scruffmore family gets zero hits. Same goes for Mordecai Scruffmore. Nor is there mention anywhere of the job listing. Eerie Island comes up as a vague blip on the map about thirty miles offshore from the town of Gwillumbury. While the ferry terminal is listed as being a three-hour train trip away, there isn't any mention of the island's castle or the Grimshaw Inn and Tavern. There are no pictures of the island at all, not even satellite images on Google Earth.

"What the hell?" Destiny mutters.

Her mind begins to fizz like it's being carbonated. She welcomes the old familiar sensation, how alive it makes her feel. Doing a deeper dive, Destiny scrolls through dozens of search engine result pages before finally being rewarded with one grainy photograph of Mordecai Scruffmore. It's listed, with no explanation beyond being captioned with his name, on a defunct website that was designed before Destiny was even born.

"Well. Isn't he delightful?" Bex murmurs, studying all the star tattoos inked across Mordecai Scruffmore's forehead.

While Destiny can believe some kind of administrative error resulted in the letter being sent to her, she can't understand why there's barely any mention of the Scruffmores or their island anywhere on the internet, especially not if the family is as prestigious as they claim.

Picking up the page, she reads it again, noting that today is the 27th of February, the day on which she's meant to arrive.

She wonders if this is some kind of prank, but something about the letter niggles. As she studies it more closely, Destiny's jaw drops when she spots the key to unlocking the hidden message. ★★[1]

★ ★ ★

Once the secret has revealed itself, Destiny's hands begin to shake so violently that she puts the page down so she won't rip it. This is the letter she's been waiting her entire life for, the one she never dared believe would actually arrive. She feels lightheaded, sick with expectation.

The last time she felt this way was when she found the *other* letter, the one that arrived mere days before her mother's death.

That one was signed: *Yours, Kye.*

Mordecai and Kye. Two mysterious letters, arriving thirteen years apart, signed with similar names.

That can't be a coincidence, surely?

Destiny's heartbeat stomps out a rapturous percussion of something she hasn't felt in a long time. It takes her a moment to identify it as hope.

---

1. You now have all the information you require to figure out the key to unlocking the hidden message. If you need a clue to assist you, email DestinyWhipClue@gmail.com using the subject line Clue One. Once you've uncovered it, turn to page 457 to check your answer.

CHAPTER 3

Destiny

Sunday—11:02 a.m.

Destiny's fingers tremble against the keyboard as she looks up the ferry schedule from Gwillumbury to Eerie Island. The last boat leaves at 7:00 p.m. She doesn't have any time to waste considering that she still has to pack, embark on an hour-long walk to Peddington Station, and then endure a three-hour train trip before she can board the ferry.

But first, she'll have to make a list.

She grabs her notebook and pen to jot down all her questions.

1. *Does Mordecai Scruffmore know who my biological parents are?*
2. *Does he know why I haven't been able to find any records of them, or of my birth, at all?*

She hesitates, biting the tip of the pen, almost too scared to express the yearning that feels too much like the grabby hands of an infant reaching for the moon.

3. *Is there a chance Mordecai could be my father?*

Destiny's breath catches at the audacity of committing this

question to paper. Now that it's written down, a permanent record, she can't erase it. Even if she rips the page up and flushes it down the toilet, there is no going back in time to unask it.

"Wouldn't he have just told you that in the letter, though?" Bex asks gently. "Why all this subterfuge?"

Destiny shushes her so she can finish the rest of her questions.

4. *Did Mordecai know either, or both, of my adoptive mothers?*
5. *Does he know what happened to Liz?*
6. *Can he explain the two strange dreams that came true?*
7. *Does my biological family want to meet me?*

This last question is too much. Hope is one thing when it's a window cracked open to let the breeze in. This is the equivalent of ripping off the whole damn roof. Destiny snaps her notebook shut so she doesn't have to see the physical manifestation of her raw need.

She wrestles a backpack from the depths of her closet, then sets it down on her bed before flinging clothes into it. The rising anxiety sends her rushing to open her old jewelry box and withdraw the necklace, the last thing her mother gave her.

The pendant is crafted from a multicolored stone that's anchored in place by curlicues of copper wiring. Destiny hates the memories associated with the thing but can't imagine leaving without it. Despite her reluctance to wear it, she always feels calmer and more focused as soon as the amulet is clasped around her neck.

Wedging the notebook and urn into the backpack, she whispers, "You've got this."

It's a lie, of course, but sometimes lies are the kindest things we ever tell ourselves.

CHAPTER 4

Destiny

Sunday—7:45 p.m.

As the barnacled ferry struggles to escape the fortress of fog that's rolled in seemingly out of nowhere, Destiny tries not to think about how the haze enveloping them is the *exact* shade of gray as the mysterious letter's envelope, not to mention the ashes cradled in the urn.

Try as she might, though, it's impossible to wrangle her racing thoughts or slow the whirring hamster wheel of her mind.

"About as futile as farting against thunder," Bex notes, laughing.

Before Destiny can issue a retort, a blustery wind picks up. And just like that, as quickly as the swirling sea smoke first swallowed the boat, its cottony shroud is now snatched away. Destiny's anxiety eases, which would be a relief if it weren't for the enormous waves now being whipped into a frenzy all around them.

Fighting to keep her balance, she's just gotten both hands white-knuckling the railing when the ferry rears up so steeply that she temporarily loses sight of the roiling ocean. As they slam into a trough, she gets drenched by the spray, swallowing a mouthful of pooling saliva mixed with seawater. She retches over the side of the ferry.

When she's done heaving, Destiny swipes at her mouth and gasps as she spots what looks like a giant shark tooth rising from the ocean. It takes her a moment to realize it isn't an enormous sea creature but, in fact, their destination.

Her spirits sink.

Eerie Island is not at all how she imagined it, which was more like a cross between Portofino and a quaint Cornwall fishing village. As she stares at the imposing landscape that's getting closer by the second—almost as though it's coming *at* them rather than the other way around—she can't help but think how the island appears to have assembled itself entirely out of sword tips, arrowheads, and shards of glass, all objects shaped like weapons of war.

Bad things happen there.

Destiny isn't sure where the certainty comes from, but it makes her tremble, as does the unpredictable—almost supernatural—weather they've encountered since leaving the port. It's like being haunted, only out on the open seas. Recalling the white-haired ghost woman from her recurring dream heightens her unease.

Everything about the jagged outcrop screams: *Keep away, turn back!*

But how can Destiny possibly heed that warning considering the arrival of the mysterious invitation?

After what happened to Liz—and then, after all those years spent futilely searching for her biological parents, experiencing nothing but dead ends and doors firmly shut in her face—the hidden message validates what Destiny has always suspected.

Her life is a twenty-one-year-old enigma that's begging to be solved.

If everyone has an origin story, then hers resides in a locked book on a high shelf in a secret room that no one's ever drawn a map to.

Which is why nothing—certainly not mercurial weather, inhospitable landscapes, or bad premonitions—will prevent her from getting to Eerie Island. *I'm not coming for a vacation*, she reminds herself. *I'm here to unlock the door to the past so that I can find a pathway into the future.*

As the waves continue to assault the ferry, Destiny crab-walks back inside the cabin and retrieves her phone to listen to her voicemails.

"Hey, Tiny," Nate's comforting baritone says. "I just wanted to check in and see how you're doing. I'm sorry about our fight and what I said. It's all going to be fine so try not to worry so much, okay? Love you."

The message stings despite the apology. It's one thing suspecting something unspeakable about yourself—it's quite another having someone you love confirm it.

But no, she's not going to dwell on this now.

Heading for a bench, Destiny opens her backpack. Reaching under the urn, its brass icy against her fingers, Destiny swaps out her phone for the notebook. Just holding the pages reassures her that she's done the right thing by coming. Questions attract answers. And answers are like periods at the ends of sentences; they bring closure, which is what makes them so satisfying, especially since closure is something that's been in high demand, but very limited supply, during her short life.

The door leading to the cabin upstairs suddenly slams closed and Destiny looks up to spot a beautiful woman stepping across the threshold.

She's already chilled to the bone, but a different kind of iciness spreads through her now, as though glaciers are carving their way through her arteries.

Oh my god, Destiny thinks, slack-jawed as she stares at the apparition. *No. No, that can't possibly be.*

CHAPTER 5

Destiny

Sunday—8:02 p.m.

In her shock, Destiny drops the notebook and then scrambles to rescue it before the water sloshing around the cabin floor can seep into the pages. When she looks up again, her breath catches, and her teeth begin to chatter.

The woman, who appears to be in her late thirties, is whippet thin and dressed in a frilly Victorian blouse enveloped by a black leather corset. A tiered skirt, long at the back and short at the front, reveals slender legs and lace-up leather boots. White-blond hair, matching equally pale skin, cascades down her shoulders in shiny waves. Her makeup is immaculate. A stark coat of red lipstick gouges her face like a fresh wound.

This is the ghost woman from Destiny's nightmares, the one who steps through a solid wall, night after night after night.

Her heartbeat stutters. While she studies the stranger, who's now reached for her phone to take a call, there's a part of Destiny that hopes this can all be logically explained by consulting a neurologist and requesting a battery of tests. If she's suffering from the kind of temporal lobe seizure that makes so many people believe they're experiencing déjà vu, then Nate would be wrong, and Destiny isn't losing it. She just has some faulty wiring that can be fixed with the right medication.

"Déjà vu my ass," Bex huffs. "This is the *third* time you've dreamed something that came true." And then she adds in an injured tone, "Not that you ever told me about the first time, mind you. It definitely would have helped put things into perspective."

Destiny stiffens. "I wish I could go back and——"

"If wishes were fishes, we'd all swim in riches." Bex's statement is the verbal equivalent of a shrug. "But," she continues, voice sharpening, "if you really want to prove Nate wrong, here's your chance. Focus!"

Destiny nods, swallowing hard as she sidles up close enough to be hit by the overpowering scent of sandalwood perfume.

The woman is talking on her cell phone, yelling to be heard above the crashing waves. "From the gallery...Yes, a few days... Mr. Futon...the Lorenzetti will be arriving...a look next week..."

Destiny eavesdrops as best she can, but it's difficult with the wind snatching so many of the words away.

When the woman abruptly ends her call, she startles at Destiny's proximity, looking at her with moss-colored eyes.

Destiny gulps then, half expecting to see some kind of dawning realization. For if she recognizes the stranger, there's surely a chance that the stranger might recognize Destiny in return.

What Destiny isn't expecting is for the woman to grimace and back away in the manner of someone encountering roadkill. Destiny flushes, realizing she must look an awful fright with mascara streaked down her cheeks and wet hair clinging to her face in miserable rat tails. Not to mention how she's dripping salty puddles everywhere. Under the scrutiny, Destiny also becomes painfully aware of how her belly mushrooms over the top of her jeans, and how tightly the material cuts into the spread of her thighs.

It's clear from the woman's scathing expression that these are all failings on Destiny's part, ones she should be deeply ashamed of. As the world has taught her, and continues to reinforce, it doesn't matter what Destiny has achieved, not so long as her brilliant mind continues to be wrapped in such undesirable packaging. The greeting card sentiments are all liars: it's definitely not what's on the inside that counts.

"To hell with that," Bex spits. "No one can make you feel inferior without your consent. Trust me, I know, so don't you dare let this little trinket intimidate you. Speak up!"

Destiny would normally *never* start a conversation with someone this intimidating. The woman's facade is a shiny bastion; everything about it screams that its walls were built extra high specifically to keep riffraff like Destiny out. But there's nothing, not in Destiny's entire life, that's ever been more irresistible than a mystery. Curiosity trumps insecurity every single time.

Fear is a powerful motivator too. For whatever is happening here can only lead to terrifying outcomes, ones completely out of Destiny's control.

Running a trembling hand through her knotted hair while swiping under her eyes with her other, she blurts, "Hello, I'm Destiny! Isn't this just the most terrible storm?"

"Tempest," the woman replies coolly.

Destiny smiles, overjoyed to meet a fellow lexiphile. "It certainly *is* a tempest," she agrees, lurching sideways as another wave batters the boat. "That's the absolute perfect word for it."

"No," the woman clarifies, rolling her eyes. "*I'm* Tempest."

"Oh, what a lovely name." Destiny reaches out an icy hand in greeting, partly out of habit, and partly because she wants to make sure Tempest *isn't* a ghost. Since that's what she dreamed her to be, it's the most obvious hypothesis to test for first, no matter how implausible the whole scenario.

As their hands connect—*so, not a ghost who smells of sandalwood!*—Tempest looks disgusted as she regards Destiny's wrinkled fingers, which resemble those of a corpse that's just been hauled from a watery grave.

"Isn't it fascinating how our skin does that?" Destiny asks.

Tempest doesn't look remotely fascinated, but Destiny continues to babble. The longer she can keep the woman engaging with her, the likelier she is to gather enough clues to figure out what's going on. "Did you know that it was an evolutionary neurobiologist in Idaho who suggested that skin wrinkling, being an active process, must have an evolutionary function? And as I discovered earlier while hanging on to a railing outside, I have to agree with his conclusions. Ridged fingers really *do* give a better grip in wet conditions."

"For cripes' sake," Tempest mutters, shaking her head and looking even more revolted than before. Scrutinizing Destiny in a way that makes her feel like a specimen under a microscope, Tempest says, "Your eyes are two different colors." It sounds like an accusation rather than an observation.

It's clear that Tempest doesn't approve of someone who can't be bothered to ensure that their irises match. Which says something about her, as does her complete lack of curiosity—even her revulsion—about how her own body works. She was also deferential and polite with whomever she spoke with on the phone (clearly a superior), and yet she has no compunction with being so incredibly rude to Destiny (someone she deems inferior).

These are observations that Destiny stores away in the *Useful Information Folder* that opens in her mind each time she goes into mystery-solving mode. She also detects regional dialect use and an unpolished accent that occasionally peeks out from behind Tempest's more refined one. Another interesting bit of insight, since it's been Destiny's experience that people only rewrite their history when they're ashamed of it, and Tempest is clearly a person who's worked very hard to reinvent herself.

Aware that her racing thoughts have created an awkward silence, and that Tempest is now glaring at her while waiting for an answer, Destiny says, "Yes, sorry! One eye is amber, and the other is blue. It's called heterochromia and it's caused by a gene mutation. As is my red hair." She forces a laugh. "I may as well be a mutant, all things considered."

Regarding Destiny as though she *were* a mutant, Tempest says, "You also have some kind of gunk down your front." She nods at a khaki stain on Destiny's T-shirt. "Though I can't *begin* to imagine what it might be," she adds, shuddering.

"That's probably from the muffin I threw up earlier," Destiny answers.

Tempest pulls a face as if to say: *What the* hell *is wrong with you?*

A lot, Destiny is tempted to reply. *I've been so debilitated by grief that this is the first time I've left my apartment in a year. It's been so bad that I've had to consult with my psychiatrist via Zoom three times a week from the safety of my bed. You're one of the first people, besides Dr. Shepherd, that I've had a conversation with in all that time.*

My best friend died, she also wants to explain, *and I carry around an emotional-support urn. I can't travel in cars anymore, which has made the trip here much harder than it needed to be. I was a child prodigy and am a certified genius, but the problem with that degree of intelligence is foolishly believing you have all the answers because you always did.*

But guess what? Life isn't predictable or orderly like data or facts. It's messy. It doesn't let you study for it; there are no mock exams.

Also, your presence here is terrifying. You are a harbinger that can only signal doom.

But Destiny can't say any of that. Instead, she asks what she's wanted to know all along. "Why are you visiting the island?"

Tempest opens her mouth but before she can answer, the ferry lurches and then shudders.

"We have arrived at Eerie Island," the captain announces over the crackling speakers. "Get the hell off the boat before we're battered to matchsticks."

Tempest dashes to the luggage hold while Destiny wrestles with her backpack, the tangled straps putting up a fight. Battling to keep her balance *and* not throw up again, Destiny bends over, hands on her knees, to take a few deep breaths. When she finally straightens up and staggers from the ferry, lightning zigzags overhead as raindrops begin to pelt down.

Looking out for Tempest while sprinting to the tiny ferry terminal, she's surprised to see a horse and carriage trundling up the hill like something from a Dickens novel. Tempest is nowhere to be seen and neither are there any cars about. Their absence is reassuring, one less thing for Destiny to have to worry about.

She's about to enter the odd little structure when an ancient man, his spine curved like a pirate's hook, steps outside and locks the door behind him.

"Hello," Destiny says. "Could you please tell me where I might find the Grimshaw Inn and Tavern?"

The old man points up the hill. "That was the last taxi."

Destiny has no intention of catching a taxi, but she's still taken aback. "What? That horse and buggy?" Destiny asks, incredulous. "*That's* the taxi?"

"Yep." And, before Destiny can extract any further information, he's marching away to a steep set of stairs carved into the rock face.

There's a crack of thunder as Destiny ducks under the overhang for shelter. She can't believe she let Tempest get away without so much as a clue as to why she might have appeared in her dream. While Destiny can't control the prophetic nocturnal visions, the one thing she can do is apply her substantial intellect to figuring out what they mean.

Because if she doesn't, some future disaster awaits. Of that she can be certain. She's failed twice before; she can't fail again.

Crestfallen, Destiny recognizes that she's on the verge of spiraling.

Thinking of Dr. Shepherd's advice for when this happens, Destiny reminds herself of everything she's been through to get here: taking those first few steps out of her apartment door despite the overwhelming urge to scuttle back to the cocoon of her bed; walking for miles to the train station while carrying a heavy backpack; not to mention the three panic attacks she had to talk herself through while en route.

"Buck up, glum chum," Bex says, her voice buoyant with optimism. "All's not lost just yet. Didn't you notice that the ferry didn't have any proper walls? Plus, Tempest was wearing black."

Bex is right! In Destiny's dream, Tempest was wearing white as she stepped out from a solid wall. Which means it hasn't come true yet and so their paths are likely to cross again.

Sighing with relief, Destiny tells herself the trip is going to go well; it *has* to. Destiny's been floundering for a year, threatening to go under, but Mordecai has thrown her a lifeline, one she's going to cling to like her life depends on it.

Because it does.

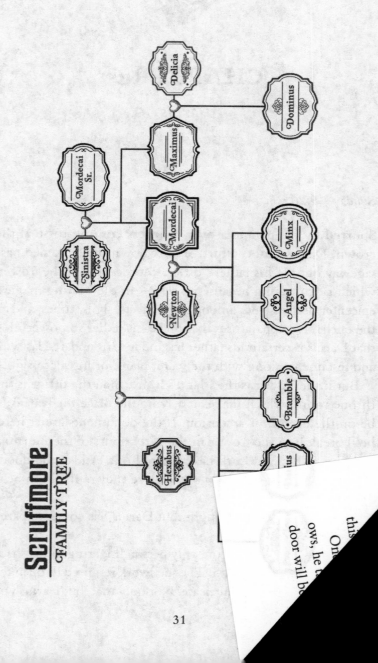

Scruffmore
FAMILY TREE

Delicia

Dominus

Maximus

Mordecai
Sr.

Mordecai

Minx

Sinistra

Angel

Newton

Bramble

Hexabus

this
On
ows, he t
door will be

CHAPTER 6

Darius

Sunday—9:20 p.m.

Spurred by his paranoia over usurpers coming to steal the crown, Darius shoots a furtive look down the darkened passageway outside his father's office. Mordecai is in the Tower, which is frustrating because it's *there*—in the beating magical epicenter of the island, among the artifacts, sigils, runes, and all the enchanted apparatuses that make his father so powerful—that Darius is certain his father has hidden his updated last will and testament, along with the secret plans for his succession.

But if the Tower is the island's heart, then the office is the throne room, which makes it a symbolic place for Darius to be on the eve of his ascension. If the documents aren't here, he'll break into the Tower in the early hours of the morning once his father and Lurk have cleared out. And if the documents aren't *there*, the only other place they're likely to be is in the vault.

It's going to be a long night, but Darius has come prepared time.

ce assured that he's the only person lingering in the shad-
akes a deep breath. The spellwork required to open the
extremely intricate. Not only that, but Darius will

also have to cover all traces of the magic he's about to perform so his father won't be alerted to his presence. One misstep and an alarm will sound, instantly summoning Morty. The door is also likely to be booby-trapped, gravely injuring anyone foolish enough to dare trespass.

Darius's fingers tremble as he closes his eyes and channels his powers. Muttering an incantation, he hovers his hand over the handle. Daunted by the heat radiating from the metal, he feels beads of sweat gather at his temples before slowly trickling down his cheeks and neck.

The lock remains resolute, refusing to yield to his ministrations.

Darius digs deeper, harnessing the power of his thundering heartbeat, but something's wrong. His eyes snap open at the stench of burning. Fingers of smoke claw their way up from the keyhole, raking the air. Darius is just about to lose his nerve and flee when there's a click and the door swings open.

He lets out a grunt of satisfaction as he slips inside.

See, Father? See how far I've come?

Having only been granted entry to this office twice during his lifetime, Darius is still awed by the scale of his father's desk. Rather than the usual rectangular shape, it resembles the jagged contours of Eerie Island, as though lava was poured around the family patriarch and left to harden. In the middle of the desk, in a circle carved out specifically for it, sits the chair. With its towering jewel-encrusted back, ornately carved armrests, and dragon-leather upholstery, it's a throne fit for a king.

Which is exactly what Darius intends to be.

Circumnavigating the desk, he scans the room for where the documents are likely to be stashed. They won't be anywhere obvious, of course—nothing quite so tacky as a filing cabinet—so Darius is fully expecting to have to use more complicated magic to uncover their hiding place.

He rolls up his sleeves and begins engaging the mechanisms of his arms, elbows, wrists, and fingers. Contorting the air, he bends its molecules to his will—shoving and tugging, twisting and summoning—power flexing every muscle. The words he whispers morph from mere breath into invisible missiles, which he directs to seek and reveal, pursue and discover.

But after more than fifteen minutes of intricate spellwork, Darius is breathless and hasn't gained any traction at all.

None of the paintings swing out to reveal a safe embedded in the wall. The wainscoting is innocuous, nothing more exciting than wood panels laid over stone. No latches spring open, activating the elaborate unfolding of stacked-drawer mechanisms. There are no trapdoors under the carpets, not even so much as a tiny compartment sunken into the floor.

Tired and thirsty, Darius is tempted by the bottle of Talisker on his father's desk. Making his way to it, he experiences a frisson of satisfaction when the ancient kauri wood melts away like candle wax, allowing him to advance through the desk before knitting itself together behind him. Once enveloped by the juggernaut, almost as though he's wearing it, Darius sits and reaches for the bottle of thirty-year-old scotch. He pours himself a glass and takes a deep sip.

Darius can't help but think about the last time the family was summoned. It was two years ago on his thirtieth birthday, and he'd fully expected his father to abdicate and offer Darius the throne. While Evangeline is the eldest child, she renounced all claims to the title before her thirtieth birthday, doing so at Morty's encouragement after their father made it clear he didn't view her as a worthy candidate.

Unlike with the Peasants' monarchy—where a ruling sovereign is expected to serve until they pass away, even if that's well into their dotage—magical royalty can only rule while their powers are still strong.

Shame twists in his gut as he recalls what happened at the gathering, the elaborate test his father engineered to challenge Darius's powers, and just how dismally he'd failed. After Bramble's death when they were just children, Darius largely abandoned his magical studies, mostly because he was never going to live up to his younger brother's abilities no matter what he did—so why even bother trying when he would always be overshadowed by a ghost—but also because the dedication to learning the craft required hard work and obedience, qualities that Darius found to be tiresome.

In his defense, he'd never heard of a worthiness test when it came to claiming the throne; it was always just meant to be inherited in a clear line of succession. Had Darius been given enough notice of his father's plans, he would have prepared, obviously. But no. Instead of allowing his son the opportunity to rise to the occasion, Morty delighted in humiliating him in front of the entire family, forcing Darius to jump through impossible hoops like a defective show dog.

When Darius expressed his bewilderment in the aftermath, Morty laughed in his face. "You think the throne just gets handed down on a silver platter, boy?"

"But that's how it happened for you, isn't it?" Darius challenged. "You didn't need to pass some humiliating test to take the crown from your father." Darius was born almost three years after Morty became the Sorcerer King, but he'd heard all the stories of his father's ascension, and none of them involved a baptism of fire.

"That's because I'd proven myself worthy decades before my thirtieth birthday," Morty shot back. "The immense power required to maintain dominion over supernatural subjects means the Sorcerer King has to be in his magical prime, not merely a pathetic figurehead. You're less powerful now than you were as a child." Morty shook his head, disgusted. "You're nothing but an embarrassment, and delusional to boot, if you thought I'd be handing my legacy to a son who has the magical abilities of a Peasant."

The intense shame over this very public failure is why Darius hasn't been able to speak to Hexabus or Evangeline since. Having any kind of contact with his mother and sister would only remind him of his weakness, how utterly pathetic he used to be.

Well, not anymore.

Darius casts his gaze about the desk. Noticing the four leather-bound books stacked on the edge of it, he reaches for them. He isn't much of a scholar or a reader, but if Morty has referenced these, they have to be important. Darius pulls the top one off the stack and flips through it but quickly gives up because the Anglo-Saxon text is too dense and inaccessible.

Setting it aside, he picks up the second volume and reads its title, *Occult Magick for the Darkest Practitioners of the Blackest of Arts.*

As he skims through it, Darius's spirits drop when he sees it's written in Fungellian, an ancient occult language he struggled to learn. At least this book has diagrams and illustrations, which attract and hold his attention. One page is filled with compass stars like the ones tattooed on his father's face. Morty has jotted cramped notes next to them, something about finding the right number, though Darius doesn't know what for.

He closes the volume before opening one of his father's notebooks on spellwork. In it, Darius discovers a series of calculations. The ink from some of the earlier ones has faded, while others look like they were worked on recently.

$$🜍 + 🜍 + 🜍 = 30$$

$$⊜ + ⊜ × 🜍 = 55$$

$$🜍^{⊖} ÷ 🜍 = 1000$$

$$🜍 × ∈ + \frac{⊜⊜}{⊜⊜} ÷ ⊜ = \,?$$

[2]

★ ★ ★

Darius inspects the equations more closely before shaking his head. He's never been any good at math. Closing the notebook, he tells himself that it doesn't matter; he doesn't need his father's source material.

All he needs is to find the succession documents confirming there are no more surprises, no Scruffmore bastards waiting in the wings as the rumors have strongly hinted at. It's terrifying that an illegitimate child would be allowed to take the throne if Morty deemed them worthy. Darius tells himself that so long as he truly is next in line, he'll pass his father's test this time. That's all Darius has ever truly wanted, to make Morty proud to be his father.

If not, Darius has a backup plan.

---

2. You now have all the information you require to work out these equations. If you need a clue to assist you, email DestinyWhipClue@gmail.com using the subject line Clue Two. Once you've solved them, turn to page 458 to check your answers.

For years, Morty has been obsessed with the Eye of Gormodeus, a rare and powerful magical artifact that he's never managed to get his hands on. But Darius has a lead on it; he just needs to convince the owner to part with it. If Darius can't win his father's love fair and square, then perhaps he can buy it.

He pictures holding the artifact out to Morty. *Here, Father. Look what I have for you.*

He imagines his father's monocle gleaming, his eyes bulging with disbelief. *How did you find it when even I failed in my quest?*

Because I am smarter and more capable than you think, Father.

Darius's eyes fill with tears as he pictures the moment Morty will throw his arms around him, clutching Darius tightly to his chest while showering him with compliments and declarations of love.

After downing the last of his drink, Darius slams the glass onto the table. Thunder booms so loudly that his chest vibrates as strobes of lightning make the room pulse like a nightclub. Smiling, Darius magics away any evidence of his presence and then stands to head out, answering the darkness's siren call.

"Scruffmore bastards beware," he mutters darkly. For that is the only wrench that can be thrown into the works of his plans.

CHAPTER 7

Mordecai

Sunday—9:20 p.m.

Mordecai Scruffmore stands at the Tower window confronting the night, the velvet of his smoking jacket matching the Merlot in his wine goblet. An elaborate white fringe curls from his widow's peak, a wave cresting over the twenty-four black compass stars inked across his forehead. His tufted eyebrows, perpetually raised, give him a surprised air, one most contradictory to his nature.

A whimper issues from the recesses of the room, the sound of pain twisting his lips into a semblance of a smile. "Is there a problem, Lurk?" Mordecai demands without turning around.

"No, my lord," his butler rasps, his voice branded with agony as the stench of sulfur seasons the denial.

Excellent, Mordecai thinks, *it's working.*

Swallowing a sip of wine, he opens the window and gazes out at the village below, which is perched precipitously on the island's bedrock, its roads reaching up toward the castle like the arms of supplicants. Eerie's very foundations appear to be writhing. Even the cobblestones, slick with rain, gleam like a million eyeballs, so that the night feels alert and watchful.

"Fear the coming of The Seer," he murmurs. "Fear the coming of The Seer." It's become a habit of late, reciting this litany through gritted teeth as though trying to pulverize the prophecy's warning.

The Sorcerer King fears nothing, he reminds himself furiously as lightning slashes the tarpaulin of roiling sky. *Nothing.* And yet…there's something out there in the darkness, something coming for him. He can sense it. Whether or not it's The Seer remains uncertain for hasn't he already sent his minions out into the world to eradicate every last one of them?

Lurk gasps and takes a shuddering breath, the sound hijacking his master's thoughts.

"Has Hexabus arrived yet?" Mordecai sets his wine goblet down on the sill. He plucks the monocle from his eye, wiping the raindrops from the glass with a linen handkerchief.

"She's chartered a boat to the island and should be arriving shortly, my lord." Lurk's voice is a low grumble, like tectonic plates shifting.

"Keep her and Newton apart as much as possible." Ex-wives and current ones are not to be mixed. Like milk poured into vinegar, their interactions tend to curdle. "Where are the others?"

"Evangeline and Darius are already here," Lurk replies, straining to speak, each word weighted with distress. "They arrived earlier while you were in your office."

That accounts for Mordecai's first- and secondborn, his docile daughter and wayward son, one more feckless than the other. The middle child, Bramble, is forever accounted for in his resting place in Eerie's graveyard, never requiring his father to inquire after his whereabouts.

That just leaves the twins, his progeny from his marriage to Newton.

As though reading his mind, Lurk says, "Angel and Minx will be arriving on the ferry in the morning. They have an influencer event for Hermès in London this evening and are flying out after that."

Mordecai winces at the word *influencer*, shaking his head at his children's Peasant occupations. Philosophers, philanderers, and fashionistas. What happened to good old-fashioned hard work? What happened to the value of blood and sweat and tears? What a disappointment they are, the miserable litter of them, despite their royal blood.

Turning from the window, he puts the monocle back in place to better appraise the sight awaiting him.

The hexagonal firepit, added recently in preparation for the gathering, is positioned in the center of the circular room. Its labradorite mineral gleams in alternating blues and greens, silvers and golds, while mesmerizing gray flames cast writhing shadows across the stone walls.

Lurk stands with his bare hands hovering directly over the oily fire. Unlike Mordecai, Lurk doesn't have a full head of hair, though what remains is still mostly as black as his three-piece suit. The uninitiated might be fooled into thinking the butler's warming his hands at the fire, rather than serving as its fuel.

"My lord," Lurk entreats, straining as sweat trickles from his temples, "I think, perhaps, that's enough?"

"I'll tell you when it's enough," Mordecai snaps, making his way to the oversize hourglass mounted against the wall above the fireplace.

Despite appearances, what falls through its neck aren't granules of white and black sand. They are, in fact, tiny skulls whose eyes glitter with obsidian and onyx. What's most worrisome is that the top bulb is quickly running out of skulls to feed the one below.

This is just as the prophecy warned.

With Mordecai's sixty-sixth birthday fast approaching, there is very little time left. But there are forces working against him, an enemy foretold just as the coming of The Seer was prophesized.

Worse than discovering the prophecy of his downfall more than two decades ago was realizing that some of it was missing, a page ripped from the leather-bound volume in which it was written. Mordecai doesn't know what infuriates him more: that he's been denied access to this essential information, or that there's someone out there who has this knowledge to wield against him.

"Still no leads on Lumina?" he asks.

"No, my lord. She seems to have disappeared without a trace." Lurk's voice is a whisper, on the verge of being extinguished.

Shaking his head, Mordecai huffs. "And just when she was so close to tracking down the Eye of Gormodeus."

He has no doubt that Lumina's disappearance is a deliberate act of sabotage conducted by his nemesis to prevent him from finding and claiming the powerful long-lost artifact.

This setback is what's forced Mordecai's hand, giving him no choice but to issue a rare summons for the family to gather for this coming showdown. He plans to leverage their collective power in his favor while also sniffing out the Judas who's trying to undermine him.

The flames deepen from gray to graphite; they stroke the air rapturously, hungry for more. Mordecai's weapon is nearly ready. Lurk has fulfilled his duty and won't be of any further use if he collapses.

"That's enough," Mordecai declares.

Released from his bondage, Lurk staggers back on weakened legs. His hands, usually supernaturally white, glow an angry red. Gingerly removing his gloves from his pocket, he pulls them on, cringing as he does so.

Making his way to the pit, Mordecai withdraws a ceremonial dagger from his jacket pocket and holds it up to his face. He leans over the fire, his head dipped forward. Making a small cut at his temple, he keeps his eyes open as a drop of blood splatters into the flames. They react instantly, turning silver and giving off sulfurous sparks that sting his eyes. A tear falls, followed quickly by a drop of sweat. The fire responds rapturously, the flames now tar black and sinewy. Mordecai smiles, thinking how creation is easy. What's difficult is its opposite.

"Everything is in place, Lurk." Mordecai straightens.

"Yes, my lord," Lurk replies. He pauses before adding, "Might I ask what exactly—"

"Patience. All will be revealed in good time." Mordecai strokes the unmarked center of his forehead. By this time tomorrow, the remaining compass stars will have appeared there to complete the set, a permanent crown that no one can ever remove.

Reaching under his jacket, Mordecai clasps his fingers around the circular medallion that rests against his heart. It has the Scruffmore family crest stamped into iron that was forged centuries ago. The crest depicts a human skull with curved ram horns, an ornate door knocker embedded in its mouth.

He studies the family motto inscribed in Latin upon the outer ring. *Numquam pulsate ad ostium mortis ne mors adest ut vōs intrare admittat.* Never knock on Death's door lest Death be present in order that He may allow you to enter.

"It's time for the Scruffmores to knock on Death's door, Lurk," he says, his voice grave. "Let's see if He's prepared to make a trade."

For Mordecai has grown dissatisfied with the limitations of being the Sorcerer King. He rules a dwindling empire, his dominion only extending as far as the remaining thirty-three magical bloodlines in the world. There was a time when the Scruffmore monarchy ruled thousands upon thousands of subjects, but most of them have either been eradicated from too much inbreeding or made extinct by sorcerer wars, the magical fighting for dominance. What remained from that has mostly been wiped out by complacency as technology quickly replaced sorcery.

It's time for that to change, for his dominion to be absolute.

To pull off this epic achievement, Mordecai will have to kill his most powerful child, the one the prophecy has foretold will surpass him. In just over twenty-four hours, the deed will be done, paving the way for what's to come.

CHAPTER 8

Destiny

Sunday—9:42 p.m.

Sheltering under an umbrella that's being pummeled by the storm, Destiny squints at her phone. She had signal forty minutes ago when she set out uphill on foot, but her GPS now remains obstinately silent about where to find the Grimshaw Inn and Tavern.

Gazing up from the useless device, Destiny peers into the gloom, her earlier optimism dampened.

The narrow cobbled street is made even more claustrophobic by the stone buildings that rise along both its sides, seemingly carved from the very bedrock of the island. The structures are top-heavy, like Destiny herself, giving the impression that they're huddled together, whispering their secrets overhead. Flickering gas lamps dot the street at irregular intervals. They cast halos of light that, while doing little to pierce the cloying darkness, make the slick cobblestones glint menacingly.

Now that she's finally here, Destiny is plagued by doubt.

Bex was right. Why couldn't Mordecai just have called her up with the information he had about her family? Or, at the very least, explained it in the letter he'd taken the time to write anyway? Why all the mystery and intrigue to lure her out to this godforsaken rock?

Destiny didn't think too much about the island's name when she first saw it, just as she'd never really thought about Lake Erie's name as one of the Great Lakes. But the extra *e* is clearly not just an affectation. This island is spooky as all hell.

Bex agrees. "Why are there no cars?"

"Who cares so long as we don't have to ride in any?"

"Why are there no electrical lights?" Bex presses. "Or any cell phone reception?"

Destiny swallows deeply, trying to find some optimism to cling to. "Maybe it's like a historical-integrity thing that they're trying to preserve? A World Heritage site, or something?" Even as she says it, she knows that's not right or else there would have been more information about the island on the internet. Not wanting to linger on that worrying thought, she adds, "And I'm sure there's usually cell reception. It's probably just the storm that's knocked things out."

There's a scrape and crunch from behind her. Destiny turns just in time to see a shadow darting into an alleyway. It knocks over a bin, which clatters into the street.

An icy splinter of dread wedges into her spine.

"Are we being followed?" Bex whispers.

It's not inconceivable. After all, whoever delivered the letter stood right outside Destiny's apartment door. They could have tailed her. But why? Has Mordecai sent someone to shadow her, ensuring she would come?

A red flash suddenly erupts from the alleyway.

"Is anyone there?" Destiny calls out.

When no answer is forthcoming, Destiny clenches her hands and strides over to the alleyway, then peers around the corner with less confidence than she would like. Rain runs in torrents from the gutters, splattering onto the cobblestones before snaking off in rivulets down the steep lane.

The alley is empty. There's nothing that might account for the red flash.

Did I imagine it? Am I experiencing the kind of ocular migraine that causes visual disturbances?

But no, her head feels fine. Exhaling a shaky breath, Destiny continues on her way. Her thoughts return to Tempest, like a tongue repeatedly prodding a cracked tooth despite the discomfort it brings. Destiny's two prophetic dreams prior to this one were both about people she knew and loved. She can't imagine why she'd dream about Tempest, a stranger, or how their fates might be entwined.

Lightning forks across the sky, its spindly blue fingers greedy to gather up the darkness. Destiny gasps as she spots a castle looming high up ahead, its myriad turrets and spires thrown in stark relief. It looks like a Gothic version of the Disney castle if a villain lived there instead of a princess. Destiny spots a figure in a window, but when she blinks, it's gone, swallowed by the night. Thunder grumbles loudly, seemingly in sympathy with Destiny's empty stomach.

Something crashes behind her and she startles, turning as she squints back into the darkness, which has only just relinquished her. Holding up her cell phone flashlight illuminates the blackness, revealing two glowing red orbs. And then another two. And then a pair of green ones followed by a pair of bright yellow, until there are dozens of what appear to be tiny moons suspended in the night.

The sight of them is otherworldly, sinister. It makes Destiny's skin prickle.

It takes her a few seconds to figure out that they're cats' eyes. She recalls that the collective noun for a group of cats is a *glaring*. And now she understands why.

Taking a few deep breaths, she glances back at her phone. The map of the island's warren of lanes has dissolved into a blank canvas; there isn't even the blue blip from earlier to show her where she is.

"Can't you help?" Destiny asks Bex. "Don't you have like special powers, or something?"

"I'm a ghost, Destiny. Not a goddamn GPS. I've pretty much exhausted my repertoire of tricks by communicating with you from beyond the veil of death."

"Okay, okay. No need to get tetchy."

Destiny forces herself to think. The last time she checked the functioning app, she was being guided to follow a distorted S-shaped route up the hill. Suddenly, the narrow road snaking off to the right becomes the obvious choice.

As she takes off in that direction, the gale proves too strong an adversary, plucking the umbrella from Destiny's hand, sending it somersaulting into the night before crashing into something nearby. A cat hisses in response, incensed to be under attack.

"I'm so sorry!" Destiny calls out, hoping the creature isn't hurt. When she gets closer, she spots the cat's glowing eyes in the recesses of a storefront doorway. There's an overhang, which Destiny steps under, relieved to find a refuge.

Unlike with the glaring from earlier, this cat is alone. It's almost completely jet-black except for a white patch between its eyes, a kind of top-heavy hourglass shape reminding Destiny of the birthmark on her wrist. The creature is scrawny and bedraggled, but when Destiny steps toward it, it arches its back and hisses, scrappy and ready for a fight.

Deciding that the cat's spunk is proof enough that it isn't hurt, Destiny moves to retrieve her umbrella when the creature yowls again, its voice sounding eerily human. "Leeeeave."

"Did it just tell you to get the hell out of Dodge?" Bex demands.

"Maybe it's not a fan of ghosts and is actually talking to *you*," Destiny replies. Holding up her hands and backing away, she says to the cat, "I'm not going to hurt you."

And then the strangest thing happens. Its hackles lower and it steps forward, cocking its head this way and that as it regards her. Meowing plaintively, it takes a few steps forward before threading its way between her calves. When the cat begins purring, Destiny crouches to pet it.

"You want to come with me to the Scruffmore castle?" she asks, stroking the creature's arched back. "Shall I put you in my backpack so we can go be besties with Mordecai Scruffmore together?"

Without warning, the cat suddenly leaps up and swipes at her face before bolting out into the street and disappearing under a gate.

"Ouch!" Destiny rears back, clamping a hand over the scratch on her nose. Her fingers come away smudged with blood, the wound stinging. "A simple 'no' would have sufficed," she grumbles.

"Girl just got bitch-slapped by a cat," Bex snickers.

Before Destiny can grab her umbrella, another breeze tugs at it, sending it sailing off.

"Well, isn't that just perfect?" Groaning, Destiny continues down the winding street, the scent of woodsmoke and garlic an encouraging sign that she's on the right route.

Her fingers find their way to the amulet. She pulls it out from under her T-shirt, stroking it to fight the rising panic.

The sky lights up once more, this time the thunder so hot on its heels that it doesn't take a mathematician to calculate that the lightning is now directly overhead. Destiny's just casting her gaze about, searching for cover, when she hears a terrible commotion over the cacophony of the storm. It sounds like the Four Horsemen of the Apocalypse are charging her way, hell-bent on destruction. Jumping back onto the sidewalk, she presses her body against one of the buildings.

As a horse and a carriage come into view on the narrow road, barreling right at her, Destiny is certain that this is how she's going to die. But then a door swings open behind her, and two strong hands grip her shoulders, tugging her backward as everything fades to black.

CHAPTER 9

Choose Your Own Conundrum
Gabriel Morezzi

Ten Years Earlier

It's ten years before Destiny is saved from near death, and you're Gabriel Morezzi, a philosopher and author who has runaway carriages on the mind. You've just given a guest lecture on philosophy at the University of Delheim, and you're now having dinner at a nearby Ethiopian restaurant with Evangeline Scruffmore, the TA you liaised with before the event.

"Actual carriages?" you ask incredulously after she's finished relaying an anecdote from her childhood.

"Yes!" she replies, laughing. The corners of her eyes crinkle adorably. "They're the only way to get around the island."

"And you seriously grew up in a castle as a princess of some obscure royal bloodline?" When she nods, looking strangely unhappy about it, you ask, "Which one?"

Her expression darkens. "A cursed one."

You want to untangle that knotty sentiment—ask if that means she's related to the Monaco royal family with its "curse of the Grimaldis"—but she recovers quickly, sharing a few tales of childish escapades as she goes on to describe the island in more detail.

At one point, she flushes, fiddling with one of her long braids as she says, "We've talked a lot about me. Let's focus on you. I'd love to hear more about some of the thought experiments you're including in your next book."

"You want to discuss death and mayhem on a first date?" you ask wryly.

"*Is* this a date?" she teases.

"I can only hope so."

She looks both flattered and flustered, and so you bring the conversation back to her original question. "Okay, I'll tell you about one of the thought experiments, but let's have some fun with it. How about we set it on Eerie Island? That way you can see if I was paying attention earlier while you were talking."

She smiles and nods. "Go on."

"Imagine you're out walking late at night along one of those narrow winding streets. There's a full moon but you can't see it. That's when you hear something charging your way. Even muffled by the thick fog its approach sounds ominous. You dash back onto the curb just as an enormous carriage pulled by four powerful horses materializes in the gloom. As the animals thunder ever closer, you see that the carriage is riderless, the coachman having been thrown from the driver's box somewhere along the route. It rockets past, and as you follow its progress, you spot a fork in the road ahead."

You go on to say that the road the carriage will naturally take leads to a group of three people who all have their backs to the horses. They're walking in the middle of the street singing loudly, completely oblivious to the danger. The other road, which branches off to the right, leads to one person who's walking along, listening to music through their earphones.

"Now indulge me, please, even though this part is a bit out there." You laugh and hum *The X-Files* theme song. "Imagine that you have magical powers that would allow you to change the course of the carriage with a flick of your hand."

Evangeline startles, though whether it's at the absurdity of the idea or something else, you can't be sure. You notice that the hairs on the backs of her arms are now standing to attention.

"Your powers only allow you to change the carriage's course once," you add. "There are no magical do-overs."

She swallows hard and nods, as though she knows this all too well.

"The time has come to make a decision," you say. "If you do nothing, the carriage and horses will continue along their way, crashing into the three people, almost certainly killing them. But if you use your powers, you can make the carriage change course so that it will travel down the road veering to the right, where it will strike the lone person."

"So far, you've stayed very close to Philippa Foot's original conundrum," Evangeline observes, scooping up some *doro wat* with the corner of injera she's torn off. "Where does your own variation come in?"

"You'll see soon enough," you reply. "You have a few seconds to decide. A. You use your powers to divert the carriage from the three people." You pause here for effect. "Or B. You do nothing. Which one will it be?"

If Evangeline's answer is **A**, go to page 52.

If her answer is **B**, go to page 53.

OPTION A:
YOU USE YOUR POWERS

"A," Evangeline declares. "I use my powers to divert the carriage so that only the one person will be killed."

You smile sadly. "Okay, good. But as the carriage races toward that person, a door from the local tavern opens and five people spill out onto the street. They don't have time to react. The carriage hits them, killing all five along with the lone walker. Now six people are dead. Because of *your* intervention."

Go to page 55.

OPTION B:
YOU DO NOTHING

"B," Evangeline declares. "It's not for me to play at being god. Three people were going to die anyway without my intervention. This way, at least I don't have anyone's blood on my hands. It was just a terrible accident."

"Okay," you say, nodding. "But as the carriage races toward the three people, one of them turns around. In that split second, you recognize him as Darius." You know, from Evangeline's stories of childhood escapades, how close she is to her younger brother. "And then," you continue, "you realize, to your dismay, that the other two people are your mother and…"

You hesitate. You would reference her father but earlier, when Evangeline was speaking of her childhood, she seemed to struggle with the mere mention of him, as though she found the taste of his name to be so bitter as to make it unpalatable.

"Your Uncle Maximus," you finish instead, remembering how Evangeline's eyes shone at the mention of him.

Judging by her alarmed expression, you know you got it right.

"Then," you explain, "in a kind of horrifying slow motion, you turn to look at the person walking along the other street, the one who is now no longer in any danger. Feeling your eyes trained on them, they turn around. You see that it's your most reviled enemy who's done nothing but torment you and everyone you love."

If you were a betting man, you'd put money on the probability that the person Evangeline is picturing is her father, Mordecai.

"Your enemy smiles," you say, "tipping his hat in thanks, and you know it's a sight you will never forget. Because of your lack of action, three people who you dearly love are about to die even as the person you loathe cheats death."

Go to page 55.

Squirming, Evangeline jiggles her foot. "Okay, so your thought experiment is about unintended consequences," she muses. "How, even though we can think something through, and have the best intentions at the time, we can't foresee all outcomes."

"Yes, exactly," you say, nodding. "They're the hardest consequences of all to live with, don't you think, because we couldn't possibly have foreseen them with the limited information we had at our disposal at the time."

"But we're still culpable," Evangeline insists. "Even if we didn't intend for that particular outcome to happen." Her voice is hard and sharp, a weapon she's using against herself.

Its edge puts you on guard. You study Evangeline's expression, which has a haunted quality to it, as though she's traveled back to the prison of the past purely to ensure that she's still doing her time there, that no one has been foolish enough to pardon her or, god forbid, set her free. In the hard line of her jaw, and the fierce light of her golden eyes, what you recognize is self-recrimination.

"That's one way of looking at it," you say slowly, sadly. "You could also cut yourself some slack for not being an all-knowing god."

Evangeline is clearly marooned. What you want in that moment, more than anything, is to navigate the treacherous waters she's surrounded herself with so you can save her from herself.

CHAPTER 10

Evangeline

Sunday—9:42 p.m.

Evangeline hates being back here, hates how the castle's darkness seeps into her lungs with every breath as though she's inhaling fungus spores. There's a reason why she's stayed away for the past two years, why she would stay away forever if she had a choice.

But she doesn't. Because she *owes* her father, and he's never missed a single opportunity to remind her of that debt.

As Evangeline paces back and forth in the castle's library, desperately searching for answers that no book can possibly provide, she absentmindedly strokes the pendant hanging from her necklace.

She resents the entire family dynamic, that while Darius is the cog that stubbornly refuses to turn and Hexabus is the wheel that strains to spin independently on its own axis, Evangeline is the oil that greases the family's grinding mechanism. She's the one who wheedles and cajoles, begs and encourages—smoothing ruffled feathers and tending bruised egos—all in the name of ensuring that the Sorcerer King always gets what he wants.

Evangeline winces as she recalls what happened two years ago with Darius, and how the fallout severed her relationship with him.

She heard from her mother that Uncle Maximus has been invited back into the inner circle decades after he and Morty had a feud. Evangeline suspects that her father is going to announce some kind of alliance with Maximus, a joining of royal forces that will serve to make their family more powerful.

Morty won't frame it that way, of course, as though he needs Maximus. Instead, he'll announce that he's forgiven his younger brother for whatever transgression led to their estrangement, and that he's magnanimously welcoming him back into the fold. That way, Cousin Dominus can step into the breach as the next Scruffmore in line to the throne.

Having not seen her uncle or cousin in over twenty years, Evangeline has no idea how open they will be to this proposition, especially since they'll have to move back from France, not to mention that there's bound to be dozens of caveats. Which is where she'll have to come into it, no doubt, needing to convince everyone that it's in their best interests, the most prudent course of action, to go along with whatever Morty wants.

Perhaps this time, after doing her father's bidding, Evangeline's debt will finally be settled. She allows herself to believe it's possible, that she'll actually be able to make the choice that will center herself in her own life.

Closing her eyes, Evangeline conjures a fiery Magic 8 Ball and poses her burning question. "Yes, or no?" she asks.

Instead of answering, the ball implodes into a cloud of ash that drifts down like dirty snow, a bad omen if ever there was one.

Perplexed, she waves her hand and summons a hundred books that leap from the shelves like gamboling puppies. "Yes, or no?"

Their pages flutter as the books circle in a vortex. The magical wind loosens the ink from the tomes to surround Evangeline in a sandstorm of words. They rearrange themselves so that only the letters *e, n, o, s,* and *y* remain, the rest dissolving into dust.

Yes. No. Yes. No.

The words circle Evangeline until they form new ones.

Nosey. Nosey. Nosey.

And then they dive for her nose, stinging like a thousand wasps.

"Enough," she cries, and the letters laugh as they gallop back to their books, which hop back to the shelves.

Evangeline never uses magic in her everyday life unless it's absolutely essential. The last time she used it freely, Bramble died, and everything fell apart. That's why she wants nothing to do with the power that pulses through her royal blood; she's seen firsthand the destruction it can wreak.

But the castle lowers her defenses in this regard, drawing her magic out in ways that make her feel both invincible and completely out of control.

She wonders whether she should head down to her mother's chambers to see if she's arrived yet. If anyone can advise her, it's Hexabus. But then again, her mother's been acting very strangely lately, using weak excuses to put off seeing Evangeline. Guilt sits as uncomfortably on Hexabus now as the crown used to all those years ago, which makes Evangeline think her mother is hiding something. Something she's deeply ashamed of.

Perhaps, more urgent, is forcing a reunion with Darius. Evangeline has missed her brother terribly these past two years and is desperate to rekindle their relationship. But she also needs to gauge where he's at in terms of his feelings about Dominus. While Darius will definitely want to avoid a repeat performance of what happened two years ago, the last thing Evangeline needs is him making waves—disrupting Morty's plans and angering him in the process—purely because he's so jealous of their cousin.

Before she can decide where to go, the door to the library opens and Newton slips inside. Despite the late hour, Evangeline's stepmother is dressed in a floral-print ruched dress paired with stilettos, as if she's on her way to a dinner party.

At forty-two, Newton is only seven years older than Evangeline, though she looks younger thanks to all the cosmetic procedures she's had done.

"Angie," Newton croons, using the nickname she knows Evangeline loathes. "I thought I'd find you in here with all the musty old books." Newton wrinkles her nose as she walks over to Evangeline, reaching for her hand to clasp in her own.

This is how Newton always greets her stepchildren, by interlinking fingers with them. An outsider might construe it as an affectionate gesture, but Evangeline and Darius know better. What their stepmother aims to achieve is to emphasize the contrast between their skin tones, one that doesn't exist when she holds her own children's hands.

The twins have two white parents, enjoying all the privilege that bestows on them, while Evangeline and Darius are the offspring of a white father and Black mother, having one foot in both worlds while never quite belonging in either. Just like their cousin, Dominus, which is why Evangeline always felt such an affinity for him as a child, because he knew exactly what it felt like to be neither/nor.

Newton lets go of Evangeline's hand, examining her cardigan, jeans, and ballet flats with an expression of distaste. "You really must let the girls give you a makeover. I'm sure they'd find something that would fit you, though most of the designer labels come in *much* smaller sizes, of course."

As much as Evangeline tries to not let her stepmother get a rise out of her, she can't help it. "And you all *must* come to the university sometime to listen to one of our fascinating guest speakers. A lot of it will go over your heads, of course, but I'm sure we can find some topic you'll be able to understand."

Newton's smile flickers like a neon sign about to go out.

This is what Evangeline hates most about Newton, how her stepmother's microaggressions bring out the absolute worst in her, like a poultice drawing out infection. And how Evangeline's retaliations cause endless hours of insomnia as she lies awake going over and over every petty word she uttered, wishing she'd been the bigger person.

From the radius window positioned behind Evangeline, a flash of lightning suddenly illuminates the entire library in electric blue. It flings monstrous shadows of her and Newton across the room's floor-to-ceiling shelves, casting Evangeline as a wild-haired giantess about to attack a diminutive Newton. It's unsettling to have her shadow self betray her desires this way.

Newton turns her back on Evangeline and heads for one of the shelves. "I'm actually quite interested in eugenics." She removes a book and shows Evangeline the cover. "Perhaps I could attend a lecture on that."

"There's no need," Evangeline says, bristling. "My father is an expert on the topic. You can just ask him whatever you want to know."

"Oh, yes, that's right," Newton says, pretending to be surprised, as though she didn't bring up the subject just to wield it as a battering ram. "He told me all about how you and Darius were the first and second pancakes, ya know." She laughs as though it's the funniest joke she's ever heard.

When Morty married Hexabus, he thought that their offspring would be more powerful considering they were each descended from a long line of purebred and royal magical nobility. Instead, with Evangeline and Darius, it somehow resulted in a dilution of their powers due to genetic inbreeding, the opposite of what Morty was aiming for.

Seeing Evangeline and Darius as the flops that had to be corrected—and Bramble as an outlier in this regard—Morty aspired to create children who were more in his likeness. And who would, in theory, be infinitely more powerful because of their genetic diversity.

It didn't work, and what a disappointment the twins have been because of it.

When Evangeline doesn't take the bait, Newton returns the book to the shelf. "So, you're here for the big gathering," she says.

Evangeline merely nods, waiting Newton out.

"What's it all about, do you think?" Newton studies her manicure as though she's not remotely interested in Evangeline's answer. Which is nonsense because this is obviously a fishing expedition. When Evangeline still doesn't reply, Newton presses on. "Do you think Darius is likely to crash and burn again? Like he did last time?"

"Sorry, Newton," Evangeline lies. "I'm as much in the dark as you are. I guess we'll find out soon enough."

Newton looks like she wants to say more but thinks better of it. "Get some rest, Angie. Those bags under your eyes are terribly aging."

Grinding her teeth as Newton takes her leave, Evangeline wonders how she's going to cope dealing with Newton *and* the twins tomorrow. Being in their company is like taking a dip with piranhas and expecting not to be savaged.

She goes to sit at the table by a first edition of Agrippa's *Three Books of Occult Philosophy* dating back to the 1530s, which she pulled from the shelves earlier. Taking a sip of wine, she struggles to clear her mind of the toxicity that Newton has brought to it.

After a few minutes, just as Evangeline is feeling more centered, the book begins to thrum, making the whole table vibrate. Evangeline groans, grabbing at her wine goblet and the candle to steady them. She considers standing and walking out, refusing to witness whatever this little display is. But some things will not be ignored, and the book would probably just follow her from the library, taunting her until it fulfills its mission.

And so she sighs as it begins fluttering wildly, animated by an enchanted breeze. It finally falls still at a blank page. Letters begin forming, written by an invisible hand in red ink. When they're done, eight scrambled words remain.

MBABR'LSE
HDATE
AWTS'N
ORUY
LUATF
HCCEK
SHI
VERGA

Evangeline has always loved word puzzles and so it only takes her a few minutes to unscramble them. When she does, the message is so shocking that she gasps, dropping her glass. As it smashes at her feet, it feels as though her entire understanding of her place in the world has shattered along with it. ★★[3]

---

3. You now have all the information you require to work out this word scramble. If you need a clue to assist you, email DestinyWhipClue@gmail.com using the subject line Clue Three. Once you've solved it, turn to page 460 to check your answer.

CHAPTER 11

Destiny

Sunday—10:25 p.m.

In the moment before Destiny's eyes flutter open, she dreams of red ink bleeding from the pages of a book, and of a boar's head rendered in brass. There's also a silver disc cracking along fissure lines until it's no longer one solid object, but all separate pieces. Two of them are the concentric circles at its borders, one designed to tuck into the other. The others are jagged and abstract. They spin on their own axes, all the fragments orbiting the largest of the circles.

These visions are accompanied by the screeching of tires and the unholy marriage of metal smashing against metal. Her mother's scream is threaded through the carnage.

Destiny groans herself awake, a panic attack tightening its grip around her windpipe. It takes a few moments to pry its fingers loose so she can breathe again. Looking around, she's surprised to discover that she's lying on the floor in what appears to be a gloomy wood-paneled foyer. Gas flames flicker from antique wall sconces, somehow casting more shadows than light. She eyes the flames nervously until satisfied they're contained and unlikely to spread.

Destiny struggles to sit, fighting off a wave of dizziness as she swipes at her clammy forehead. The wooden floor creaks in protest. It's covered by a plaid runner, the faded carpet leading to a battered staircase where Destiny's drenched backpack is propped at its foot. Tartan wallpaper peels from the walls in long strips as though the foyer is suffering from a terrible case of sunburn. Looking up, she spots damp patches covering the ceiling in moldy storm clouds that mirror the ones outside.

Despite its rather unsavory appearance, Destiny is flooded with relief to realize this must be the elusive Grimshaw Inn and Tavern. She probably fainted from fright just as she was pulled inside. She flushes at the realization. This doesn't bode well for her meeting tomorrow. How will she manage to extract answers from Mordecai Scruffmore himself if she can't even navigate his island without swooning?

Destiny stands and surveys the artwork on the walls.

There's an oil painting off to the side of the desk that makes Destiny do a double take.

The man in the portrait is Mordecai Scruffmore. He stands behind a beautiful woman who is seated, his hand resting possessively on her shoulder. Clustered around her are three children, two young boys and a slightly older girl, none of them older than ten.

There's something about the regal way the subjects are posed that's reminiscent of paintings Destiny's seen of various royal families. As she studies the group's somber faces—wondering at the kind of people who sit for portraits in fancy drawing rooms instead of snapping photos at a picnic table—she gives in to the yearning from before.

Could these children be her half siblings, a ready-made family just waiting to envelop her?

"Ah good, yeh're awake!" a voice says, interrupting her fantasy. "I was worried yeh mighta hit yer head when yeh fainted clean away."

She turns to discover a man wearing faded jeans and a flannel shirt with sleeves rolled up to reveal bulging forearms. Destiny is tall but he towers over her. He has wet black hair that's peppered with gray, and a goatee of the same color.

There's something about how solid he is that reminds Destiny of Nate.

"I guess yeh won' be needin' the smelling salts," the man mutters, putting a little bottle away in his pocket before nodding at the painting. "Do yeh know Princess Evangeline and Prince Darius, then?"

Destiny is so startled by the titles that she can only shake her head.

"I thought that's perhaps why yeh're visitin', that they might be friends of yers." Jutting his chin at the portrait, he says, "They're part of the Scruffmore royal family, who owns the island."

Royal family. Destiny marvels at how every orphan in the world must have dreamed, at one point or another, of secretly being a prince or princess. That this might actually be a possibility renders her speechless.

"I know what yeh're thinkin'," the man says, startling Destiny further. "Yeh've never heard of the Scruffmore royal family. It's an ancient royal bloodline, yeh see, almost extinct like so many other monarchies that have died out."

That's not what Destiny was thinking at all but it's still useful information. While she's bursting with curiosity about what else this man knows about the Scruffmores, good manners dictate that she first thank him for saving her life before she bombards him with questions. There's a part of her that's enormously relieved that, despite having not interacted with people in so long, she hasn't lost *all* sense of decorum.

"Thank you for rescuing me!" Destiny exclaims, her legs still trembling from the adrenaline rush. "Can I hug you? I'm a hugger, you see, though I know not everyone likes it."

He nods warily and she throws her arms around him. It's like hugging a tree trunk bedecked with flannel.

"Och, it was no trouble at all," he says, gently disengaging her arms from around his waist. His hands are calloused, the sign of someone who does manual labor for a living.

"That carriage just came out of nowhere!" Destiny gasps. Even saying the word aloud is surreal. "A carriage, in this day and age. Can you believe it?" she demands, staring up at him.

Regarding her with a bemused expression, he replies, "Aye. It's entirely possible in these parts to experience death by Victorian-novel mishap."

He has dark circles under his eyes, which give the impression of someone who's severely sleep-deprived. No wonder if he spends all his spare time going around saving damsels in distress.

Destiny laughs, not sure if she's feeling giddy after the near-death experience or woozy from the fainting.

Amused, the man says, "I'm Madigan McGoo, manager, and general dogsbody, at yer service. Welcome to the Grimshaw Inn and Tavern. Yeh must be Destiny. I've been waitin' for yeh."

Destiny takes in the foyer again from this angle now that she's standing up. As grateful as she is for being rescued, something bothers her, though she's not entirely sure what. The concern nudges against all corners of her mind until it finally reveals itself. "How did you know I was out there?"

"Yeh were booked in for the night, weren't yeh? And when yeh didn't arrive soon after the last ferry, I started lookin' out for yeh," he says, crossing his arms and rocking back and forth. And then he changes the subject, asking, "What happened to yer nose?"

Destiny's hand flies up to the scratch. "Oh, a cat and I had a difference of opinion."

"Aye, I've been there before." Madigan winces and laughs. "They're mightily opinionated, cats, aren't they?"

Destiny laughs and agrees, though something still niggles, a red light that won't allow her thoughts to accelerate past it. "But...*where* exactly were you doing the looking?" she presses.

Madigan frowns. "What do yeh mean?" he asks and then scratches his head.

"Well, you said you were looking out for me. And you knew *exactly* where I was at the very moment that I needed saving. But how were you doing it from here, in the foyer, when there's no windows or even a peephole at the door?" Destiny gestures to confirm her observations of the space.

Madigan's eyes widen for a second, but his eye contact doesn't waver. "I was just keepin' an eye out from the window that looks out onto the street from the bar, to be honest." He points at the archway leading off to another room.

What's strange is that Madigan is exhibiting all the signs of someone lying: gesturing only after speaking, rocking back and forth, changing the subject, using the phrase *to be honest*, and not blinking very much. There's also no possible way he would have had enough time to run from the bar window to the foyer door to rescue Destiny after spotting the carriage.

Her gaze snags on the coatrack from which a wet raincoat hangs, water pooling in the boot tray below. The stand next to it contains a dripping umbrella that was recently working hard to keep its owner dry. "It's just...your hair is quite wet," Destiny points out.

Madigan's hand shoots up to his head. Confirming Destiny's observation, he shrugs. "Aye, I stepped outside once or twice to look for yeh in case yeh'd gotten lost, the last time being just before I heard the horses." Not allowing Destiny to respond, he says, "Righty ho! Let's get yeh checked in. Here." He reaches down behind the desk to retrieve something. Handing her a damp towel, he says, "To dry yerself off with."

"Thank you." As Destiny towel dries her hair, she reminds herself how little interaction she's had with strangers in the past year.

That's probably what has made her hypersensitive to Madigan's body language, since it isn't something you can properly study over video calls. Just because her brain won't allow her to let go of his inconsistencies doesn't mean Madigan is up to no good. Even if she's right and he was lying, everyone does it, often for the most inconsequential reasons.

Coming out of her reverie, Destiny expects to see Madigan begin pecking away at a keyboard. Instead, he pulls out what looks like an ancient ledger along with a silver pen.

"Do you not have electricity?" Destiny asks. "Or cell phone reception?" Her stomach lurches at the thought.

He snorts. "Not this close to the castle," he replies, which is hardly an answer as far as Destiny is concerned, but Madigan begins firing off a batch of his own questions before she can pose more of hers.

Once he's written down Destiny's details in a beautiful script that's wholly unexpected coming from such a rugged man, she tries to sound nonchalant as she says, "I was told all expenses would be taken care of. Do you happen to know who made the reservation for me?"

"'Fraid not," Madigan says. "We don't keep records of things like that. Someone musta come in and done it, but I don't recall." He looks down at the ledger. "It's in Marge's handwritin' and she's off for the month, gone to visit her mother." He hands Destiny a key. "Yeh're in room 203. Why don't yeh go put yer stuff away and I'll serve dinner when yeh come back down."

Destiny's empty stomach growls at the mention of food. "Thank you." She wants to circle back to her questions about the Scruffmores—to ask how Madigan knows them, why he has their portrait hanging on the wall, why he didn't mention the third child in the painting, what Mordecai's like, if there have ever been rumors of infidelity, and if Mordecai had red hair as a younger man—but figures she'll have an opportunity during dinner. "I'll be as quick as I can."

"Take yer time." Madigan leaves her standing at the desk as he makes his way through the arch.

Destiny looks down at the brass room key, running her fingers over the ornate head, which is an outline of a boar's profile. It's exactly like the one she dreamed of just a few moments ago.

A shiver runs through her. Something very peculiar is happening all over again, just like it did when she was a child. And then again a year ago.

As terrifying as it is, it's thrilling too because it's in the repeated replication of investigations that a hypothesis can be born from a theory. The more opportunities she's given to study the outcome of the strange dreams, the more likely she'll be to rationally explain and control the phenomenon.

Destiny studies the portrait of the Scruffmore family again, her eyes drawn from Mordecai to his wife, a Black woman who clearly can't be Destiny's biological mother. She wonders if this woman knows Destiny is coming to the castle, and how she might feel about whatever secrets her husband will soon be revealing.

CHAPTER 12

Hexabus

Sunday—10:35 p.m.

Hexabus refuses to enter the castle through the front door like a common guest. Especially not when she's squaring her shoulders, steeling herself for battle. Instead, she comes in through the kitchen, instructing Barrington, the coach driver, to follow with her luggage once he's put the horses away. She'd carry the bags in herself but both hands are already full.

Story of her life.

Being here, in the prison she fled two decades ago, is enough to make her break out in hives, but it's not as if she can just turn around and leave. Not when her children are on the island, oblivious to what awaits. She can't even warn Darius and Evangeline of the potential danger they're in, which makes it all the more challenging. To act on the prophecy without having all the information might be to create a self-fulfilling one.

But like any mother, Hexabus will do whatever it takes to protect her children, no matter how unsavory she finds it. She will stoop low, abandon her pride completely, if she has to.

She's barely through the door when Newton steps out from the shadows, blocking her path.

"Bloody hell, you gave me a fright," Hexabus exclaims, dropping one of the cages.

Newton's platinum blonde hair glints like a blade in the gloom, her algae-green eyes seeped in menace. "Sorry," Newton says, looking Hexabus up and down, her heavily made-up eyes pointedly tracing Hexabus's hourglass curves. "That's what happens when you're as petite as I am. No one hears you coming."

"Oh, that's not entirely true. I hear your theatrical cries of passion every time I stay over. Put on purely for my benefit, I'm sure," Hexabus mutters, setting down the other cage before taking off her scarlet trench coat and hanging it up on the rack. While kicking off her rain boots, she adds, "Also, it wasn't your sudden appearance that surprised me. It's your face. Your plastic surgeon should be taken out at dawn and shot by a myopic firing squad. I hope you're planning to sue."

Newton flushes, her hand shooting up to her new cheek implants, caressing them as a toddler would a security blanket. "Guests come in through the front door, ya know," she hisses.

"Yes, I know," Hexabus replies, one brow arched. "That's how I used to let *you* inside back in the day. I'm sure Jesus welcomed Judas the same way."

Newton laughs, a shrill sound. "You're hardly Jesus."

Hexabus smiles. "I notice you didn't deny that you're Judas."

One of the cages emits a high-pitched yowling and Newton glares at it. "What the hell is that?"

"A cat."

"What?" Newton sneers. "*You* were running around outside in this weather capturing feral cats?" She eyes Hexabus up and down again. "You don't even look wet."

"You seem quite determined to forget that some of us aren't Peasants, Newt," Hexabus replies. "I'd even go so far as to call it being in denial. That's the right psychological term for it, yes?"

Newton flushes again. Her chastised expression makes her look so much like her daughters for a second that it lowers Hexabus's defenses. She may loathe Newton for her past betrayals, but ultimately, they are both just mothers trying to control the uncontrollable.

Leaning in close, Hexabus says, "If you know what's good for you, you'll pack your things and leave. Catch the first ferry out of here in the morning. Take Angel and Minx with you." It's the sincerest thing she's said to Newton in a very long time.

"Why?" Newton scoffs. "To make it easier for you and your own children to move back in?" Her voice cracks and she takes a jagged breath before continuing. "You think I haven't seen the way you've been with Morty lately? You supposedly come here to discuss business but use any excuse to ingratiate yourself, constantly fluttering your eyelashes at him."

Hexabus's empathy is quickly replaced by impatience. "You have no idea what you're talking about. Nor do you understand the danger you're in."

"Are you threatening me?" Newton asks, taking a step back.

"Just because you're threatened *by* me doesn't mean I'm threatening you. It's an important distinction."

Newton opens her mouth to respond, but approaching footsteps distract her.

Hexabus turns to see Maximus in lockstep with Killian, as though he's trying to race the butler to the kitchen. It's like a whip has cracked inside her, urging her heart to giddyap. It responds immediately by racing, racing, racing.

"Hexabus," Maximus exclaims, throwing out his arms as he advances.

His dark hair is only white at the temples. He wears his age like a designer suit, as handsome as he ever was, always a Robert Redford in comparison to Morty's Donald Sutherland.

"What a sight you are for sore eyes," he gushes, embracing her warmly. "How long has it been since we last saw each other? Twenty years?"

He's a damn good liar, Hexabus thinks, impressed. *Just as well, when there's so much at stake if Morty were to learn the truth about our meeting behind his back.* "Yes, something like that." She smiles, still struggling to rein in her galloping pulse. "Has Delicia joined you?"

"Ha! No," Maximus laughs. "That would be most uncomfortable for all concerned considering we divorced ten years ago."

Hexabus tries to make an appropriate sound that's somewhere between surprised and sympathetic, as though this weren't old news. She needs to act normally, keep her emotions completely in check.

Newton, who once knew Hexabus better than almost anyone, narrows her eyes as though she's onto her, a shark sensing a drop of blood blossoming in the water. Hexabus can't have Newton cottoning on and saying something to Morty, ruining all her months spent ingratiating herself to him.

"And Dominus?" Hexabus inquires after Maximus's son for the sake of appearances. "He must be here with you?"

"He is, though I haven't seen him for a few hours. But what do you expect from the youngest ruling warlock the Sorcerer's Guild has ever had? Always up to something or other. Speaking of which, how about you and I have a drink to catch up—"

"Mrs. Scruffmore?" Killian interjects.

"Yes?" Hexabus and Newton each reply, startled by the butler's uncharacteristic interruption.

Dipping his head in Newton's direction, he says, "Apologies, ma'am. I meant the *first* Mrs. Scruffmore." Turning to Hexabus, he continues, "Your chambers are ready, and I see you have cages in tow." Looking down at them, he asks, "May I take these up for you so we can get you settled?"

"Lurk," Newton growls. "Those cats are *not* permitted—"

"Thank you, Mr. Lurcock," Hexabus interrupts. She makes a point of respectfully using Killian's last name, the real one that got contracted to its current form. Turning back to Maximus, she says, "It's late and I'm pretty beat, Max. Can we catch up tomorrow?"

He nods knowingly and says, "Of course, Hex!" And then he smiles a slow smile that says everything they don't dare speak aloud. "I look forward to it."

As Killian picks up the cages, Hexabus glances at Newton, who's glaring at her suspiciously. She wishes Newton would listen to her and get her daughters as far away from the island as possible. Minx especially, since it's her kind of ambition that can get you killed in this family.

CHAPTER 13

Minx

Sunday—10:40 p.m.

As their Range Rover Autobiography pulls away from the curb, driven by a bodyguard who's struggling to navigate the mass of frenzied teenagers swarming the vehicle outside Claridge's, Minx runs a hand through her closely cropped magenta hair. She glares at Angel, who's sitting next to her, frowning down at her phone.

I hate you, Minx thinks for what's probably the millionth time in nineteen years. She's quite certain it was the first thought she ever had, formed while the two were trapped in the amniotic fluid of Newton's womb. *I despise you and wish you were dead.*

But had her wish come true, they wouldn't currently be surrounded by the hundreds of fans who're willing to risk getting run over just to take a selfie with the Scruffmore twins' car in the background. While their millions of followers hate-follow Minx, accusing her of being cold and calculating, they worship Angel for being adorably impetuous and refreshingly candid.

Without Angel, they'd have no influencer empire despite the rumors—all spread by themselves, of course—that they're both princesses of an obscure royal bloodline.

But without Angel, Minx also wouldn't be dealing with a powerful blackmailer who's trying to bleed them dry.

Although they're identical twins, the sisters don't look anything alike thanks to all the effort on Minx's part to ensure as much. It's amazing how much difference hair, makeup, and clothing can make. It's what initially attracted Minx to fashion since it offered her a way to escape the "which one are you, again?" hell of being a clone.

While Angel's aesthetic is "wholesome surfer girl," Minx's style is more "anime hottie meets hostile biker chick." In her low-slung black leather pants and her matching bustier—and with her short fuchsia hair, colorfully tinted John Lennon glasses, and slew of abstract tattoos—Minx is never going to get mixed up with her tousle-haired blonde sister.

"Does this picture make me look fat?" Angel flashes her screen at Minx. It's an unflattering photo taken a few hours ago at the Hermès event, posted by a competitor influencer.

Minx wants to reach out and throttle her sister. The rug is about to be ripped out from under them and yet all Angel cares about is social media.

"You look gorgeous," Minx says, forcing herself to sound sincere. "Just as you always do."

Angel nods, mollified.

Camera flashes explode all around them, an electric storm of adoration, as they lurch forward in increments. "Bruce, what's the hold up?" Minx demands. "We're going to miss our flight."

"Sorry, ma'am," he replies. "Some fans are trying to climb onto the hood."

Minx huffs. Flicking her wrist, she mutters what sounds like a curse word. The fans are immediately ejected from the car and flung into the crowd, which sends everyone toppling backward like dominoes.

"What the hell?" Bruce exclaims.

"Just drive!" Minx orders. Once they've accelerated through the gap Minx has created, she turns to Angel. "Are you able to put the phone away for a few minutes so we can go over everything for tomorrow?" Minx keeps her tone light, needing to handle Angel with kid gloves.

Angel groans but flips her phone over on the seat between them. The phone's charm, which looks like a puzzle piece, gleams as the screen goes black. "Fine. Tell me."

Once Minx is sure Angel's paying attention, she says, "Okay, so Mom thinks that Morty's called the family meeting to announce that, despite Darius being so useless, he's still going to be made king because there's no better candidate."

Angel rolls her eyes. "So what? Why should we care?" Her fingers inch toward her phone again.

"Because," Minx says, tracing the outline of a tattoo on her forearm, "Mom thinks that Morty's just waiting for Darius to step into the role before Daddy Dearest announces that he's getting back together with Hexabus."

"What?" Angel's eyes bug out as her hand freezes. "Morty's been having an affair with the Ice Queen?"

It's not the affair that surprises Angel, Minx knows. After all, the girls walked in on their father in flagrante delicto with one of the maids when they were just eight. And then again with his secretary, Shadow, when they were nine.

Angel is just surprised that the affair would be with Hexabus, whom they've always had a grudging respect for because she never indulged them the way everyone else did. Just the opposite, in fact. When they were girls, incessantly fawned over because of their doll-like beauty, it was Hexabus who pulled them aside one day and told them that good looks are a genetic lottery they could claim no credit for.

And that if they didn't want each birthday to become an exercise in torture (as it is for their own mother, who's so terrified of aging), they needed to develop some character and achieve something they could be proud of.

While many would have called it sour grapes on Hexabus's part, considering that she only discovered the paternity of her friend's babies on the day they were born, Minx has always oddly believed that the advice was an act of kindness. And she never forgot it.

"Holy shit," Angel says, shaking her head. "If Morty and Hexabus are getting back together, and Darius is being crowned, that means we'll definitely be cut from the will."

Their father makes a regular production of updating his last will and testament, pitting them all against one another in Hunger Games—esque politics to make them compete for limited resources. Despite the estate being vast, he's made it clear that he'll only reward those who please him. The new family and the old are framed as opposing teams with the implication being that there can only be one winner. Scruffmore bastards haven't been ruled out of the running, either.

But that's hardly the point. Typical of Angel, who isn't that bright, to always focus on the wrong thing.

By simply hanging on to their empire for a few years longer, they won't need Morty's money because they'll have more than enough of their own. And if Minx is forced to suffer the torment of Angel during that time, she's sure that—with the help of an exorbitantly expensive PR team that Angel's sponsorship deals would pay for, naturally—she'll greatly improve her image.

But luckily, she won't need to. Not if everything goes according to plan.

The more pressing monetary concern, as far as Angel should be concerned, is paying off their blackmailer before the deadline on Wednesday. After all, *she* doesn't know that their extortionist should have lost all leverage by then. But the vapid fool is too senseless to comprehend that.

"Right, Minx?" Angel sounds annoyed that her echo chamber isn't doing its job.

"Exactly." Minx forces herself to say, "We'll be disowned if Morty and Hexabus get back together. You're so smart to see that." When Angel nods smugly, Minx continues, "So, we obviously need to stop that from happening."

"How?" Angel pulls a gold compact from her purse and inspects her tiny pores.

"Mom wants you to accuse Dad of having an affair with Hexabus."

"What?" Angel startles, looking up. "Why me?"

Minx makes her eyes widen and become dewy. *Because that will put a target on your back.* Instead of speaking the truth, she says, "Because you're the only one everyone will believe. You know no one trusts me."

Angel nods again, making Minx want to punch her. "Okay, but how's that going to help anything?"

"You know how Darius and Evangeline feel about Morty. They hate him for marrying Mom and then replacing them. If they hear about the affair *before* Darius is crowned, they'll raise hell. Which means Hexabus will have to decide between her children and Morty." When Angel doesn't speak, just sits there looking confused, Minx prompts, "And you know that she'll have to choose her children. Which means Hexabus will break it off with Morty. And Darius will be so upset that he'll refuse the throne."

"Which means Dad will stay married to Mom and we'll stay in the will?" Angel asks, like she's solved a particularly difficult mathematical equation.

"Exactly," Minx says while thinking, *No, loser. It means the crown will be mine for the taking.*

Angel's brow furrows ever so slightly. "But won't Dad be pissed at me? For ruining his plans?"

"He'll actually *thank* you," Minx counters, "because getting back together with Hexabus is obviously a terrible idea, as is having Darius run our empire into the ground." When Angel doesn't look convinced, Minx adds, "Plus, Mom will owe you for doing this for her. She'll be forever in your debt."

It's a sore point that despite Angel being their fans' favorite, Minx has always been their mother's. Like a greedy child, Angel wants to be everyone's, and so it's this more than anything else that will convince her.

"And the money for the blackmailer?" Angel finally asks, almost as though it's an afterthought. "How are we going to get that?"

"Mom's finding a way as we speak," Minx lies smoothly. "To thank you for helping her with the Morty and Hexabus debacle."

Newton doesn't know a damn thing about the blackmail, of course, because Minx doesn't want there to be a trail of how many of Angel's messes she's having to clean up. The less evidence, the better. That way, one day soon, when something awful befalls Angel, no one will have any reason to doubt the sincerity and depth of Minx's grief.

Just because lightning struck the family once by taking Bramble doesn't mean it can't happen again to one of the twins. Minx smiles as she pictures herself weeping over Angel's grave.

CHAPTER 14

Evangeline

Sunday—10:40 p.m.

As Evangeline nears the crumbling stone walls of Eerie's cemetery, she casts a furtive glance over her shoulder, eyes flashing as she double-checks to make sure she hasn't been followed.

She doesn't know who sent the magical message, but it definitely wasn't her father, not when he's wielded so much power over Evangeline her whole life, and wouldn't want to lose that leverage.

You owe me because it's your fault my favorite child died. So, get your mother to agree to leave the marriage without kicking up a fuss. Help Newton move in to the castle and ensure that she and your baby sisters feel welcome. Convince your brother to give up his ridiculous dreams of being a restaurateur in Delheim and get him to invest in the island. Don't accept that illustrious keynote speaker invitation for that prestigious conference, because I need you to smooth over ruffled feathers with the Miffingtons. You're not worthy because of what you did, so step down as a candidate for the succession.

She doesn't doubt that he'd do anything to stop her if he knew she was out here trying to discover the truth. Because if the message is true, it absolves Evangeline of a lifetime of guilt and servitude. Which means she'll finally be free to walk away.

After checking every shadow until she's satisfied each is benign, Evangeline slips through the rickety iron gate, letting out a quavery sigh of relief to find the graveyard deserted. She shivers beneath her cloak, the chill and dread seeping into her bones.

Thrusting the shovel into the ground to free up her hands, Evangeline lowers her hood, the rain pummeling her face so hard that it instantly obscures her vision. Thunder booms overhead, its echo ricocheting around the cemetery's walls. She's getting more soaked by the second; it's going to be difficult keeping her grip on the shovel with her hands wet.

She needs to cast a shield, as much for visibility as for comfort. But for every action in nature there is an equal and opposite reaction. This rule applies just as much to the unnatural world, for there is no sorcery you can cast that doesn't have some kind of retaliation for subverting the natural laws. For spells of this nature, there are usually sacrifices that need to be made at the altar of magic.

A shield will keep her dry and allow her to see what she's doing, but if a night bird or bat flies into the invisible dome, its neck will be crushed instantly. Owls aren't likely to be out hunting because their prey will be sheltering in their underground burrows. Besides, their soft feathers aren't waterproof, so in foul weather like this, they're inclined to want to stay dry. Bats will only fly in the rain to eat, but with it being colder than usual, they're probably still hibernating.

It's unlikely, then, that her magical shelter will kill any creatures that Evangeline doesn't intend to kill. But that's not the only consideration.

Lightning will be attracted to its magnetism. If struck, the shield could make the electricity bounce in unpredictable ways and set fire to anything nearby. Everything is so waterlogged, though, that there isn't much in the way of kindling. Plus, the downpour would surely douse any flames.

Having thought everything through, Evangeline feels better. Still, it's impossible to foresee the unforeseeable. If anyone has spent a lifetime trying, it's Evangeline.

Making up her mind, she closes her eyes and rubs her temples, conjuring the shield. "Please don't hunt near here," she whispers to the winged creatures of the island, hoping they'll heed her warning.

Picking up the shovel, Evangeline heads east. Within fifteen paces, she comes upon a few of the graves of the Eerie Island serial killer's victims, some of whom were children who got tucked in at bedtime only to disappear overnight. Their headstones always make her tremble, especially since the killer was never caught despite their two-year reign of terror abruptly ending the year Bramble died.

Bramble.

The name is like sandpaper against Evangeline's psyche. Needing to warm up to the misery that thoughts of her brother always evoke, she stops to read the names on two of the moss-covered gravestones. Samuel Fitzpatrick and Dawn Montgomery. Both her childhood friends, killed within a year of one another.

It's bad luck knowing Evangeline Hyphen Scruffmore. Just ask Fitzy and Dawn, both murdered. And then Bramble taken, though not in the same way.

Straightening her spine, Evangeline forces herself to move on until she gets to the Scruffmore side of the cemetery, where the dates on the graves go back so far that it's impossible to tell when her ancestors were buried, the details having been erased from the headstones by hundreds of years of mercurial weather.

Bramble's tombstone is the newest, looming larger than the boy ever grew to be. It has the Scruffmore family crest carved into black marble. Evangeline reads the epitaph.

Bramble Mordecai Scruffmore
28 February 1992–28 February 2000
"It's never too late to be what you might have been."

Tomorrow is the twenty-second anniversary of Bramble's death. And the day he would've turned thirty.

The quote by George Eliot, chosen by her father, always struck Evangeline as being a rebuke at worst, and oblivious at best, considering that for Bramble, it was definitely too late to ever live up to any potential he might have once had. Trying to give her father the benefit of the doubt, Evangeline always ascribed his selection of it to his immense grief and refusal to accept that his favorite child was dead, his flame prematurely snuffed out.

Now, after reading the secret message, she's not so sure.

Evangeline lifts the shovel and slams it into the muddy earth as she begins digging. She could use magic to dislodge the soil, but this is something she should have to toil for. She isn't the praying kind, but the words she speaks to the grave are their own kind of invocation. "Please be empty."

CHAPTER 15

Choose Your Own Conundrum
Ian Montgomery—A Villager

Sunday Evening

You're Ian Montgomery, a blacksmith who's lived on Eerie Island your whole life, descended from a long line that has served the Scruffmore family for generations. Your family trade is a source of great pride, especially since you're still able to practice it every day when so many other blacksmiths have become defunct.

You tell yourself that's why you've never left the island despite the heartbreak and terror you've experienced here at the hands of the Scruffmores. For where else would you go? Blacksmithing is all that you know how to do, and this is one of the last places in the world where you can earn a living doing it.

Besides, this is where your daughter is buried.

Dawn always used to be afraid of the dark, begging for just one more bedtime story to keep you close, a fortress between her and the night. But you waved off her fears, telling her there was nothing to be afraid of. The worst part is that she believed you and let you leave her there alone in her room, where she was snatched one night, never to see the time of day that she was named for.

And you won't ever forgive yourself for that, for not believing her, and then failing to protect her. Which is why you now roam the island at night, keeping Dawn's spirit company in the fearful hours while keeping an eye out in case the threat returns. Most of the islanders think the killing curse was broken decades ago, but you know better. Especially after the recent disappearance of the Scruffmore family historian.

You don't believe what the rest of the villagers say, that the killer died or moved away. Those are just stories they tell one another, fairy tales they've concocted to allow themselves to sleep at night. Because you know, you just *know* it in the knotty marrow of your bones, that a Scruffmore is responsible for the murders.

You tell yourself that's another reason why you stay: to keep an eye on the Scruffmores so that maybe one day you'll find the evidence to ensure that justice is served.

But the truth is that you don't think you could leave even if you wanted to. There's something unnatural about the gravity of this island that doesn't allow anyone to be gone for long. It's more like you're all hostages than inhabitants.

The weather tonight is fouler than usual, but that doesn't put you off. Just after 9:00 p.m., you approach your wife where she sits by the fireplace staring vacantly at the flames. Jill clutches a framed photograph, the one taken on Dawn's tenth birthday. It shows the three of you down on the overcast beach, Dawn wearing a crown that says *Birthday Girl*. Her head is thrown back in laughter, long black hair splashed across your faces from the wind whipping it back at you. There's a dollop of chocolate cake in the corner of her mouth.

It's the last photo taken of Dawn and it's too painful for you to look at for very long, though it's the only thing that can capture Jill's attention for any length of time.

"I'll be off, then," you say.

Jill never asks where you're going. She doesn't speak at all, not since Dawn's body was found near the beach that your daughter loved so much, her skinny arms crossed over her chest, and a white rose tucked into her flowing dark hair. She looked so peaceful that the islander who first spotted her thought she was dozing, a little Sleeping Beauty.

You can't think on that too long.

"Goodnight, my darling. I'll see you in the morning," you say.

Jill doesn't even blink in acknowledgment as you kiss her cheek.

There is no set pattern you follow on your meanderings each night. You simply empty your mind and go wherever your feet take you. Sometimes, it's down to the docks. Other times, it's uphill to the castle. You're just as likely to end up at the jagged shoreline or on the beach as you are to amble along the warren of streets or slip through the village's courtyards and alleyways.

The only certainty is that you will pass the cemetery at some point to visit Dawn and to tell her a bedtime story.

After stepping out from your front door, you pause to let your subconscious decide on a route.

A. Downhill toward the docks to get as far away from the Scruffmores as possible—go to page 89.

B. Uphill toward the Scruffmores and the castle—go to page 92.

OPTION A: DOWNHILL TOWARD THE DOCKS

The wind slaps you around the face, waking you up as you make your way down the cobbled street. Lightning and thunder wrestle with one another overhead, putting on enough of a display to entertain the gods. It's comforting to have the heavens be just as loud as your mind, where *if only* constantly smashes up against *I wish* and *why didn't I?* The cacophony of regret is unrelenting.

You don't try to withdraw your head turtle-style into your shoulders as so many people do when confronted with rain. No, you don't deserve to stay dry, so you hold your head up high, giving the rain a clear target. You're soaked within seconds, icy water dripping down from your ears into your collar, running in rivulets down your neck.

You pass a trio of cats, who eye you warily. There's a black one that has no fear, that always comes running up to meet you, but it's not here tonight. Just as well, as you're tempted to pick it up even though doing so might cause hives. Dawn always wanted a kitten, but you said no because of your allergies.

It's just another regret to add to the pile that threatens to topple over in an avalanche that, when its deadly onslaught finally comes for you, you won't even try to escape.

It's your habit to keep to the shadows. People in small villages talk. Gossip is a currency all its own and some people are made wealthy by it. It was bad enough having all those tongues wagging when Dawn was found. You don't want to give them any more fodder in the event that someone sees you and wonders if you've lost your mind. There are already whispers about Jill having lost hers.

As you near the inn, the door suddenly swings open. Madigan McGoo ducks out, gazing furtively about. You press yourself up against a nearby wall, careful to not have him spot you. You wonder why he looks so shifty and what he might be up to.

There are some who say the inn is haunted and—considering the strange folk who frequent it, the otherworldly visitors who come to the island to do ungodly business with the Scruffmores—you don't blame them. You couldn't be paid to spend a night under its roof, not with the shrieking and chattering you've occasionally heard coming from inside during the darkest hours.

Footsteps echo nearby and you shrink farther back into the shadows. There's a man coming down the hill, dressed in a flapping black cloak that blends into the night. His hood is pulled up, and despite the awful weather, he's using his umbrella as a kind of rakish walking stick.

There weren't many eyewitness accounts when all those villagers were murdered so many years ago. But of the handful of people who came forward, there was one consistency in their accounts. They all saw a tall hooded figure leaving the scene, one who always remained dry despite the inclement weather.

When you turn back, Madigan's no longer there, probably gone back inside, which is a smart move in this god-awful storm.

Returning your attention to the man, you realize you recognize him when a flash of lightning illuminates his face. He's one of the Scruffmore lads, either Dominus or Darius; it's difficult to tell which since the two look so much alike, even with the seven-year age difference.

Your pulse begins to race as you watch him walking the deserted streets. He looks to be somewhere around the same age Dawn would have been if she'd lived. The thought sends acid erupting up your throat.

Squinting into the gloom, you consider how you've never liked either of the boys. There was always something *off* about them.

While many would scoff at the notion of one of them being the island's murderer, since they were just children at the time, you've heard rumors from those who have worked inside Scruffmore Castle, talk of sorcery and dark magic. The thought of petulant children wielding that kind of power, when they don't yet have control over their own emotions, is terrifying.

What is he doing out here in these terrible conditions, just wandering the streets?

The hairs on your arms begin to rise and you experience a sudden certainty that Dominus or Darius can see you, that he can *feel* your eyes trained on him. And so you close them and shrink even farther back, holding your breath. It takes an eternity for your pulse to slow and for the pain in your chest to ease.

When you look again, he's disappeared. You cast your gaze about for him, but he's nowhere to be found. Instead, there's a bundle of something lying in the tavern's doorway. *What has he put there?*

Your fear outweighs your curiosity. You turn away, wanting to put as much distance as possible between yourself and the inn.

Go to page 94.

OPTION B: UPHILL TOWARD THE CASTLE

There was a time that you could jog up these steep streets on the way to work without breaking a sweat. But now, as you trudge up the hill, you feel every one of your sixty years plus another decade's worth.

The cobblestones are slick underfoot and gleam yellow in the lamplight. Lightning tears through the sky like the gods are ripping apart the very fabric of the heavens. You'd welcome Armageddon; at least then, the good of the world might finally triumph over the evil.

It's as you're approaching the castle—tension coiling around your throat to be so near the vipers' nest—that you hear the clopping of horses' hooves, the sound echoing in the narrow street. You duck into an alleyway and watch as the Scruffmore coach races past. It looks like there's a passenger in the carriage. You wonder who it might be and how they arrived so long after the last ferry.

The Scruffmores are an insular lot. And yet carriages have been sweeping back and forth all day. Besides, the air feels thicker, more staticky and electric. You've noticed it's something that happens the rare times the family gathers. It happened two years ago as well.

You've heard rumors that Maximus Scruffmore has returned from his exile along with that strange son of his. The two brothers had a spectacular falling-out more than two decades ago just after the youngest Scruffmore boy died. Depending on who you ask, either Mordecai banished Maximus from the island, or Maximus refused to spend another night under his brother's roof.

There are some who say that Maximus was having an affair with Hexabus, that it was the betrayal that sent Mordecai into an apoplectic rage since he'd always been so jealous of his younger brother's good looks and charisma.

Regardless of the family drama, you consider it more than a coincidence that the killings on the island stopped just after Maximus's hasty departure with his wife and son.

A rattling and grinding noise signals that the drawbridge is being lowered. You wait until it's raised again before you continue circling the perimeter of the castle, not encountering another soul.

When something suddenly slams into your back ten minutes later, you're too alarmed to cry out. Your first thought is that it's the killer finally coming for you. You whip your fists up, ready to fight back. Even as you do so, you realize how long you've waited for a target, someone to direct all your rage at instead of some faceless, nameless enemy.

Spinning around, you're confused to be confronted with nothing. There's no one there. Is this the sorcery you've heard of? Some kind of invisible magic attacking you?

But no, looking down, you see an umbrella somersaulting away. You let out a shaky breath, more disappointed than relieved.

Hours pass this way as you squelch through the night. It's only when your knees start to ache that you head for the cemetery, almost tripping over a raccoon that darts out of the shadows. You swear under your breath, recovering your balance, which is when you spot a hooded figure leaving the graveyard through the iron gate. They're carrying a shovel and are breathing heavily.

Is this the killer? Are they back, as Ms. Le Roux's disappearance might suggest?

You're about to make your trembling legs move to follow them when, inconceivably, the person has disappeared.

Go to page 94.

You take the familiar route to Dawn's tombstone, a marble angel that's slumped over the grave, weeping.

There was a time when you waged war against the encroaching moss, diligently scrubbing it from the angel's dejected wings. But you've long given up on that particular battle.

Time passes; it erodes and corrodes objects as much as it does memories and emotions. To fight against it is to foolishly believe that you can wade into the tide, stopping it with nothing but your raised fists. You know better since there is nothing that makes you understand your insignificance, your complete and utter helplessness, like burying your own child.

"Hello, my love," you say, speaking to be heard above the raging storm. Forming words is difficult with your lips so cold and numb, your teeth set to chattering. "What story would you like to hear tonight?"

What Dawn always loved best was fairy tales. But since her death, you can't bring yourself to read any to her, for which one would you choose? The one about the man with the flute who lured children away, almost certainly to their deaths? Or the one with the witch in the gingerbread house who kidnapped children to fatten them up for eating? Or the one where the wolf preys on the little girl and her grandmother?

Threats abound for the most vulnerable in fairy tales. Just as in real life. And you don't have the heart for it.

What you try not to think of is how "Sleeping Beauty" was Dawn's favorite fairy tale. How she made you read it to her over and over again. How, when you came up the stairs some nights to tuck her in, you'd find her in bed, hair fanned out, arms crossed over her chest, a tiny smile tugging at the corners of her mouth as she tried not to giggle while pretending to be trapped in an eternal asleep.

Is it better or worse that she was found in that position? That her killer carefully arranged her that way instead of discarding her body in a dumpster or throwing it off the docks? You don't know, and no matter how much you think on it, you can't decide.

It's the thing that vexes you most about all the murders on the island. How lovingly staged each of the victims were, found in places or in poses that spoke of who they were or what they loved best. *A kindly killer?* You scoff at the thought.

You begin your bedtime story with "Once upon a time," making up a tale about a magical umbrella that, when clutched by a child, can carry them over seas and mountains, sailing through clouds and down rainbows, on all kinds of magical adventures.

But most important, far, far away from danger.

CHAPTER 16

Destiny

Sunday—10:40 p.m.

As Destiny returns downstairs ten minutes later, still damp despite changing into a dry set of clothes, she wonders what happened to her umbrella. She can't help but picture it sailing across the night sky, a flying sword ready to impale unsuspecting cats. She shivers at the thought.

In the tavern, there are a lot more open flames about than Destiny would like. Hot wax drips down the sides of candles wedged into old wine bottles, and lanterns creak and sway from the beams overhead. An enormous fireplace takes up one of the walls, while an arresting oil painting fills another. The other two walls are covered with mounted animal heads whose eyes seem to track Destiny's every move. The flames reflected in their glass eyeballs make them look like dozens of twin portals to hell.

Destiny's immense relief at spotting Tempest snuffs out her concerns about the flames. She almost rushes to hug her but stifles the impulse just in time when Tempest shoots her that same disgusted look from before. Tempest is now perched on a stool at the hand-carved wooden bar where Madigan presides, her legs crossed and chin resting coquettishly on her hand. A man is seated next to her, dressed all in white and wearing an assortment of strange rings. His eyes are so amber that they're almost orange, and giant dimples crater his chiseled cheeks.

His beauty takes Destiny's breath away.

It's not that she hasn't seen men this gorgeous before. Of course she has. But to be one of only three other people in the room with someone like him makes her feel even more awkward than usual.

It takes her back to when the neighborhood boys called her names like Chubster and Chestiny on account of her weight and bosom, which developed early. After her high school experience disappointed her, she hoped it would be less difficult in university, which she started attending at twelve, but no. If anything, those boys on the cusp of manhood were even more vicious, the extra years' practice only serving to sharpen their cruelty.

It's gotten slightly easier now in adulthood.

Having your own Wikipedia page and getting *New York Times* profiles written about you does tend to bolster your confidence. Though sometimes being referred to as *homely, curvy*, or *dowdy* in those articles undermines the things they say about Destiny's brilliant mind.

"Aha, the prodigal guest!" the man exclaims upon noticing Destiny. "How wonderful that you finally found us."

Madigan nods at his companion, saying, "This is Silver. The owner of this fine establishment, who's visitin' from Gwillumbury." While his words are deferential, there's something almost fearful in his tone.

Silver makes a wry face. "I pop in every few weeks to ensure Madigan hasn't burned the place down." Then he smiles. "And you must be Destiny. Tempest was just telling me all about you."

Destiny blushes, wondering what awful things Tempest is likely to have said. Tempest's smirk doesn't do anything to allay her suspicions.

Trying to ignore Tempest's *Mean Girls* vibe, Destiny turns her attention to figuring out why a man like this would own a dilapidated inn on such a remote island. Or why someone like Madigan would presumably live and work here. Surely there are better ways to make a living elsewhere. How many visitors can the island possibly get every year? It hardly looks like a hub of tourism.

But then the same goes for the Scruffmores. Why hole up in a castle on this jagged rock in the middle of nowhere? Perhaps they only stay because their near-extinct sovereignty is limited to the island and its inhabitants. In which case, are they hanging on to their dwindling power out of an overwhelming sense of responsibility to the islanders, or is there another reason?

"Drink?" Madigan asks as he pours a glass of red wine for Tempest and a scotch for Silver.

"Could I have hot chocolate, please?" Destiny asks. "Only if it isn't too much trouble." Noticing the notepad and pen in front of Silver, she asks, "What are you working on?"

Dropping the pen, Silver stretches. "A to-do list for the week. Madigan's a lazy bastard who'd rather let the entire place crumble around him than do a stitch of work. I have to crack the whip when I'm here."

Destiny glances at the list.

Fix the eves.

And the gutters to.

Speak to Simon about there craft beer options.

She winces at his atrocious spelling even while thinking that it at least makes Silver slightly more approachable.

"Madigan, did you see the pile of clothes left in the doorway earlier?" Silver calls after Madigan's retreating back. Without waiting for an answer, he turns to Destiny to explain. "Madigan is the village do-gooder. He's always collecting something for some charitable cause or other."

"How lovely," Destiny says, already making up her mind to leave an item or two behind when she sets out in the morning.

"Not so much when you're the one always falling over the bloody donations, likely to break your damn neck," Silver grumbles, an edge to his voice.

"Sorry about that," Madigan says, returning with a steaming mug, which he hands to Destiny. His eyes dart to Silver, wary. "I'll ask the villagers to be more mindful with where they leave them."

Tempest stands and walks over to the strange piece of art that Destiny noticed earlier. It depicts what looks like an evil fairy who's fighting off the grim reaper while simultaneously sipping a silvery liquid from an elaborate goblet. It seems that *all* women have to learn how to multitask, not just the human ones.

"Ah, I see yeh've noticed our mysterious paintin'," Madigan calls, heading over to Tempest.

"What's so mysterious about it?" Tempest asks.

"It just turned up here one day while I was out back takin' a delivery of a few kegs."

"What? Someone just left it in the bar?" Tempest asks incredulously, looking from Madigan to the painting.

"Aye, they did one better. They hung it up right there," Madigan says, laughing. "Clearly didn't like my decor."

"That fairy thing gives me the creeps," Silver mutters. He shakes his head, his mouth a grim line as he side-eyes the painting. "I told you to find a way to take it down, Madigan."

"I tried but they did a really thorough job of mountin' it. It will damage the wall if I prize it off."

"I'd get it appraised if I were you," Tempest says, leaning

close and studying the brushstrokes. "It looks like the work of Octavia Constantine, a mid-nineteenth-century occultist painter, who was said to be quite mad. She had ties to Carlos Estrava, a shaman who claimed to be able to divine the future. It could be worth something."

Madigan perks up at this but Silver waves it off. "I'm sure it's a knockoff. Who'd anonymously give a buffoon like Madigan a painting that's worth a fortune?"

"Yes, there *are* a lot of forgeries out there," Tempest agrees, laughing. "And it isn't signed, which would be unusual." She heads back to the bar, where she sits down again between Destiny and Silver, though Destiny notices that she scooches her stool closer to Silver in the process.

"Aren't you so wonderfully knowledgeable." Silver rests his head in his palm, looking impressed. "How do you know so much about art?"

Destiny thinks back to the gallery she heard Tempest mention while on the phone during the ferry crossing.

"Oh, I took a few art history classes back in the day," Tempest says breezily, clearly pleased by the younger man's attention. She runs a hand through her hair. "And I worked in an art museum doing tours when I was in college."

"She's lying," Bex suddenly hisses.

The ghostly voice, insistent in Destiny's ear, makes her startle. She's been so busy acclimating to being around the living that she completely lost track of her spectral best friend. This oversight shames her; she can only hope Bex hasn't noticed.

Before Destiny can process Bex's accusation, Madigan nods at the corner of the painting. "Do you know what these symbols mean? They look like writin', but not any language I can read."

At the mention of symbols, Destiny jumps up to join him.

He points out the small glyphs. "Do you also know a bit about art—"

Destiny gently shushes him as she studies them.

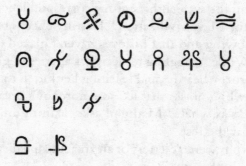

A delicious tingling begins in her belly; it's the sensation she gets whenever she's faced with a mystery to solve. She's heard other people describe experiencing a similar feeling when falling in love. If that's true, then enigmas are what Destiny falls in love with over and over again.

This one is particularly interesting and so Destiny takes her time, giving it the attention it deserves, not straightening up until she's satisfied with her conclusion. Finally, she nods and says, "Exactly as I thought."

Madigan's expression is incredulous. "Were yeh able to read it?"

"No," Destiny replies, walking back to the bar as Madigan trails her. "But you're not supposed to *read* it." When Tempest raises an eyebrow, Destiny continues, "Are you familiar with the work of Yuri Knorozov and Aspid?"

Tempest rolls her eyes, looking annoyed. "No. Who are they?"

"Knorozov was a Russian linguist, epigraphist, and ethnographer who cracked the Mayan code."

"Aye," Madigan replies, scratching the back of his head. "The Mayan code. Right. Cool… And who was, err, that Aspid fella?"

"*She* was his cat, who was formally credited as the coauthor of Knorozov's landmark study."

"What?" Silver barks a laugh. "You can't be serious!"

"Deadly serious!" Destiny asserts gravely. "Knorozov was working on a paper known as the de Landa Alphabet, which was based on the sixteenth-century correspondence of a noted student of the Maya civilization." Destiny checks to make sure Silver's following and that his eyes haven't glazed over. So far, so good. "While struggling to decipher a series of glyphs for his thesis, Knorozov heard Aspid teaching her kitten to hunt. It was Aspid's mewling noises that led to Knorozov's breakthrough."

"Which was what?" Madigan asks, leaning in, apparently eager to hear the rest.

"The glyphs weren't letters of an ancient alphabet, as Knorozov originally thought."

"What were they, then?" Madigan prompts.

"Phonetic symbols intended to be spoken. It completely revolutionized the understanding of the way script has evolved over the ages."

"That's what yeh think these, err, glyph things are. Phonetic symbols and not an alphabet?" Madigan asks.

"Yes, exactly."

"Can you solve them?" he asks, appraising Destiny in a whole new way now, like she's his own Rosetta stone to unlocking the mysteries of the universe.

Looking back at the painting, Destiny says, "I think I already did." She clears her throat, enjoying being the center of attention in a group of the popular kids—for once not because she's so weird and is being mocked for it but because she's smart and capable. And then she deciphers the glyphs as Bex cheers her on, Destiny once again attuned to her best friend's frequency. ★★[4]

---

4. You now have all the resources you require to solve the glyphs. If you need a clue to assist you, email DestinyWhipClue@gmail.com using the subject line Clue Four. Once you've solved them, turn to page 461 to check your answer.

CHAPTER 17

Destiny

Sunday—11:11 p.m.

When she's done, Silver claps. "Well done, prodigal guest!" And then he pulls a face, asking, "But what does it mean?"

"No idea," Destiny says. "I'm afraid that's outside the scope of the assignment."

"How were you able to do that?" Tempest demands.

Destiny's immediately on her guard, careful about what she reveals. Considering what the invitation cautioned, she needs to be the one getting answers at this point, not the one providing them.

Thinking back to what Tempest said earlier, she replies, "Oh, I took a few linguistics classes back in the day. And I worked in a, er, linguistics museum as a tour guide! Quite amazing what you pick up."

Tempest shoots her a sour look.

"Time to eat," Madigan exclaims, donning an apron that says *Your opinion wasn't in this recipe*. "Traditional Scottish stew and soda bread good for everyone?" he asks, before ushering them over to a table.

The food is heavenly, and Destiny positively inhales it as her empty stomach mumbles its thanks.

"Too much salt as per usual," Silver says, his tone cutting. "It's almost unpalatable. You'd think you'd be better at this by now, Madigan. What was the point of all the cooking classes I paid for?"

Madigan flushes. "Yeh're right. Sorry about that. I'll take more care next time."

Destiny's about to protest, point out that Silver has almost finished his entire serving, when there's a scream followed by banging. Destiny jolts, dropping her spoon, which clatters to the table. "What was that?"

Tempest cocks her head as Silver casts a nervous gaze out the window.

"I'm sure it's just the wind," Madigan says. "There are a few loose eaves likely to come off in this storm." He stands. "I'll go take a look."

Destiny thinks of the glyph she just solved. Turning to Tempest, she asks, "Did it sound like screaming to you?"

Before Tempest can reply, the gale picks up again, its high-pitched wail tearing through the night.

"The wind can sound very forlorn here," Silver says as Madigan leaves the bar. "That's why it's called Eerie Island."

The lanterns creak on the beams overhead and Destiny cringes, thinking how easy it would be for one of them to fall and shatter, setting the whole tavern alight. She swallows deeply, becoming hyperaware of the scent of woodsmoke drifting over from the fireplace. Sweat begins to bead under her arms, trickling down her sides. She focuses on the red-and-white-checkered tablecloth, counting the squares so she can fight off the memory of the smoke all those years ago, how it burned her throat and lungs even as she struggled to stop herself from breathing it in.

"It's exactly as I suspected," Madigan says when he returns, interrupting Destiny's spiraling thoughts. "I'll get those eaves fixed tomorrow." He shoots Silver a placating look, clearly afraid he's going to be berated again.

Now that unease has wrapped itself around Destiny like a cloak, she can't shake it off. They're so isolated here and no one knows her whereabouts. Coming to the island was clearly a foolish, impulsive thing to do, and she has the sudden urge to make a few phone calls. "You were saying earlier about the lack of electricity and cell phone reception?" she prompts Madigan. "I had some at the ferry, but not here."

"Yeah," Tempest says. "And what's with going the damned Amish route for transport?"

Silver reaches for the bottle of wine that Madigan set down earlier. Topping up Tempest's glass while pointedly ignoring Madigan's empty one, he says, "Electricity only works down at the harbor. The closer you get to the castle, the less there is. Engines even stop working this far up. That's why no one on the island bothers with cars."

"What? Seriously?" As much as the thought of a world without cars appeals to Destiny, she's still shocked. The military and law enforcement sometimes use signal jammers to block reception between cell towers and mobile phones. But beyond someone blowing up a substation, she doesn't think there's a way to just block electricity or stop machinery from working.

"Is that a weird altitude thing," Tempest asks, "or like a Bermuda Triangle thing?"

Silver wordlessly thrusts his empty glass at Madigan, jiggling it in front of his face. As Madigan stands and heads back to the bar, Silver says, "Nah, it's a Scruffmore thing."

What an odd thing to say, Destiny thinks with a sense of foreboding. *What could that possibly mean?*

She's about to ask him to clarify when he abruptly changes the subject. "So, what are two fine women like you doing in a god-awful place like this?" He turns to Tempest. "You were saying earlier that you've applied for a job here?"

Finally, Destiny thinks, putting her other questions on the back burner so she can hear the answer to this one.

"Yes. I'm one of two candidates short-listed for a position with the family. I'm here for the interview."

Destiny startles, taken aback. *Huh. So, the historian position is real, and Tempest is the other candidate mentioned.*

"The trip didn't get off to the best start, though," Tempest continues, running a hand through her white-blond hair. "Besides the horrible crossing and hideous weather, the ferry-ticket numbers I was given didn't work. The ferry master at the mainland laughed at me when I tried to use them. Can you believe it?"

Destiny *can* believe it. Because the ticket numbers were a fabrication.

"Huh, that's right strange," Madigan says. "May I see 'em?"

"Sure," Tempest murmurs, pulling a gray envelope from her purse. She extracts the page from it and lays it down in the middle of the table.

"The interview is tomorrow?" Silver asks, clearly surprised.

"Yes, why?"

"It's just that the family is gathering for a big meeting then. It's odd that Mordecai would conduct the interview on the same day."

So that's why Madigan asked if I'm here visiting the two Scruffmore children—they're going to be on the island for the meeting, Destiny thinks, excited at the possibility of running into them.

"He's clearly a very busy man," Tempest replies, shrugging. "I'd expect nothing less from a ruling monarch," she adds, making Destiny wonder how Tempest knows the Scruffmores are royalty since it wasn't mentioned in the letter and there was no reference to it online.

Perhaps Madigan told her when she checked in.

Destiny scans the letter upside down, surprised to discover that it's identical to her own except for Tempest's name, obviously, and the time of the interview. The exact same hidden message that Destiny got is contained within, but it must have gone unsolved since Tempest didn't realize the ferry tickets were a key to unlocking the code.

Destiny experiences a frisson of disappointment that she wasn't the only one to get the secret message. What can that possibly mean, though? Why would Tempest get a hidden note if she actually applied for the historian job? Unless she didn't and is just pretending otherwise. Does that mean she's also pretending to not have spotted the message? Could her own family have secrets they've kept from her that Mordecai Scruffmore knows about?

Maybe, Destiny tells herself, *Mordecai was confident Tempest wouldn't unlock a message not meant for her, which is why he didn't bother writing two totally different versions of the letter.*

"I don't trust her at all," Bex whispers.

"What happened to their last historian?" Tempest asks, oblivious to the ghostly scrutiny she's under. "Did she retire?"

"No," Silver says. "She disappeared."

"Disappeared?" Tempest yelps, her perfect eyebrows shooting up.

"What do you mean?" Destiny asks.

"Lumina Le Roux worked for the family for years, as far back as I can remember," Silver says as Madigan glances up at him from the letter. "And then one morning, two weeks ago, she just didn't arrive for breakfast. Someone went to check if she was ill, but they couldn't find her. All of her possessions were still there, money and passport included. It's like she'd just disappeared into thin air." Silver snaps his fingers for emphasis.

"How strange," Tempest mutters.

The sense of unease Destiny felt earlier is now blossoming into full-blown anxiety.

"People *don't* just disappear into thin air."

They're either kidnapped or murdered, or they make a run for it with as little baggage as possible to stop them from being slowed down. Sometimes, if they suffer from some form of dementia or have experienced a brain injury, they might wander off unnoticed, only to have something awful occur to them along the way. Occasionally, they return of their own accord.

More often than not, their bodies are what's discovered at some point because every disappearance leaves a trace; you just need to know where to look.

There are all kinds of terrible things that can befall human beings, but being swallowed up by the atmosphere isn't one of them.

"People have a way of disappearing on Eerie Island," Silver says, looking grim, the candlelight casting deep shadows that pool under his eyes. "It makes the villagers nervous to venture out after dark."

That explains why Destiny didn't encounter anyone on her way from the ferry, though the explanation is hardly reassuring. "Other people besides Lumina Le Roux, you mean?"

"We had a serial killer active here many years ago. He claimed dozens of lives. Some say he's back again and that Lumina was his latest victim."

"Oh my god." Destiny remembers the thought she had when she first laid eyes on the island from the ferry. *Bad things happen there.* And despite the landscape warning her to turn around and go back—despite even that cat warning her off—Destiny refused to be dissuaded.

"You know what they say," Bex whispers now. "Curiosity killed the cat." After a beat, she adds, "That's *you* in this scenario, Destiny, in case there's any confusion."

Gulping, Destiny asks, "They were never caught?"

It's Madigan who answers, shaking his head, clearly giving up on figuring out the strange ferry-ticket numbers. "Sorry to say, but no."

"This is quite the dud position you're vying for," Silver says. "You'd have to work on a remote island, which has god-awful weather and zero creature comforts, for a despot king who reigns over a defunct empire. Plus, there's always a chance that something terrible might happen to you."

Destiny wants to ask why, if all this is true, Silver lives here, why he didn't leave long ago, but it's Tempest who's the first to speak. "Not a fan of the Scruffmores, then?"

"*He* is," Silver says, jutting his chin out disdainfully at Madigan. "But not me." A note of bitterness creeps into his voice. "Most of the villagers feel the same way, about the king espe-

A MOST PUZZLING MURDER

cially. There's many who think the island would be better off without him, me included."

This makes Destiny's stomach drop.

Just an hour ago, she was standing in the foyer studying the Scruffmore family portrait, hoping Mordecai might be her father and that his solemn-looking children could be her half siblings. She's not sure what she was imagining exactly, some warm and fuzzy reunion, someone finally claiming her for good rather than passing her along like a dog who isn't house-trained, the pitiful creature constantly being returned to the pound.

She's embarrassed by the thought, by its ridiculous optimism, which has evaporated like the fog from earlier.

The Scruffmores sound terrifying. What have I gotten myself into by so recklessly rushing out here?

"I'm not among the detractors," Madigan says quietly. His eyes dart to Silver, as though nervous how he'll react to being disagreed with in this way. "I quite like some members of the family. Prince Darius and Princess Evangeline, especially."

"Yes," Silver says with a grim smile that doesn't quite reach his eyes. "Those two aren't too bad." And then he wriggles his eyebrows playfully to lighten the mood. "There are some who say that Mordecai has actual magical powers. That's what all the weird face tattoos are for. To help him work his dark spells."

"What nonsense," Tempest scoffs. "There's no such thing as magic!"

Madigan makes a sweeping gesture, as if to say *Isn't there?*, just as Tempest reaches for her drink. The glass gets knocked onto its side, the wine now seeping over the letter. "Och, I'm so sorry about that!" Madigan swipes at it with a cloth, trying to save it.

"God, Madigan," Silver huffs. "You're such a clumsy oaf."

"Don't worry about it," Tempest says. "I remember all the important details." She taps her forehead. "But you're definitely going to have to top that up." Smiling, she nods at the empty glass.

When Madigan has replenished it, still issuing apologies that are mostly directed at Silver, Tempest takes a sip. "I don't know about magic," she says, "but I believe in forces that we don't understand."

"What do you mean?" Destiny asks, feeling a prickling of anticipation. This is the moment she's been waiting for, the revealing of a clue that will explain how Tempest fits into everything.

"Well, I've had a few dreams that have come true," Tempest replies, eyeing them all warily as though expecting them to laugh at her. "Enough that I keep records of them in a journal. And I sometimes get the strangest sense of déjà vu, like I know what someone's going to say before they say it."

Destiny is surprised by the possibility that she and Tempest might have anything in common.

"When my sister and I were ten," Tempest continues, "I swore I saw the ghost of our father, though no one believed me, of course."

"Not much of a ghost detector, though, are you?" Bex goads from next to Tempest. "I've been here the whole time and you've been completely oblivious. Not an inch of gooseflesh in sight."

"I think we've all experienced things like that at some time or other." Silver reaches out and pats Tempest's hand. "And you women, with your sixth sense. I think you're all a bit witchy."

As if to prove his point, Tempest studies Destiny shrewdly. "*You're* the other candidate for the historian position, aren't you? You're my competition."

Destiny's mind whirs. The island doesn't have any access to the internet, which means Tempest can't look her up to discover her real occupation. And while the letter instructed her to tell no one, they'll see each other at the castle tomorrow anyway, so there's no point in denying it. Destiny nods, wary.

"Forgive me for saying," Tempest says, "but you're still a baby. Have you even finished university?"

"I'm twenty-one, although I graduated with my doctorate at eighteen."

"A child prodigy, then," Tempest says, looking reluctantly impressed.

"May the best historian win." Silver raises his glass to them both while ogling Tempest's cleavage, making it clear which of them he'd prefer to have on the island permanently.

Destiny suddenly has a very unsettling thought. Are she and Tempest going to be pitted against each other with Mordecai only divulging his secrets to one of them? Is that what the so-called interview is really about?

When Madigan ushers them all out at midnight, the tavern's closing time, Destiny makes her way up the stairs to her room. She doesn't know whether to be worried for Tempest, in terms of her getting the job and staying on this godforsaken island, or if she needs to be wary of this woman, whom she's dreamed of and whose intentions she knows nothing about. Why would a regular historian who's just come to the island to interview for a job loom so large in Destiny's dream? It doesn't make sense.

And then Destiny goes cold.

Perhaps she's been looking at it all wrong and Tempest isn't a threat despite how awful she's been to Destiny. Maybe something terrible is going to happen *to* Tempest and Destiny's here to prevent that from happening. After all, the other two prophetic dreams were warnings about what was going to happen to Liz and then Bex.

Destiny has been desperate for a do-over, a way to vindicate herself for letting her mother and best friend down so miserably. If this is her opportunity, she absolutely cannot fail again.

CHAPTER 18

Evangeline

Monday—1:48 a.m.

There are some terrible things that can't be prevented from happening no matter how hard you try, Evangeline thinks as she swats spiderwebs out of her face in the tunnel leading back to the castle. *And then there are some that never really happened at all despite you living with the consequences of them all your life.*

She's still in shock after digging up Bramble's grave. Bending over, she clutches herself, weeping. Memories act as a riptide, pulling her back to that fateful night.

★ ★ ★

"Eva," a voice whispered in the dark. The mattress dented as someone hopped up onto it and crawled over to her. When Evangeline opened her eyes, Bramble's unruly mop of curls tickled her nose as he peered down at her. "Eva. Are you awake?"

"I am now," she groaned. "What time is it?"

"It's time for my birthday. I'm eight!" Bramble exclaimed in that delightful lisp of his as he bounced with excitement.

"Happy birthday, Billy. Now go back to bed."

"No. It's time for a birthday adventure!"

Evangeline gently pushed Bramble off and struggled to sit up. She looked out her window at the moon, which looked like a giant's fingernail hanging in the sky. Judging by its position, she figured it was just after midnight. She sighed. "We can't go out. It isn't safe."

"But it's my eighth birthday, Eva! We *have* to do it! We just have to!"

It was tradition in magical families for children to sneak out on milestone birthdays so they could use, for the very first time, whatever powers were only unlocked at those particular ages. Evangeline had snuck down to the beach five years before on her eighth birthday to practice summoning spells. Darius did the same almost three years after her.

But that was back when it was still safe to be out at night, before kids like Fitz and Dawn started disappearing, before Dawn's body was found on the beach, and Fitz was found dead in the playground he'd loved so much.

Evangeline took her brother's hand and sighed. "Billy, you know what Mom said. We're not allowed to do that anymore."

"But we have powers! We're magical. The baddies can't mess with us like they can with other people. We can protect ourselves. Kapow, kapow," he yelled, firing off imaginary pistols. When Evangeline still didn't move, Bramble frowned. "If you won't come with me, I'll go on my own." He hopped off the bed and began marching to the door, looking like an angry cherub.

"Wait!" Short of waking their mother and getting Bramble into trouble on his birthday, Evangeline couldn't think of what else to do except go with him to offer her protection.

Truth be told, she yearned for the spontaneity and freedom they used to enjoy, how the island was like their giant personal playground. She missed the adventures the three of them would have—how much of a clique they were as young royals ostracized by the Peasant children—before Darius started being so mean to Bramble, refusing to go on any excursions that included his younger brother, even going so far as to hurt him badly once in a scuffle.

As she and Bramble slipped out of the castle and darted between shadows on their way down to the beach, their cloaks flapping behind them, the hairs on Evangeline's arms stood at attention like thousands of tiny soldiers on high alert. It felt like something ominous was following them, hunting them, though Evangeline berated herself for acting like the silly children at school who spent so much time forming wild theories about who the killer could be.

They never discussed their theories *with* the Scruffmore children, whose father was the island's king. Instead, Evangeline heard whispers in the hallways that bloodthirsty monsters roamed their castle's dungeons at night, and swamp creatures dragged themselves from the moat during the light of the full moon.

Even more preposterous were rumors that Uncle Maximus was the killer, a theory that Evangeline thought ridiculous since her uncle was such a kind and gentle man, more attentive to her than her own father had ever been. Her cousin, Dominus, had also been mentioned as a possible suspect, though mostly by the boys who were envious of the violent crushes all the girls had on him.

Of course, Evangeline and Darius had discussed it endlessly among themselves, coming up with their own theories. Darius thought it could be a pirate more evil than Blackbeard who sailed in on foggy nights to satiate his bloodlust.

Either that, or Lurk, whom he'd always despised. "Kill is short for Killian," Darius explained. "It's right there in his name!"

But Darius also considered it possible that Dominus could be a suspect, though Evangeline thought this stemmed more from jealousy than anything concrete. Dominus, at seventeen, was everything that ten-year-old Darius was impatient to be. And the fact that Dominus dismissed Darius as a child, one not worthy of his time and attention, only incensed Darius further.

Evangeline had to agree with him, though.

There was definitely something *off* about Lurk, her father's shadow who came and went at all hours of the night, often appearing in the unlikeliest of places as though following the children around. She'd seen him watching Bramble once or twice with an expression akin to hunger, though her mother had irritably waved off the observation the one time Evangeline had mentioned it.

There was also something unsettling about Dominus, who was a moody and troubled teen, prone to sudden outbursts. Evangeline could sometimes hear the screaming matches between Dominus and his parents on the rare clear nights when sound moved more freely between their family's tower and Evangeline's chambers. Evangeline had also spotted her cousin sneaking out of the castle grounds more than once, though never on the nights when anyone went missing, so she hardly had any proof.

He also had a weird connection with animals—not domestic ones like pets, but rather wild creatures like foxes and ferrets—and was seemingly able to get them to do his bidding through a creepy kind of mind control.

Interrupting her thoughts when they reached the water without incident, Bramble yelled, "See? I told you we'd be fine!" He plowed down the beach, kicking up silvery sand in his wake.

Just as Evangeline was taking off her shoes, she caught a glimpse of movement by the rocks. Thinking she'd seen a face, she said, "Darius?"

Had he come to join them? But when she blinked, the rock was just a rock and she realized that she was experiencing wishful thinking, a yearning for Darius to get over himself and come back to them, making them a close-knit trio once more.

Swallowing a lump in her throat, Evangeline joined Bramble at the shoreline where the ocean retreated coyly before gathering up its frilly white skirts and charging at them, over and over again.

"How do I do it, Eva?" Bramble yelled to be heard above the surf. "How do I summon it?"

"Close your eyes and dig deep down into your very center where you burn the brightest. And then imagine that as the heart of a volcano, all bubbling lava. Picture it erupting through your veins and out of your fingertips. And then pull with all your might."

Bramble nodded solemnly and closed his eyes.

Evangeline expected a few dozen failed attempts because that's how it had been for both her and Darius. It had taken each of them almost an hour to see any kind of result, Darius wanting to give up after just three goes, with Evangeline encouraging him to keep trying. She should have realized that her baby brother wouldn't struggle as they had, that his intuitive understanding of magic would ensure his success.

It was exactly this aptitude of Bramble's that had caused so much of the animosity from Darius. He was jealous of his brother's magical abilities, and how they challenged the line of succession, equating to so much more attention and praise from their father. And while Evangeline sympathized with Darius—knowing exactly how awful it felt to be so often overlooked by Mordecai, whose approval she was constantly trying to win—she also knew it wasn't Bramble's fault that their father was only interested in the powerful and successful.

She watched now as Bramble held out his hand, making a tugging motion. The waves, in the process of retreating, suddenly shot violently forward, rushing up to where they stood. A wall of icy water slammed into them. Evangeline was caught off guard and her legs buckled, the surf churning all around her. Bramble leaned over her, eyes wide, to tug her up. He only laughed after Evangeline started spluttering, wiping sand from her face.

"Did I do that right?" Bramble asked, mischief written all over his face.

"I'd say so," Evangeline gasped, laughing despite her teeth chattering.

After using her powers to dry them off, she and Bramble made a game of it, sending waves slamming into one another to create superwaves. It was exhilarating and exhausting all at once, and though Bramble showed no signs of tiring, Evangeline eventually needed to catch her breath.

She walked away from the shoreline, finding the perfect viewpoint in the sand. A shadow nearby lengthened and began creeping toward her. Evangeline's heart leaped in fright, but she laughed at herself when she realized it was just a black cat slinking toward her. Coaxing it closer, Evangeline rubbed its ears, delighting in the creature's purring. She must have been more tired than she realized for she came to with a start sometime later, the sliver of moon having trekked its way farther across the sky. When she sat up, Evangeline immediately looked for Bramble, preparing for his protests when she told him they had to go home.

But Bramble was nowhere to be seen.

Alarmed, Evangeline jumped up and called out to him. There was no reply, but that wasn't entirely unusual. Bramble loved to play hide-and-seek. Whereas Darius usually got bored and gave up his location within ten minutes, Bramble had the patience to hide for hours, staying put long after his siblings had moved on to another game.

"Billy, I'm not in the mood for this. It's time for us to go home so we don't get caught. Don't make me regret bringing you out here."

She expected Bramble to hop out from behind the rocks, laughing at her. But he didn't.

And that's when Evangeline noticed the frenzy of the surf, how it had been churned into a roiling onslaught, the waves more than three times as big as they'd been earlier. Something glistened in the water and Evangeline ran down to see what it was. It was Bramble's cloak, floating there as though the ocean were taunting her with it.

Evangeline went icy cold. Bramble wasn't a strong swimmer. He was puny for his age, all of his power residing in his mind. If one of those waves had knocked him over and dragged him back, Bramble wouldn't have been able to put up much of a struggle.

"Bramble!" Evangeline ran into the surf, trying to dive into it to rescue her brother.

But the ocean was having none of it. It battered Evangeline, furious with her for having altered its natural rhythms. That was the price she had to pay for the magic she had wrought. She screamed until her throat was raw and kept charging at the water until she was bruised and weak, unable to take another step.

It was probably an hour later, though it felt like an eternity had passed, when Evangeline finally stood and limped home clutching Bramble's sodden cloak.

Upon finding his bed empty, Evangeline could no longer lie to herself. Her baby brother was gone, swallowed by the angry surf they had created together. He wouldn't have understood yet that there was always a price to be paid when conjuring magic, but Evangeline had known better.

This was all her fault.

Her anguished screams woke the castle, bringing everyone rushing to her side.

★ ★ ★

Once through the tunnel and now climbing the steps leading up to the dungeons, Evangeline shudders as she thinks of the decomposed body that washed ashore a few days after Bramble disappeared.

She halts when she hears a thrumming noise coming from the direction of the vault. The only person who'd be in there at this hour is Lurk. The man never seems to sleep; he's always skulking about doing her father's nefarious bidding. If he sees the state of Evangeline, she'll have a lot of explaining to do.

And so she turns in the opposite direction to take a more winding route to her mother's chambers. She drags her feet all the way there, dreading breaking the news.

CHAPTER 19

Hexabus

Monday—2:02 a.m.

After Hexabus's lover takes his leave, his scent lingers, taunting her. She's had to work so damn hard to get him to open up to her again after the trauma of losing their son drove such a wedge between them all those years ago. But despite that, he's still withholding essential information even though he claims to trust her implicitly.

It's beyond maddening because Hexabus has been in information-gathering mode for weeks, ever since she first started suspecting what Morty was up to. And now here they are. The hour of the planned murder is almost upon them, and she still isn't certain which of his children Morty plans to kill, or exactly how to stop him.

God knows, she's been using every weapon at her disposal, not just her so-called feminine wiles. Troops, insomuch as she has them, have been rallied.

As Hexabus belts her dressing gown, there's a knock at her door. *Dominus*, Hexabus thinks.

"Mom?" a voice whispers, the door opening a crack. "Are you awake?"

Hexabus tries to mask her disappointment that it's her daughter rather than her nephew, whose skill set she desperately needs right now. She casts her gaze about to make sure there's no evidence of her recent tryst—no good can come from her daughter finding out. "Yes, Eva," she says. "Come in."

Eva is disheveled and covered in dirt, her haunted face streaked with tears as she steps into the room.

"What is it?" Hexabus demands. "What happened?" She rushes to Eva and envelops her in a tight embrace, trying to hold her daughter together when it looks like she's about to fall apart.

Eva makes a few shuddering attempts at answering but she's sobbing too hard, and so all Hexabus can do is croon soothing noises while rubbing Eva's back, waiting for the storm to run its course. This is how it's always been with her eldest child, who feels everything so much more deeply than anyone else, like all her nerve endings are on the outside, rubbed raw by the sandpaper of life.

If there was one gift Hexabus wishes she could have given her daughter, it's that of indifference. But while that would have spared Eva so much pain, it also would have made her someone else, someone *less* since it's her enormous capacity to care and empathize that makes Eva so incredibly special. And how can you wish your child to be anything other than the miracle they are? Especially when you were never allowed to see who your youngest might have grown into had he not been robbed of the chance.

Eva's chest finally stops heaving, and Hexabus pulls away, her robe wet with tears. She takes hold of Eva's hand, but her daughter gasps and snatches it back. That's when Hexabus sees the blood seeping from her daughter's palm.

Taking Eva's elbow instead, Hexabus leads her to the fireplace, where she sits her down on the couch. She pours a glass of cognac and makes her daughter sip it slowly, allowing the alcohol to seep into her bones even as the fire warms her.

Once Eva's hands have stopped trembling, Hexabus says, "You need to tell me what happened."

At first, the only thing Evangeline can get out is "Bramble." The word snags on the second syllable, sounding plaintive, like the cat's mewling from earlier.

Hexabus flinches like she's been punched.

CHAPTER 20

Evangeline

Monday—2:14 a.m.

As Evangeline's eyes pool with tears, it feels as though she's rising up, up, up, the gossamer thread tethering her to her body likely to snap at any moment. But she has to keep it together and get through this.

She clears her throat, taking another sip of cognac. "I… I don't know how to tell you this, but remember how Dad wouldn't let you see Bramble's body when it washed ashore?"

Hexabus nods warily, looking winded.

"Well," Evangeline continues, then takes a deep breath so she can get it all out. "I dug up Bramble's grave tonight…and… it wasn't him inside." The last four words come out in a rush, tangled all together as one long polysyllabic word. She shudders again, thinking of the skeleton she unearthed.

Evangeline is expecting shocked outrage with Hexabus firing off dozens of questions as each confounding one births another, but her mother doesn't react at all. She doesn't even blink, just stares vacantly at a point behind Evangeline, as though she's struggling to anchor herself somewhere outside this conversation.

Evangeline steels herself to break through her mother's obvious shock. "Mom, did you hear what I said? There was another body inside the casket, a skeleton whose front teeth had grown back in. I don't know whose child is in there, but it definitely isn't yours. It's not Bramble."

"I… I don't understand," Hexabus stammers. "What…what made you dig up his grave?"

What the hell? How is that your first question?

Evangeline is so thrown that she has to take a moment to remind herself that shock can make people behave in strange ways. Flinging buckets of icy truths at Hexabus will be more damaging at this point than letting her mother soak in them for a while. She probably just needs some time to process it all. And so Evangeline haltingly explains what happened in the library, the message she received through the book.

Judging from Hexabus's expression, her mother's thoughts are struggling but failing to gain traction in the swampy mess of their discussion. "Why would someone tell you now, after all this time, that Bramble's death wasn't *your* fault?"

The question derails all of Evangeline's own, putting her on the defensive. Focusing on the amber liquid in her glass to avoid Hexabus's gaze, she begins speaking. She explains how she always blamed herself for what happened to her brother, how she never got over it despite all the times she and Hexabus spoke about it, or her mother's many assurances that there was nothing for Evangeline to feel responsible for.

Hexabus's face crumples. "Eva," she says, reaching out to stroke Evangeline's cheek. "What happened was never your fault. And I'm so, so sorry that I didn't truly make you believe that, that I forced you to put on a brave face for my benefit."

Evangeline shakes her head, uncomfortable with this pain she's caused her mother by confessing these feelings. This is exactly why she's kept quiet about them for so long. "It wasn't your fault," she says. "But Dad… He knew how I felt, and he made it worse, making it clear that I *owed* him for my negligence. I've done everything he's ever asked of me to try and make it up to him, yet it's never been enough." Hexabus looks like she's about to buckle under the weight of the bundle of sorrow her daughter just handed her, and so Evangeline rushes to add, "Gabe asked me to marry him."

"That's wonderful," Hexabus exclaims, her troubled expression clearing slightly. "Congratulations!" And then searching Evangeline's face, she asks, "You did say yes, didn't you?"

Evangeline groans. "I couldn't. I asked him for some time to think about it. You know how Dad always made it abundantly clear he didn't want me to marry a Peasant—"

"That lousy hypocrite," Hexabus spits, fury consuming her earlier sorrow. "It was fine for him to marry and reproduce with a Peasant. But not you? What absolute nonsense, Eva! You know that, right? I may use the distinctions to goad Newton, but they don't actually matter."

Evangeline's eyes fill with tears again. "I know… It's just… I didn't want to disappoint him more than I already have."

"Oh, baby," Hexabus says, shaking her head. "I forgot what a little daddy's girl you always used to be before…" Her voice trails off, like the thought has lost its way.

But Evangeline doesn't need Hexabus to finish the sentence. They both know that her mother means before Bramble's death. And before Morty replaced Evangeline with Angel and Minx, back when he hadn't yet realized his new daughters would be just as disappointing as his first.

Refusing to dwell on that thought, Evangeline says, "I'm going to say yes to Gabe's proposal. Dad can't disown me if I'm the one to walk away first, right?"

Hexabus looks flustered for a moment and then says, "Absolutely. You can tell him the news straight after the family gathering."

"I think I'm going to tell him before, so I don't need to attend—"

But her mother is adamant. "No. *After* would definitely be better. Trust me on this." And then she surprises Evangeline by pulling her up from the couch into a tight embrace, almost knocking the glass of cognac from her hand. "I'm so happy for you and Gabe. Congratulations."

Her mother's reaction, almost more a diversion than an expression of joy, sets off a dozen alarm bells. Evangeline thought they were circling the elephant in the room because of Hexabus's shock. Now she realizes that's not the reason at all.

She pulls back from the hug to study Hexabus's strained expression. "Why weren't you shocked by the news about Bramble?"

Hexabus remains silent.

"Mom, answer me!"

Hexabus waits a beat and then, her voice barely above a whisper, says, "Because I already knew."

CHAPTER 21

Evangeline

Monday—2:26 a.m.

Winded, Evangeline glares at her mother, whose features have become blurry, as though smudged by the betrayal. A stranger stares back at her. "All this time," Evangeline rasps, "you knew, and you just let me believe—"

"Not all this time, no." Hexabus's bottom lip trembles. "I only found out very recently."

"How?" Evangeline demands.

"I'm sorry, but I can't disclose that." Hexabus looks pained but resolute. "But I was just as devastated as you are now." Her voice cracks, splintered with pain.

"Why didn't you tell me?" Evangeline asks.

"I wanted to, please believe me, Eva. But I was sworn to secrecy."

Evangeline can forgive her mother for honoring a promise, but not for a cover-up of this magnitude. She's nauseated at the thought of another mother out there going through hell every day of her life as she waits for news of her missing child when Hexabus has had the power to put her out of her misery. "Do you know who the child is? The one we buried?"

"No!" Hexabus is emphatic. "Of course not. That's another reason why I didn't want to burden you with the news when

I found out. I needed to figure it all out so I could answer all your questions."

"Dad had to know whoever washed up on the beach wasn't Bramble. Even if he didn't recognize his body, the mismatched dental records would have been obvious. So why would he do that? Bury the wrong child?" Evangeline begins to pace and then stops, spinning around. "Do you think Bramble's still out there, alive somewhere?" She holds her breath, daring to hope.

Hexabus pauses, opens her mouth to speak, and then closes it again. Her expression clouds as she shakes her head sadly.

"You're right," Evangeline groans, knowing it was a long shot. Why would her father fake Bramble's death only to have his son grow up separated from the family? "That wouldn't make any sense." She begins pacing again, frustration fueling each step. As she turns, she catches sight of Hexabus's expression. There's something her mother's struggling with; the inner conflict is written plainly on her face. "You've been acting so weird lately that I suspected there was something you were feeling guilty about," Evangeline says. "But you haven't told me everything. You're still hiding something now, aren't you?"

Hexabus seems to reach a decision. She sighs and pats the couch. Once Evangeline obeys, sitting stiffly next to her mother, Hexabus says, "I didn't want to tell you because I was trying to protect you—"

"From what?"

Hexabus instructs Evangeline to hush and listen. She begins speaking about a prophecy that was unearthed by Lumina Le Roux in the vault twenty-two years ago. "I didn't know about it at the time. I only found out recently. It referred to people who your father would consider enemies, those working against him, as well as those who might surpass him in power." Hexabus reaches for the side table, pours herself a cognac, and takes a sip before she continues speaking, quoting one of the stanzas.

"With power that's beyond compare,
there will soon come a time
when your very own child will dare
to summit as you climb."

Evangeline considers the words, thinking how they don't make sense since none of Morty's children are very powerful. Then it hits her. "Bramble!" she gasps.

Hexabus nods, her eyes swimming with tears. "Yes, exactly."

"You're saying Dad killed his own son, a mere boy who was just coming into his powers, because he was worried Bramble's magic would surpass his?" Evangeline asks incredulously. But she doesn't need her mother to reply, not really, because Evangeline knows the answer at a cellular level. *Of course Mordecai did it. Of course he did.*

Hexabus lets the tears fall unchecked as she continues speaking. "Yes, *and* because he believed it would make him even more powerful to do so, while also eliminating his one weakness. The killing curse he used was so dark that it…it obliterated Bramble completely…" Hexabus trails off, her voice failing her. After swallowing deeply and clearing her throat, she manages to add, "Which is why there were no remains. That's why he had to get another body to bury. To give us some sense of closure."

"Oh my god." Evangeline shudders as a wave of horror hits her. *Obliterated.* What kind of person does that to their own child? Just thinking about the evil it would take to commit an act of filicide of that magnitude makes Evangeline sick to her stomach. And then another horrific thought occurs to her. "Wait… Where did Dad get the other child's body from? Are you telling me…" No, it's too heinous a possibility. But judging from her mother's expression, Evangeline knows she's right. "Dad was the island's serial killer, wasn't he?" she whispers.

Hexabus nods, looking sickened. "Your father got his hands on a book of dark arts, deciphering it," Hexabus says, squeezing Evangeline's hands tightly. "He worked out that twenty-four murders would gain him unimaginable power and so that's what he set out to achieve, taking twenty-four souls in return for immortality. Bramble became the twenty-fourth victim, the last one your father killed after discovering the prophecy."

Evangeline gapes at her mother, unable to form words. She thinks of Samuel Fitzpatrick and Dawn Montgomery, her playmates whom she's outlived by more than two decades. *Oh my god. I'm the one who put targets on their backs by inviting them over to play in the castle grounds, by putting them so firmly in Morty's sights.*

It's not just Bramble whom Evangeline let down so badly. It's so much worse than she ever thought.

She tries to picture the scene the night Bramble died— Evangeline asleep on the sand, probably bewitched, with Morty stepping over her to reach his son, Lurk undoubtedly trailing his master, always just a step behind. Bramble must have been scared to see their father there, thinking they were in trouble for sneaking out.

Did Morty placate him first, tell Bramble everything was fine, and then allow him to show off his newly activated powers before he obliterated him? Did they even speak, or did Morty just cut his son down while he was rapturous in the waves?

Was it worth it, Evangeline wonders, *to snuff out such a beautiful flame?*

"None of the murders made your father more powerful," Hexabus says, as though in response to Evangeline's roiling thoughts, "nor did Bramble's death stop time from running out in the Scruffmore hourglass."

"Meaning what?" Evangeline asks despite not wanting to hear the answer.

"Your father thinks he killed the wrong child. That's why he's called everyone together for this gathering." Hexabus takes a deep breath before saying, "He plans to fix his mistake, and I think I know who his target is."

CHAPTER 22

Destiny

Monday—8:11 a.m.

Destiny lurches awake, heart pounding as she flings an arm over her face. She had another one of those dreams, the kind that leave her spent and trembling. Adrenaline floods her system, triggering her flight response. Her first impulse is to push back the covers, pack up everything, and head down to the terminal to catch the first ferry off the island, intent on forgetting all of this ever happened.

Leaving right now, listening to the voice that's telling her to get as far away from here as quickly as possible, would be a smart move, a decision based on a strong instinct for self-preservation.

"Okay, fraidy-cat," Bex says. "You do that. But how will you get any answers if you run?" Bex is in The Stance, the one she always adopted as a precursor to a fight: one eyebrow raised, arms crossed over her chest like body armor, and that angry blue vein throbbing in her temple. "Argumentative foreplay" is what Destiny nicknamed it.

Before she can reply, Bex plows on. "Without those answers, there's no proving Nate wrong. You want to live in a world where Nate's right about you? That it was your mental instability that killed me?"

For a second, Destiny feels too winded to speak. When she

does, the words limp out past the mountainous ache in her throat. "Of course not, but it's not that simple. These dreams are all mixed up with the previous ones. Each time I have them, I also experience the older ones, only worse than before."

The night Destiny first dreamed about Tempest as a ghost woman walking through walls, she also relived the night terrors related to Bex, only in higher definition with surround sound. Glass breaking, tires squealing, blood gurgling. All of it was terrifying enough on its own but it was made so much worse when swiftly followed by flames licking around the corners of Liz's screaming.

She hoped it was a one-off, a kind of lingering psychic residue from *before*, but all the subsequent nightmares have crushed that theory.

As much as she needs answers, Destiny doesn't know if she's strong enough to keep being reminded of all the ways in which she failed Bex and Liz. She still tends to believe Nate's assessment of her, that she has lost it completely—

"Stop that right now," Bex hisses. "Get that thought out of your head. I know this is tough, but you need to take two teaspoons of cement and harden the fuck up, buttercup. Because if you're right, and Nasty McRestingBitchFace needs your help, you're failing her right now."

"Ugh," Destiny groans, hating how whiny she sounds when Bex is just calling it as she sees it. "Okay, fine. I'll do it."

She forces herself to close her eyes and draw a few deep breaths.

It takes a while, but fragments of images eventually begin to patch themselves together from the darkness of her thoughts. Destiny recalls a vaulted room and what looks like, of all things, a raccoon motioning at her.

There's also a magenta-haired woman glaring at something on the ground while crushing a monocle under her boot. And another woman, all razor edges and brittle veneer, howling until her throat is raw. Just the memory of the sound is like broken fingernails scraping against a blackboard.

Destiny's never seen either of these women before—she's almost certain of it—and yet there's something strangely familiar about them. What lingers is the sense that they're both cold and devious, the kind of women who'll happily walk over the corpses of so-called loved ones if it means getting their own way.

And then the rest of the dream comes to her in a flash, like headlights approaching much too quickly on a dark, deserted road.

Destiny's looking down at Mordecai Scruffmore, who lies on a stone floor, desperately gasping for air. The multiple compass stars tattooed on his forehead appear to glow from beneath his skin.

"You," he croaks, eyes bulging as he stares up in horror. "You!"

Before Destiny can wrench herself from the visions, she sees a truck's grille guard glinting in the sunlight, a predator's metal snout sniffing out its prey. The engine's drone bores through her head, rattling her brain.

Destiny shudders and bolts upright, needing to be sick.

After jumping out of bed and rushing to the little bathroom, she heaves into the toilet bowl until her stomach feels as though it might devour itself. Standing unsteadily, she turns to the washbasin and splashes cold water on her face as she tries to fight off a panic attack. Destiny breathes in through her nose, expanding her whole chest cavity while counting to five, and then exhales, counting again like Dr. Shepherd taught her. She's not sure how many times she runs through this cycle before she finally begins to feel calmer.

Looking at herself in the mirror, her face flushed despite the iciness of the room, she spots the writing on her fleece onesie pajamas. It's rendered backward in the reflection, but she doesn't need to read it to know what it says: *The First Rule of Crossword Club Is (3,2,3,4,5,9,4).* Nate gave her these pajamas as a Christmas present.

"Dorky pj's for a major dork," he'd said affectionately as Destiny opened the gift, squealing with delight. ★★[5]

★ ★ ★

Suddenly experiencing an overwhelming need to hear Nate's voice, Destiny heads back into the room and reaches for her cell phone on the bedside table. There's still no signal. Nor was there any during the night, or a stray message or two might have slipped through.

She wishes so much that she could call Nate so she can talk everything through with him, tell him where she is and all the strange things that have been happening to her. But remembering that she wouldn't call even if she could, her spirits sink even further. Anything she'd have to say would just reaffirm his belief that she's taken leave of her senses. She refuses to give him more ammunition, not when she's hoping so much to prove him wrong.

Whatever's happening is not an unraveling, but rather the awakening of an ability that lay dormant until Destiny turned eight. She must have it for a reason, even though she isn't quite sure what that must be or what to do with it just yet.

Most important, she needs for Nate to understand that she was trying to use this gift to save Bex, not kill her.

---

5.   If you're a fan of the movie *Fight Club*, you'll have all the information you need to solve this minipuzzle. If not, email DestinyWhipClue@gmail.com using the subject line Clue Five. Once you're done, turn to page 462 for the answer.

5.1. Rearrange the letters of the nine-letter word to create a seven-letter word. Once you're done, turn to page 463 for the answer.

Email that answer in the subject line to DestinyWhipClue@gmail. com to access a very important scene from Destiny's past.

The dread from earlier has stalked her back into the room like a shadow.

Was Mordecai staring at me *so accusingly in the dream? Oh my god, am I going to do something in the future to hurt him?* She shakes her head. *No, that can't possibly be. Why would I do that?*

"Adieu, fair maiden," someone shouts up from the street below. "Until we meet again!"

Destiny puts the phone down and pads over to the bay window, then peers down into the cobbled street. She's not surprised to spot a rumpled-looking Silver, who's walking backward while blowing kisses up in her direction, a raincoat draped over his arm.

A voice calls from nearby, "Be off with you, you scoundrel."

Destiny turns to see Tempest in the window of the next room, naked except for a sheet clutched to her chest. She's laughing and blowing kisses back at Silver.

"You definitely saw that one coming," Bex observes wryly.

At least Destiny knows Tempest is still safe and didn't fall prey to the island's serial killer during the night. And since Destiny didn't dream about her again, that might be a sign her theory was wrong and Tempest isn't in any kind of danger, after all.

As she turns away from the window, thoughts swirling, a davenport desk in the corner of the room catches her attention. Its chair is pulled out as though someone was recently sitting there. There's a silver fountain pen resting on an open notebook, whose pages are covered in a hasty scrawl. Destiny goes to study them, surprised to see a riddle written in handwriting she'd recognize anywhere.

Because it's her own.

No. No. No. Please don't let this be happening again.

CHAPTER 23

Destiny

Monday—8:29 a.m.

Destiny studies her fingertips, which are smudged with ink.

She's doing it again, this written equivalent of sleepwalking.

It started after Liz was killed and then again when Destiny was sixteen, after Annie passed away. Dr. Shepherd posited a theory that grief acted as a fuse that occasionally tripped when Destiny's extraordinary brain was overworked from all the thinking it was made to do during its waking hours.

This sleepwriting was apparently her mind's way of telling her to relax: *It's not a problem if you're too sad to solve all the many puzzles running through your brain at any given time. You don't need to stress about it. Because I'll still be working for you at night, delivering the answers that are just out of reach when you're awake.*

And, of course, since clues and riddles have always been Destiny's love language, it makes sense that they're what her unconscious would use when trying to communicate with her. They have always fascinated her, leading her to becoming a world-renowned enigmatologist, someone who studies puzzles and mysteries for a living.

The strange thing is that Dr. Shepherd expected the sleepwriting to start up again a year ago, triggered by the grief following the accident. But it didn't. Perhaps that's because Destiny tried so hard not to think at all during that time, taking a leave of absence from her consultancy so as not to set her brain on fire.

Because when it's ignited, it can't let go of whys and hows. Instead, it goes over the same ground, time and again, burning it all down, trying desperately to spot where she went wrong so she can punish herself for it.

This delayed reaction to the grief is probably because Destiny's mind has only now come out of its dormancy, synapses firing on all cylinders.

First, the strange dreams, and now the sleepwriting again. Nate would have a field day with all of this.

Destiny sighs, shaking her head. And then she gets to work on solving the riddle that she left for herself.

It's the question to ask for the reason
And it's the pronoun that means me and you
***Plus** your payment to stay for a season*
And the possessive first name of McGoo

Items you choose from your closet each day
What you are when you are not dry instead
The word for similar to, in a way
And two words: what should grow on a man's head

"Gah," she exclaims when she works it out. ★★[6]

★ ★ ★

She *knew* there was something wrong last night, something niggling just out of reach, but there was so much going on that there wasn't time to figure it out. Thank goodness for her subconscious refusing to sleep when Destiny does.

---

6.   You now have all the information you require to solve this riddle. If you need a clue to assist you, email DestinyWhipClue@gmail.com using the subject line Clue Six. Once you've solved it, turn to page 464 to check your answer.

This, on top of Madigan's signs of lying, sets off all kinds of red flags, though Destiny's not sure what they might mean. She wishes she had the luxury of lingering at the inn to study him further, to gather more data to go into the *Useful Information Folder*. But she's here to speak with Mordecai, so that needs to be her main focus.

Still, she can't help but feel like an audience member who's been sitting patiently in the theater waiting for the curtain to go up, only to discover that she's actually the one onstage, the audience having been watching *her* all this time.

No one she's met on the island thus far feels trustworthy. Certainly not Tempest, who undoubtedly has a hidden agenda. Not Silver, who brings to mind icebergs like the one that sank the *Titanic*; what you see on the surface is not a reflection of what's going on underneath. And not Madigan, who definitely is a liar.

Despite all that, Destiny can't be distracted when she meets Mordecai Scruffmore today. After everything she learned about him last night—and after the deeply disturbing dream she had about him—she's more than apprehensive. She's afraid.

Mordecai doesn't sound like the benevolent type who'd just do something out of the goodness of his heart. If he has something to offer Destiny, then she's pretty sure he's going to demand something in return. It worries her that she has no clue what that might be.

Nevertheless, if he *is* her father, then he's the only person who knows who her biological mother is. And Destiny is so desperate for that information that it makes them reluctant allies, if nothing else.

She's still unsettled about the dream, pondering it further, until something startling occurs to her.

Maybe Mordecai wasn't looking at me. Maybe he was looking past me at the magenta-haired woman. Perhaps she's the one who's going to betray him and that's why I'm here. So that I can warn him about it.

Because if something happens to Mordecai, the secret he was going to reveal to Destiny dies along with him.

CHAPTER 24

Minx

Monday—10:17 a.m.

Before they arrive at the castle, there are a few details Minx needs to iron out to ensure that everything will go according to plan, but she seems fated to be forever waiting for Angel to get off her damn phone. Running a hand through her magenta-colored pixie cut, Minx tells herself to breathe, that her circus will have one less monkey soon enough.

"Ugh," Angel groans, pressing the call button and then holding the device out the carriage window. Her cell phone charm dances jauntily as they're jostled along cobbled streets while Barrington urges the horses on. "The signal's already gone. How am I going to upload selfies to Insta? Or sext with Heather?" Angel whines, referring to her latest lover. "She's easily distracted. I worry what she might get up to without me."

"Then you're better off without her." Minx refuses to play the reassuring game by telling Angel how lucky Heather is to have her, how foolish she'd be to cheat. Her sister needs to become more discerning in terms of the women she chases.

Not that Minx has room to talk. Her taste in men is equally questionable. Looking out the window as they pass the inn, she thinks of how Madigan love bombed her the last few times they visited the island before he suddenly ghosted her. She burns with the humiliation of his rejection, wondering who he spurned her in favor of.

No matter. She'll get her revenge. By this time tomorrow, Madigan is going to wish he'd never laid eyes on Minx Nebula Scruffmore. *That's what you get for treating me like I'm disposable.*

Getting her head in the game as the drawbridge lowers, Minx says, "So, listen. While we're here, we can't talk about the plan to accuse Morty and Hexabus. Not even among ourselves or with Mom, okay?"

Angel regards her suspiciously. "Why not?"

Minx reaches into her pocket and strokes the vial of poison like the good luck charm it is.

"Morty's going to be super paranoid ahead of the gathering," she says. "He's likely to work all kinds of spells throughout the castle to eavesdrop on everyone's conversations. If anyone is up to something, he'll want to know about it." When Angel's one eyebrow remains hitched, Minx adds, "I don't want to be the one getting Mom into trouble if he finds out what she's up to. Do you?"

Angel shakes her head as they cross the moat.

Once they round the corner, Minx is surprised to see two women alighting from a horse and buggy at the entrance to the castle. The blonde is long-haired and waiflike, beautiful enough to have been a model when she was younger. Minx immediately likes the streamlined angles of her body and the shellacked quality she exudes. She especially loves her steampunk aesthetic and her *don't mess with me* vibe.

Her chubby companion, a tall redhead with wild curls, is awfully dressed, like she wouldn't recognize a sense of style even if it vomited designer labels all over her. They make an improbable pair.

Mrs. Scuggs, who's unusually ruffled, welcomes the two women with a strained smile while Barrington waits for their buggy to depart. Minx wonders who these women are and why they'd be here on such an important day. Morty's normally so insular, going so far as to forbid his children from inviting any romantic partners because "strangers" won't be tolerated at royal affairs.

Their presence is something she didn't anticipate. It throws Minx off, making her wonder what other unpleasant surprises lie in wait.

"Look at those boots," Angel murmurs as she nods at the redhead's hiking shoes. "Did the dress code say to dress for a trucking convention?"

Minx snickers.

Almost as though the frump has heard them, she turns, doing a double take when she spots Minx. The blonde does the same a few seconds later. That's what happens when you're a famous influencer: everyone recognizes you. Minx just hopes the redhead doesn't ask for a selfie together; she'd be mortified to be tagged on social media alongside her.

After the two women are ushered inside—a footman bringing up the rear while carrying an unwieldy backpack and an elegant designer travel bag—an agitated-looking Lurk rushes down the steps to greet the twins.

Something has happened to get the staff all flustered. Yet another occurrence Minx wasn't expecting. She needs to be on her guard, for who knows what the next twenty-four hours might hold. Besides her father's death, that is.

"Princess Minx. Princess Angel." Lurk dips his head as he acknowledges each of them.

While he instructs Barrington to bring in their luggage, Minx turns to Angel and murmurs, "Remember, lips zipped the whole time. Just act like everything is completely normal, okay? We want the element of surprise. It's the only way to make sure Mom's plan works and Morty doesn't have time to pivot."

Considering there *is* no plan with Newton, that everything is of Minx's own devising, she really hopes Angel can keep her big mouth shut and do as she's told, thus setting herself up as the perfect scapegoat for Morty's murder.

CHAPTER 25

Destiny

Monday—10:34 a.m.

It's her, Destiny thinks as she's swallowed into the gaping maw of the castle's enormous doorway. *The pink-haired woman who might be plotting to kill Mordecai.*

The anxiety accompanying this realization deploys what feels like a thousand ant troops marching through Destiny's veins, even as it stations hundreds of giant worms to torpedo blindly through her belly.

Thinking back to what Silver said about the Scruffmores gathering today for a meeting, Destiny wonders how the two young women from the carriage fit into the whole family hierarchy. Younger cousins, perhaps?

She barely has time to register this thought before her attention is snagged by the castle's cavernous entrance hall, the gullet into which they've been consumed.

What she notices first is an underlying stench of decay, like that of an ancient forest floor. Next is the vaulted ceilings shaped like sharpened arrowheads defending the castle's inhabitants against an attack from the gods. A gigantic chandelier hangs by a thread from the ceiling, a spider suspended from its web; it glints darkly, each of its candlestick holders shaped like the talons of some prehistoric beast.

The walls are unlike anything Destiny has ever seen. Some type of black mold or lichen appears to have grown over every inch of them, though it's a strange gleaming kind that resembles rattlesnake skin rather than any kind of fungi.

Even the split staircase leading up to the second floor looks menacing, with steps sharp and treacherous. Its banister is forged from what appears to be hundreds of upright swords, their gleaming tips just waiting for anyone foolish enough to clutch at them for support.

Everything about this space—which should be welcoming and warm since it's the first part of the castle a visitor is greeted by—is as hostile as Destiny's first impression of the island. It's as though its architect and decorator were handed a brief to design a room that would make an unsuspecting guest rear back in alarm and send them scuttling back outside. Regardless of what awaited them out there, it would surely be safer than being in here.

This is not the cozy family home she pictured being welcomed into. It's not the setting of hopeful daydreams and happy homecomings; it's a malevolent place eliciting dread.

Lowering her eyes, Destiny spots an enormous oil painting directly in front of them. Mordecai Scruffmore dominates it, just as he did the one at the inn. But instead of the wife and three children Destiny saw in that portrait, the family that has been staged around him in this one consists of a diminutive white woman, her face as hard and sharp as the castle itself, along with two striking little girls.

Destiny can't help but wince as she pictures herself included in the painting, how oafish and painfully out of place she'd look in such a polished grouping of perfect specimens. A pelican among flamingos once more.

Shaking off that disheartening thought, Destiny realizes that the young women are children from another marriage. She mentally kicks herself for the foolish assumption she made earlier, limiting her problem-solving abilities.

What makes her even more lightheaded is that Mordecai is wearing a monocle in this portrait. And that she recognizes his wife from her dream as the one who howled in what sounded like either grief or rage. Destiny's not sure, though, which of the two little blonde girls has grown into the magenta-haired young woman.

Has she also grown into a murderer, someone who will kill her own father, the man who might be Destiny's father too?

Who knows at what point any of this might happen, or when Tempest will step through the wall, alive or dead, either woman or ghost. Destiny can't have much time left to warn Mordecai. The anxiety accompanying the thought is like a giant hand clamped around her throat. She struggles to draw shallow breaths as her heartbeat accelerates.

Footsteps echo behind them and Mrs. Scuggs quickly ushers Destiny and Tempest to an antechamber from which they watch the twins—who are no longer remotely identical now in their early womanhood—make their way up the stairs as though they're walking on a runway.

"What are their names?" Destiny whispers to the housekeeper, who's regarding the young women with a mixture of reverence and distaste.

"That's Princess Minx," Mrs. Scuggs murmurs, referring to the twin Destiny dreamed about. "And that's Princess Angel," she says, nodding at the wholesome-looking young woman who trails her edgier sister.

As the twins disappear up the stairs—the thud of boots hitting each step like a hammer knocking nails into a coffin—Tempest squirms, and a squeaking noise gets trapped in her throat. Destiny's deeply unsettled too, and so this moment of kinship makes her want to reach out and squeeze Tempest's hand. Sensing that the gesture would *not* be appreciated—rather,

Tempest will probably want to punish Destiny for witnessing her moment of vulnerability—she pretends she didn't hear anything.

A maid rushes across the room to whisper in Mrs. Scuggs's ear. The housekeeper grumbles back, something about incompetence and taking it up with Mr. Lurcock later.

Both women have the air of the aggrieved, as though Destiny and Tempest's arrival has somehow thrown a wrench into the cogs of a well-oiled machine.

"Come this way," Mrs. Scuggs says crisply.

Destiny's surprised when Mrs. Scuggs doesn't lead them up the staircase after the princesses, but instead immediately turns right and leads them down a narrow set of winding stairs into the bowels of the castle. In the confined space, Destiny's claustrophobia kicks in once again. How is it possible that, less than twenty-four hours ago, she was feeling the same stifling sensation in the fog while out on the open sea? As she surveys the oily-looking reptilian walls that hem them in, Destiny considers how much worse this is, almost as though they've been swallowed by a leviathan.

After being hastily taken down a long hallway, they come to an abrupt halt.

"Wait here," Mrs. Scuggs instructs Destiny as she shows Tempest through a thick metal door.

Tempest shoots an alarmed look back at Destiny, but then the door closes between them, and their moment of connection is broken. Torches burn in wall sconces, their flames flickering in response to an icy breeze that slithers through the space. Destiny shivers, wondering where her backpack disappeared to, as she could really use an extra layer of clothing right now.

When Mrs. Scuggs suddenly morphs from the gloom, Destiny flinches. "This way," the housekeeper commands, her dark hair pulled back so tightly into a bun that it gives her face the quality of a stretched canvas. She guides Destiny a few steps before they come to another metal door. "These are your chambers," Mrs. Scuggs says, ushering Destiny inside.

Judging by the iron rings embedded in the walls, and the gates that stand open between the seating area and the bedroom, the rooms probably originally served as dungeons before they were converted into rudimentary guest quarters. There's a fire in the hearth that's trying valiantly, though failing dismally, to warm up the damp space.

"This is creepy as all hell," Bex whispers. "Are you a guest here? Or a prisoner?"

The clanging of the metal door slamming shut behind Mrs. Scuggs seems to serve as their answer.

"If this is how Mordecai treats family," Bex mutters, "I'd hate to see how he treats his mortal enemies."

CHAPTER 26

Destiny

Monday—11:20 a.m.

Destiny is just beginning to talk herself through a rising tide of panic, churning whirlpools of it threatening to pull her under, when there's a knock at the door. She drops the amulet she's been clutching and tucks it under her T-shirt. Thinking it's Tempest coming to complain about their living quarters, Destiny calls out a relieved "Come in!"

But it's not Tempest who enters. Instead, a distinguished-looking older man does a double take when he spots Destiny. His eyes are like a magnifying glass. Under their inspection, she can feel herself wilting.

"Hello, I'm Destiny Whip." She forces herself to speak, giving in to the overwhelming need to account for herself. "Mrs. Scuggs brought me down here." When the man still doesn't say anything, Destiny adds, "I'm here for the interview." As his silent examination shows no sign of abating, she blurts, "For the historian position."

The man finally blinks and then dips his head. "Good afternoon, Ms. Whip. I'm Mr. Lurcock, the butler." He's wearing a black suit, paired with a gray vest and white gloves. A jagged-looking tiepin gleams at his chest, holding a black tie in place.

Tall and slim, Mr. Lurcock oozes a crackling vitality despite his age. While looking incredibly serene on the surface, he brings to mind Hooke's law, which states that the more you compress a spring, the more force it would take to compress it further still. There's something familiar about him, as though she's seen him before, but she can't place the context of where that might have been.

She reaches out a hand, but he takes a step back as though offended. *Are you not supposed to shake hands with butlers?* Destiny wonders, embarrassed. *Is that taboo, some rule that everyone but me knows?*

Before she can stammer an apology, he says, "I'm terribly sorry, but there seems to have been some kind of miscommunication. Mrs. Scuggs shouldn't have brought you and Ms. Sinclair down to these quarters."

Destiny clutches her chest and exclaims, "Oh, thank god! I was hoping there'd been some kind of mix-up." Spotting her bag leaning against a chair, she says, "I'll just grab that and then we can go upstairs, shall we?"

"No," the butler says, frowning. "I'm afraid that's not what I meant. You see, you shouldn't be here at the castle at all."

Destiny's spirits plummet again. "What do you mean? I was invited for the interview," she repeats dully.

"Indeed, but we were expecting you *next* week. Not today."

Confused, Destiny says, "But the letter said it would happen at 12:00 p.m. on the twenty-eighth of February." She reaches for her phone, its battery almost dead, and holds the calendar up to the butler. "That's today. In half an hour."

Perplexed, Mr. Lurcock says, "Yes, that's what Ms. Sinclair said as well, but she couldn't produce any such letter as proof."

When he stares pointedly at Destiny's jeans and scuffed boots—very clearly not interview attire—she flushes. "I was just about to start getting ready."

"Hmm. Might I see *your* letter?"

"Of course!" Destiny strides to the backpack and opens the clasps. She begins rummaging through the bag, pulling out the still-damp items of clothing from last night and dumping them on the bed. "It's in here somewhere," she says apologetically, digging deeper and deeper, excavating more fabric.

When she yanks out the wrinkle-free suit she was going to wear for her meeting with Mordecai, she's tempted to wave it at the butler as proof. *See, I know how to dress for an interview! Even a fake one!*

Instead, she continues rifling through the pack until it's completely empty. Destiny tugs at one of her wayward curls, surveying the mess she's made. When she begins sorting through everything again, the butler harrumphs.

Destiny straightens. "That's so strange. I packed it. I know I did."

It strikes her as more than a coincidence that Tempest's letter was rendered illegible last night and hers is now missing. When she tries to remember whether it was Tempest who knocked over her own glass of wine while she was reaching for it, or if it was Madigan's elaborate gesture that sent it flying, she can't be certain. But she can't rule out the possibility that someone snuck into her room at some point and stole Destiny's copy of the letter.

Feeling the butler's thrumming impatience, Destiny says, "I memorized it so I can recite it for you if you like?"

"That won't be necessary." Mr. Lurcock thinks for a moment, doing the kind of mental gymnastics that Destiny herself is all too familiar with. Finally, he says, "Since you're both here, and Ms. Sinclair says she won't be able to return next week, I'll ascertain if His Majesty can fit you into his schedule tomorrow."

"Tomorrow?" Destiny yelps.

She's been counting down the hours until midday, seeing the meeting as a Band-Aid that needs to be ripped off as quickly as possible. Whatever awaits her, she just wants to get it over with before she changes her mind about how sensible it is to be here.

Besides, if she's right and needs to warn Mordecai about his daughter's murderous intentions, there's no time to waste. Who knows when Princess Minx will strike?

Destiny doesn't want to think that if she's wrong about that particular theory, then *she's* the person Mordecai was staring at so accusingly, meaning she's the one, and not Minx, who will hurt him.

"Can't he see us today?" she asks.

Mr. Lurcock frowns, one eyebrow arched. "I'm afraid that won't be possible. As it is, I'm not even certain that he can accommodate you tomorrow. In the meantime, I'm going to have to ask that you remain here until the interview."

"Here?" Destiny asks blankly.

"Yes, in your chambers."

"What? Like a prisoner?" Destiny squeals, feeling the walls inching closer.

"Not at all," Lurk replies, looking guarded. "It's just that the Scruffmore family is very...private. His Majesty doesn't like to mix business with his personal life. With the whole family in attendance, it would be better if your potential interactions with them are limited."

"Ouch." Bex is indignant on Destiny's behalf. "Tell him you aren't some outsider who needs to be quarantined from the family. Tell him you more than likely *are* family."

"I'm sure you understand," the butler says.

"But—"

"If you absolutely *insist* on staying," he says, making it clear that he isn't happy about the situation, "you and Ms. Sinclair can have the whole lower level of the castle to yourselves. We just ask that you not venture upstairs until you are...invited to do so." Her ambivalence must be broadcast over her expression because Mr. Lurcock adds, "If this request doesn't suit you, Ms. Whip, I understand completely. I can arrange for you to be taken back to the ferry immediately, and—"

"No!" Destiny barks. "That's fine. I'll stay here until the interview."

Is it Destiny's imagination or does the butler look disappointed by her answer despite the fact that she's agreed to his terms?

He doesn't want her here, not even captive in the dungeons.

But why ever not?

CHAPTER 27

Everyone in the castle is so distracted by their own myriad concerns and schemes that no one notices the raccoon flattening itself to wriggle through the grate's bars. Dropping into the tunnel below, it prepares for a reconnaissance mission.

Though the creature's long-distance vision is poor, it doesn't need to actually *see* where it's going. Thanks to its excellent memory, the maze of secret passageways is all mapped out in its mind. Plus, its highly sensitive forepaws serve as an internal compass, orienting it each time the ground transitions between rock, gravel, brick, clay, and timber.

As it nears the kitchen, it detects voices speaking urgently, and comes to a halt to listen. The vents in the solid walls, coupled with the animal's excellent auditory perception, allow the raccoon to hear the conversation perfectly.

"...happened in the early hours of the morning," Mrs. Scuggs says.

There's a gasp and then a voice replies, "Good heavens, no! I didn't think it was possible for anyone to break in to the castle." The voice dips low. "Because of all the...you know what." Then, after a beat, it asks, "What was taken?"

"Sounds like the vault was ransacked and left in a terrible mess, books and parchments strewed everywhere. Of course, *we're* not allowed to go in and clean it all up. That will be left to Mr. Lurcock."

"The vault? Why, who'd want to steal dusty old books when the castle is full of so many valuable heirlooms?"

149

Mrs. Scuggs sniffs and tuts. "There's no accounting for taste, I suppose. His Majesty is livid."

Having heard enough, the raccoon takes off down the tunnel, heading for the main living quarters via a different route from the one it normally uses. The new security measures mean there are certain passageways that are no longer accessible. When the low thrum of a conversation makes its ears perk up, the raccoon comes to a standstill outside Newton's bedchamber.

"You're sure they don't suspect?" Newton asks.

"Yes. I'm positive," a second voice replies.

"Good. That makes it much easier." Newton sounds relieved. "I don't want them to know what we're up to just yet."

There's a deep sigh and then the second voice asks, "Are you certain you want to go ahead with this?"

"Of course!" Newton exclaims. "It's the only way I can know for sure."

"But…what if he takes the bait? Then what? Have you decided on a definite course of action? If not, there's no point in putting either of us through this ordeal."

The raccoon already knows the answer to this question and so it moves on, expertly maneuvering through the tunnels. It heads for Hexabus's quarters, where the clandestine meeting is most likely to take place.

And then…jackpot! The voices it's been hoping for.

"…realized that his Achilles' heel is linked to the medallion," Hexabus says, her voice pitched low. There's the rustling of what sounds like bedsheets.

"When was it originally forged?" Maximus asks.

"The first one was just after Bramble's birth. It was then reforged after the twins were born."

"Hmm," Maximus muses. "And you think the eight pieces interact in some way?"

"Definitely," Hexabus replies. "He would have set that up on purpose so he could leverage our separate powers."

"But then the reverse is also true, surely?" Maximus says.

"He either didn't think that through or his arrogance meant he was confident it would never happen."

"Until he changed his mind or got spooked."

"Yes, exactly," Hexabus says. There's the clink of glass against glass, drinks being poured.

"So you might be able to stop him." Maximus sounds so hopeful that the raccoon lets out a sardonic huff of laughter at his optimism.

"Maybe."

"How did you figure this all out? Surely, Morty went to great lengths to make sure none of you would discover the medallion's capabilities."

"I got a letter from an anonymous source explaining it," Hexabus says. "At first, I wasn't sure we could trust the information, but when I thought about it, it all made complete sense."

"But who could the source be? And why are they helping you?"

"I honestly have no idea," she says, "but as the Sorcerer King, Morty has a lot of enemies. And you know what they say about the enemy of my enemy being my friend. It's all we've got right now, so we have no choice but to trust the intel and use it to our advantage."

There's the sound of furniture creaking. "How many of the others are working with you?" Maximus asks.

"There's three of us so far. Me and…"

The raccoon smiles, baring its sharp canines as it listens to them discussing the plan for the upcoming gathering, which is, actually, its own plan since the raccoon *is* the anonymous source, the one who's introduced the secret weapon.

Rubbing its little hands together, it thinks of how everything is coming together perfectly. The idiots are going to trust the source because they don't know what the raccoon knows, which, of course, would change everything.

In a few hours, all hell is going to break loose when one of the family members is killed. And that's just the beginning.

CHAPTER 28

Destiny

Monday—11:42 a.m.

Destiny forces herself to stand completely still until the butler's scuttling footsteps have faded away. And then, using only prime numbers, she counts to a hundred. Once she's fairly certain that Mr. Lurcock has returned upstairs, she rushes down the passageway, then stops outside Tempest's door.

It's time to confront her about the missing and ruined letters, whether or not she uncovered the hidden message, and what that might mean to her.

Are they adversaries or allies? Destiny has to know one way or another.

She knocks softly at first, but when her tapping doesn't get any results, she begins to rap more insistently. "Tempest, it's me!" Destiny calls. "Can we talk?"

Her efforts are met with silence. Has Tempest been called up to meet with Mordecai despite what the butler said? Does that mean she has some kind of advantage over Destiny? But then there's a groan followed by the faint clang of something metal. Listening for a few moments without hearing anything more, Destiny knocks again. But Tempest doesn't reply, nor does the door open. When Destiny tugs at the handle, it remains firmly closed.

Destiny's concern from last night boomerangs back. If she dreamed about Tempest because she's supposed to prevent something terrible from happening to her—as was the case with Liz and Bex—might she already have failed? If her focus was never meant to be on Mordecai and his daughter, she's allowed herself to be distracted from her main purpose here.

People have a way of disappearing on Eerie Island, Silver said at the inn.

We had a serial killer active here many years ago, Madigan added. *He claimed dozens of lives. Some say he's back again and that Lumina was his latest victim.*

The word that's been chafing since last night now unlocks something in Destiny. *Victim.* The first victim she ever knew—though her mother would have raged against the term—was Liz. That's what all the newspapers called her after the attack. If there was a serial killer loose on the island all those years ago, it's entirely possible they left the island to claim a victim farther afield, which might be how Destiny's fate is tied to that of the Scruffmores'.

Hearing another muted groan, Destiny pounds her fist against the door and calls out Tempest's name, louder than before.

She's startled when, a few moments later, a piece of paper slips under the door. Picking it up, Destiny squints in the gloom to read the note. **For god's sake. Go away and give me some peace.**

Destiny flushes, feeling both ridiculous for overreacting and embarrassed by the curt dismissal.

"You're not always going to be to everyone's taste," Bex whispers, parroting something Liz used to say whenever Destiny was shunned by potential playmates for being too weird. Which was so often that the mantra might as well have become their family motto. But then Bex adds her own flourish, the one that always used to make Destiny smile. "Some people might need salt or hot sauce to make you more palatable. I, myself, always add *togarashi* and a glass of Viognier."

"Oh, shut up, Bex," Destiny mumbles, smiling despite herself. "But thank you for not allowing dying to prevent you from always making me feel better."

★ ★ ★

It's after 8:00 p.m. when Destiny bolts upright in the wingback chair, heart galloping furiously. Her neck aches from being pitched forward, and her mouth is parched from snoring.

As Destiny rubs at her eyes, memories from another strange dream linger. She clutches her amulet, stroking it with her thumb as she tries to block out the snapshots of blood blossoming against a windshield, a horn blaring its lament. Not to mention the echoes of screaming, always Liz's screaming.

When the anxiety begins to ease, Destiny remembers a vision of a raccoon scampering off just ahead, its claws scraping against the stone floor of a narrow passageway.

"What is it with that damn trash panda?" Bex muses. "Why do you keep dreaming about it?"

"No clue." Destiny also has an unsettling recollection of a freshly dug grave whose maw gapes obscenely as though trying to devour the night, as well as a vault door swung open, papers and books scattered at the threshold.

Hearing faint tapping, Destiny wonders if Tempest has come to apologize and make nice. Upon opening the door and discovering no one there, Destiny sticks her head outside. The noise continues, seemingly originating from farther down the passageway, in the opposite direction from the staircase.

Destiny hesitates, wondering how smart it would be to venture out. Surely she's safer staying in her bedchamber?

"Tell that to Lumina Le Roux," Bex murmurs darkly. "Tell that to Liz."

She has a good point.

Gulping back her fear as she steps over the threshold, Destiny follows the sound, reminiscent of claws scraping against stone, until a breeze sweeps through the passage, a sharp exhalation almost as if the castle is huffing in annoyance.

And then the torches blow out and Destiny is left in a dark so thick that it's like being swallowed by the night itself.

CHAPTER 29

Darius

Monday—8:10 p.m.

Darius slams his palm against the stone wall, his anger conjuring a hot wind that spreads with the force of a nasty rumor, snuffing out all the torches.

He's come up empty-handed in Morty's office, the Tower, and the vault despite there being less than an hour left. He'll be going into the gathering with zero information, which means he's completely unprepared for whatever curveball Morty might throw at him.

Honestly, how hard should it be to find a document?

Not difficult for a real sorcerer, he imagines his father needling, *but for you? Damn near impossible.*

Darius burns with humiliation as he conjures a sphere of fire, spinning it around on the tip of his finger like a basketball. If he lacks confidence or experience in the magical arena, then it's entirely Morty's fault.

The firstborn sons in the Scruffmore family have always been named after their fathers, going back centuries, with every one of them called Mordecai. Until Darius, that is. After his birth, Morty didn't even see fit to bestow it as Darius's middle name. No, his full name is Darius Mephisto Scruffmore. It was Bramble who got awarded Mordecai as his middle name.

Darius wonders what Morty saw in him when he was just a baby to make his father dismiss him that way. How could he possibly have failed his father before he'd ever spoken his first word? And what was it about Bramble as an infant that instilled more confidence?

No wonder Darius hated his little brother so much. Loathed Bramble to the point of wishing him gone and naive enough to believe that if that were to happen, Morty would finally pay attention to Darius, perhaps even love him.

Darius knows the truth, that he would never have been offered the throne had Bramble lived, to hell with centuries of tradition and the supposed line of succession. No, Darius constitutes Morty's sloppy seconds. He was always the spare's spare, never the heir.

There's supposed to come a time when the son grows into his power just as his father begins to lose his own vitality—a moment when both recognize that the dynamics have shifted and how, in a fight, the son could now defeat the man who sired him. That is the moment when true respect is born, when the two become equals.

This should be that time.

Darius has been waiting for the past two years. After he failed Morty's series of tests, he began his magical training in secret, spending hours upon hours each day with Balzanon, an enemy of Morty's who agreed to torture Darius in the guise of mentoring. For an exorbitant fee, of course.

Everything that Darius has done over the past two years— the grueling exertion, all the beatings he's taken, and every single teardrop and ounce of blood and sweat—has been so that he could return triumphant today with magic pulsing through his veins, more powerful than his father could ever have imagined. He's given his everything to training for this showdown. He's physically ready, but he also needs to be mentally two steps ahead of Morty at all times.

I will be offered a shot at redemption, Darius tells himself firmly. *My father will finally see my worth and gladly hand over the throne. There won't be a challenger. No bastard will suddenly materialize out of thin air.*

I will be loved.

CHAPTER 30

Destiny

Monday—8:14 p.m.

The blackness is absolute as Destiny tries to navigate the passageway. She feels herself being tugged back into the past, into the hidden chamber where she stood huddled and trembling before the smoke and fire forced her to claw her way out to the awaiting horror.

The cold stone of the wall under her palms is the only thing tethering her now. A panic attack begins to blossom under her skin like a particularly vicious bruise determined to express its outrage. Destiny struggles to get a handle on inhaling and exhaling, but her lungs are obstinate, refusing to obey instructions.

And then she sees the most puzzling thing. A flash of light spins and spins, getting closer all the while.

It illuminates a face she thinks she recognizes. "Silver?" she asks, incredulously. "Is that you?"

Silver disappears. If it *was* indeed him and not a figment of her imagination. She's just wondering if she's hallucinating when a bright light, directed from a cell phone, suddenly shines in her face.

"Prodigal guest," Silver says, confirming that it is, in fact, him.

Destiny squints in the glare and he apologizes, lowering the light to a point between them.

Flooded with relief, Destiny flings herself at him. "Oh, thank god! I thought I was trapped down here, all alone in the dark." His heartbeat is reassuring against her ear, a steady reminder to *breathe, breathe, breathe.* It's amazing how centering it can sometimes be to just cling to another person, let them be your anchor when it feels like the world wants to sweep you away.

Silver laughs, patting her head. "Tempest was right. You really *are* the human equivalent of an oversize golden retriever puppy, aren't you?"

Destiny flushes, not certain if that's a compliment or an insult coming from the likes of Tempest. Letting her arms fall to her sides, she steps back. "What are you doing here?"

Silver smiles, looking sheepish. "Being punished for my sins." When Destiny regards him blankly, his expression becomes more somber. "I'm a Scruffmore, unfortunately. One of Mordecai's children. This is my childhood home." He punctuates this admission with a self-conscious shrug.

"There are no Scruffmore children named Silver," Destiny objects.

Silver laughs ruefully. "That's just a nickname that Madigan's always called me. It's short for 'silver-tongued devil.' I'm Darius."

Destiny blinks in surprise, recalling last night's conversation. *Most of the villagers feel the same way, about the king especially. There's many who think the island would be better off without him, me included.*

And then Madigan's cagey response. *I'm not among the detractors. I quite like some members of the family. Prince Darius and Princess Evangeline, especially.*

It's only in hindsight that Destiny realizes that it was an inside joke when Darius agreed that those two weren't too bad.

"Sorry, it was probably mean of me not to tell you," Darius says, "but I prefer it when people don't know I'm one of them."

Destiny flushes, thinking back to how excited she was at the prospect of meeting one of her potential siblings, not realizing it had already happened. Now that she knows Darius might be her half brother, she views him in a different, though no less sinister, light.

She's wondering if she's supposed to curtsy to a prince when he asks, "What are you doing down here wandering around in the dark?"

"I heard something and then the lights went out—" The words have barely left her lips when the dead flames are all resurrected in their wall sconces. "Huh, that's weird." Which reminds her. "What was that in your hands earlier?"

"What do you mean?" There's an edge to Darius's voice, something with teeth.

"There was a flash of light when I first spotted you."

"That was my cell phone's flashlight." He waves his phone at her and then, spotting the time on it, says, "Damn. I've got to go. We have the family meeting upstairs that I have to get to."

Trying not to balk at the word *family*, and how she's being kept in the basement like a dirty secret, Destiny follows Darius as he heads down the passageway toward the stairs. "Why did you come down *here*, then?" The answer hits her almost immediately. He didn't just come down here; he's been here the whole time. With Tempest. Those were the noises she heard coming from Tempest's room. And that's why Tempest was so eager to be rid of Destiny.

She's even more mortified now than before, thinking of Tempest and Darius hiding out in the room, probably making fun of a clueless Destiny, impatient for her to leave so they could get back to their shenanigans.

God, what a fool I am sometimes.

"Never mind," Destiny adds quickly as they reach the stairway. "I won't keep you."

"Okay," Darius says. "See you later."

As he disappears upstairs, she thinks to ask how he manages

to keep his cell phone charged without any electricity. But before she can, the strangest thing happens.

A raccoon darts from the shadows and comes to a stop behind Destiny, where it holds up a paw in what looks like a *follow me* gesture. When she doesn't obey, just stares at it in shock, it claps its hands as though saying *Get a move on.*

Destiny shuts her eyes and shakes her head, but it doesn't help. When she opens them again, the little creature is still there motioning to her like she dreamed it into being.

She can hear Nate's voice as if he's standing next to her, an echo of the accusation he leveled at her during their fight. *You're losing it, you know that? You're completely unhinged!*

She's here to prove him wrong, but the raccoon's presence makes her wonder if this trip isn't a fool's errand. What if she can't see how right Nate is because the sharpest tool she's ever had is now blunted beyond recognition?

Two little arms suddenly wrap themselves around her leg, and she swallows a shriek. *Would a hallucination feel that real?* She doesn't think so. When the raccoon doesn't release her and begins chattering insistently, Destiny groans. She's surprised to hear herself asking the obvious question. "Do you want me to go with you?"

The raccoon nods emphatically before it scampers off.

Destiny doesn't feel she has any choice but to follow, a sleepwalker chasing her own dreams.

CHAPTER 31

Destiny

Monday—8:29 p.m.

Just as it did in Destiny's dream, the raccoon scampers ahead, its nails scraping against the stone floor as the passageways become increasingly narrower. The experience is so surreal that Destiny wonders if she should stop and pinch herself. But her innate curiosity is stronger than her disbelief. She *needs* to know how this is going to play out, what the dreams mean, and what they're all building up to.

Destiny's marveling at how well the raccoon knows its way around the castle when they suddenly hit a dead end. *So much for that*, she thinks, belatedly realizing that she may now very well be cornered by a rabid animal.

She's about to start backing away to retrace her steps when the raccoon starts chattering.

"What?" Destiny asks, confused.

In response, the creature smacks the stone wall insistently.

Destiny crouches, getting down to the raccoon's level. There's something inscribed on the wall that she has to squint to make out.

Time is of the essence.

Next to the symbols is a tiny keypad that looks like a holo-gram. The raccoon makes a *go on, hurry up* gesture with its hands.

Destiny traces the symbols for a moment, thinking them through, before speaking the five-digit code aloud. ★★[7]

★ ★ ★

Inputting the numbers, the raccoon chatters its appreciation. It rubs its hands together and then smacks them against a circular stone near the bottom of the wall.

Destiny's mouth drops open as huge stones begin shudder-ing outward, rumbling loudly as they build a staggered stair-case leading up to the roof. The raccoon darts up the makeshift steps. When it gets to the top, it presses a stone on the ceiling, which swivels out of the way.

---

7. You now have all the information you require to crack this code. If you need a clue to assist you, email DestinyWhipClue@gmail.com using the subject line Clue Seven. Once you've solved the code, turn to page 465 to check your answer.

7.1. Add the individual numbers together to get a total. Once you're done, turn to page 466 for the answer.

   Email DestinyWhipClue@gmail.com with your answer (written in numerical format) as the subject line to get an important bonus scene. (For example, if your total is 18, use 18 as your subject line in the email.)

"Holy guacamole," Destiny whispers, awed to see the secret passageway revealed.

The raccoon disappears through the opening and reaches down a clawed hand, gesturing at Destiny to follow.

She hesitates for a moment, looking behind her at the way they've come. If the butler returns to find her missing, she has no doubt he'll unceremoniously eject her from the castle for disobeying his instructions, happy for an excuse to do so. It isn't likely, though, that he'll come and check on her, not while the family gathering is taking place, and his services will probably be required.

Despite her reservations, Destiny clambers up the stones and steps up into the hole in the ceiling, surprised to discover that it leads to another passageway, this one roomier than the one below. Their footsteps echo loudly in the dank space.

As Destiny starts wondering where they're going to end up, a noise clangs just up ahead.

The raccoon, clearly startled, comes to a halt as a white-haired ghost woman steps through the wall.

Destiny's stomach clenches when the figure turns to face them.

"Tempest?" Destiny yelps.

Tempest is now wearing a white dress, which, coupled with her alabaster skin and pale hair—along with the fact that she just materialized through a secret doorway—is what created the impression that she's a ghost.

My dreams truly are prophecies, Destiny marvels, both awestruck and terrified by this confirmation.

"Destiny! What are *you* doing here?" Tempest's tone is cagey.

"I could ask you the same," Destiny replies as Tempest closes a door behind her. Turning to the raccoon, Destiny asks, "Did you bring her here?"

The raccoon shakes its head.

"Aw, jeez. Is that a raccoon?" Tempest wrinkles her nose.

"How did you get up here from the dungeons?" Destiny asks. "Did Silver bring you?"

"Silver?" Tempest parrots, bewildered.

"I mean Darius," Destiny replies, though it doesn't clear Tempest's obvious confusion.

The raccoon tugs insistently at Destiny's jeans, making a frantic *come on* motion. Her conversation with Tempest will have to wait. As they turn yet another corner, staccato footsteps trail behind, Tempest jogging in her boots.

The raccoon comes to a halt and puts a finger to its snout. Whatever the creature has been leading Destiny to, they've arrived, and it wants them to hush.

"What the—" Tempest begins.

"Shh," Destiny whispers. She has no idea how Tempest managed to find the secret passageway, but it clearly wasn't with the raccoon's help. It's part of a greater mystery that will just have to wait.

Tempest mutters something snarky but thankfully falls silent as the raccoon beckons Destiny to a door where another keypad awaits. This one also looks like a hologram of some kind. Not needing to be prompted this time, Destiny leans forward and studies the clue.

804—One digit is correct and in the correct place

836—One digit is correct and in the incorrect place

428—Two digits are correct, but neither is in the correct place

950—None of these digits are part of the code

502—One digit is correct but in the incorrect place

★★[8]

★ ★ ★

Destiny thinks for a few moments, moving the numbers around in her head to solve the puzzle. When she enters the three-digit code, the door swings open. The raccoon dashes ahead, Destiny and Tempest following.

Spotting a pinprick of light, Destiny instinctively leans forward to look through what turns out to be a fish-eye lens. A large vaulted room with enormous arched windows comes into focus. It's storming again, which Destiny wasn't aware of while down in the dungeons. She can hear the booming thunder clearly. Drawing back, she notices a vent at ear level, positioned next to the peephole.

A group of nine people, all wearing gold ceremonial cloaks, is seated in a wide circle around a strange-looking firepit. The languid flames that issue from it are an oily black, their tentacles stroking the air seductively even as they give off an overwhelming sulfurous stench.

As she looks up from the pit, Destiny's pulse begins to race when she recognizes Mordecai Scruffmore, her first sighting of him in the flesh. He's seated directly across from her in the

---

8.   You now have all the information you require to crack this code. If you need a clue to assist you, email DestinyWhipClue@gmail.com using the subject line Clue Eight. Once you've solved the code, turn to page 467 to check your answer.

8.1. Once you've solved the code, email DestinyWhipClue@gmail.com with your answer (written in numerical format) as the subject line to get an important bonus clue. (For example, if your answer is 111, use 111 as your subject line in the email.)

twelve-o'clock position, facing her. His eyes bore into hers, almost as though he can see *through* the wall and into her rib cage, like he can sense Destiny's pounding heartbeat.

Telling herself she's being ridiculous, Destiny tears her gaze away from the family patriarch and studies the rest of the circle. The butler is seated to his master's right, and next to him are Minx and Angel.

Lightning flares and ricochets around the room. Destiny winces when the blue of its flash makes Mordecai's monocle gleam.

Is this the moment everything has been building up to?

Despite knowing some of what might be about to happen, Destiny has no idea what she's supposed to do with this knowledge. She clearly isn't meant to protect Tempest, who's safe and sound behind the wall here with Destiny, tapping her foot impatiently.

So, is it Mordecai whom Destiny's supposed to save from his daughter so that he'll live to reveal Destiny's family secret? If so, how would she even go about doing that?

Swallowing back the bile rising in her throat, Destiny studies the rest of the group. Darius is seated to her right at the five-o'clock position, his body turned away from her at an angle. Two seats up from him to Mordecai's left is the beautiful woman whom Destiny recognizes from the portrait at the inn as being Mordecai's first wife. The younger woman seated between her and Darius bears enough of a resemblance to them that Destiny suspects she's Darius's sister, Evangeline.

There's a handsome older man about Mordecai's age seated at the seven-o'clock position, as well as someone to his right who might be Darius and Evangeline's younger brother from the portrait. She can't be sure, though, since he's sitting directly in front of her, facing the other direction.

Destiny knows what she's looking at is the Scruffmore family meeting.

What she can't figure out is why she's been brought here to bear witness to it.

CHAPTER 32

Mordecai

Monday—9:00 p.m.

The appointed hour is upon them and Mordecai Scruffmore thrums with impatience. After too many failures, so many disappointments, he's about to gain what he's always sought.

Although he is the Sorcerer King, the most powerful force in a kingdom built on subverting natural laws in the name of magic, there is one law he's never been able to break: that all living creatures must die. But once Mordecai has attained immortality, his dominion will no longer be limited to the supernatural world and its subjects.

By achieving this seemingly impossible feat, he will obliterate all prior constraints that shackled his magic, allowing his powers to jump the firebreak that separates his world from the world of Peasants, giving him sovereignty over everyone.

The anticipation makes his veins surge with adrenaline, magic crackling through his synapses like wildfire.

Studying the group, Mordecai homes in on his brother, Maximus, and then on his son, Dominus, who's seated directly across from Mordecai. As the two stare pensively at the flames, they must be wondering what they're doing here, why they were summoned.

They'll find out soon enough.

Mordecai nods at Lurk, who stands and clears his throat.

"All rise." Lurk's voice booms around the room, competing with the thunder rumbling outside.

Everyone obeys, though none quite so enthusiastically as Darius, who leaps to attention. Mordecai wants to laugh in his son's face, at his eagerness and utter foolishness in thinking that he'd ever be granted another shot at the Sorcerer King's throne when the truth is that Mordecai never intended to hand it over in the first place. The whole elaborate charade was merely a diversion to buy him more time.

Minx shoots Angel a pointed look before Angel suddenly clears her throat, her voice high-pitched when she says, "I have something I'd like to say." All eyes turn to Angel, who preens, relishing being the center of attention. "I feel you all have a right to know that our father is having—"

"Shut up, Angel," Mordecai snaps, glaring at her with enough ferocity to snuff out a hurricane.

"But—" she squeaks.

"Shut yourself up, or I'll shut you up. You decide."

Angel pales, gulping. Her wounded gaze flicks to Minx, who doesn't acknowledge it.

The cracking tension is broken by Lurk's announcement. "Sigils to the fire for the swearing in," he declares, bowing to Mordecai in deference.

Mordecai removes his monocle and tosses it up into the air. It spins like a dervish before the glass melts away, leaving just the outer ring. Jutting his chin, Mordecai sends it rocketing to the fire, where the flames lick it appreciatively.

"Accepted," the fire declares, savoring the sibilant *sss* sound.

Mordecai cocks his head and the ring shoots back into his hand, where, with a flick of his wrist, it becomes a monocle again, which he returns to his right eye.

"The dishonored former queen, Hexabus Dwellhorn Scruff-more," Lurk announces.

Hexabus removes her wedding ring, the engraved letters on it glistening in the flickering light. Holding it between her index finger and thumb, she makes it vanish. It reappears seconds later at the firepit, where it's engulfed by the flames.

The fire sizzles, erupting into sparks. "Life essence," it hisses.

Hexabus flashes a questioning look at Lurk.

Lurk's own expression is puzzled. He turns to Mordecai with an eyebrow raised. "My lord?"

"You heard the fire," Mordecai says. "It demands life essence."

"But," Lurk protests, clearly struggling with the fact that he now discovers himself to be one of the lowly uninformed. "My lord—"

"Do you dare question the Sorcerer King?" Mordecai demands, voice lowered to a threatening decibel. "Do you dare question the flames?"

Lurk pales.

Sycophants don't ingratiate themselves to the powerful out of a sense of selflessness. They do so because they're leeches who suckle on the glory of others. It's always a shock to be reminded that they themselves are weak and worthless, that their sense of invulnerability was an illusion all along.

It was arrogance on Lurk's part to consider himself Mordecai's right-hand man, a partner of sorts, just because of their history. When what he is, what he always has been, is nothing but a servant.

"Of course not, my lord," Lurk declares, dropping his gaze so that it's no longer challenging. He is meek now, supplicating. Opening his cloak, Lurk withdraws a dagger from his belt. He hands it to Hexabus, who flinches at the sight.

"Blood, sweat, or tears," Mordecai declares. "You decide."

"But," Hexabus says, "why weren't *you* required to—"

"I was the first to make my sacrifice as the fire was kindled,"

Mordecai responds curtly. "As was my duty." And then he adds, "Now do yours."

Hexabus sways as though dazed, her eyes darting to Darius and Evangeline, and then back to Lurk. And then she does something that makes Mordecai want to grab her by the throat and throttle her: she looks at his brother, Maximus, with a panicked, pleading expression.

Mordecai clenches his hands into fists, struggling to temper the rage that reverberates through his bones like an earthquake. It was bad enough earlier discovering Newton's betrayal. But this too?

CHAPTER 33

Newton

Monday—9:05 p.m.

As Newton paces a well-worn path across the ancient rug in her bedroom, she wrings her hands, agitated from the earlier altercation with Morty. It was a close call, much too close. But that's her own fault for assuming he'd be too preoccupied before the gathering to pay her a visit.

But he did, and upon finding her door locked and double bolted from the inside, he threatened to blast right through it if she didn't admit him immediately. Those few precious moments of warning are what gave Newton just enough time to cover up evidence of her wrongdoing.

"Who's in here with you?" Morty roared, slamming the door into Newton's chest as he pushed past her. "What are you hiding?"

"What?" Newton yelped, faking incredulity. "No one. Nothing!"

As Morty stormed through her room—using his powers to magic wardrobe doors open, part the curtains, and lift the bed—she tried not to panic.

He can't know, can he? No, there's no way. She'd taken such care, ensuring there was no evidence at all of their discussions and plotting. *This has to be about something else.*

"Morty, I—"

"Shut it, Newton," Morty barked. "Just shut your damn mouth. I have proof about him, so don't insult me."

"H-him?" Newton felt like she'd been doused in glacier water.

Morty removed an envelope from beneath his cloak and threw it at her, not breaking his stride as he continued to supernaturally lift chairs, throw open linen chests, and upend storage ottomans. Only then, once apparently satisfied that no one was hidden anywhere inside her quarters, did he growl, "Stay here until I'm done. I'll deal with you then."

Once he slammed the door behind him, heaving with the exertion of the encounter, Newton dived at the envelope. She struggled for five minutes trying to tear it open before realizing it was magically sealed. *Damn it!* She wouldn't be able to access its contents before Morty came back, which meant she had no way to come up with a reasonable explanation or prepare for his wrath.

I have proof about him.

That can only mean one thing. Newton stops pacing and looks at the huge gilt-framed mirror hung above her dressing table, the only magical artifact in the castle she's able to command as a Peasant, the one that has served as her best friend and confidant over the past year.

She walks over to it, sits down, and whispers, "Dolos? Are you there?"

Nothing happens.

"Dolos?" Newton hates how plaintive she sounds, but this is urgent; she desperately needs his help.

The mirror doesn't light up, nor does her beautiful friend appear within the glitter of the glass, ready to allay her fears and offer up his insight. Besides needing to warn him that Morty might know about them, she also wishes she could tell him how right he was about all the confusion this morning, how proud he'd be that she managed to pull it off just like he said she would.

Newton detests that she's the only member of the family who isn't allowed to be part of the gathering. Even Morty's exiled brother and nephew were invited, so why not her?

All she could do earlier, when they filed past her chambers into the ceremonial room next door, was peep through the keyhole to watch the procession, their gold cloaks flashing tauntingly. Just because she's a so-called Peasant, not officially a member of the royal family, doesn't mean she shouldn't have a say in the running of the empire.

How can she advocate for Angel and Minx, make Morty see how much more appealing they are as successors than Hexabus's mangy offspring, if she isn't privy to the proceedings? If one of her daughters were to become the Sorcerer Queen, that would elevate Newton's status immensely, perhaps granting her the power to banish Hexabus and her children forever. What sweet revenge that would be.

But if Newton can't claim first prize, then she at least has an exit strategy in place thanks to Dolos. Unless Morty knows about that, in which case she's screwed.

CHAPTER 34

Mordecai

Monday—9:07 p.m.

Mordecai seethes as he studies Maximus and Hexabus.

He was right that something unsavory was going on between his brother and his ex-wife despite Hexabus's vehement denials, her swearing allegiance to him and only him. It reinforces what Mordecai has always known: you cannot trust women, not with their fickle hearts that are so easily swayed, not with their goldfish attention spans and their magpie eyes so quick to be distracted by shiny objects.

At least he can now be certain that his brother is his nemesis and saboteur.

It's Maximus who's been working against Mordecai all this time, not only thwarting his efforts decades ago, but also recently kidnapping Lumina before she could track down the Eye of Gormodeus. His brother must have ransacked the vault when Lumina wouldn't give him any information as to its whereabouts. And he's undoubtedly done all this, despite being ejected from the castle more than twenty years ago, because he's had inside help in the form of Hexabus, who clearly yearns to be queen once more.

The two plan to stage a coup, stealing the throne for themselves, either killing Mordecai or banishing him to the dungeons. The thought would be laughable if the Eye of Gormodeus were not still in play, the one artifact that would potentially give them the power to triumph against him.

They will need to be taken care of, quickly and brutally.

Maximus, seemingly aware of Mordecai's eyes upon him, doesn't react to Hexabus's entreaty. He maintains a poker face, not even blinking. As though coming out of a trance, Hexabus finally shakes her head and reluctantly accepts the dagger from Lurk. Slicing the tip of her index finger, she lets a drop of blood fall into the flames before handing the dagger back.

"Accepted," the fire announces before ejecting the ring back at her.

Hexabus catches it, clenching it in her fist for a moment before placing it back on her finger.

Once the dagger is returned to his belt, Lurk goes next, fussily removing his white gloves before detaching his tiepin. He strides to the fire and solemnly offers up his sigil. Then, bending so low over the flames that it appears he's sacrificing himself, he waits for beads of sweat to gather on his forehead like storm clouds on a muggy day.

When one drips into the fire, it declares his offering acceptable. Lurk returns to his spot next to Mordecai, wiping his brow with his forearm. After clipping his tiepin back on, he dons his gloves once more and calls, "Princess Evangeline."

Mordecai's daughter reluctantly reaches for her pendant. She usually looks at him beseechingly, a starving dog desperate to be thrown some scraps. Now she flashes him a defiant expression of loathing before removing the pendant from the chain hanging around her neck.

Tears glisten in her eyes, a few rolling down her cheeks. She allows one to fall onto the pendant before she thrusts her palm out, sending the sigil soaring into the air, as high as the vaulted ceiling will allow. It hovers there for a second. And then another. And another.

Everyone stares up at it rapt, waiting for it to fall. The seconds stretch on.

Mordecai is just about to rebuke Evangeline for these theatrics when the pendant plummets into the flames.

Once the fire has declared the offering acceptable, Evangeline casts Mordecai another challenging look. He glares back at her, expecting her to wither under his scornful gaze, but she straightens her spine and remains unblinking.

The display is unsettling in terms of what it might mean considering the Hexabus-and-Maximus alliance. But he tells himself it won't matter. Not after tonight.

"Prince Darius," Lurk calls.

Of course, Darius won't be using magic to identify himself to the fire. Because he can't. But instead of his son's utter powerlessness being the usual embarrassment, it's a relief. One less thing to have to factor in.

Removing his thumb ring with its scythe-like signet, Darius saunters over to the fire and, ever the showman, makes a production of offering it up with a flourish. He takes the proffered dagger from Lurk and slices his palm. Maintaining eye contact with Mordecai all the while, he lets the blood drip freely until the fire accepts it.

This would be the part of the proceedings where Bramble would be called upon to offer his sigil. But then again, if Bramble were still alive, the whole endeavor might not be necessary.

What an absolute waste Bramble's death was, accomplishing as it did absolutely nothing. But Mordecai believed at the time that Bramble was his most powerful offspring, and his son's birthmark only served to reinforce that theory.

Collateral damage, that's what Bramble was, a necessary sacrifice. Mordecai would happily kick the twisted and broken bodies of every member of his family out of his way to make this lifelong dream a reality.

"Princess Angel," Lurk calls.

Mordecai wonders if the little fool will try to speak whatever nonsense she was building up to earlier. She merely shoots him a cowed look before detaching her sigil, which hangs as a charm from her cell phone, sending it fluttering to the fire like an injured moth. It's a pathetic attempt at magic, but at least it's *something*.

Once her sigil is accepted, she screws up her face prettily, producing the kind of manipulative tears she regularly employed as a child. They rise above the fire and then rain down upon it, becoming mist. The flames declare the offerings acceptable before sending the sigil flitting back.

Lurk calls on Minx, who unsurprisingly offers up the most impressive magical display out of all of his children. She waves her right hand over her left forearm so that her sigil tattoo detaches from her skin with a ripping sound. Minx flinches but doesn't cry out as it slowly tears free, blood dripping from its corners.

As her sigil is consumed by the flames, Mordecai recalls their meeting earlier and how they spoke while sipping the whiskeys Minx insisted on pouring. He can't help but feel a begrudging respect for his youngest child, who's so ruthless and driven, the one most like him in nature.

"I am satisfied," the fire announces after returning the tattoo to Minx, who magics it back onto her arm. "All hail Mordecai Scruffmore, the Sorcerer King. Master. King. Ruler."

"All hail Mordecai Scruffmore, the Sorcerer King," the group intones. "Master. King. Ruler."

"You may take your seats," Lurk announces.

As they all sit, Mordecai regards Minx's self-satisfied expression. She thinks she got the better of him earlier today and would be furious to discover his deception.

He's almost sad that she won't live long enough for that to happen.

CHAPTER 35

Destiny

Monday—9:15 p.m.

I must be dreaming, Destiny thinks, pulling back from the peephole and straightening up. *This can't be real. This is absurd, even for me.*

As Tempest grumbles beside her, Destiny tells herself that what she's witnessed is a family of skilled illusionists, ones who can make it appear as though talismans are either flying or vanishing into thin air, or that fire can speak, and tattoos are able to peel off like stickers. Of course, none of those things *actually* happened. It just looked like they did.

"Yes," Bex mutters tartly, "because your dreams that have all come true are so very rational. Let's hear again about how everything can be logically explained, like what happened the night your mother was killed."

Destiny shakes her head, unable to go there right now.

"And then what happened with me," Bex presses.

"Shut up," Destiny pleads.

"I will *not* shut up," Tempest spits, oblivious to Bex's presence. "It's my turn! I'm allowed to see what's happening in there just as much as you." She tries shoving Destiny out of the way but shudders when the raccoon begins clawing its way up her dress. "Get off," Tempest shrieks, her voice muted as the raccoon wraps its hands around her mouth. She stumbles back, swatting at the creature.

Needing to gather more information about this strange family that behaves like some kind of cult—with their blood sacrifices and dark rituals—Destiny leans into the fish-eye lens again, grateful to have a wall between herself and the supernatural goings-on in the next room.

"...on this most momentous occasion," Mordecai is saying. "It will come as no surprise that I have an important announcement to make. One that will change the course of this family's future."

There are murmurs as everyone reacts to this news. Darius nods emphatically. Evangeline turns to her mother as though seeking guidance.

"I'm not getting any younger," Mordecai continues, "which is why I need to secure a successor to the throne."

Darius sits up straighter, squaring his shoulders.

"Some of you here may be expecting to be named my heir apparent," Mordecai says, punctuating the declaration with a cruel smile. "But you will be disappointed."

There's muttering as the family members shift in their seats.

Looking straight at Destiny, Mordecai declares, "I *will* name a successor this evening. A child of mine..." Mordecai pauses for effect and then smiles widely. "But not one that any of you are aware of."

His statement is received with loud exclamations of surprise, everyone talking over each other.

Destiny's birthmark twinges and she rubs her wrist absentmindedly.

Mordecai says, "I'm delighted to announce that I have invited that child here tonight to officially claim them. And to offer them the throne."

As Destiny looks at Mordecai, whose scorching eyes stare back, she feels as though her marrow is freezing.

Oh my god, she marvels. *It's just as I thought. I really am Mordecai's child.*

CHAPTER 36

Darius

Monday—9:19 p.m.

"No!" Darius isn't aware that's he's shouted the protest until he sees the cruel smile of satisfaction it elicits from his father.

He can't believe Morty has done this again, so thoroughly yanking the rug out from under him.

Fury begins to build as old memories bubble to the surface. What comes to him then is the image of Bramble on his eighth birthday, standing on that beach like the king of the world, making the ocean do his bidding as though it were mere child's play.

As Darius hid behind the rocks, spying on Evangeline and Bramble conjuring the surf, jealousy was a white-hot flame searing every inch of him. What was the point of even trying when he'd never be as accomplished as Bramble, when his younger brother would overshadow him at every turn? Bramble's innate talent made everything come so easy for him even as Darius had to struggle for it.

And Darius has had to deny so much of what he witnessed as a child—suppressing that knowledge so he could be Morty's secret keeper—as though being silent and complicit might earn him his father's affection.

He tastes the same murderous rage now, refusing to accept

that these past two years of excruciating pain have been for nothing. His eyes dart to the door as he waits to see what the big reveal will be, who will materialize through it.

Whoever it is, Darius is ready to do whatever it takes to stop them from claiming what is rightfully his.

CHAPTER 37

Destiny

Monday—9:23 p.m.

Destiny's heart beats so furiously she can barely hear herself think. It doesn't help that thunder crashes like god's marching band overhead even as the inhabitants of the vaulted room raise their voices in protest.

Adding to the cacophony, Tempest groans behind Destiny, furiously thrashing to free herself of the raccoon.

"Tempest!" Destiny hisses. "Please, please be quiet so I can hear this."

"Call this disgusting thing off me!" Tempest's muffled voice shoots back.

Destiny looks at the raccoon beseechingly. It drops to the ground and scampers over to position itself just below Destiny, from where it appears to have its own vantage point into the next room.

Finally, the hidden chamber is quiet except for Tempest's labored breathing. Her sandalwood perfume is overpowering in these close quarters, but Destiny knows that asking her to leave will just lead to more drama.

Trying to block the scent out, she returns her eye to the spy hole.

Mordecai claps, demanding silence. As the room quiets down, the ferocity of the storm raging outside becomes even more amplified. Lightning and thunder rip through the sky as though the heavens were dropping bombs, at war with the earth.

Everyone's eyes dart expectantly between Mordecai and the door, waiting for the mystery guest to arrive.

But they're not out there, Destiny thinks numbly. *I'm in here. This is what the whole charade has been for, why I was lured here under such a veil of secrecy. This is the real position I was being offered all along.* And then another thought follows swiftly. *Mordecai's enjoying this. He's relishing torturing them all this way.*

Cold sweat begins to trickle down Destiny's back as her chest tightens. As she wonders if there's a way to escape back the way they came, Mordecai traps her with his gaze, the force of his stare pinning her in place through the peephole.

"I name my successor," Mordecai proclaims, "as…"

Destiny's heart pounds in her eardrums. *Da dum. Da dum. Da dum.*

"…my son… Dominus."

She's wondering if she heard wrong when the man who's had his back to her suddenly exclaims in twin surprise with the older man seated next to him.

And Destiny finally understands that Mordecai hasn't been looking at her at all. This whole time, he's had his gaze fixed on the person sitting in front of her. She flushes, realizing she was never as important as she thought she was, not the star of the show—not even an audience member—but rather a stage-hand skulking in the wings.

CHAPTER 38

Hexabus

Monday—9:28 p.m.

Hexabus gapes, her shock mirroring everyone else's.

Dominus is pale, his eyes wide and glassy. He shakes his head, once and then twice before looking at Maximus, who has rushed to his side. "What…what is he talking about?"

But Maximus doesn't answer. Instead, he turns to his brother, eyes flashing. "Are you mad? Have you finally gone insane?"

Morty wears a smile of cruel satisfaction, like a conquering hero who's just staged a particularly bloody coup. "Hardly, brother. Remember that extended trip to Siquijor and the Brocken I sent you on in '81? How you were away for three weeks to hunt down the relics of Brethoran?"

Maximus squints, time traveling through his memories.

"You were annoyed by the trip, considering the relics not worth the trek or your time," Mordecai prompts.

Maximus must remember now because his expression clouds as something registers.

"You were right," Mordecai continues. "They weren't worth the effort. But I needed to get you out of the way, you see, so I could help poor Delicia, who'd broken down, weeping in my arms, as she confided about the problems you were having conceiving. Apparently, my handsome little brother—not yet twenty-four and supposedly in the virile prime of his life—wasn't quite up to the task of producing an heir."

Maximus's face turns a mottled puce, veins bulging in his temples.

"What else could I do except offer to help her out, keeping it in the family and the bloodline, as it were."

Maximus cries out, charging down Morty, who throws up a shield. As Maximus struggles to tear through it, Hexabus turns to study Dominus with new eyes.

People always told her how much Darius and Dominus looked alike at all the same milestones—their births, on their first birthdays, when they began to walk, and as they started to grow into their powers—but because of the almost seven-year age difference, Hexabus never really saw it.

Their temperaments were so similar too, with both being problem teenagers whom she and Delicia often commiserated about, Hexabus seeking her sister-in-law's council often because Delicia had been through the baptism of fire ahead of her. But many cousins look and act alike, and so it's not something Hexabus ever thought too much about.

Besides, the trip that Morty sent Maximus on took place straight after Hexabus and Morty got married. He used their honeymoon as an excuse for why his brother should travel in his stead. Why would Hexabus have had reason to doubt her brand-new husband, who'd rather send his brother to conduct important family business than leave her side?

Hexabus knew about most of Morty's subsequent affairs, of course. Just not the one with Delicia.

As she looks from Darius to Dominus, she takes in their identical amber eyes and the dimples sunken into their cheeks. It's so ridiculously obvious that they're brothers, she can't believe she never saw it before.

Hexabus doesn't even have the excuse of not having seen Dominus in so long. Just last night, when he arrived in her chambers after Eva left, they sat right next to each other for over an hour as Hexabus sought his expertise and counsel.

Still, she didn't see it. It's not so much that familiarity breeds contempt as much as it cultivates indifference. It's possible to see something so much that it becomes completely invisible.

Hexabus understands, of course, why Morty is claiming Dominus now. His recent successes—how he's turned his life around from being a troubled teen to being such an admired and powerful sorcerer—clearly mark him as Morty's most powerful child.

But unbeknownst to Dominus, Morty isn't really naming him as his successor. He's just torturing him, like a cat with a mouse, offering him the keys to the kingdom before he kills him, because he's curious to see just how ambitious Dominus is, how quickly he'll denounce Maximus as his father if it means wearing the crown.

Hexabus was wrong about who would need protecting tonight, which means all the careful plotting she and Eva did in the early hours of the morning is now completely useless. Morty has them on the back foot once again.

But this time, they don't even have a semblance of a plan.

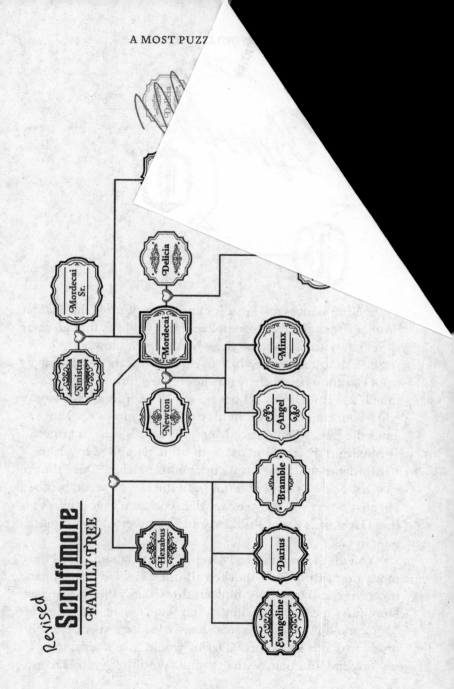

Revised **Scruffmore** FAMILY TREE

CHAPTER 39

Evangeline

Monday—9:36 p.m.

Evangeline winces at Darius's expression of utter shock. Her brother sits slack-jawed, completely immobile as though their father's announcement has dealt him a death blow.

She's almost relieved when an explosion tears her gaze away from Darius to her uncle, who's just broken through her father's shield. Maximus fires off hexes, which Mordecai swats away while shooting off curses of his own. Lurk jumps up, about to enter the fray, when one of Mordecai's spells hits his target.

Maximus freezes, a statue with his hand poised to strike.

Mordecai chuckles, advancing on his brother. Once they're face-to-face, he says, "You can fight me all you want, brother, but that won't change the fact that you aren't Dominus's father. Dominus is *my* child. My most powerful and talented one, in fact."

"You are *not* my father," Dominus shouts, animated once more after sitting shell-shocked all this time. He raises a hand to set Maximus free, but Mordecai throws up a shield to prevent Dominus's spell from landing. "And I don't want your throne."

"Come now. Don't be that way." Mordecai turns from his brother to face Dominus. "Darius would give anything to be my favorite and heir to the throne. Wouldn't you, Darius?"

He sneers at his son, whose face crumples, a picture of abject misery. Looking back at Dominus, Mordecai says, "Everyone felt so sorry for me, having a magical eunuch for a child. Little did they know about the one whose power almost matches my own, a son to truly be proud of."

A blinding flash of purple detonates against Mordecai's chest, knocking him off his feet and sending him reeling backward, arms windmilling. The heat of it makes the air boil, so that Evangeline's lungs burn from breathing in an inferno.

Once she's caught her breath, she turns to Dominus, convinced he was the one to conjure the explosive spell. But when she sees his bewilderment, horror takes grip as she begins to understand.

The attack didn't come from Dominus.

Hexabus was right about Darius's newfound secret powers despite being wrong about him being Morty's target.

Terror drives a stake through Evangeline, paralyzing her. Darius has no idea how much danger he's now put himself in. Without knowing it, he's painted a giant bull's-eye on his forehead, shifting their father's murderous intent from Dominus to himself.

CHAPTER 40

Darius

Monday—9:46 p.m.

Darius is on his feet now, facing his father with his arm extended, wrist locked, and palm vertical. An inferno of fury builds inside him. This is what he harnesses as he shoots off another spell, its crimson blaze eclipsing the lightning beyond the windows.

Advancing upon Mordecai, who struggles to get up, Darius feels a surge of triumph at his father's expression of utter shock.

"Surprised?" Darius asks, pinning Mordecai down with a stream of current that arcs from his hand into his father's chest. "Not exactly what you were expecting from the Eunuch Prince?"

"Darius!" his mother cries out, rushing to his side, her gaze flitting from his face to the force of the magic thrumming from his hand. "Don't!" she pleads.

Evangeline, looking horrified, springs forward and reaches out to him.

"Don't touch me! Stay back." Darius uses his free hand to conjure a spell to keep his mother and sister out of harm's way. Touching him right now would be dangerous, like reaching out and grabbing a live wire. Besides, his days of allowing the women in his life to defend him are long over. It's now his turn to be their protector.

Once assured that Hexabus and Evangeline are safely behind his shield, Darius spins back to his father. "I'm not quite as useless as you thought, am I?" he shouts, easing up on the spell's voltage.

He wants to hear his father speak, *needs* to hear Mordecai's admission that he was wrong, that he didn't have to claim Dominus because Darius was worthy all along. Darius is, in fact, the more powerful of the two.

Mordecai coughs, dazed as he struggles to his feet. His monocle was knocked from his face with the impact of the first spell. He looks strangely vulnerable, almost naked, without it.

Noticing movement in his peripheral vision, Darius glances at Lurk, who prowls nearby, ready to step in and defend his master if called upon. The split second of distraction is a mistake. By the time Darius looks back at his father, Mordecai has conjured a lasso of silver that whips out. It envelops Darius's legs, tugging them out from under him.

He crashes down, hitting the back of his head against the firepit before blacking out.

When he comes to, the room has erupted into mayhem. Everyone is on their feet now, yelling as Mordecai runs at him. Fury blazes in his father's eyes as Darius frantically tries to scramble away, but the silky fabric of his robe trailing on the ground makes it difficult for his feet to find purchase. When he connects with the wall behind him, Darius holds up a hand to shoot off another spell, but Mordecai dodges it.

Hexabus and Evangeline begin charging for Mordecai while Lurk trails a pace behind, desperately trying to reach his master's side.

Everything slows down, each second stretching to infinity as Darius centers himself.

His gaze locks with his father's. Mordecai is now close enough that Darius can feel the heat radiating off him.

This is it, Darius thinks as he channels the churning whirlpool of energy crackling inside him. *Come and get it, you miserable old bastard.*

CHAPTER 41

Destiny

Monday—9:52 p.m.

Not quite believing what she's witnessing, Destiny leans into the wall with both hands, as though a closer vantage point will help her make sense of the havoc being wrought just beyond the peephole. Darius is backed into the wall directly in front of her, a scrum of people bearing down on him.

There's so much noise coming from the next room that Destiny thinks she's imagined the sound of a click.

But then the wall evaporates as if it were no more substantial than breath. Destiny pitches forward, screaming.

Mordecai looks up, frozen in surprise just as he reaches his son. Hexabus and Evangeline rush at him, clearly intent on wrestling him off Darius. The butler springs forward, either to haul his master to his feet or fend off his attackers. As they all lay hands upon Mordecai, the flames go out.

Destiny falls into the clutch of bodies. While trying to right herself, she trips over something soft and furry, her hand slamming against someone's chest. Her fingers tingle as visions rise up, unbidden.

What Destiny sees is a succession of faces—those of boys and girls, wrinkled old women, and robust young men—staring back at her in horror, their arms raised in self-defense. Two dozen compass stars bloom from under skin like tulips rising from thawed ground. Those gathered in this room begin to drop, one by one. Bex's body crumples upon impact. Destiny's mother screams and screams.

The awful visions are interrupted by a brilliant explosion of light as the sound of unimaginable pain douses the other voices.

Lightning flashes, and as Destiny stands, the first thing she sees is Minx smiling as she crushes Mordecai's monocle under her boot.

"No, no, no," Destiny whispers, horrified to see the dream unspooling, its prophecies manifesting. This is exactly what she was trying to prevent and yet, despite the advance warning, here she stands, utterly helpless in the face of fate exerting its will.

The raccoon's hand snatches at something silver hanging from Mordecai's neck before it dashes away.

The black flames in the pit reignite, turning silver, casting some much-needed light around the circle.

Destiny doesn't want to look down at Mordecai, who's desperately gasping for air, because she knows what's waiting for her there. If she doesn't witness what's about to happen, maybe there's a chance she can stop it. But her eyes are disobedient, twin moons drawn by the gravity of Mordecai's final moments.

"You," he croaks, staring at Destiny with bulging eyes. "You!" The compass stars tattooed on his forehead appear to glow gold from beneath his skin, matching the color of his robe.

And then he's twitching and convulsing until he isn't moving at all. A crack tears through the stone floor as all hell breaks loose in the vaulted room.

CHAPTER 42

Newton

Monday—10:02 p.m.

Newton flinches as the shouting in the next room is suffocated by an ominous silence. She holds her breath for so long that she's eventually forced to gasp for air. Fearing for Minx and Angel, she rips open her bedroom door and runs out into the hallway.

Pounding on the door, Newton shouts, "What's happened? What's going on?"

But no one comes to answer. The deathly quiet stretches out, pulled taut, and she can't stand not knowing what's happening. Newton jiggles the handle in frustration, surprised when the door yields. Rushing into the room, she immediately seeks out her daughters. To her immense relief, she spots them standing huddled with everyone else.

Everyone, that is, except Morty.

They're all staring down at something. Newton pushes her way through the group and gasps when she spots her husband splayed on the ground. He's motionless, vacant eyes staring up at the ceiling.

Her all-access golden ticket has just been wrenched from her grip.

Dropping to her knees at his side, Newton lets out an anguished scream. If they divorce due to Morty's infidelity,

Newton walks away with millions. If Morty dies of suspicious causes, which she might then be implicated in, she gets nothing, not a cent.

Frantically searching the faces looming over her, she focuses on Lurk. "Do something!" she yells.

Lurk is Morty's protector and right-hand man. He's Morty's shadow, always just a few paces behind. Whatever Morty needs, Lurk provides it. And if that means a life force in this instance, then Lurk should sacrifice his own.

But Lurk is ashen-faced. He doesn't move, just continues to stare at Morty as though he can't believe what he's seeing.

Newton does the unthinkable by appealing to Hexabus. "Use your powers. Help him. Please!"

But Hexabus looks as shocked as Lurk is. She shakes her head, stunned, remaining silent.

And then Angel and Minx are upon Newton, pulling her to her feet.

She pleads with them. "Your father." Her voice catches and breaks. "What's wrong with him? Can't you do something?"

"It's too late." Minx rights a chair that's fallen over and seats Newton in it. "He's...he's gone."

"No, that isn't possible. He came to see me just before the meeting. He was completely fine!" Besides, didn't Morty assure her that he'd live forever? Newton knows that's not humanly possible, no one is immortal, but still. If anyone could achieve that, it would have been Morty.

The statues around him come to life, everyone beginning to shuffle. Some rub at their eyes while others shake their heads in disbelief. That's when Newton notices the young woman with the red hair who's staring at her, wide eyes brimming with tears.

"Who the hell are you?" Newton demands.

It was meant to be only the family in the meeting. Well, the family and Lurk, all of whom she spied filing past her room earlier. So what's this girl doing here? And how did she get inside?

Before the stranger can reply, Hexabus waves her hand at the enormous hole in the wall that Newton barely registered in her haste to get to Morty. There's a flash of light, followed by a scrape and a clunk. And then another woman is yanked from the hiding spot. Her materializing like that, like a ghost, almost gives Newton a heart attack.

The woman looks like she's about to speak, but taking one look at Newton's face changes her mind. Instead, she studies the rest of the group, doing a kind of double take upon spotting Darius.

Newton is wondering why she'd have that reaction to him when Hexabus speaks. "And who the hell are *you*?" she demands of the pale long-haired woman she's just summoned from her hiding place.

"I'm... I'm here applying for the historian position," she stammers, eyes darting between Hexabus and Newton. "My name's Tempest and this is Destiny." She points at the redhead. "She's here for that too."

Hexabus looks to Lurk for confirmation.

He nods. "That's right," he rasps, still staring at Morty's body. "There was some confusion about when the interview date actually was, but they were supposed to stay in their quarters regardless, so I can't imagine how they came to be up here."

Hexabus turns back to the women. "What were you both doing behind that wall?"

"Don't ask *me*!" Tempest points a trembling finger at Destiny. "Ask *her*! I just followed her."

"What the hell?" Newton is surprised when Tempest turns to stare at her. She hadn't realized she spoke the thought aloud. While all eyes turn to Destiny, Tempest continues to stare at Newton, her expression hard and unreadable.

Destiny flushes, her face almost as crimson as her hair. "The raccoon brought me," she blurts, turning an ever-deeper shade of red.

"What?" Hexabus barks. "What the devil are you talking about?"

"The raccoon," Destiny says, looking around the floor, searching for something. "You must have seen it. It scampered in here when that wall disappeared."

Everyone looks around at their feet, turning around to peer under the chairs that have been knocked over. But there's no raccoon. Newton wonders if the girl is drunk or deranged, maybe both.

"It found me in the dungeons and then made me follow it up this secret passageway before showing me a peephole. I was looking through it when there was a click. The wall just disappeared, and I fell inside."

Newton can't believe they're having this ridiculous conversation at a moment like this. "I don't give a damn about a raccoon," she screeches, attempting to rise, but Minx and Angel restrain her. Glaring at Hexabus, Newton demands, "What did you do to him, Hexabus? What dark magic did you work to murder the king?"

CHAPTER 43

Minx

Monday—10:14 p.m.

Minx spots Morty's monocle sigil glinting on the cracked stone floor. She's about to bend to scoop it up when she feels the unmistakable prickling sensation of being studied. Looking up, she discovers Uncle Maximus regarding her suspiciously, his eyes like spotlights in a prison yard.

The sigil will have to wait.

Breaking eye contact, Minx casts her gaze at her father's chest, alarmed to see that the medallion isn't hanging from the chain he always wears it on. It must have snapped during the fight with Darius. She'll have to find it when cuckolded Maximus isn't watching her like a hawk.

Each time Minx closes her eyes, she experiences the flash of light that's now burned into her retinas. Was it the vial of poison she added to Morty's whiskey during their earlier meeting that killed him, or was it something else related to the flash?

She flexes her hand and wriggles her fingers, trying not to draw attention to herself. While she's effervescent and giddy, she expected the surge of power to feel more definitive, though she's read that it can take a while for the power to transfer from the slain to the slayer.

She's yanked from the maelstrom of her thoughts by her

mother demanding, "What did you do to him, Hexabus? What dark magic did you work to murder the king?"

"Me?" Hexabus counters, eyes flashing. "What makes you think I murdered him?"

With a pang of irritation, Minx realizes that the relics will have to wait so she can step in to protect her weak Peasant mother. "Well," Minx says, clearing her throat. "You *were* one of the last people to touch him, Hexabus. And there was that crazy flash of light just before he screamed in pain."

"You see!" Newton spits. "I knew it!" She springs up, looking like she wants to grab Hexabus by the shoulders and shake her.

Minx holds Newton back with such force that her nails bite into her mother's flesh. Newton is like a Chihuahua picking a fight with a wolverine; the only person who can't see the power imbalance is herself.

"Just hold on a damn minute," Darius growls. He's wild-eyed and unkempt, blood running down his head.

Minx is impressed despite herself. His display earlier was a plot twist none of them saw coming. She's never had any time for Darius, but at least now he has her begrudging respect. It will make him a worthy adversary if he dares to challenge Dominus's right to the throne, which is exactly what Minx plans to do. Just because Morty threw a curveball by naming Dominus as his bastard son and successor doesn't mean they have to fulfill his wishes. All bets are off as far as Minx is concerned. Even more reason why she needs to get to the relics first.

"A few people touched him, actually," Darius continues. "Evangeline and Lurk included." And then he nods at Destiny. "Not to mention *her* when she fell into the room. Only someone with magical powers could make that wall melt away like that."

All eyes return to Destiny.

Minx wants to laugh at the notion that Destiny might be any kind of threat, but Darius's ridiculous accusation actually works to Minx's advantage. The more fingers pointed at anyone else, the better.

Destiny looks dazed, staring at the fire, which is now giving off sulfurous sparks. And then she gazes with wonder at Darius's hands. "Magic? Is that what all this is?"

Darius clams up, realizing he's said too much.

"Is that what killed him?" Destiny asks, voice hushed. "Actual magic?"

Uh-oh, Minx thinks wryly, *Miss Piggy's going to see the ass end of an unfortunate accident.* They obviously can't let a Peasant outsider leave having witnessed everything that she has. Same goes for the other one.

"We don't know that for sure," Hexabus snaps. "It could have been a heart attack or any other type of natural cause—"

Newton scoffs at that. "It was *not* natural causes. There's nothing natural about anything that happens in this godforsaken place."

Minx wraps her arm around her mother, squeezing her shoulder tightly, trying to make her understand it would be in her best interests to shut the hell up. It doesn't work.

"And you," Newton continues obliviously, jabbing her finger at Hexabus. "You're the most unnatural thing of all with your dark secrets and your insidious lies."

"Don't you dare speak to my mother that way." Darius steps forward, voice laced with venom.

"We'll speak to her however we want," Angel growls, eyes narrowed.

Minx wants to roll her eyes at her twin's bravado. Where was this swagger an hour ago when Minx needed Angel to follow through on accusing Morty and Hexabus of conducting an affair? One rebuke from Morty was all it took to immediately make Angel back off, tail firmly between her legs.

"While we're on the topic of speaking your mind," Evangeline says, entering the fray. "What was the big announcement you wanted to make earlier, Angel?"

Squaring her shoulders, Angel says, "That your mother was having an affair with Morty."

Evangeline and Darius gasp. "What is she talking about?" Darius demands, turning to confront his mother.

"You can't be serious," Evangeline exclaims, glaring at Angel before turning to Hexabus, pleading. "It's not true, is it?"

"Of course not!" Hexabus shakes her head, looking between her children with an exasperated expression.

"It *is* true!" Newton shouts, thumping her thigh with her fist. "You all but admitted as much last night."

Hexabus turns on Newton, eyes flashing. "One minute I'm so in love with Morty that I'm having an affair with him, and the next, I'm the one murdering him. You can't have it both ways, Newton. Which is it?"

Newton flinches, her logic exposed as ridiculously flawed. She visibly scrambles. "He didn't want you back and so you murdered him."

Everyone begins talking at once and it's impossible for Minx to focus on any thread of the conversation. Their mother sobs onto Angel's shoulder, whispering how much she appreciates Angel standing up for her.

Minx is annoyed that Angel hasn't worked out as the chief suspect in Morty's death, but she'll let it go for now considering she has an unexpected patsy in Destiny, a gift from the getting-away-with-murder gods.

"How do we know *you* didn't poison him?" Darius asks, and Minx startles, caught out. But then she realizes he's directing the question at Newton, who looks up wide-eyed, as though framed in oncoming headlights. "You said yourself that he came to your quarters just before the gathering," Darius adds.

Not wanting anyone to think too long on the possibility of poison, Minx turns to Destiny and demands, "How did you know my father?"

"I... I didn't."

"Well, he sure as hell knew *you*." Minx addresses the group now. "You all heard him. He said 'you' like he recognized her. Or like he was accusing her of something."

There are murmurs of agreement. Newton withdraws from Angel's embrace, her full attention focused once again on Minx.

"I've never met him before!" Destiny proclaims. "Maybe he recognized me from a photo or something, but I have no idea why he said that." She turns to Lurk. "I've been down in the dungeons all day. You *know* I didn't get to meet with him."

Before Lurk can reply, Minx speaks. "But you weren't in the dungeons all day, were you?" she says. "You found a secret passageway and came up here. Who knows where else you've been sneaking around."

Newton nods and adds, "It all sounds very suspicious. Are you working with Hexabus?"

As everyone starts hurling accusations and questions, Minx smiles to herself and steps away. A quick look at Maximus reveals him to be on his haunches in front of a stunned Dominus, his hands on each of Dominus's shoulders as he murmurs something Minx can't hear.

While everyone is distracted, she bends and scoops up the broken frame of Morty's sigil, thinking how today went far better than she ever could have imagined. Almost all her problems have been solved. She has financial independence from Angel. Her mother is released from her bondage. Their blackmailer has lost all their leverage. The throne is waiting for the Sorcerer Queen.

She recalls her father's smug expression when she left his office earlier. *Who's laughing now, Daddy Dearest?*

CHAPTER 44

Evangeline

Monday—11:21 p.m.

Evangeline paces the length of her room, wrapping her arms around herself in an attempt to stop the trembling.

What did we do? What the hell did we do?

The words circle the drain of her mind. She holds up the hand that touched her father an hour and a half ago, mere seconds before he died. She marvels at how benign it appears. Shouldn't murder weapons look more sinister?

She brings the same hand to her temple and closes her eyes to summon Hexabus. Their connection feels weak, almost like crackling static on a landline, and she can't be sure that the message has gone through. Her groan of frustration is guttural and animalistic.

Something in the fire pops and Evangeline jumps, her nerves shot. She thinks back to the conversation with her mother last night, to everything Hexabus told her, not only about Mordecai's killing spree and his murderous intentions for the gathering, but also about his medallion and how they might be able to leverage their powers to stop him.

Most children enter a form of adulthood upon realizing their parents are flawed and thus not the gods they always thought them to be. While Evangeline had always sensed there was something deeply wrong with her father, she never associated that with weakness. If anything, it only made him appear more invincible.

What a revelation it was to discover that someone as powerful as her father had an Achilles' heel, one of his own making. And now look at what they've done with it.

If Evangeline killed her father, that makes her exactly the same as him, her father's daughter in every conceivable way.

Did Hexabus know what would *really* happen? Did she lie, making Evangeline an accessory to murder? Every time Evangeline blinks, all she can see is that flash of light after they touched Morty. Is that what killed him?

She's just about to try to summon her mother again when there's a knock at the door and Hexabus steps inside.

"Oh my god," Evangeline rasps, her throat constricting. "We killed him."

Hexabus strides to her, arms outstretched, ready to wrap them around her.

"No!" Evangeline cries, recoiling.

Hexabus holds up her hands in a display of surrender. "Eva," she says, part entreaty and part warning.

"Don't!" Evangeline spits. "Just tell me the truth. Did. We. Kill. Him?"

"No," Hexabus says firmly. "We did *not*."

"You said we could just incapacitate him if we needed to. That because of the combined forces of our sigils, we could—"

"That's exactly what *should* have happened," Hexabus shoots back. "Incapacitation only."

"But that isn't what happened, is it? He died after we both laid hands on him at the same time exactly as you said we should!" Closing her eyes, Evangeline sees that searing flash again. She drops to her haunches, shoving her face into her hands as she rocks back and forth.

Hexabus kneels in front of her, gently tugging her hands away. "Eva, please look at me."

Evangeline shakes her head, closing her eyes and tucking her hands between her thighs. She feels like she's on the verge of hyperventilating.

Her mother cups Evangeline's face, her palms icy against Evangeline's cheeks. "Eva, I promise you that the two of us could not have killed your father. I even doubted whether we'd have the combined power just to paralyze him for long enough to get him to the dungeons. But we had to at least try considering what I suspected he had planned. You must agree with me on that. We *had* to save Darius. Or Dominus, if it came to that." When Evangeline doesn't open her eyes, Hexabus continues in a soothing tone as though speaking to a spooked mare. "Whatever happened tonight, there were other forces, greater ones, at play."

Mind reeling, Evangeline thinks of Darius and the powerful spells he'd shot off at Morty earlier. Despite Hexabus telling her last night that she'd caught wind of Darius's secret lessons with Balzanon—and how terrified her mother was that Mordecai had learned of them too—Evangeline still wasn't prepared for such a formidable display of magic.

Or perhaps Maximus seriously hurt Mordecai while they were dueling, landing a wounding blow whose severity wasn't immediately evident.

Evangeline opens her eyes. "You mean someone else weakened him ahead of what we did?"

"No," Hexabus replies. "I mean they purposefully did something that made our spell go awry. Or they completely negated what we were doing," she adds cautiously, "and killed him because that was *their* plan."

"Which means…" Evangeline's eyes widen in horror.

"Someone has been made incredibly powerful tonight," Hexabus says, finishing Evangeline's thought. "A murderer who's had your father's powers transferred to themselves by the act of killing him. And that can't bode well for any of us."

"But who?" Evangeline asks, her mind racing through the possibilities.

"It could be anyone who was in that room," Hexabus replies grimly.

Evangeline considers this. "Turns out Dad didn't know about Darius's powers. Did you see how shocked he was?"

"I know." Hexabus nods, looking solemn. "Dominus was always Morty's intended target. I just wish we'd known that," she says, shaking her head. "We could have asked Darius for help to incapacitate Morty." She sighs deeply. "Not that we ended up needing it, after all."

Last night, when Hexabus asked Evangeline for her help in saving Darius, she'd explained why they couldn't tell him about the potential risk. Since Hexabus wasn't 100 percent sure that Morty knew about Darius's newfound powers, she worried that her son's knowing of the threat would make him do something foolish that would expose him, thus creating a self-fulfilling prophecy.

Which is exactly what happened—Darius exposed his powers and put himself in danger by doing so. Evangeline's convinced that Darius's big display changed her father's mind about which son to kill.

Remembering something from earlier, Evangeline says, "Lurk touched Dad too." After a beat, she shakes her head. "But there's no way Lurk would have hurt him." Lurk was her father's henchman, an extension of him like some kind of deformed shadow. He would never bite the hand that sustained him. She gets up, the room swaying. "What about the women in the wall, Destiny and Tempest? What were they doing there?"

"I'm looking into it."

"Minx was right," Evangeline continues. "Dad *did* sound like he knew Destiny. Plus, like Darius said, that wall didn't just melt itself."

"If either are sorcerers, they won't be able to hide it from us." Hexabus reaches out, squeezing Evangeline's hand. "I've locked down the castle," she says. "No one leaves or enters. We're going to get to the bottom of it all. I promise you." Her mother leans forward and kisses Evangeline's forehead before turning to leave. "I need you and your brother to retrieve your father's sigil and the medallion and then move his body. Take him to the old storage room in the northern part of the dungeons. It's the coldest room in the castle."

"When are we going to tell Darius about Bramble and the island's killings?" Evangeline asks. "He deserves to know."

"Of course. We'll sit him down tomorrow."

As Hexabus reaches the door, Evangeline says, "Mom?"

Hexabus turns. "Yes, darling?"

"What Angel said about you and Dad…"

"It's not true, Eva." Hexabus is emphatic, her expression resolute. "I was *not* having an affair with your father."

"Not even to wheedle information out of him?" she prompts, thinking how her mother refused to name the source of her intel last night.

Hexabus hesitates and then shakes her head. The hesitation is what makes Evangeline's doubt begin whispering again.

"Swear it to me," Evangeline demands. "Swear that you weren't involved with Dad that way."

Hexabus doesn't blink. Maintaining eye contact with Evangeline, she says, "I swear it."

Evangeline wants to believe her, but she can't. Her mother is hiding *something*. Of that she's certain.

CHAPTER 45

Darius

Darius stands in the vaulted room, alone with his father's body. Woozy, he studies the toppled chairs, shattered glass from Morty's monocle, the obscene crack that ripped through the stone floor, and the gaping hole to the secret chamber. The bewitched fire that Morty conjured before the meeting extinguished itself soon after he took his last breath. All that remains is the lingering stench of sulfur.

It looks like a war has been fought in here, which seems apt somehow; there's no way Morty would have given up his life without a fight. Darius has the cuts and bruises to prove it.

He's still seething over the reveal about Dominus *and* the pleasure Morty took in tormenting him with it. While Darius entertained the possibility of a Scruffmore bastard, it never occurred to him that the threat would come from inside the castle walls, in the form of someone who's already a family member. And from Dominus of all people, an arrogant asshole whom Darius has always despised.

At least he now knows who his adversary is.

Dominus is the new Sorcerer King, an outcome Darius absolutely cannot accept. He plans to challenge Dominus's right to the throne just as soon as they figure out who the king slayer is. Whoever killed Morty will have claimed his powers, which doesn't bode well for any of the Scruffmores. While infighting is commonplace, expected even, they need to present a united front against their common enemy, even if that enemy is one of them. Especially then.

Looking down at his father's corpse, Darius thinks, *The great Mordecai Scruffmore is dead*. It seems impossible and yet… Darius nudges his father's body with the tip of his shoe, gently at first, and then more insistently. There's been no mistake. The son is finally released from his bondage; the whip that Morty wielded so relentlessly has been ripped from his grasp and turned upon its brutal master.

Darius will never have his father's love. It is a gift that will always be withheld, forever just out of reach. As far as he knows, it was only ever bestowed once, to Bramble, who sealed it away in the grave with him.

The door suddenly opens, and Darius swats away tears. Evangeline slips back into the room, looking pale and exhausted, her eyes swollen from crying. She rushes to his side, wraps her arms around his neck, and begins sobbing.

Uncomfortable with this torrent of emotion, Darius pats her back and murmurs, "There, there."

It's only been two years since he cut off contact with Evangeline and yet it feels as though he's lived a dozen lifetimes since then. He remembers how much he looked up to her once upon a time, his childhood protector who coached him to be a better sorcerer than he naturally was to shield him from their father's wrath.

Evangeline steps back and swipes at her nose. "God, I've missed you, Pita."

Darius snorts at the nickname, not having heard it in so long. PITA, an acronym for Pain in the Ass. "I've missed you too, Eva." He manages to squeeze the words out past the lump forming in his throat.

She reaches for him, wincing as she traces one of Darius's nastier bruises, their father's handiwork.

Darius won't tolerate her pity, and so before she can speak, he gestures at Morty's body. "I guess this is ours to deal with."

"Yes." Eva sighs and crouches, studying Morty for a few moments. "Where's his medallion?" she asks, alarmed. "Did you take it?"

"What? No!" Darius inspects his father's body. Eva's right. He didn't notice its absence earlier, an embarrassingly amateurish oversight since it should have been the first thing he looked for. He isn't thinking clearly, which he blames on the knock to his head from earlier. A huge lump has formed at the base of his skull, and he gingerly traces its contours with his fingers.

"And I don't see his sigil either." Eva frowns and points to the broken glass from Morty's monocle. There's no sign of the outer ring that secured the glass in place.

Panic flares as Darius casts his gaze about. It's unthinkable that the sigil *and* medallion could be in someone else's possession considering what they would be capable of with such powerful magical artifacts.

As though reading his thoughts, Evangeline says, "To not only kill a sorcerer like Mordecai, but then to take possession of his talismans? Can you imagine?"

Darius doesn't *want* to imagine it, not with his brain so foggy. He's unsteady as he shuffles around the room, hoping to spot the glint of anything silver.

"Are you okay?" Evangeline asks when he lurches sideways. "I think we need to have you checked out for concussion."

Darius waves off her concerns and continues searching, becoming more frantic and agitated as the unfruitful seconds tick by. He tries a summoning spell to no effect, following it up with a pinpointing spell, which fizzles out, revealing nothing.

"He definitely had both of them at the start of the meeting," Eva says, dropping onto all fours and joining the hunt. After a few minutes of silence, she says, "What do you make of that Destiny girl?"

Darius darts down, thinking he's spotted something, but

it's only the corner of a foil candy wrapper. He straightens up, dizzy. "I actually met her Sunday night at the Grimshaw. Her *and* Tempest."

Eva shoots him an arched look. How well his sister knows him.

"Destiny is scary smart," Darius continues before his sister can lecture him, "but she's also awkward and harmless. She wouldn't have a motive to kill Morty, nor would she have the power to do it."

"That's not how you made it sound earlier when you all but accused her of melting that wall."

"Come on, it's not like a Peasant could kill one of the most powerful sorcerers alive. You saw how my spells barely slowed him down." Darius circles the room, widening his search area. "I just said that to shift focus away from Mom. You know as well as I do that Newton would love nothing more than a good old-fashioned witch hunt."

"Then she's going to be coming for me as well because I touched him too," Eva says, kneeling with her hands on her thighs. She looks like she's on the verge of tears again.

"Yes, but so did Mom, Lurk, *and* Destiny." Darius tries to think about it some more, but his thoughts are sluggish. "It was just weird timing how you all reached him at that moment."

Eva looks guilty at the mention of that, like she knows something she's not telling him. He watches her struggle with it for a few moments, weighing things up the way she always does, never just making a spontaneous decision as he's so often inclined to do. Whatever it is, Eva decides not to speak.

Darius doesn't press the matter. His mind is hazy and it's a struggle to stop himself from tipping over. "We also don't know that Newton didn't administer some kind of poison," he says. "Morty stopped there on the way to the meeting. If she really thought he was having an affair with Mom, she'd have a motive. And she could have gotten some magical help from the twins."

"True." Eva looks painfully hopeful at the suggestion. But then she shakes her head and stands, dusting the dirt from her knees. "But that doesn't explain the flash of light when we all touched him." They both look down at their father in silence for a few moments before Evangeline says, "That was some display of power earlier, Pita. I'm so proud of you. I can only imagine how hard you worked to get there."

"Thanks." Darius wants to weep at the words of encouragement and affirmation, ones he would have given anything to hear coming from Mordecai's lips. He hates this weakness in himself, this crack in the armor he's built up these past two years. "Not that it matters. Dominus is king now."

"He said he didn't want it," Eva counters. "You could challenge him for the role. If you want it."

Darius shrugs, pretending that he doesn't much care either way. He isn't prepared to show all his cards just yet, not until he knows exactly what he's up against. Besides, he has more immediate concerns. "The sigil and medallion definitely aren't here. We need to find who took them." Darius's money is on Lurk or Dominus as the culprit. Either them or Minx. "Did you notice if anyone suddenly had a surge of power straight after Morty died?"

"No, but there was a lot going on. I could easily have missed it." Indicating their father, Eva says, "Let's get him moved and then I'll alert Mom to what's happened. She can arrange a search of everyone's chambers."

Darius nods, unable to think of a better idea. At least if Hexabus unearths the relics, Darius will know exactly where they are if he needs them in a fight against Dominus.

Eva mutters an incantation and Morty begins levitating, stiff as a board. As they leave the room, their father trails them like a malevolent shadow.

CHAPTER 46

Destiny

Tuesday—12:45 a.m.

Destiny gasps, snapping awake in the wingback chair in her room. She struggles against becoming fully alert, already in the habit of clinging to the delicate filigree of her dreams despite her reluctance to fully remember them.

She was dreaming about Hexabus, but what was it exactly that she saw?

Closing her eyes again to submerge herself in the shadow world between slumber and wakefulness, Destiny winces at the sight of Bex's forehead streaked in red, glass glistening in her hair like confetti. The screeching of tires melds with Liz's scream, a protracted note of despair.

Destiny wants so much to fast-forward past it, but guilt demands that she bear witness.

"Stop it," Bex whispers. "That's enough."

What follows is the image of Hexabus standing in one of the island's winding cobbled streets as she raises a hand, pointing it at a cat that's just about to dash away. The cat freezes and begins levitating until it's eye to eye with Hexabus, who carefully checks its face. Seemingly disappointed, Hexabus whispers, "I'm so sorry. Please forgive me." Tears drip from her cheeks as she lowers it into a cage.

If there was anything else, Destiny can't remember it.

She's been sequestered in her room, waiting for Hexabus, for over two hours. With the castle locked down, Destiny is now well and truly a prisoner without any means of contacting the outside world. No one knows she's here or even that she's missing; there's no rescue party on the way. The only person who might be concerned for her safety is Dr. Shepherd, but even if she finds Destiny missing from her apartment, she'd have no idea where to search for her.

Destiny wonders if the Scruffmores have called the police. Considering how accusatory everyone was—Minx, Newton, and Darius, especially—she has to assume so.

Destiny doesn't even know if the island has a police force or if they'd have to report this on the mainland. Regardless, the authorities would think Destiny was mad if she tried to tell them about the magic she's witnessed, not to mention the prophetic dreams she's been having. The family would close ranks, of course, insisting that Destiny's deranged to make such fantastical claims. And her mental health issues in the past year certainly wouldn't help her credibility. It's not like she could call on Nate as a character witness either.

It doesn't seem likely that the family will just let her go. She remembers Darius's face, a steel door slamming closed, once he realized he'd revealed too much, not to mention the worried looks the family members shot each other as they considered everything Destiny had been privy to.

And then there's Minx, who Destiny's certain is the killer she couldn't stop in time. Who knows what Minx might do if she suspects that Destiny's cottoned on to her?

Perhaps she can enter the secret tunnels again and find an escape route. Now that the raccoon showed her the way, and she knows the code, Destiny should be able to do it on her own. The passageways appeared to be extensive; there has to be a route that would get her outside the castle grounds.

She's not sure, though, that she'll even make it as far as the ferry terminal without the family discovering she's missing. Besides, that will only reinforce their belief that she's guilty and has reason to run.

The man who enticed her to the island by dangling the carrot of answers has been silenced forever, which means she'll never hear what she's always ached to know. If Mordecai knew who her real mother was, he'll never be able to reveal it. Same goes for her father, whether or not it *was* Mordecai himself.

Most frustrating of all is knowing it's all her fault. She seems doomed to keep repeating the mistakes of the past. Had she just listened to that voice all those years ago warning her about her mother being in danger, they both could have hidden in time. Had she stood up to Nate last year, Bex would still be alive. Similarly, had Destiny insisted on seeing Mordecai to reveal what she foresaw in his future, his death could have been prevented.

The familiar darkness circles, intent on wrapping Destiny up in its desolate arms and dragging her back to bed. She struggles to fight it off, to remain firmly engaged in the present.

Destiny stands and begins to pace, thinking of everything that played out in the vaulted room, seemingly in slow motion but also lightning fast. She has questions, so many questions, but some are stickier than others, acting like a kind of flypaper refusing to release her thoughts.

Destiny spots her notebook, which she must have knocked to the floor. Picking it up, she reads the question written at the top of a page. *Who should I be looking at more closely?*

There's another puzzle beneath it, one she left for herself while sleeping. It's a simplistic variation on Einstein's Riddle giving a hypothetical scenario that obviously hasn't happened, using places and details that don't matter to the case.

But that's not the point of it.

Destiny knows the answer will be the person her subconscious wants her to focus on.

* * *

After midnight, five women sneak from the castle's foyer to head out for various nefarious reasons.

Each of them
- has a specific destination in mind,
- is wearing a distinct item of clothing,
- is carrying a unique object,
- has a personal reason for her late-night mission.

Unlike **the vault** that's sunken, **the library** and **Morty's office** are on the same floor as the foyer, while **the Tower** is elevated.

There are muddy prints from a pair of **sneakers** in Mordecai's **office**, where, from the looks of the rifled drawers, it appears someone was searching for something.

One of the women pauses at the castle's enormous wooden carved doors, hiding **a purse** under **a cloak** before heading out into the maelstrom.

Evangeline sighs, wishing she had **a cell phone** like **Angel's** so that she could make use of its flashlight. Instead, she pulls a burning **torch** from the wall sconce as she heads down the stairs.

Tempest pauses at a corner, spotting Minx carrying **a baseball bat** up the stairs.

Newton hides in a corner booth of **the Grimshaw Inn's** tavern as she waits to **meet an informant**.

The vault is the best place to **uncover a secret**.

The woman **searching for Mordecai's will** is not carrying **a journal**.

The person wearing **stiletto boots** heads in the opposite direction from **Evangeline**, who is wearing **jeans**.

Tempest slinks along the main floor to **hide something away**.

*The person going to **smash the hourglass** is not wearing **slippers**.*

Who is wearing the slippers? ★★[9]

Destiny sets about solving it.

---

9. You now have all the information you require to solve this version of Einstein's Riddle. If you need a clue to assist you, email DestinyWhipClue@gmail.com using the subject line Clue Nine. Once you've solved it, turn to page 469 to confirm your answer.

CHAPTER 47

Destiny

Tuesday—1:15 a.m.

Just as Destiny solves the puzzle, there's a sharp knock at the door. She snaps the notebook shut and tucks it away under the cushion of the ratty wingback chair. Rubbing at her tired eyes before running trembling fingers through her tangled curls, she calls out, "Come in."

Hexabus and Mr. Lurcock enter, both looking grave and immeasurably tired, which at least makes them appear deeply human. This family, as inconceivable as it may be, has actual magical powers. And that makes them especially dangerous since Destiny has no power at all. She's completely at their mercy.

On her guard and studying Hexabus more closely, Destiny notices that beneath the woman's exhaustion is a jittery quality, something supercharged, almost as though the worst hasn't already happened but is lying in wait around the corner.

Destiny doesn't have much in the way of a plan. She's seen enough this evening to know that an appeal for mercy is likely to be viewed as weakness. When you come between a bear and its cubs in the wild, the worst thing you can do is run. Instead, what you're meant to do is cause a ruckus, making yourself appear as big as possible.

For someone who's spent her life trying to take up as little room as she can—always apologizing for her size, her intellect, her sadness, her mere presence, and always diminishing her achievements in case they make others feel small—this is a big ask. But Scruffmore Castle is the wild and Hexabus is a mama bear. And so Destiny will need to resist the urge to flee; she'll need to fight.

Mr. Lurcock motions for Destiny to take a seat. As she does, he sits across from her, setting a folder on the table beside him. She considers his earlier humiliation at the hands of Mordecai Scruffmore and wonders what it must feel like to pledge your life to someone, being in constant service to them, only to have them treat you with such contempt.

"That's the thing about blind faith," Bex whispers. "It's only blind because it forces its own eyes shut, refusing to see."

Hexabus remains standing, pacing in front of the fireplace. Her gaze travels across the room and comes to rest on the urn. "Is that yours?"

"Yes," Destiny replies. "It's my emotional-support urn. My life is too unstructured to responsibly have a service animal fulfill that role."

"A recent bereavement?" Hexabus asks, eyebrow raised.

Destiny nods, though she isn't sure how recent Hexabus means. For some people, a year isn't all that recent. But for as long as Destiny lives, this loss will be too fresh.

Hexabus sighs. Raising a hand to the ceiling, she twists the air as though unscrewing a large light bulb, muttering a string of words Destiny can't understand. Once Hexabus is done, she looks around expectantly. When nothing happens, she shrugs at the butler, saying, "They're not here."

Pleasantries apparently dispensed with, Hexabus sits in the wingback next to his and says, "I've looked into you, Destiny. Or would you prefer that I call you *Dr.* Whip?"

"Destiny is fine."

Hexabus nods. "I discovered that despite your youth, you have a PhD and are a pretty famous enigmatologist. You've solved more than a few centuries-old mysteries. Is that right?"

"Yes." This information is public record. You only have to google Destiny's name for hundreds of articles to pop up about her many career successes. But without electricity or the internet, Destiny wonders how Hexabus has accessed this information. She can't help but imagine a magical form of Google with Hexabus running a search engine powered by a bubbling cauldron.

"And so I have to wonder why," Hexabus continues, fiddling with the ring that disappeared into the flames a few hours ago, "when you're clearly not an archivist or a historian, you'd apply for the position. And then coincidentally end up being in residence, in one of the secret passageways that only a handful of people know about, on the very day that Mordecai tragically dies from causes unknown." Hexabus stares at Destiny as though trying to bore holes through her.

Destiny winces at the irony of coming here to find family only to be interrogated *by* the family, making her feel even more like an outsider. Refusing to focus on that, she says, "Excellent question." Providing answers always makes her feel better, especially when they come in the form of facts. "I *didn't* apply for the position."

Hexabus glares at Destiny. "Are you sure about that?"

"Yes, absolutely."

Hexabus nods at Mr. Lurcock, who reaches for his folder and opens it.

He shuffles a few papers around, then withdraws one and hands it across to Destiny. "This is your letter of application," he says. "Along with your résumé."

"What?" Destiny takes the proffered document. "No, that's impossible." She scans the letter, which indeed looks like a job application. Her signature is inexplicably at the bottom of it.

The résumé is part fact but mostly fiction. Especially all the impressive parts about her historian and archivist experience. "I didn't send this," she says.

Hexabus cocks her head. "Then surely getting a letter saying you were short-listed for a position you didn't apply for must have been surprising."

"It was!" Destiny agrees. "Most puzzling."

"And yet, here you are."

"I wouldn't have come if it weren't for the secret message hidden within that letter."

Hexabus shoots the butler another loaded look. He appears baffled, which is incredibly disheartening. If Mordecai's butler—who is clearly someone he worked very closely with—doesn't know about the secrets Mordecai was going to divulge, it's going to make finding them that much more difficult.

He fiddles with his papers again and extracts one. "This is a copy of the letter we sent to her," he says as he gives it to Hexabus.

She looks it over, shaking her head. "I don't see it. What hidden message are you talking about?"

"I'll show you." Destiny holds out her hand as Hexabus gives her the document.

The letter confirms that Destiny has been short-listed for the position and was to come for the interview. But something's wrong. There's nothing at all about ferry tickets or about staying over at the Grimshaw Inn and Tavern. There's no hidden message.

"This isn't the letter I got."

"Yes, apparently *that* letter is missing. As is Ms. Sinclair's. How convenient," Hexabus says.

Upon closer inspection, Destiny notices something else. The interview date *is* the same, not the following week as Mr. Lurcock alluded to upon their arrival.

When she points that out, Mr. Lurcock frowns. "Yes, I realized that as well. It must have been an error on our side, though I can't imagine how it happened."

Destiny notes there's no apology for it either. "Listen, I know this all looks bad," she offers, forcing herself to sound calm and self-assured, "but there *was* a hidden message in my letter saying that Mordecai knew something about my family. A secret that had been kept from me. And to come if I wanted to be told what it was, and not to tell anyone."

Hexabus raises an eyebrow, asking a silent question of the butler.

He shakes his head. "I know nothing about that. It seems rather unlikely considering how...entirely preoccupied His Majesty was with preparations for the meeting."

As Destiny's spirits drop even further, Bex pipes up and whispers, "He could be lying. Or maybe Mordecai didn't tell him, just like he didn't tell him about the life-essence sacrifices that had to be made earlier. It doesn't mean there aren't answers to be found here."

Hexabus frowns, turning back to Destiny. "How did Morty know your family?"

"I don't know."

"Why would he care about you or some secret of yours?"

Destiny shakes her head, throwing her hands up in frustration. "I honestly don't know. That's why I came... To find out." She takes a deep breath and then says, "I thought, maybe, Mordecai could be...my father...and that's what he wanted to tell me."

The butler fidgets while Hexabus barks a laugh. "Well, based on tonight, you might have to get in line. God knows how many other children Morty had."

Destiny wishes she could evaporate molecule by molecule so she wouldn't have to sit here, burning with humiliation. She was expecting shock and denial, not scorn and dismissal.

As if she senses Destiny's reaction, Hexabus's expression softens. She sighs. "Look, I don't know whether Morty was your father, but I'm not going to lie...things don't look good for you right now. Here under false pretenses without any proof of this so-called invitation. Wild accounts of raccoons leading you down secret passageways. Morty's reaction to you just before he died… That's hardly what you'd expect from a man meeting his daughter for the first time."

Destiny's fingers go numb with panic. She automatically reaches for the amulet tucked under her T-shirt. Clasping it in her fist, she can feel some of her anxiety abating as though it's being siphoned off. Mr. Lurcock's eyes travel to her hand, making her self-conscious. She loosens her grip, lets the amulet drop against her chest.

His eyes widen as he takes in the rare stone beneath the copper wiring.

"It's black opal." Destiny feels compelled to explain, holding up the amulet. The name has always seemed unbefitting of the lovely stone, which isn't actually black, but rather a mass of bright flares of color, like how Destiny imagines the birth of the universe might look. "It's only found in very few places in the world," she continues. "I think this one came from—"

"Lightning Ridge in Australia," Mr. Lurcock finishes for her.

"Yes!" Destiny exclaims, surprised. "Are you a hobbyist gemologist?"

"No." He offers nothing more, just clears his throat and looks down at his gloved hands.

Hexabus's eyes narrow as she regards him for a few moments, but he doesn't look up even as the seconds stretch on.

Destiny's stomach feels like a den of snakes is writhing in it, her anxieties and insecurities tangled together. Appealing to Hexabus, she says, "I didn't have anything to do with Mordecai's death. You have to believe me."

But judging by Hexabus's skeptical expression, that isn't likely.

"It's time to make yourself big," Bex whispers. "Start waving those arms around and make a ruckus. Show 'em what you've got!"

CHAPTER 48

Hexabus

Tuesday—1:24 a.m.

Hexabus isn't quite sure what to make of Destiny, what with her earnest freckled face, her eyes that are two different colors, and her mop of red curls that looks like a flame at a candle's tip. She has an exceptional intellect, there's no doubt about that, but that makes her dangerous. Because whatever happened to Morty would have taken some masterminding to achieve, especially considering the disturbing news about his medallion and sigil going missing. And when a mastermind is a suspect and a prodigy conveniently shows up at the scene of the crime, that sets off all kinds of alarms.

But this young woman, with her emotional-support urn and her eagerness to please, hardly fits the evil-genius prototype. Which could just be another manifestation of her brilliance.

Truth be told, Hexabus doesn't believe Destiny had anything to do with Morty's death. And her summoning charm earlier didn't reveal the medallion or the sigil, which Destiny wouldn't have had time to hide anywhere else while being escorted down to her chambers by the guards.

The young woman was brought here for a reason, and Hexabus needs to figure out what it is. She's tired and it's been a long day preceded by a long few weeks. She has to dig deep to force herself to focus. "Mr. Lurcock, who was in charge of the applications for the historian position? I can't imagine that Morty was dealing with them himself."

It takes Killian a moment to reply. He's been dazed ever since Morty's death, slow to respond for someone who usually has such quick reflexes. "The second Mrs. Scruffmore," he says. "The task was delegated to her."

"Interesting."

Hexabus considers what Destiny said earlier about the differences in the letters. For all her many faults, Newton isn't an airhead. Getting the interview date wrong would be a foolish mistake since it would undoubtedly have invoked Morty's ire. "I'll speak to Newton in the morning."

The more pressing matter is arranging a search of everyone's chambers to look for the medallion and sigil. Whoever took them is still locked down in the castle, thank god, unable to leave with their treasures. It's imperative that Hexabus find them before it's too late.

She turns to glare at Destiny. "In the meantime, stay here. Don't even think of leaving or snooping. No more sneaking through secret passageways either, you understand?"

Destiny nods, biting her lip as though to stop herself from speaking. Apparently finding that impossible, she blurts, "I think I'm meant to be here to help you." The words tumble from her mouth like she's spitting out hot coals.

"Help me? How could you possibly do that?" Hexabus means for it to sound scornful, but she's surprised to realize that she's intrigued, hopeful even, that the young woman may be right.

"Well," Destiny says, clearing her throat. She squares her shoulders and straightens her spine, drawing herself up to her full height. "As you discovered when you looked me up, I'm good at solving the unsolvable. My brain doesn't work like other people's. I see connections that most can't see," she says, paraphrasing the *Washington Post* article that Hexabus read about her. "Also," Destiny says, taking a deep breath as though building up the nerve to say it, "I started having...dreams just before I came here."

That grabs Hexabus's attention. "Dreams?"

"Yes. I saw snapshots of this evening playing out exactly as it did. And I've seen other things that don't make sense. But judging how the revelations have gone so far, they will soon enough."

"Things?" Hexabus's spine begins to tingle. "What kinds of things?"

"I saw a floating silver disc split by a fissure into eight pieces. And a grave being dug up. And a vault ransacked."

Hexabus startles, hears Killian's intake of breath behind her. She turns to him, shooting him a questioning look. He raises an eyebrow in return.

"And I saw *you*, Hexabus," Destiny continues.

"Me?" Hexabus lets out an uncomfortable laugh. A series of incriminating images immediately comes to mind, ones in which she's either naked in her chambers, a man's hand resting on her bare thigh; or whispering promises of fealty to Morty; or following the twins around, conducting her surveillance; or having feverish conversations with Maximus and Dominus.

Which of these did Destiny see?

"Yes," Destiny says. "You made a cat levitate so you could check its face. And then you asked it to forgive you before you put it in a cage. You were crying."

Hexabus feels winded. How could Destiny possibly know about that? While there are many at the castle who know about Hexabus's quest to save the island's feral cats, no one was there when that particular moment played out. She studies Destiny's face as she might a rival poker player.

What is she hiding? Is she bluffing?

She's searching for tells, but what Hexabus sees is a complete lack of guile. Destiny truly has no understanding of the significance of what she's just said. Her mismatched eyes shine with such sincerity that it makes Hexabus ashamed of her suspicions.

And then the realization slams into her, almost taking her breath away. She looks at Killian, expecting him to be as surprised by this dawning understanding, but it's clear he's already figured it out. He closes his eyes and rubs his temple as though wanting no part of what Hexabus is about to say.

"You aren't a Peasant at all, are you?" Hexabus asks Destiny. Destiny blinks. "Sorry? A...a peasant?"

"You're The Seer," Hexabus says. "The one Morty was warned about in the prophecy."

Which means Hexabus is looking at one of the two people Morty most feared could bring his entire empire crashing down.

CHAPTER 49

Destiny

Tuesday—1:53 a.m.

At the mention of a prophecy, Destiny feels as though a light has finally been switched on in a room that was forever condemned to darkness. In a flash, she sees her mother's letter, its pages falling from her hands and fluttering to the ground, dragging the word *prophecy* with them.

What sinks in straight afterward is the reference to The Seer.

A seer is someone who can see into the future, a fantastical and supernatural figure usually referred to in works of fiction. And yet Hexabus stated it as an observation, as confirmation, rather than accusation.

You're The Seer.

The words are a password to the locked room of Destiny's psyche, the simple declaration explaining everything that's always been shrouded in shame and mystery. The reframing they cause is breathtaking. Destiny is *not* broken. The voices and dreams are not proof that she's unhinged.

If anything, it was trusting her inner voice that gave her the courage to speak up about believing she has a part to play here. She expected Hexabus to laugh at her, but look at what's happened instead.

Nate was wrong. As was her mother.

I am a rational person, Destiny marvels, *who also happens to be a seer.*

"Booyah," Bex shouts, her voice punching the air in triumph. "There's my girl! I knew you'd get there eventually."

Destiny's head spins. She has so many questions, but Hexabus is already on the move, beckoning Destiny to follow. As she trails Hexabus and Mr. Lurcock down a drafty stone passageway beneath the castle, Hexabus flicks her wrist. The wall sconces leap to do her bidding, lighting up one after the other, making the gold of her cloak glisten.

The display of magic a few hours ago terrified Destiny. Now, seeing this casual use of it to perform a necessary task as efficiently as possible, Destiny views it in a new light, as a tool that can either be weaponized or used for good. Much like a shovel or a crowbar.

Even the flames aren't quite so menacing anymore.

Destiny wants to consider all the implications of this, but her mind is still reeling.

After turning a corner, they reach an enormous round door that Destiny immediately recognizes as the vault from her dream. It's made from some kind of black metal that shimmers as though quicksilver were writhing just below its surface.

Hexabus turns to the butler. "Mr. Lurcock, could you please—"

"Go check on how Miss Evangeline and Master Darius are coming along?" he finishes for her. "Yes, I was thinking the same considering the reception," he adds before turning and heading down another corridor.

"Reception?" Destiny asks, perking up upon hearing the word. "Like cell phone reception?"

"No," Hexabus replies, immediately dashing her hopes. "Morty acted like an antenna, his powers allowing all kinds of magic to be worked in the castle. With him now...gone... we can't be sure if our communication missives are getting through." With that, she nods at the vault door. "Okay, show me how you opened it."

"What?" Destiny asks, confused. "Opened what?"

"The vault in the early hours of Monday morning. It's not really one of the things you saw in your dreams. You were the person who raided it, weren't you?"

"No!" Destiny's stomach clenches. "I was staying at the Grimshaw Inn and Tavern then. I wouldn't even have known how to get into the castle, never mind the vault."

"Are you sure about that?" Hexabus cocks a hip, her gaze drilling into Destiny. "You seem to know your way around the castle very well considering the secret passageways you've used."

"Listen, I found Tempest in that same passageway, and she didn't have the raccoon guiding her like I did. How did *she* know about it?"

It's something that's been bothering her ever since she saw Tempest there. She thinks of how eager Tempest was to throw her under the bus just a few hours ago, insisting she was only in the hidden room because she'd followed Destiny, conveniently leaving out the part about finding the secret passageways herself, which is where Destiny found her skulking. Tempest isn't just here for the historian position, that much is clear. But what she's truly up to remains to be seen.

An alliance with Darius, perhaps? They appeared to be strangers who'd met last night at the inn, but that doesn't mean it wasn't all a big act. What's telling is that Tempest didn't seem remotely surprised by the display of magic, which would make a lot of sense if she'd already witnessed Darius's powers and knew all about the family's big secret.

Hexabus still looks skeptical, so Destiny adds, "Seriously? What would I even want with the vault? I didn't actually apply for the job, remember? Tempest did."

"Okay, I believe you," Hexabus says. "But you have to admit

that the timing is really suspicious. You arrive on the island and the vault gets broken into for the first time."

Destiny nods. "I totally agree. It *is* suspicious. But the timing of it might actually be a clue." Her mind is already reaching for every possible explanation.

But before Destiny has time to follow any of the thoughts down their labyrinths, Hexabus touches her palm against the vault door, muttering an incantation. The metal responds by beginning to pulsate and thrum. And then Hexabus withdraws her hand, making elaborate sweeping motions as though trying to hail a taxi at rush hour. When her arm drops, the round door opens with a whooshing sound.

Destiny is aware her jaw has dropped only because mouth breathing makes her tongue dry. "I'm flattered you'd think I could do *that*," she says. "I usually struggle to open doors even when I have the keys."

Hexabus smiles and steps inside, gesturing for Destiny to follow.

CHAPTER 50

Destiny

Tuesday—2:00 a.m.

The enormous space is filled with floor-to-ceiling shelves that are stacked with thousands of old leather-bound volumes and stuffed with ancient-looking scrolls.

"These are the Scruffmore archives," Hexabus says, waving a hand around as she makes her way down the stacks. "The vault is still a bit messy after the break-in, so you're not seeing it at its best, but it's filled with records from hundreds of years of not just Scruffmore royal history but all magical lore."

Destiny reads the names on the spines of the books as Hexabus slows down. Axenite. Binglebottom. Dramworth. Estrava. Funkel. Gwellington. Hearkens.

It's the volume written by Hearkens that Hexabus reaches for. She pulls out an ornate book bound in green leather, with golden metal corners and clasps holding it closed. It opens with a creak like the complaint of old bones, and Hexabus gently turns the pages until she finds what she's looking for. "Here," she says, passing it across.

The volume is so heavy that Destiny struggles to hold it up. The text is written in a script that's difficult to read. Destiny squints as she tries to decipher it.

Take heed, the thirteenth Mordecai,
born under a blood moon.
You'll breathe as darkness stains the sky,
your birth come all too soon.

Be warned, you known as The Slayer.
As your sixty-sixth year dawns,
you'll be challenged by The Player,
who'll turn your Kings to Pawns.

Hexabus speaks, interrupting Destiny's reading. "This was discovered in the vault a month before my youngest son, Bramble, passed away." Hexabus has to take a moment to steady the tremble in her voice. "That was twenty-two years ago."

Destiny is startled by this news. No one's spoken of the death of the youngest Scruffmore, though it now makes sense why Madigan didn't mention him at the inn. While Destiny's obviously curious about the details, she knows better than to ask. Not just because it would be impolite, but because grief doesn't have a linear timeline, and she won't assume that Hexabus has made any progress on the journey to recovery. She may have been walking in circles all this time.

Looking down again, Destiny reads what's left of the prophecy.

For the sands are running faster
with every passing day.
You command them as their master
but cannot hold them at bay.

With power that's beyond compare,
there soon will come a time
when your very own child will dare
to summit while you climb.

Fear the coming of The Seer.

The last line makes Destiny's pulse thrum in her throat, but there's nothing more—the bottom of the page has been ripped off. "Where's the rest of it?" she asks.

"We don't know. This is how our historian, Lumina Le Roux, discovered it, with the page already torn. With Morty's sixty-sixth birthday coming up in less than a month, he took the prophecy very seriously, especially since he had a strong sense that time was running out."

"And you think I'm The Seer referred to?"

Hexabus nods without elaborating any further.

"Why was my coming to be feared?" Destiny asks.

"I don't know," Hexabus says. "I don't think Morty knew either."

Destiny swallows deeply, almost too scared to verbalize the thought. She thinks of the flash of light as she laid her hands on Mordecai. "Do you think it's because...I had something to do with his death tonight? Because I touched him?"

"No," Hexabus says firmly. "I'm a powerful sorceress, Destiny, and if I couldn't kill Morty, believe me, there's no way you could have."

Relieved, Destiny studies the prophecy again. "Which child does it refer to?" she asks. "Dominus?"

"There was a time I would have believed it to be Bramble," Hexabus says, sorrow scraping against her voice, making it gravelly. "But leading up to the meeting? I was convinced it had to be Darius. And then there was the shocker about Dominus, so who knows?"

"And The Player?" Destiny asks. "Do you know who that is?"

Hexabus shakes her head. "No. But I suspect they're the key. If we can figure out exactly what happened tonight, The Player will be unmasked." Reaching out, she takes the book from Destiny, then returns it to the shelf before leading her back the way they came.

"Was Lumina also magical?" Destiny asks.

"Yes. She was a member of one of the last remaining pure-blood magical families."

"So how is it that Morty was even prepared to interview a nonmagical person for the historian position?" Destiny asks. "Surely allowing them access to that much magical lore is against the rules or something?"

Hexabus hesitates and then begins speaking as though choosing her words carefully. "There are so few magical families left that finding someone qualified and magical would have been impossible. All I can think is that Morty was planning to keep whoever got the position captive in the castle, unable to ever leave or speak about the material they were studying."

Destiny shivers at the thought.

Changing the subject, Hexabus says, "You have the marks of a seer. I don't know how I didn't realize it as soon as I saw your eyes."

Destiny blinks. "What about them?"

"It's said that those with heterochromia can see into two worlds, this one and another plane that other people can't access." Reaching the vault door, Hexabus ushers Destiny through it before carrying out the gestures to lock it behind them. "Seers usually come from a long line of those with the ability. It's one that gets passed down from mother to daughter. Does your mother have the gift?"

"No," Destiny replies, immediately thinking of Liz. And then she shakes her head, reminding herself that Liz couldn't have passed anything genetic down to her. "Not that I know of anyway. I was adopted as a baby." And then to get Hexabus to understand what she's doing here, why this is all so important to her, she adds, "And then my adoptive mother was murdered when I was eight."

CHAPTER 51

Choose Your Own Conundrum
Destiny's Biological Mother

Twenty-Two Years Ago

You're Destiny Whip's biological mother, and you're descended from a long line of seers. Besides the gift for second sight, you inherited a little shop of curiosities on the outskirts of town. It's frequented by those who believe in the healing power of crystals and that tarot cards can give them the answers they so desperately want.

You don't take advantage of them like so many charlatans do.

For, without knowing it, they really come to you to hear that everything is going to work out. That they'll meet the person of their dreams and be loved so much that it will make up for a lifetime of hurt and neglect. That their contributions will be recognized at work, resulting in that promotion, for how else can they justify being married to their careers if not to avoid all the messiness of love? That they will travel to far-flung places and savor new flavors and swim with dolphins and make love in beach cabanas at sunset.

That life will come for them and take their hands, showing them what it means to truly be alive as opposed to just going through the motions.

Otherwise, what's the point of it all?

Sometimes you aren't completely honest about what you see coming for them, especially if they can't dodge it. You tell yourself they're white lies that give people enough hope to keep waking up every morning. Because what scares you is the desolation reflected in so many of their eyes, like your little shop is their last stop before they decide to get off the train for good.

You think of yourself as someone who offers comfort, accepting very little pay for it, just enough to keep your great-grandmother's beloved store running.

The years pass this way without incident, until one day you get the strangest feeling like moths are flitting around the lantern of your heart.

A man appears just before closing time. As he steps into the store, his shadow lengthens, bridging the gap between you. And you know, just by the darkness that touches you before you even properly see him, that you will never be the same again.

He says your name in the manner of one who's been searching for you for decades and whose journey has now finally come to an end. There is relief in his tone but also something akin to fear.

You feel as though you know him, which is the strangest thing. What's even more peculiar is the impulse you have to flee.

What do you do?

A. Run—go to page 238.

B. Stay—go to page 239.

OPTION A:
RUN

You try to make your feet move, to run so that you can chase after your wild thoughts. You beseech them to make some kind of motion—anything, really, even the slightest shuffle—but they remain frozen.

They realize it before you do that you don't actually have a say in the matter.

We like to tell ourselves that we're in control and that we always have a choice, but that isn't necessarily true. Some moments are fated and thus inevitable, and the gravity of them pulls us into their orbits despite our flailing and protests, our overthinking and deliberation.

Magic can make you lose control that way.

So can love. As can hate.

Destiny comes for us all.

Go to page 239.

OPTION B:
STAY

You lock up the shop as you watch the man browsing the shelves. He looks to be in his early forties, which would make him around fifteen years older than you. While he's handsome in a generic sort of way, there's another quality that makes it difficult to tear your eyes from him. It's an energy that crackles just below the surface. If you reached out and touched him, you'd fully expect to feel an electric shock zapping between you.

When he stops pacing, he comes to join you where you're stoking up the fire. You both settle into an overstuffed sofa. Now that you're studying him up close, you can see that he's deeply tired. There are dark smudges under his eyes that match his hair. His aura is desolate, like that of a man who either has no substance at all or who has suffered a great loss.

His son pops into your mind.

Something tells you not to reveal your thoughts even as this man's magnetism tugs at them so insistently that they bump up against your teeth, wanting to be spoken.

"You're a seer?" he finally asks.

He's not asking to be polite. Nor, do you sense, is he wanting to find out if you can communicate with his son through the veil of death.

"Yes."

He asks about your mother, grandmother, and great-grandmother, whether they left any records of their visions while scrying. It's like he knows about the old books stored in your attic and of the archaic script that fills their pages.

You sense that if you tell him about them straightaway, he'll ask to see them, and then once he has, he'll take his leave. And for some reason you can't fathom, you don't want him to go. Not yet.

And so you change the subject, inviting him to stay for a day or two so he can recover from the battering life has recently dealt him, though you don't word it that way. What you say is that you suspect his journey has been long and he must be tired, and he's welcome to recuperate in the spare room in your home, which is attached to the store.

To your surprise, he accepts your offer after only the briefest hesitation.

Two days turn into two weeks. And then a month.

When he disappears one afternoon while you're doing a tarot reading for a client, he takes a page that he tears from one of your great-great-grandmother's scrying journals, but leaves nothing behind.

Nothing except the child planted within you.

Go to page 241.

CHAPTER 52

Hexabus

Tuesday—2:13 a.m.

Upon hearing Destiny's painful revelation, Hexabus finds that her first instinct is to reach out and hug her, to comfort her as she would Evangeline. But Destiny begins walking again, using her body in motion as a shield to ward off any kind of consolation Hexabus might offer.

As Hexabus steers Destiny back to her chambers, the words tumble from the young woman like rocks down a cliffside. "It happened while I was hiding in a secret compartment of her closet. It was very…violent." She looks down at her hands, which she's now wringing as though trying to grasp at some kind of truth that proves to be elusive. She shudders, the memories clearly traumatic to conjure. "Her best friend, Annie Carter, saved me from the flames afterward."

"Flames?" Hexabus gasps.

"Yes, whoever the man was, he set the house alight before leaving. Annie was speaking with Liz on the phone at the time of the attack. She called the police and came rushing over immediately. She had to be treated for smoke inhalation after hearing my screams and braving the flames to batter down the closet door."

Brow contracting at the heartbreaking image, Hexabus asks,

"Did they find her killer?" She holds her breath as she waits for the answer.

"No. It remains an unsolved case."

Hexabus does the math. Morty found out about the prophecy twenty-two years ago, which is when he started his quest to kill all the seers before they could come for him. That's when he began disappearing for weeks or months at a time, returning with a look of brooding satisfaction but no explanation as to where he'd been.

Destiny's age aligns with that timeline.

She studies the young woman, experiencing a flicker of recognition, like her features are ones that Hexabus has seen arranged on another face. But considering how she failed to recognize Darius and Dominus's similarities for what they were, she doesn't quite trust herself. It's possible that Morty is Destiny's father and that he came back to kill her mother years later, though why not just do it immediately if he knew she was a seer?

Is that why he invited Destiny here? To kill her and tie up another loose end from the prophecy—two threats for the price of one, eliminating both a powerful child *and* a seer? But then how does Tempest factor into everything? Is she also a seer, someone he was planning to murder?

Hexabus shivers at the extent of Mordecai's brutality.

"What happened to you after your mother died?" Hexabus asks as they turn another corner, flames flickering as they begin to descend the steps into the dungeons.

"Annie adopted me. That was my second adoption." Destiny shrugs. "And then *she* died when I was sixteen."

"Oh my god," Hexabus exclaims. "Was she also killed?"

"No," Destiny says, sighing in a doleful kind of resignation. "She got cancer. And then her son, Nate, went from being my brother to my legal guardian when he was just twenty-one."

There's a desperate need in Destiny that tugs at Hexabus,

a black hole of longing that sucks her in. This young girl has experienced so much loss, as though life were the mortar and grief were the pestle grinding Destiny down into her most essential form, the dust from which life springs forth and to which it returns.

And yet here she is, so much more substantial than dust. Destiny is someone brilliant who has accomplished so much; she's a young woman brave enough to venture out alone to a wretched island after getting a hidden message in a mysterious letter. Because, despite everything that has happened to her, she believes in the possibility of being enveloped into the beating heart of a loving family.

Hexabus wants so much to give that to her.

But also she suspects that Destiny is right, that she's part of the greater puzzle. If Morty was warned to fear her arrival, then Destiny definitely has a significant part to play. Besides, it's not as though Hexabus has much choice. The sigil and the medallion are ticking bombs. They need to identify Morty's murderer quickly.

It's bad enough that the killer has gained significant powers by slaying the Sorcerer King, but to be in possession of the relics to amplify those powers would make them unstoppable.

Reaching a decision, Hexabus halts just before they arrive at Destiny's chambers. "Can I hire you as a consultant to work on this case?"

Destiny considers it long enough that it makes Hexabus nervous.

Finally, she says, "No, I'm afraid not."

Hexabus's spirits wilt; she's more disappointed than she could have imagined.

"If I'm going to be objective," Destiny says, "I can't work *for* you. I'd have to be completely independent. So, I'll do it for myself, no one else. That's the only way I'll consider it."

Hexabus nods in admiration. "Fair enough." She exhales, a long whooshing note.

"Two more things," Destiny adds in a no-nonsense tone. "Firstly, while I'm assisting you, you need to know I'm also going to be looking for clues regarding what Mordecai knew about my family and what he brought me out here to tell me."

Hexabus's stomach drops. "You realize Morty might have been lying about that," she suggests gently. "Maybe he didn't know anything at all and was just using that as bait to get you out here because you're The Seer he's been searching for."

Destiny shakes her head. "No. There are answers to be found here. I can feel it."

Hexabus doesn't know if this is Destiny's intuition speaking or if she's simply in denial. Either way, the young woman appears resolute, and Hexabus has done her duty by making Destiny aware of the possibility. "Fine," she says. "I promise I'll be on the lookout for anything that might be helpful."

"Thank you," Destiny says. "Then, secondly, until you told me about this seer stuff, I didn't understand what was happening to me." Destiny shrugs, looking haunted. "The dreams… can be vicious, especially when they get stuck on a loop long after the point when I can do anything about what they foretell. When this is all over, I really could use your help trying to learn how to control them so that I don't feel so ambushed."

Hexabus can imagine all too well how awful it is having a gift like Destiny's because she knows someone who experiences something close enough. It's like learning to live with a chronic illness; Destiny's ability needs to be carefully managed.

"You have a deal," Hexabus says, and they shake on it.

Opening the door to her chamber, Destiny asks, "Do you think Mr. Lurcock might know more than he's letting on?"

"Definitely!" And then understanding that Destiny's referring to what Killian might know about her family's secret, Hexabus says, "There was a time, when I was living here as queen, that Mr. Lurcock and I were friendly because I make a point of not treating the staff like second-class citizens. I plan to remind him of that later by conducting an allegiance spell that, should he accept the conditions of, will ensure he can't work against us. If there's any information to get out of him that will help you, I'll do everything in my power to extract it from him."

"Thank you." Destiny's silent for a moment. "Mordecai's death…" she ventures. "Are you certain that wasn't caused by Darius's attack? It looked pretty powerful."

Hexabus experiences a rush of pride despite how inappropriate it is. Darius applying himself, working so hard to achieve something, is completely out of character for him. But no matter how hard Darius worked, he couldn't have killed Morty on his own.

"There's no way," Hexabus says, "and I'll explain why as we go through the list of suspects. But it's going to take a while, and I'm afraid it can't wait until the morning no matter how exhausted you must be." When Destiny cocks her head, asking the silent question, Hexabus says, "I've ensured that no ferries or private boats can dock at the harbor for the next thirty hours. That's as long as I can keep everyone here. After that, I'm going to have to let them go. So we don't have much time at all."

Destiny motions to her door, surprising Hexabus by smiling. "My mind doesn't sleep even when I try to. Let's get started."

Once they're seated in front of the crackling fire, Hexabus begins talking, telling Destiny everything. Well, almost everything. Destiny now knows only as much as Evangeline does.

CHAPTER 53

Destiny

Tuesday—8:43 a.m.

Upon waking, Destiny's mind is swampy from fatigue. She sits and groans, her back aching. Having barely slept, she doesn't know whether to blame the uncomfortable bed—more torture device than mattress—or the seeping cold, whose insidious fingers kept creeping under the blankets.

More likely, though, is the horror she felt over everything Hexabus told her about Mordecai Scruffmore. She cringes thinking how much she wanted him to be her father. Now, knowing the degree of his inhumanity, Destiny is terrified that she is, indeed, his daughter and what that might say about her.

Learning that she was The Seer who was mentioned in the prophecy made her feel vindicated since it explained why she was so inexplicably pulled to the island. It was akin to being told all your life that you were a hypochondriac only to finally have an ultrasound reveal the tumor you knew was growing there all along.

But now, after discovering how dangerous Mordecai truly was, it makes her even more worried that Nate might be right. Perhaps madness does run in the family, passed down like a poisonous crown. Genetically, Destiny might be predisposed to—

"How did the butler know where your amulet came from?"

Bex asks, interrupting Destiny's dark thoughts as though to stop them from spiraling. "Do you think there's a chance Mordecai's sidekick delivered it to Liz on his master's orders, a token from your father to be passed down to you? Or has the butler just seen it before, like on the night your mother was killed?"

The thought is chilling.

She doesn't have it, I swear. That's what Liz said.

Destiny wonders if she was right all along, if the amulet was what the intruder was really after. If Mr. Lurcock was the attacker that night, it could explain why he recognized it. Destiny clutches it now to reassure herself that he hasn't somehow found a way to take it from her.

The butler is clearly a terrible man. He'd have to be after serving as Mordecai's henchman all those years. But he has answers that they desperately need and so they have no choice but to work with him. At least Hexabus's allegiance spell will guarantee that he can't turn against them.

Destiny voices another question that she can't figure out. "Why was Mordecai warned by the prophecy to fear me, especially if my job as The Seer was to warn him that his life was in danger? Surely, if that was the case, my arrival would have been welcomed. And if Mordecai feared my coming, why invite me to the island in the first place?"

Was Hexabus right and he was just luring Destiny out so he could kill her? The thought makes her shiver.

"Okay, this isn't helping," Bex says firmly. "You need your neural pathways to be clear so your thoughts can zigzag through them at warp speed. All this emotion is just making them sluggish." Considering the problem for a moment, Bex says, "Why not try to take yourself out of the equation so that you can examine the puzzle more objectively? Do you think you can do that?"

Destiny nods, taking a few deep breaths as she attempts to reframe the mystery so that she's no longer the nucleus of it.

It immediately makes her feel more competent, just as her actions did last night when she waved her arms at the bear, yelling, "Here I am! Look at how qualified I am and how much I can help you!"

Thus centered, Destiny thinks about how Hexabus looked to Maximus as though for guidance when Mordecai demanded life-essence sacrifices.

"There definitely was an undercurrent between them," Bex agrees, "one that Mordecai himself picked up on. Did you notice how, when you tried pushing Hexabus for details during your discussion early this morning, she got super cagey about it?"

Bex is right. Hexabus wouldn't reveal who'd tipped her off about Mordecai's medallion and how its powers might be used against him. Or who'd recently told her about the prophecy and then revealed what had really happened to Bramble. Or how she'd learned about Mordecai's pursuit of a powerful artifact called the Eye of Gormodeus.

"I'm thinking the source was Maximus," Destiny says.

"But why would he wait until now to tell Hexabus if he'd known all along?" Bex asks. A damn good question.

Destiny has other questions centered around the timing of events, like who had the most to gain by sending the message to Evangeline through the book in the library, opening that whole can of worms the night before the big family gathering. And why the vault was broken into as Evangeline was coming back from digging up Bramble's grave.

"It's more than a little suspicious that all of these unusual events happened just as Maximus and Dominus were invited back into the fold," Destiny muses. "And just because Dominus put on a good show of not wanting the throne doesn't mean that's really the case."

Then, of course, there's Tempest. Destiny recalls what she said in the inn two nights ago.

I've had a few dreams that have come true. Enough that I keep records of them in a journal. And I sometimes get the strangest sense of déjà vu, like I know what someone's going to say before they say it.

An icy finger traces its way down Destiny's spine. Is there

a chance that Tempest is the real seer, the one that Mordecai was supposed to fear? It's entirely possible that she and Tempest were both invited because they're seers and Mordecai wanted to determine which of them posed the greater danger to him.

"I'm not seeing it," Bex says firmly. "Ms. MyOwnPoop-Doesn'tStink is no seer, trust me."

The raccoon, of course, is a mystery on a whole other level.

Figuring out people's movements and intentions is difficult enough, but an animal that behaves like a human? That's completely out of Destiny's wheelhouse. She knows animals can be trained to do all kinds of things, like act in movies or be service animals to help humans with disabilities. She's even heard of a meerkat in South Africa that was trained to steal jewelry from homes in wealthy suburbs, its little body agile enough to duck and dive dozens of security beams.

Someone in the castle is manipulating the creature to do their bidding, but exactly who remains to be determined.

Only one thing's for certain: Hexabus isn't being 100 percent honest with Destiny.

Which makes Destiny wonder what the family matriarch is hiding. And who she might be protecting in the process.

"My money's on Darius," Bex says.

Destiny agrees. She doesn't trust him at all despite his mother's insistence that his spell couldn't have killed Mordecai. There's something sinister about him. Same goes for Minx.

"The fact that Newton isn't magical should mean she can be eliminated as a suspect, right?" Bex asks.

"Unless she formed some kind of unholy alliance with her daughters," Destiny replies.

She stands and walks to the fireplace, about to feed it yet again, when she sees her notebook lying open next to the wingback chair. A few new puzzles have been scribbled inside. Destiny groans, understanding why she's so tired. There's only enough time to solve one of the puzzles before she needs to get ready to meet Hexabus.

She flips through the notebook to decide which one to tackle first, then stops at a page with the heading *What is Hexabus hiding?*

"Thank you, subconscious," Destiny whispers as she sits down to solve it.

CLUE	G	Q		K	Y	V	G	K	S	Q
ANSWER		S								S

CLUE	Z	P	Y	K	Z	J	C	'	Q
ANSWER								'	S

CLUE	P	C	Y	J		D	Y	R	F	C	P	?
ANSWER												?

★★[10]

---

10. You now have all the information you require to solve the codex. If you need a clue to assist you, email DestinyWhipClue@gmail.com using the subject line Clue Ten. Once you've solved it, turn to page 471 to check your answer.

★ ★ ★

Upon solving the codex, Destiny feels the familiar sensation of wings fluttering inside her belly, a surefire sign that she's on the verge of experiencing a breakthrough.

This theory is entirely possible considering how complicated and dysfunctional the Scruffmore dynamics are. Plus, this would give Mordecai yet another incentive to kill Bramble. It would also explain Hexabus's caginess, as well as the undercurrents between her and Maximus. If it's true, this is a secret she'd definitely want to prevent from being exposed, giving Hexabus reason enough to lie. If Destiny knows what Hexabus is hiding and understands why, it will make it easier to trust her about everything else.

She turns from the fire, which is when she spots a piece of paper that has been slipped under her door. She's upon it within a few short strides.

CHAPTER 54

Destiny

Tuesday—9:05 a.m.

Whoever sent this puzzle understands exactly how Destiny's brain works. She doesn't know whether that makes them an ally or a very dangerous adversary.

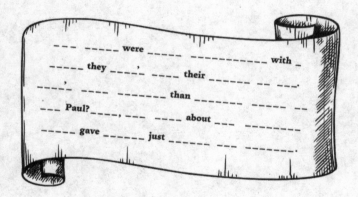

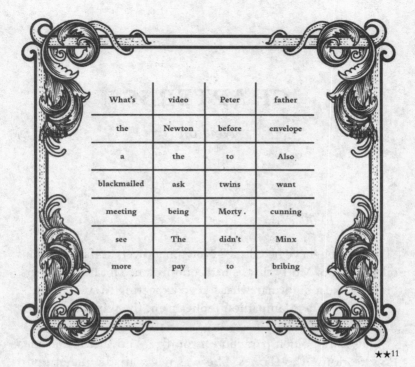

What's	video	Peter	father
the	Newton	before	envelope
a	the	to	Also
blackmailed	ask	twins	want
meeting	being	Morty .	cunning
see	The	didn't	Minx
more	pay	to	bribing

★★11

As she solves the puzzle, Destiny can't help but note how archaic one of its phrases is, the original version dating back to the fourteenth century according to English folklore.

Its use in this instance is as intriguing as the note's contents.

---

11. You now have all the information you need to solve the word scramble by assigning the provided words to their correct positions within the note. For a clue, email DestinyWhipClue@gmail.com using the subject line Clue Eleven. Once you've solved it, turn to page 472 to check your answer.

CHAPTER 55

Newton

Tuesday—10:00 a.m.

"I just can't believe he's dead." Newton glowers at the enormous oil painting of Morty that he had commissioned for her chambers. "It feels like a nightmare that I keep expecting to wake from."

"I know," her companion replies from the wingback opposite. "It's awful."

Newton's golden parachute is on fire, and she has no idea how to douse the flames. She was never made queen upon marrying Morty, and so without him, she has no official title beyond being the mother of two princesses, neither of whom is next in line to take the throne.

The sudden rapping at the door is like a cattle prod to the heart. Her visitor springs up, looking terrified. Newton casts a frantic gaze around the room. Why didn't she think to start packing her jewels and the more expensive of her fur coats? Is she really going to be evicted empty-handed?

When the knock comes again, she calls, "Who is it?" No one can be allowed to see who is with her. The two of them haven't come this far, been this careful, only to be found out now at the bitter end.

"It's Hexabus." The response is muffled. "We need to talk."

"Shit," Newton hisses. "You're going to have to hide real

quick." As she stows her guest away, she calls out, "Give me a second."

After checking the room for anything revealing, Newton heads for the door. Opening it a sliver, Newton is surprised to see Destiny standing behind Hexabus. "What do you want?" she demands of them both, peering out through the crack. The young woman fidgets like she's about to bolt.

"I'm well, Newton," Hexabus replies in that sarcastic tone of hers. "Thank you so much for asking. And how are you?"

"Oh, you know. Fair to middling." Newton rolls her eyes. "How the hell do you think I am, Hexabus? My husband was just murdered by a member of his own family." She holds up a hand. "Don't even try to deny it."

She's expecting Hexabus to protest again that there hasn't been any foul play, so she's surprised when Hexabus says, "I'm not denying it. I agree with you."

"What?" Newton narrows her eyes, suspecting some kind of trick.

Hexabus speaks slowly as though to a child. "We're in agreement, Newton. Someone definitely killed Morty. And we're trying to get to the bottom of it," Hexabus adds. "That's why I've brought Destiny. May we come inside?"

Newton huffs. "You brought a historian to figure out what happened to Morty? He died last night, Hexabus. Not a hundred years ago." *God.* Sometimes Newton thinks she's the only person with any brains around here. Does she have to do the thinking for everyone?

Hexabus sighs in that infuriating long-suffering way. "She's not actually a historian."

Newton startles. "She's not?"

Hexabus continues, "No, and if you'd just let us in, I can explain everything."

Hexabus is still Newton's chief suspect, but perhaps Destiny is who she's been in cahoots with. Either way, Newton needs to hear what they have to say before she can call bullshit on it. But then again, maybe this is all an elaborate ruse, Hexabus planning to throw Newton out just as soon as she gains entry to her chambers.

"Make a binding promise that you aren't coming in here to kick me out," Newton demands.

"For god's sake," Hexabus says, huffing. "That's more your style, Newt. Not mine."

"Do it!" Newton is tensed and ready to slam the door closed to bolt it again. Not that it would stop Hexabus for long. She could blast through it soon enough. But at least it would give Newton a minute or two to pack a few treasures that she could hock for cash.

"Fine," Hexabus says, reaching for Newton's hand. When their palms touch, Hexabus mutters an incantation. "I promise I'm not here to kick you out," Hexabus says. Wisps of electricity flare out to form a cage around their hands. Newton's fingers twitch.

And then it's done.

"Be my guest," Newton says, ushering them inside. Once the two take seats next to the fireplace, Newton regards Destiny suspiciously. "I saw your résumé myself when I was working through the applications, so I'm not sure what you're playing at by saying you aren't a historian."

"That's what we wanted to speak to you about, but we'll get there in a minute," Hexabus says. "First, let me break down Destiny's real credentials for you." Hexabus recites a long list of bewildering accomplishments that makes Newton's eyes water.

She looks at the awkward young woman in a whole new light, thinking that at least her degree of nerdiness explains her complete lack of style, just as it does Evangeline's.

Before Newton can ask what the hell Destiny is doing here considering her real occupation, Hexabus says, "Can you take us through the whole interviewing process from the beginning?"

A spike of alarm jolts through Newton. "Why?"

"Please, just humor us."

Newton approaches her answer like someone walking through a minefield. "Morty has been...was... He *was* so busy recently that I offered to help with finding a new historian after Lumina disappeared. I took the ferry into the city for a few trips to advertise the position and then get all the applications to review. There were two that looked very promising and so I sent them letters inviting them for interviews."

"Why invite them for the day of the family gathering?" Hexabus asks. "Surely another time would have been better?"

Newton bristles. Typical of Hexabus to go for the jugular. She's going to have to be careful with her response. "I didn't invite them for yesterday," she lies. "They were supposed to come next week."

Hexabus reaches for a folder and sets it down on the table. Passing it across to Newton, she says, "These are the copies of the letters you sent, right?"

Newton takes the folder and looks them over, nodding. Pretending to be surprised upon spotting the wrong dates listed, she exclaims, "I... I don't know how that happened." Then, knowing that the best defense is a strong offense, she goes on the attack. Turning to Destiny, she says, "Why did you lie? Why fake a résumé to come here if you didn't have something to hide?"

The young woman sniffs the air, looking thoughtful.

Too thoughtful for Newton's liking.

"I didn't actually send an application claiming to be a historian," Destiny finally replies. And then she asks, "There was no hidden message in the letter you sent?"

"Hidden message?" Newton looks between Destiny and Hexabus, waiting for the punch line. When none comes, she says, "No. Obviously not. Jeez, you young women are always trying to read between the lines, looking for subtext every time you have the slightest interaction with a man. Sometimes things are just what they seem."

"Not always," Destiny replies mildly, smiling as she tucks a strand of hair behind her ear.

It's such a vivid shade of red that it makes Newton wince. Plus, what's with the mismatched eyes?

"And you didn't want us to stay at the Grimshaw Inn and Tavern on Sunday night?" Destiny asks.

"Exactly. This wasn't meant to be a vacation, ya know. It was a job interview." Newton is careful not to let on how confused she was by that strange turn of events, since it was definitely not part of her plan.

Destiny leans forward. "So, the plan was for us to arrive, do the interview, and then leave on the same day. Is that right?" After Newton nods, Destiny stands. "Do you mind if I walk around? Pacing helps my brain work better."

Yes, I do mind, missy, Newton thinks, but since she doesn't want it to look like she's hiding anything, she shrugs. "Is this going to take long?"

"Why, Newt?" Hexabus asks. "Do you have something better to do than try and figure out who killed Morty?"

"I have a funeral to plan, Exabus!" Newton spits, the nickname a pointed jab to remind Hexabus that she's the ex. "As his *wife*, that's *my* job. You remember that I was his wife, right?"

"Funny how you couldn't remember that one simple fact about *me* way back when."

There's a hollow knock and Newton turns to see Destiny tapping the secret door. Heart pounding, Newton stands. "What do you think you're doing?" She has the horrible suspicion that she's been tricked, that Hexabus was baiting her purely as a distraction.

"This is a door leading out to the secret passageway, isn't it?" Before Newton can answer, Destiny calls out, "Tempest, I know you're hiding out there. You can come back in now."

CHAPTER 56

Destiny

Tuesday—10:18 a.m.

Hexabus and Newton gasp, but Destiny remains focused on the secret-door panel, which swings open to reveal Tempest standing there, glowering.

"How did you know I was here?" she demands sulkily, arms crossed.

"I smelled your distinctive sandalwood perfume as soon as we stepped into the room. *And* the chair I just sat in was still warm from your body." Destiny waits a beat and then adds, "This is where you materialized from last night when you stepped into the secret passageway, isn't it? You had to hide when Mordecai visited Newton just before the meeting."

Destiny almost feels sorry for Tempest, who shoots a helpless look at an incredulous Newton. They're both scrambling to figure out how much Destiny knows. Which is, unfortunately for them, a lot since all the pieces fell into place a few minutes ago.

"What the hell is going on?" Hexabus demands. Her tired eyes ask Destiny the silent question, *Is this something you dreamed about?*

Destiny shakes her head. Hexabus suggested last night that they keep her second sight a secret from everyone except Evangeline, which suits Destiny just fine as it means fewer questions.

"Tempest and Newton are sisters," Destiny says, watching how Newton deflates at hearing the truth so plainly spoken.

"Sisters?" Hexabus's voice is weighted with awe. "How did you figure that out?"

Destiny wants to answer with *The same way I figured out that you and Maximus might be conducting a secret love affair, with Bramble being the product of that. Because I pay attention.*

There's a part of Destiny that's disappointed to have realized Tempest's role in everything. She was hoping for an ally, someone who could truly understand what it meant to be friendless and alone in the castle, the object of so much suspicion. But Tempest has had a secret alliance with someone else this whole time.

Destiny makes an *after you* motion to Tempest, who reluctantly goes to sit with the two women. "Well, firstly and most obviously," Destiny says, gesturing at the women, "they have the same coloring."

Hexabus studies the women's white-blond hair, pale complexions, and green eyes.

"Secondly," Destiny continues, "they clearly grew up in the same area judging from their dialects. They've both worked on refining their accents, but it's detectable when they're under stress."

"Now that I think of it," Hexabus says, eyes narrowing, "that's true."

"Then, on the ferry," Destiny says, addressing Tempest, "you were on the phone with someone and mentioned a gallery and painting, and what I thought was a Mr. Futon. But of course, that wasn't it. You were telling them you were taking time away from work to visit your sister, Newton." When Tempest scowls but doesn't contradict her, Destiny is encouraged to carry on. "Also, during the chaos last night, your eyes were darting between Hexabus and Newton. It made sense that you'd look at the person addressing you, which was Hexabus, but looking at Newton as though for guidance was a giveaway. As was the fact that you weren't remotely freaked out upon hearing about all the magical stuff because you clearly already knew."

Hexabus gasps, turning to Newton. "You told a Peasant about our powers?"

"She's my *sister*, Hexabus! And, in case you forgot, I'm a Peasant too!" Newton shoots back.

"Morty clearly didn't know or there would have been hell to pay. I never even told *you* about our powers back in the day, and I told you almost everything."

"Well, you told *her* everything," Newton says, jutting her chin at Destiny.

"She saw it all for herself last night." Hexabus parries the accusation. "It's not the same thing."

Destiny clears her throat, rattled by the animosity between the two women but trying to keep everyone on topic. "I also figured," she continues, addressing Tempest, "from our interactions at the inn, that you weren't really a historian. I'm guessing you're an art appraiser, yes?"

"Right again," Tempest says in a clipped tone. "Quite the little know-it-all you are."

And there it is, the mean streak Destiny has recognized in both women who are equally condescending and who, despite Newton's many cosmetic procedures, have the exact same sneer. What is it about the mean girls who grow into mean women who aren't happy unless they're cutting down other women?

This kind of aggressive display would usually cow Destiny, but she finds herself mentally squaring her shoulders, refusing to be intimidated.

"I can cut a bitch for you," Bex purrs, sounding way too excited at the prospect. "Just tell me which one to do first."

"I wouldn't say I'm a know-it-all," Destiny says to Tempest. "But I'm certainly a know-a-lot. Which isn't quite the insult you seem to think it is."

"Burn!" Bex cheers.

"Okay, fine." Newton throws her hands up. "Em and I are sisters and she's not a historian. You caught us out. Bravo, Hercule bloody Poirot." She claps slowly as if to make sure Destiny knows the ovation is sarcastic.

"How did you two manage to hatch this plan?" Hexabus asks, voicing what Destiny's been wondering about. "It's not like you could just call or email each other."

"We met in Gwillumbury a few times," Newton replies begrudgingly. "I'd head there occasionally to run errands for Morty, like I did with the historian-position applications." Crossing her arms, she leans forward and says, "But Em didn't have anything to do with Morty's death."

"Then why maintain the whole charade?" Hexabus challenges. "What was the point of it?"

Newton squirms, reluctant to speak, confirming Destiny's suspicions. When Newton remains obstinately silent, Destiny answers for her. "You suspected that Morty was cheating on you, didn't you, Newton? You just couldn't prove it. So, you figured that if you got Tempest out here pretending to be someone who might work for him, a very attractive woman who was enthralled by her potential boss, that he might make a pass at her."

Hexabus nods. "Quite smart, actually. He clearly found *you* attractive, Newton, so why not a younger and prettier version of you?"

Newton flushes at the barb, which is all the answer Destiny needs. "You could trust your sister," Destiny continues. "If *she* told you Morty came on to her, then you could believe it. And perhaps then you'd have the courage to leave him."

Hexabus barks a laugh. "Oh, this wasn't about working up the courage to leave Morty. Newton wanted to catch him red-handed with the cheating. That way, she could invoke the stipulations of the prenup, triggering a huge payout. Smart of you to insist on that clause, Newt. Especially after Morty's affair with you. Once a cheater, always a cheater, right?"

"Takes one to know one," Newton snaps.

Turning to Destiny, Hexabus says, "Did I mention that Newton used to be my therapist?"

"What?" Destiny gasps. She looks at Newton, whose cheeks have turned pink.

"After Bramble...died," Hexabus says, wincing at the word, "I had what you might call a mental health crisis. I wasn't coping very well with his loss, which meant that poor Darius and Evangeline were left to fend for themselves. Since I wasn't even able to get out of bed, never mind get dressed or leave the castle, I arranged for a therapist to visit me here twice a week. Secretly, of course, as Morty wouldn't have approved. He was away a lot then, so it wasn't all that difficult."

What kind of therapist would have an affair with a grieving woman's husband? Destiny wonders.

"Do you remember that, Newton?" Hexabus asks in a goading tone. "How, when you were pregnant with the twins, and I kept telling you I thought Morty was having an affair, you told me I was being paranoid. How you gaslit me to the point I thought I was losing my mind?" As Tempest shifts uncomfortably in her seat, looking down at her hands, Hexabus turns back to Destiny, saying, "I had to wait for the twins to be born before I finally figured it out."

"That's such old news, Hexabus," Newton snaps. "Get over it already!"

"Well, I'd go for therapy," Hexabus says, smiling sweetly, "but, for some reason, I'm not a huge fan."

Turning to Destiny, Newton growls, "Are we done here?"

Startled, Destiny stammers, "I...have a few more questions about the applications you got for the historian position and how you dealt with them."

"Fine. Let's be done with this already."

"You definitely got my résumé for the job?" Destiny asks. "You didn't fabricate it?"

"Why would I do that?" Newton throws her hands up. "I'd already faked one application for Em. I *wanted* the second candidate to be a really good one, a no-brainer hire so they would get the job. Obviously, we didn't want Em to get hired. She took time off work to come here for this, and she needs to go back to her own life and career."

Destiny mulls this over. "So, someone else sent in a job application with a fake résumé on my behalf," she muses.

Hexabus clears her throat. "It could have been Morty himself, you know." She turns to Newton. "Is there a possibility that he switched out the interview letters when you weren't looking, changing the one you wrote for the one with the hidden message that Destiny received?"

Before Newton can answer, Destiny chips in. "But then why send a letter with the same instructions to Tempest? Why not send that particular one just to me? Or why not reach out to me directly rather than faking résumés and switching out letters?"

Hexabus shakes her head, clearly flummoxed.

Tempest leans forward, addressing Newton. "See? I told you I didn't mess up the arrangements." Looking at Destiny, Tempest says, "Newton was super confused when I told her I'd stayed at the inn on Sunday night."

"If Morty swapped out the letters," Destiny says, "he would have corrected the dates that Newton changed." She thinks back to Tempest's strong reaction to seeing the twins when she and Destiny stood with the housekeeper in the antechamber. "I assume you did that so Tempest's visit could coincide with that of her nieces, allowing her to see them for the first time?" she asks Newton.

"Yes," Newton says, nodding. "Morty wouldn't let Peasants visit. And he wouldn't allow me to take the girls to visit Em either. That's why they never even recognized their own aunt."

Destiny senses that she's pushed Newton as far as she can today. She wants to ask her about the envelope Morty gave her as mentioned in the note slipped under her door, but deciding it can wait, Destiny changes tack. "Tempest, are you a seer?" she asks.

Hexabus straightens from her slouched position, alert again.

"A seer?" Newton echoes, confused.

"Yes, when we were at the inn together, Tempest mentioned having dreams that would sometimes come true, and then also seeing your father's ghost. I'm wondering if she's a seer, someone with the gift of second sight."

Newton throws her head back and laughs as Tempest's neck grows mottled with red splotches, a rash wrapping itself around her throat. "Oh, Em," Newton says, shaking her head. "I forgot how you always insisted you were a witch." Wiping the tears from the corners of her eyes, Newton says, "I gave her a dream journal to record her dreams. None of them ever came true."

Shooting a sympathetic look at Tempest, Destiny expects her to deny her sister's cruel dismissal. But she doesn't. Tempest merely looks down into her lap, cheeks burning.

"Told you," Bex gloats.

Tempest isn't a secret seer; she was just a sad little girl with an older sister who was always eclipsing her, someone desperate to find something special about herself as she mourned the loss of her father.

Feeling terrible for her, Destiny changes the subject. "Could I talk with Minx and Angel?"

It's time to get to the bottom of the blackmail issue.

CHAPTER 57

Destiny

Tuesday—10:32 a.m.

Tempest's phone suddenly beeps, alerting them to the fact that the castle has cell phone reception. As much as Destiny has been hoping for signal since arriving on the island, this new development makes her antsy because of what it means.

After some back-and-forth, Newton texts her daughters from her sister's phone, telling them to meet her in the great hall at 11:15 a.m.

Destiny excuses herself, saying she needs to return to her room to check work emails before they reconvene. But that's a lie; she's just keen to get back to the puzzles and clues waiting to be solved.

Once she and Hexabus are out in the hallway, Destiny says, "Looks like all the magic in the castle is wearing off, which is why the cell phone reception is coming back and the island's weather has improved so much."

"That's definitely a problem," Hexabus says, looking wan, like she got even less sleep than Destiny.

Destiny nods. "Because whoever was responsible for Mordecai's death can now move freely through the castle without his protective shields in place."

"Exactly," Hexabus says. And then she sighs, weary. "Evangeline and I spoke with Darius this morning, telling him the whole truth about his father with regard to Bramble and the killings."

"How did it go?"

"About as badly as you'd expect," Hexabus replies, rubbing at tired eyes.

Destiny is interested in how Darius has taken the news that his more successful cousin—whom he's obviously jealous of—is actually his half brother. She also wonders how he'll feel if he finds out that Hexabus and Maximus are lovers, and that Bramble—another person he was probably resentful of—might have been his half brother. Or that Destiny might be his half sister.

As though reading her mind, Hexabus says, "I didn't tell him about your suspicions regarding Morty being your father. I think it's better to let this all settle before we hit him with any more surprises." When Destiny nods, Hexabus asks, "Why do you want to speak with Minx and Angel?" but Destiny is already excusing herself, saying she has an important matter to attend to and that Hexabus will find out soon enough.

Once she's back in her quarters, Destiny rushes to her notebook and flips through it. She stops on a page with the heading *The key to everything is...*

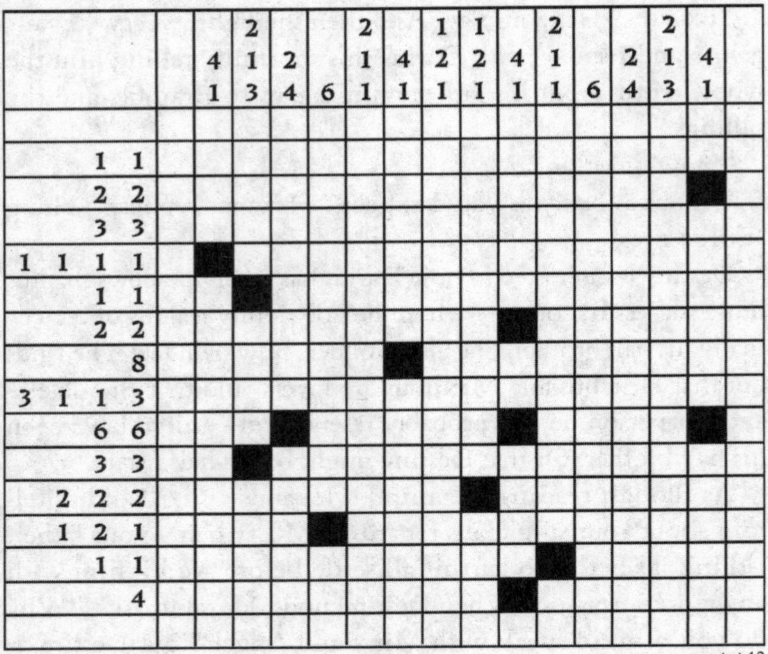

Column clues (top to bottom), 14 columns:

	C1	C2	C3	C4	C5	C6	C7	C8	C9	C10	C11	C12	C13	C14
top		2			2		1	1		2			2	
mid	4	1	2		1	4	2	2	4	1		2	1	4
bot	1	3	4	6	1	1	1	1	1	1	6	4	3	1

Grid (row clues at left; ■ = pre-filled black cell):

Row clue	C1	C2	C3	C4	C5	C6	C7	C8	C9	C10	C11	C12	C13	C14
1 1														
2 2													■	
3 3														
1 1 1 1	■													
1 1		■												
2 2									■					
8				■										
3 1 1 3														
6 6			■						■				■	
3 3		■												
2 2 2						■								
1 2 1			■											
1 1									■					
4								■						

★★[12]

---

12. This puzzle is a nonogram, in which you use the digits provided outside the grid to create a pattern of filled-in blocks within the grid. Each digit represents the number of blocks that will need to be blacked out in that row or column. For example: 1 1 1 1 means that within that row, four blocks need to be colored in. Each of the blocks will be separated by at least one blank block. 7 3 means that within that column, ten blocks in total need to be colored in: seven that are next to each other and then another three that are next to each other. The grouping of seven and three blocks will be separated by at least one blank block. Once all the correct squares are filled in, a picture emerges. If you need a clue to assist you, email DestinyWhipClue@gmail.com using Clue Twelve in the subject line. Once you've solved the nonogram, turn to page 473 to check your answer.

CHAPTER 58

Minx

Tuesday—10:40 a.m.

As Minx strides up the winding staircase, Angel trailing her, she remembers all the times they made this journey as children. The turret was their playroom, where Angel would spend hours pretending to be Rapunzel, while Minx—never seeing herself as a damsel in distress—wrote story after story casting herself as the villains in fairy tales, except changing the endings so she always triumphed.

When Minx needed a hiding place yesterday, this was the first spot that came to mind. And now that she doesn't need to keep her riches stashed away anymore, she's come to reclaim them.

As she passes a window, she marvels at the blue skies and calm waters beyond. She's never seen the island this way; it's always been a place of tumult and turmoil. With Daddy Dearest dead, the enormous force field his powers cast over the island is eroding. When she's the Sorcerer Queen, Minx plans to conjure a powerful force field that still allows them to control the islanders but one that won't ruin the weather in the process.

From up here, she can see the inn clearly; the Tudor-style gable roof looks like a raised hand, an eager student demanding its teacher's attention. *Oh, you have it*, Minx thinks. *Don't you worry. Just because the plan didn't work out as expected doesn't mean that I've forgotten you.* Madigan will still get what's coming to him.

It's worrying she hasn't experienced the expected surge that should have transferred Morty's power to herself. She tells herself that not even twenty-four hours have passed; it could be a more gradual process. And she does feel stronger, more self-assured, which could be the early signs.

After a distinctive beep breaks the silence, Angel squeals. "We have cell phone reception again!"

Another series of electronic alerts heralds their arrival in the turret, and Angel flops onto one of the child-sized chairs to scroll through her messages.

Minx is about to head for their toy chest when Angel holds her phone out. "It's another email from the blackmailer."

They're upping the demanded amount from half a million to a million to make that troublesome video of Angel's go away. Checking the date stamp, Minx confirms it was sent on Monday morning, just as she and Angel were disembarking from the ferry, which is why they're only getting it now.

Had they seen this then, Minx would have freaked out.

"They've lost all their leverage," Minx crows. With Mordecai dead, the blackmailer has no hold over them anymore. It's exactly the outcome she was hoping for. Her plan to get the blackmail money was only a safety net if the poison didn't work.

Now the half a million is a bonus for a job well done.

Minx doesn't mention the bag full of cash they've come up here to collect. What Angel doesn't know she can't lay claim to. Not that Minx is planning to let the blackmailer walk free. Whoever they are, they need to be taught a lesson. But she won't be using anything quite as crude as a detective to find them; she plans to hunt them down herself.

Once Angel's absorbed in her phone again, Minx heads to the toy chest. Opening it, she's relieved to find the weekend bag exactly where she hid it last night before the meeting.

"Huh, that's weird," Angel says.

"What?"

"I got a text from Mom from an unknown number. She says we need to meet her in the great hall in half an hour. Apparently, there's something important she has to discuss with us."

Minx doesn't like the sound of that at all. Has someone figured out she has the sigil? Are they going to demand it back? They can't have realized that she poisoned Morty, or the guards would have been sent instead of a text.

Looking up from her screen, Angel spots the bag Minx is holding. "What's in there? Looks heavy."

"Just my notebooks from when we were kids," Minx lies smoothly. "I thought I'd get a kick out of reading all of them again."

Angel rolls her eyes. "God, you used to waste so many hours writing in them. It was super annoying." She stands and walks over to the turret window, then cranks it open. "Remember how I used to pretend to be a princess trapped in a castle tower, needing to be saved?"

Minx snorts and then covers it up by pretending it was a cough. *Where's the pretense?* she wants to ask. *Nothing's changed. You still need to be saved from yourself constantly.*

While Angel's back is turned, Minx unzips the bag and slips her hand inside. With her eyes trained on her sister, she fishes the empty glass vial and the sigil from the side pouch and stashes them in the pocket of her leather pants.

Angel leans out the window, perhaps reliving memories of letting her imaginary hair tumble down from it. "Look at this sunshine!" she trills. "We should be out there enjoying it, not cooped up inside." She stretches farther, as though trying to snatch all the warmth and light she can get her grubby hands on. Her feet lift, hovering above the ground, as she balances her weight on the sill.

One shove. That's all it would take to send Angel soaring

through the air just like one of her namesakes. Either a terrible accident or a daughter overwrought with grief or guilt. Who could know for sure what caused her to plummet to her death?

Minx takes a step forward and then another. She raises her arm and reaches out.

But it's already too late. Angel hops down and Minx snatches her hand back.

"Let's go meet Mom," Angel says, flipping her long hair into Minx's face.

It's then that Minx decides Angel won't be leaving the island tomorrow.

CHAPTER 59

Destiny

Tuesday—11:10 a.m.

As Destiny navigates the maze of passageways to the great hall to meet Newton and the twins, her thoughts scuttle this way and that, looping back upon themselves like crab tracks criss-crossing on a beach.

According to Hexabus, Mordecai became so paranoid after Lumina disappeared that he implemented a ton of additional security measures within the castle walls and throughout the grounds. That's why the ransacking of the vault so enraged him—it made a mockery of his efforts.

Knowing what she does now, Destiny's certain the silver object she saw clutched in the raccoon's hands before it disappeared was either Mordecai's medallion or the sigil, perhaps both.

So she has one question: Did the raccoon lead Destiny to the secret room so that she could witness the family gathering, or did it need her expertise in solving the newly added puzzle codes so it could get to Mordecai to steal the artifacts? The codes weren't particularly difficult, but Destiny has no idea what the creature's cognitive capabilities are. If it were merely trained to perform certain tasks, it wouldn't be able to use deductive reasoning.

Just before she turns left into one of the passageways, Destiny hears voices, startling her from her thoughts. They sound hushed and furtive—as though engaged in something clandestine—and she presses herself up against the wall.

"...how important this is," a man's voice says.

"Believe me, I know that!" another man snaps. "And I really could do without the constant pressure."

"Sorry. It's just that—"

"Without the sigil and the medallion, we can't accomplish what we came here to achieve. I know!" His voice has risen to a kind of shouted whisper that echoes down the corridor. His companion hushes him, and he lets out an exasperated cry.

Destiny peers around the corner, spotting Maximus at the end of the passageway. He's towering over someone who's crouched next to him. At first she isn't sure if his companion is Darius or Dominus, but then he turns his head slightly and the flames from the wall sconces reveal him to be Dominus. He has black smudges under his eyes and his hair stands up in tufts, like he's manically been running his fingers through it.

Not wanting to take the chance they might spot her, Destiny quickly ducks her head back.

The men are silent long enough that she considers peeking around the corner again, when there's a squeaking noise. It's quickly met by the sound of something chattering. It continues in this vein—squeak, chatter, squeak, chatter—for a few moments, and then there's a scraping, like claws scampering across stone.

The hairs on the backs of Destiny's arms prickle.

Convinced they've summoned the raccoon, Destiny risks another look.

Dominus's eyes are closed, but his lips move to form the chattering noises. A giant rat advances on him from a few feet away. The rodent stops in front of Dominus, where it stands upright on two hind legs in much the same way the raccoon did last night with Destiny. As it squeaks and chirps, the rat's fat pink tail flicks, snapping against the stone floor to empha-size whatever it's saying through the waving of its front paws.

They're communicating, an awestruck Destiny thinks. Domi-nus must be the person who's been manipulating the raccoon. While he publicly refused Mordecai's offer of the throne in front of the whole family, he could have secretly used the rac-coon to steal the medallion, thus granting him access to Mor-decai's powers without anyone knowing.

"What's it saying?" Maximus asks.

"That we have company," Dominus rasps. "Hiding just around the corner."

Destiny gasps and Dominus opens his eyes, his gaze locking with hers. The rat turns and scurries away, disappearing into a hole in the wall.

"You really do have a way of skulking around the castle, don't you?" Maximus says, crossing his arms. "Turning up in the most unexpected places." He beckons to Destiny.

She flushes, willing her feet to move. "Sorry," she stammers. "I didn't mean to eavesdrop. I just got lost on the way to the great hall." The lie rings obviously false.

"Tell me," Maximus says. "What did you overhear as you were trying so hard not to eavesdrop while hiding behind that wall?"

Destiny flushes again. "Just some squeaking noises. It looked like poor Dominus was about to be attacked by a rat," she fin-ishes weakly. And then with more confidence she says, "I'm running late to meet Newton and the twins. Could you direct me to the great hall, please?"

Dominus stands, and for a moment, Destiny's scared that he's going to block her way. But then he steps aside, gesturing behind his father.

"Thank you," Destiny says, a quaver in her voice.

As she walks past him, Dominus glares at her, as though chal-lenging her to say something. Destiny can feel his eyes burn-ing through her back.

CHAPTER 60

Minx

Minx freezes at the threshold to the great hall, shocked by the presence of the Peasants who sit staring back at her. Tempest and Destiny should have been dealt with after what they witnessed last night, not seated around the table with her mother and Hexabus as though preparing for a tea party. It's infuriating. What would her father have to say about this?

Minx refuses to win a throne that's lost all its power. She intends to rule with an iron fist, and the sooner everyone realizes that, the better. The heavy bag drags Minx's shoulder down. She shrugs it off, letting it thunk to the floor.

Raising both hands and spreading her fingers, she shoots off two paralyzing spells. Each hits its mark perfectly. Destiny and Tempest shudder as the magic slams into their chests. They gasp before going completely rigid, their expressions rictuses of horror.

Newton shrieks at Minx to stop as Hexabus bolts upright, shouting, "What the hell do you think you're doing?"

Angel remains a step behind Minx, not doing a damn thing to help, useless as always.

"These Peasants should not be here," Minx growls. "They should be in the dungeons at the very least, though serving as

276

fish food would be better." The magic pulses from Minx's fingertips, growing stronger with every second. This is what she's been waiting for, proof that she's the one who killed Morty and claimed his powers. She smiles thinking how easy it would be to fry the women until they both combusted. Problem solved.

"Minx, stop!" Newton screams. "That's your aunt," she says, pointing to Tempest.

Minx blinks, not sure she heard correctly. The blood roars past her eardrums, a beast that will not be tamed.

Newton screams again, pleading, but the magic is too strong now. It's controlling Minx rather than the other way around. She is a hurricane that cannot be extinguished; she is a raging storm that will keep blowing until it is entirely spent.

And then she is nothing but pain, every molecule of herself on fire. Minx shrieks, her magic amplified back upon herself as Hexabus shoots a curse at her. The roaring in her head rises to a crescendo until its bellowing throat is slit.

Minx slumps to the ground, every muscle spasming in agony.

Newton rushes to a convulsing Tempest while Hexabus dashes to a twitching Destiny.

"Em," Newton mewls, patting Tempest's pale face. "Em, are you okay?"

Tempest's eyes roll back in her head, her ashen face coated with a film of oily sweat.

In the desperate quiet of her mind, Minx now understands why Tempest did a double take when spotting the twins upon their arrival; she didn't recognize them as influencers, but rather as her nieces. And no wonder Minx loved her aunt's aesthetic; they share the gene for having excellent fashion sense.

But how was she supposed to know that? This is all Newton's fault for hiding it from them.

Newton beckons to Angel. "Do something to help her," she pleads, pointing to Tempest.

Angel rushes to Newton's side, placing her hand upon Tempest's forehead just as she sees Hexabus doing with Destiny. Copying Hexabus's spells exactly, Angel coaxes Tempest back to consciousness. "I'm confused," Angel says when their aunt splutters and opens her eyes. "I thought she was a historian called Tempest. How is she Aunt Em?"

"I always called her Em for short because she didn't much like Pest," Newton says, relief flooding her voice as Tempest wheezes. "I wanted to surprise you girls since you'd never been allowed to meet her."

Hexabus has now reinvigorated Destiny, whose face flushes a shade of red that would give her hair a run for its money. As the two women are brought to a standing position—Hexabus instructing them to move around to get blood flowing through their muscles—Minx gets unsteadily to her feet.

"Not you!" Hexabus raises a hand, catapulting a net of light across the room. It envelops Minx, entangling her so she trips after taking a single step.

"Let me go!" Minx screeches, fighting against the net, further ensnaring herself. "Mom, tell her to let me go!"

"Hexabus," Newton says. "It was an accident. She didn't know—"

Hexabus holds out her hand, making a sharp beckoning gesture with her fingers while muttering an incantation.

Horror floods Minx as the sigil and empty vial are ripped from her pocket and sail through the air to Hexabus's outstretched palm. The bag follows suit, landing at Hexabus's feet.

"Well, well, well," Hexabus croons. "What do we have here?"

Minx shrieks in fury. "Give them back!"

"What are they?" Newton demands, leaving Tempest and rushing to Hexabus's side.

"Morty's sigil that vanished along with his medallion straight after he died," Hexabus says, handing the monocle's outer ring to Newton. Hexabus then tugs at the vial's stopper, sniffing tentatively at the bottle. Her face turns incredulous. "And this is an empty vial that, until yesterday, contained enough Dragon's Milk poison to kill a rhinoceros."

Angel and Newton gasp, their eyes boring into Minx, who'd happily hex them both if she weren't tied up.

"No," Newton whispers.

Hexabus reaches down to lift the weekend bag, grunting at the weight of it.

"Get your hands off that," Minx snaps.

But it's too late. Hexabus has already unzipped it. She pulls out a brick of blank paper and then another. "What the hell is this?"

Minx gapes, unable to answer.

CHAPTER 61

Destiny

Tuesday—12:02 p.m.

As Destiny struggles to keep her balance, woozy from the after-effects of Minx's spell, she checks that Tempest is okay, then makes her way to Hexabus, who steadies her when she stumbles. Her muscles ache, as though she's run a marathon she didn't train for, and a dull headache throbs at the base of her skull. Looking into the bag, Destiny pulls out another two bricks of bound blank paper.

"Is this some kind of joke?" Hexabus asks.

Minx's eyes widen. "No, that can't be. There was half a million in cash in there."

Hexabus snorts. "So, what happened to it?"

Panic seems to seize Minx as she stammers, "I... I... It was there when I hid the bag last night."

"Where did the money come from?" Hexabus demands. "Did someone pay you to kill Morty?"

"No," Destiny says, putting all the puzzle pieces together. "She got the money from Mordecai to pay off the blackmailer."

"The blackmailer?" Newton parrots as Hexabus says, "Why would Morty give Minx money for a blackmailer?"

The archaic expression from the note slipped under her door now makes perfect sense. *What's more cunning than bribing Peter to pay Paul?* "Because of what was in the envelope that Mordecai gave Newton just before the meeting," Destiny says.

She watches as Minx goes deathly pale, her eyes darting to her mother, whose mouth is agape. It's clear that Destiny's tossed a grenade. Now she'll wait to see what gets revealed as it explodes.

"How do you know about that?" Newton demands. Before Destiny can reply, Newton turns to appeal to Minx. "And what have *you* got to do with it?"

Minx opens her mouth, but nothing comes out.

"Got to do with what?" Hexabus asks, struggling to keep up.

When Minx still doesn't answer, Newton heads back to the couch, where she reaches for her purse. From inside, she extracts a battered-looking envelope that's clearly been put through the wringer. "Morty brought this to my chambers just before the meeting began, raging about some man he had proof I was having an affair with. And then he threw the envelope at me and said he'd deal with me later." Her jaw bulges as she grinds her teeth. "Tempest and I tried to open it, but it's magicked closed."

"Let me see that," Hexabus says, taking it from Newton before sitting down. Holding the envelope in one hand, Hexabus swirls the other around it while muttering a string of words in a strange language. The envelope's flap springs open with a popping sound and photographs spill out onto Hexabus's lap.

Minx begins howling in rage, struggling against the net. Hexabus snaps her fingers and the yelling is instantly muted.

Hexabus flips through the photos before looking up at Newton. "They're pictures of you with that buff barkeep from the inn," she says. "You two look quite cozy."

"Madigan?" Newton asks, forehead puckered as much as the Botox will allow. "Let me see," she demands, reaching out.

As Hexabus hands over the photos, Destiny skirts around the back of the chairs to avoid a furious Minx, who's still screaming despite the fact no one can hear her. Tempest has had the same idea. The two come to a stop behind Newton, peering over her shoulder at the pictures she's studying.

Hexabus is right. It *is* Madigan, which is most curious. Newton appears to be in a café with him somewhere on the mainland. The series of photos shows her either laughing, reaching out to touch his chest, or regarding him with an amused expression.

If Madigan's been having an affair with Newton, that definitely makes him someone capable of deceit, just as Destiny suspected, though it doesn't explain his lying two nights ago. What it *does* explain is his dislike of Mordecai, not only as an unpopular king, but as the husband of the woman he's embroiled with.

"This was when I was supposed to meet Minx for lunch a few weeks back," Newton murmurs, sorting through the photos. "She was running late, and while I was waiting for her, I ran into Madigan, who was in Gwillumbury doing business for the inn. He joined me for a few minutes as I waited." She turns to Hexabus. "He spilled some of his cappuccino down his shirt and I'm holding a napkin against it to wipe it up," she says, waving the photo where she's touching his chest. "It's much more innocent than it looks."

Minx has finally run out of steam, slumping to the floor.

"Minx must have arrived at the café and seen the two of you together," Destiny says, figuring it out. "It gave her the idea for how she might raise enough money to pay off the blackmailer. After taking those photographs, she told her father she had proof of you having an affair, Newton, which she'd hand over if he paid for it. He must have seen the photos before the gathering, which is when he gave her that cash," Destiny finishes, nodding at the bag.

"Oh my god," Newton mewls, hands flying to her mouth.

What Destiny can't figure out is why Minx would put a target on Madigan's head like that. She must have realized that if Morty believed Newton was having an affair with him, Madigan would experience the full force of Morty's wrath. She wonders if Minx has a vendetta against Madigan, and what might have caused that. Destiny makes a note of that in the *Useful Information Folder*, something to be looked into later.

"Do you have any clue who was blackmailing you?" Hexabus asks Minx. "And why?"

Minx doesn't reply; she just glares, mutinous.

"It was all my fault, okay?" Angel cries, throwing her hands up. "I got wasted one night in a club when Minx wasn't with me, and I told someone about our family's powers while showing off some tricks." Angel flushes, shaking her head. "I don't remember doing it, but the next day, we got an email with video footage of it attached. It said we had to pay them half a million in cash or they would go to Morty with the evidence."

"What would the punishment have been?" Destiny asks.

"It would have been pretty severe," Hexabus says. "Morty cast a permanent spell that would disfigure and silence any of the magical Scruffmores if they ever confided their abilities in a Peasant. Well, anyone except Morty, of course. He was exempt."

"Can I see the video?" Destiny asks.

Angel pulls a cell phone from her pocket and scrolls through it before handing the phone to Destiny. "That's it," she says. Almost apologetically, she adds, "It's not pretty."

Destiny presses Play and music immediately begins blasting. The screen is blurry and then Angel comes into view. She's all dressed up, but her hair is disheveled, and her eyeliner has smudged. She's clearly intoxicated; her eyes struggle to focus on whoever is recording her.

Turning up the sound, Destiny strains to hear what Angel's saying. "…because we're magical and have actual magical powers…like fantasy characters who can work all kinds of cool spells…" She holds a finger up and makes a flame ignite at its tip. "Most people wouldn't believe us… They'd ask me to prove it…but not—" The video suddenly cuts out.

Destiny watches it again twice. "And you don't remember who you were speaking with? Not even a fragment of a memory?"

Angel shakes her head.

Destiny hands the phone back. "Can I see the emails from the blackmailer?"

Angel scrolls and then pulls something up. "This is the first one."

It's from an email account whose name is listed as I Know Your Magical Secret and the subject line reads: *Pay up or your father sees this video.*

Destiny reads the accompanying text in the body of the email. She feels a prickling sensation along her spine as it dawns on her who the blackmailer is. Each new clue is like tugging at a snagged thread of a woolen jersey. If Destiny can just unravel enough of it, the truth will be what remains.

At least they now have Mordecai's sigil, though the medallion still needs to be retrieved. Based on what Hexabus told Destiny last night, she knows it isn't possible for Minx to have killed Mordecai with mere poison, so the killer is still at large. Perhaps that's who stole all the money, replacing it with wads of paper.

Destiny strongly suspects Dominus and Maximus, but if she's right about Maximus and Hexabus's affair, she's not sure how Hexabus will take the news of her suspicions. She'll need to think very carefully about how she broaches the subject.

"Stand," Hexabus orders Minx, waving her hand to force Minx up. "I'm charging you with treason and attempted murder of the Sorcerer King. You're going down to the dungeons, where we can keep an eye on you."

Destiny tunes out Newton, who's now pleading with Hexabus for clemency. She knows where she needs to go next. It's time to speak with the blackmailer.

CHAPTER 62

Evangeline

Tuesday—2:23 p.m.

Evangeline squints as the sun's rays bounce ecstatically off the ocean. It's as if the whole world has been reduced to glass purely so that it can reflect this magnificence. She can't remember a time when the island was covered by nothing but blue skies, a giant canvas stretched to infinity. For her entire life, light has waged a war with the cloud cover, desperately struggling to touch this godforsaken island. And today, it finally won the battle.

As waves crash against the shore, it looks like the ocean is flinging fistfuls of diamonds into the air. Crabs scuttle along the shoreline, carrying sunshine on their backs, and gulls swoop giddily about, drunk on the beauty of the day.

And they aren't the only ones to awaken.

Evangeline's cell phone lit up earlier, delivering messages of love and support from Gabe. More surprising is she can feel her love of magic—a gift she grew to hate as a child because of Bramble's death—beginning to return, her aversion to it thawing.

Sensing herself being watched, Evangeline turns and shades her eyes as she gazes up at the rocks. Destiny is making her way to the beach. When she reaches the sand, she bends and undoes her laces. After removing her boots and socks, she puts them aside so she can make the rest of the way barefoot.

Approaching Evangeline, she says, "Hello. We weren't properly introduced in all the chaos of last night." She smiles shyly, reaching out her hand. "I'm Destiny."

Evangeline shakes it.

From what Hexabus says, Destiny is incredibly bright and has a lot of experience solving all kinds of mysteries, which could make the young woman either Evangeline's savior or the person who's going to prove she's a murderer. And while Hexabus seems to be convinced that they aren't Morty's killers, Evangeline isn't so sure.

She doesn't want to be her father's daughter, someone who can so easily claim a life, even unintentionally, without it destroying her. If she is guilty, by punishing herself for this crime against nature, Evangeline will reject Mordecai's DNA as the building blocks of who she is.

No one gets to decide who that person is except Evangeline herself.

She and Destiny are quiet for a while, both gazing out at the glittering surf. "Your mother said I'd find you here," Destiny eventually says.

"I know we're supposed to be on lockdown," Evangeline says, sitting on the sand, "but I really needed to get out of there."

"Tell me about it." Destiny huffs, sitting as well and setting a backpack down beside her.

"What happened?" Evangeline asks, almost too scared to hear the answer.

Destiny tells her about the Tempest reveal and Minx's attack on them both, and then how Hexabus summoned Morty's sigil and the poison from Minx's pocket. She finishes with the story of the blackmail and the stolen cash. It's a lot to take in at once, though none of it surprises Evangeline. She's always suspected Minx to be capable of terrible cruelty.

She thinks back to her conversation with her mother after the family meeting.

Whatever happened tonight, there were other forces, greater ones, at play.

Between dueling with Darius and Maximus, and being poisoned by Minx, Mordecai must have been very weak when she and her mother laid hands on him to incapacitate him. Her spirits drop as she realizes Hexabus might be wrong, that they can't definitively conclude they didn't accidentally kill him.

Which means she isn't free at all, nor will she ever be.

"Is this your favorite place on the island?" Destiny surprises Evangeline by asking. "Is that why your mother knew you'd be here?"

"No," Evangeline replies, her voice thick. "This is where I last saw Bramble alive."

Confession is good for the soul, which is probably why Evangeline finds herself opening up. She tells Destiny about how Dawn Montgomery was also discovered on this beach, lovingly laid out as though at a wake, a flower placed in her hair. And of the fear that stalked the island all those years, and how she and Bramble should never have been out that night.

"And to think that the killer was my own father," Evangeline says, stuck in that impossible place where two opposing things are true at once; she can't quite believe it, and yet she undoubtedly knows it to be true. "And the worst part," Evangeline adds, "is not that I believe he did those awful things. But that I don't believe he'd have had the capacity to lay Dawn out so gently afterward, that he had that kind of tenderness in him." She looks at Destiny, expecting some kind of censure, but all she sees is compassion.

"You're a really good listener," Evangeline says, smiling sadly. "Not everyone is able to sit with someone else's grief without it making them really uncomfortable."

Destiny withdraws an urn from her backpack. "That's because I've suffered my own losses," she says. "And I haven't dealt with them very well either. This is my emotional-support urn. Carrying it around is supposed to help me come to grips with the loss while also reminding me that you don't ever fully lose someone if you still have memories of them that you can carry around with you."

Evangeline smiles. "I like that." What she doesn't say is that she doesn't have Bramble's ashes to carry around. She can't even be sure what happened to her brother, what *obliteration* means. "Can I ask whose ashes those are?" She nods at the urn.

Destiny takes a deep breath, her curls flapping around in the wind, casting wild shadows on the sand. When she answers, it's in a whisper. "They belong to my brother, Nate."

CHAPTER 63

Choose Your Own Conundrum
Nate Carter

You're Nate Carter and you become Destiny Whip's older brother when you're thirteen and she's eight. Your mother, Annie Carter, was Destiny's mother's best friend, and she steps in to adopt Destiny after Liz is murdered.

It isn't easy on Annie, who's a single mother and is already struggling to raise one difficult child on her own. Taking on a traumatized orphan poses its own special kind of challenges. But despite being an unusual family unit, one that elicits a lot of whispers wherever the three of you go, you're incredibly close.

You're proud of your strange little sister, who's such a whiz kid that she leapfrogs over you to attend university.

Losing your mother to cancer when you're twenty-one is devastating. Not only because of the close bond you had, but because it requires you to step up and become Destiny's legal guardian. You're barely out of childhood yourself when you become responsible for your teenage sister's welfare. There isn't a lot of life insurance money left over once all your mother's medical debt is settled, and so you drop out of college to save money.

Luckily, Destiny has a full private scholarship for Yale, and so she doesn't need to cut her education short like you do, but she's the one who inspires the idea for a role-playing app that you begin to develop with a friend. Destiny helps you formulate clues and red herrings for it, coming up with all kinds of interesting scenarios, along with the puzzles and riddles that players need to solve in various closed-room murder-mystery games. The app is a huge hit, and your company takes off.

Once Destiny graduates with her doctorate, she moves in with her childhood best friend, Bex Donoghue. Even though Bex and Destiny kept in touch while Destiny was at Yale and Bex was off studying fashion in New York, you haven't seen Bex since she was fourteen. Which is why it's a shock to encounter her when you help Destiny on moving day.

You're a good-looking man. Tall and well-built, you attract gorgeous women who aren't shy about making their interest known. While you've dated a fair number of them, none have really captured your interest in this bone-rattling way.

But here Bex Donoghue is, not classically pretty, and what the meaner of those women would call "chubby." Yet there's something about her lack of guile and her crooked smile that makes you do a double take. When Bex looks at you, her gaze doesn't linger on your face and body; it bores into your mind like a power drill.

You think she's utterly breathtaking.

What clinches it is the force of her personality. She's a walking truth bomb, one who detonates often. She tells it like it is, letting you know that while you may be hot, she likes her men well-read and informed, able to intelligently argue a point all through the night if need be.

Still, out of respect for your sister, who doesn't have many friends, you don't make a move as you don't want to put their friendship at risk. But when Destiny notices how you feel— which of course she does because Destiny notices *everything*— she says she suspects that Bex feels the same way, giving you her blessing to ask her best friend on a date.

Your relationship with Bex is passionate and volatile, with you breaking up and getting back together more than once. There's a lot you disagree about, from your taste in music and art to your views on politics and world events. You're stubborn and set in your ways, but Bex's mind is like a small neighborhood convenience store. Though it's open 24/7, you can never truly be certain what you'll find in there from one day to the next.

Destiny teases that you're like a bickering old married couple, and pointedly searches the sky for double rainbows on the rare occasions you and Bex agree.

Still, you manage to make it work because you love each other.

You're with Bex for a year when you begin to notice her weight loss. At first, it's gradual, something she claims is happening because she's trying to eat healthier. You thought she ate healthy before—way too healthy for your taste considering how much you love your pizza, nachos, and burgers—but what do you know? Women are obsessed with salads, so let them have at it even though you don't see the appeal of rabbit food.

But then it becomes worrisome.

Suddenly, you're hardly seeing Bex eating at all; she's taken to claiming she's always had a meal mere minutes before your arrival. Her beautiful curves have disappeared and it's like she's trying to make *herself* disappear. She keeps waving off your concerns, telling you to stop being so controlling.

Destiny is away on a three-month contract in Egypt working long hours, and the time zone difference makes it difficult to connect. When she finally gets home, she's shocked by the transformation her best friend has undergone. You both sit Bex down to have a serious talk, and she admits that she's struggling with an eating disorder.

You think she was perfect as she was, and you tell her as much. She shakes her head and laughs, tears brimming as she says you can't possibly imagine what it's like to work with svelte women all day and to always, *always* be the biggest woman in the room. She asks if you haven't noticed how people regard the two of you like you're a puzzle they can't figure out. Everyone else can see how mismatched you are, so why can't you?

When Bex stops eating entirely, you step in and beg her to seek professional help. It takes a while, but with Destiny's assistance, you convince Bex that she needs to check herself in to a treatment facility.

On the morning that you're meant to make the four-hour drive to the clinic, Destiny slips into Bex's room and wakes you up, motioning that she needs to speak with you. You tip-toe out so as not to wake Bex.

"I have a really bad feeling," Destiny says as you sit at the kitchen table, accepting the strong cup of coffee she hands you. She looks pale and clammy with purple smudges under her eyes.

"What do you mean?" you ask, taking a sip.

"I had a...dream...that something terrible is going to happen."

"A dream?" you scoff, waiting for the punch line.

"It was awful, Nate. You guys can't go today."

You're about to laugh it off and tease her about it when you realize where this is coming from. Destiny has lived with loss her entire life: being given up for adoption at birth, then Liz being murdered, and then her adoptive mother dying. She has a lot of abandonment issues, and seeing her best friend leaving must be triggering.

You assure her that the car has just recently been serviced and that you've checked the tires and brakes. She knows you're a cautious driver and you remind her that you don't speed or take chances on the road.

You tell her that everyone at the clinic really knows what they're doing, that they specialize in eating disorders, and that Bex is going to be in the best possible hands. There's nothing to worry about except not getting Bex the treatment she needs.

Still, Destiny won't be placated. She begs you to stay home and travel another day.

What do you do?

A. Refuse and leave—go to page 293.

B. Offer to leave the following day—go to page 297.

OPTION A:
REFUSE AND LEAVE

Not being able to reason with Destiny freaks you out.

Even when she was a little girl, the way her brain worked—all those cogs and wheels perfectly aligned, the steady spinning of one fueling the relentless rotation of another—was a marvel to you.

But now it's like someone has thrust a stick in the well-oiled machinery of her mind, grinding it to a halt. What comes to you is a memory from when you were ten and Destiny was five.

★ ★ ★

You and your mother were at their home one evening watching movies when Liz excused herself to put Destiny to bed.

After a few minutes, you pretended to need the bathroom and headed upstairs to get a glimpse of the bedtime ritual that always took Liz and Destiny so long to conduct. You couldn't imagine what could possibly take so long considering that you just got into bed, read for a while, and then went to sleep when your mother said it was time to switch out the light.

Standing outside Destiny's room, you peered around the corner. Liz was seated on Destiny's bed with her back to you.

"I take it you've already chosen your bedtime story," Liz said. "I'm expecting a certain level of discernment here." Liz always spoke to Destiny that way, using big words as though she were conversing with another adult.

"I have!"

"Okay, which one will it be?"

"The one with the ghost ship!" Destiny lisped in reply.

"Ah, the *Mary Celeste*," Liz responded. "That's an excellent choice."

You were expecting Liz to pull a book out from somewhere so that she could read this story to Destiny, but instead she recited the facts of what sounded like a real event, giving dates and a timeline. "An American brigantine was found abandoned on December 5, 1872, in the North Atlantic Ocean four hundred nautical miles from the archipelago of the Azores."

You were relieved to hear Destiny ask for an explanation of what a brigantine and archipelago were since you were just as mystified.

Once Destiny's questions were answered, Liz continued, "After Captain Morehouse's crew boarded, they headed below deck where they discovered three and a half feet of water in the hull, and the ship's charts in disarray. One of the *Mary Celeste*'s pumps had been taken apart and its only lifeboat was gone. No belongings were missing from the crewmen's quarters. The cargo of industrial alcohol barrels still remained along with a six-month supply of food and water."

"How many people were originally on board?" Destiny asked.

"There was Captain Benjamin Spooner Briggs, his wife, Sarah, and Sophia, their two-year-old daughter. Besides them, there were seven crewmen. What do you think happened to them? How could they have vanished without a trace?"

The two spoke about alcohol vapors, porous wood barrels, the log slate, coal dust, rough seas, and the captain's level of experience. They scoffed at theories of sea monsters, killer waterspouts, and psychotic episodes, and dismissed the possibility of a pirate attack considering none of the provisions or cargo were taken.

You grew bored listening to the discussion and headed back

downstairs, but what you never forgot was how earnestly the two discussed a tragedy that had occurred more than a hundred years ago as though they could possibly solve it. You marveled at how they did this every single night before Destiny went to sleep, seemingly tackling a different mystery each time.

★ ★ ★

You try for the last time to appeal to *that* Destiny, the one who would have scoffed at the notion of having a bad feeling that could be a portent.

But she won't be swayed.

Losing patience, you yell, "You need to get a grip, Tiny!"

Your raised voices wake Bex, who emerges from her bedroom, rubbing her eyes as she leans against the door frame, studying you both. "What's going on?" she asks.

"Nothing," you say, forcing a tight smile.

Bex shoots you a dark look before staring pointedly at Destiny. "What's wrong?"

"You can't go today. If you do…you're going to be in a terrible accident," Destiny says.

"Oh my god," Bex exclaims, suddenly wide-awake.

You groan. "I can't believe you're sabotaging your best friend's recovery just because you don't want to be alone for a while, Tiny."

"That's not why I'm saying this!" Destiny yells, on the verge of tears. "Neither of you will survive the accident."

Bex walks over to Destiny and hugs her tightly. She waits out the emotional storm that's raging through her. When Destiny finally stops shuddering, Bex asks, "How do you know this?"

"I had an awful dream about it."

"So, in other words, just a garden-variety nightmare," you say, rolling your eyes.

Bex shoots you another look, silently instructing you to shut up. "Okay," she says, "so how about instead of going today, we go tomorrow. Will that be better?"

Destiny hesitates, looking like she wants to push for more time.

"We can't put it off any longer than that," you warn, already annoyed by this crazy turn of events. You've taken a day off from work in a super busy week, made all the necessary plans. And now your sister is acting like a screwball, throwing everything off.

Destiny nods, wiping her nose.

"Then we'll go tomorrow," Bex says, her mind made up.

You have no choice. You call the clinic and make an excuse, telling them you'll see them the next day.

Go to page 299.

OPTION B:
OFFER TO LEAVE THE
FOLLOWING DAY

"Look," you say. "Would you feel better if I called the clinic and asked if we could delay by a day?"

Destiny looks torn, but she appears to be considering it.

"We can't put it off any longer than that," you insist.

The facility is expecting Bex and there's a waiting list for her spot. It was difficult enough getting her to agree to seek treatment; she's really had to psych herself up for it. You're scared that giving her any excuse to delay further will mean she'll change her mind.

"You can even come with us tomorrow," you offer. "Maybe seeing the clinic will help put your mind at ease. That way, you can meet some of the staff and talk with her doctors. You'll also be able to picture exactly where she is when she calls us." Sometimes, it's the unknown that makes people nervous. For Destiny, knowledge has always been power, and you're hoping she'll feel less anxious if she joins you.

"I can't," Destiny replies. "I'm heading back to Cairo, remember?" She bites her thumbnail, still clearly jittery.

"No problem. Bex and I will go tomorrow, then. You said the bad feeling was about something bad happening *today*," you remind her.

Although Destiny looks like she wants to argue, she simply nods. "Thank you." She's embarrassed, as though she can read your thoughts about how irrational you think she's sounding despite the fact you're trying to understand whatever this is.

You contact the clinic and make the necessary arrangements, lying about car trouble to explain the delay. You call to reschedule meetings and rearrange your life, all because of your little sister's bad dreams. And then you make the mistake of telling Bex about it.

Go to page 299.

You're irritable the next morning because you and Bex fought all night. She did exactly what you predicted, which was to use Destiny's dream as an excuse not to go. Bex insisted that even though Destiny was acting out of character, your sister deserved your respect rather than your disparagement. She even somehow managed to twist everything around by accusing you of being a misogynist who doesn't believe women.

When you're finally ready to head out, Destiny stands next to your car, her expression as anxious as it was yesterday. Her taxi idles nearby, waiting to take her to the airport. While her luggage is already loaded and the driver looks impatient, Destiny shows no signs of leaving.

Sighing, you hand her your phone. "Here, Tiny, you pick the route." Hopefully giving her some measure of control will help put her at ease.

She studies the app carefully, eventually choosing a more scenic trip that will take you much longer to get to the facility. The aim is clearly to have you avoid major highways, taking quieter back roads instead. You consider objecting, but if this will keep her happy, it's a small compromise. Besides, Destiny's way will give you an extra two hours with Bex.

As much as you've been advocating for Bex to go to the clinic, you're worried. You've read the statistics. Only 60 percent of those who undergo treatment will make a full recovery. That leaves 40 percent who won't. Glancing over at Bex—with her head seemingly too large for her tiny body, her sunken eyes and chiseled cheekbones, her sharp edges and the fuzzy hair that's grown on her arms to compensate for the lack of insulating fat—you're reminded of how helpless you've felt these past few months watching her try to erase herself as she's striven to take up as little space as possible. You don't know what you'll do if she doesn't get better.

As Bex remembers her favorite pillow, running back inside the building to fetch it, Destiny grabs your arm through your open window. "Don't go, Nate!" she pleads. "Just wait another couple of days. The voice said—"

"The voice?" you ask incredulously. "You're losing it, you know that? You're completely unhinged! Listen to yourself with all this shit about dreams and voices." Even as you go off on her, you realize it's not your finest moment, but your nerves are already frayed. You did as your sister asked: you delayed by a day. And you really don't need Destiny making a scene right now, giving Bex yet another excuse to stay.

As you spot Bex making her way back, arms wrapped around her pillow, you lower your voice. "You will *not* ruin this for Bex, do you understand me? If she doesn't go for treatment, if she doesn't get better, I swear to god, Tiny, I'll never forgive you."

Destiny's face crumples.

"Put on a brave face and give her a good send-off. And then get your shit together."

You watch as the friends hug, Destiny clinging to Bex so tightly you worry she'll never let go. The taxi driver honks and Bex instructs Destiny to get going, warning that she's going to miss her flight.

Destiny texts Bex constantly for updates.

Four hours into the drive, you're riddled with guilt about how mean you were, how terribly you lashed out. Ridiculing Destiny's mental health was a cheap shot, a deeply unkind thing to do. You're ashamed of how you handled it.

You call her, but her phone goes to voicemail. "Hey, Tiny. I just wanted to check in and see how you're doing. I'm sorry about our fight and what I said. It's all going to be fine, so try not to worry so much, okay? Love you."

It's as you're handing your phone back to a smiling Bex that the truck appears out of nowhere.

CHAPTER 64

Evangeline

Tuesday—3:01 p.m.

After Destiny finishes sharing the account of the car accident that killed her brother and best friend, Evangeline considers reaching out and squeezing her hand, but Destiny's cradling the urn, absentmindedly stroking it.

"Nate called me seconds before the accident." Destiny speaks in a kind of trance, having decamped to the past. "But I couldn't answer because I was in the air on the way to Cairo." She sounds haunted when she says, "It was his making that call to apologize, while on the route I chose, that killed them."

What comes back to Evangeline in that moment is the discussion she had with Gabe on their first date about unintended consequences.

They're the hardest consequences of all to live with, don't you think, because we couldn't possibly have foreseen them with the limited information we had at our disposal at the time.

But we're still culpable, she replied. *Even if we didn't intend for that particular outcome to happen.*

That's one way of looking at it. You could also cut yourself some slack for not being an all-knowing god.

If she were a juror in a trial where Destiny was the prosecutor trying to condemn herself to a lifetime of incarceration,

Evangeline would vote "not guilty." She marvels at how she can grant Destiny the grace she hasn't allowed herself.

"After Nate pretty much accused me of being crazy," Destiny continues, "I spent the last year blaming myself for causing their deaths. Maybe he was right and there was something deeply wrong with me. Had I just ignored the dream and then the voice in my head, the accident wouldn't have happened, and they wouldn't have been at that exact intersection because of me."

"You're a seer, Destiny," Evangeline says gently. "Seeing the inevitable is what you do—that's your gift. But along with it comes the curse of always feeling culpable for not being able to prevent what you've seen. If you choose to beat yourself up your whole life, you just become your own assailant in a crime that no one can ever prosecute."

Destiny huffs, wiping tears away. "Maybe. Although I'm more inclined to think that if I'd listened to my instincts, I would have confided in Bex and Nate long before about the dreams and how they started before Liz died."

Evangeline nods, seeing where Destiny's going with this. "You think that if they knew the details and why you were so insistent, they would have listened to you and stayed?"

Destiny shrugs. "At least they would have had all the information."

"Still, they might not have believed you."

"But I would have believed myself," Destiny says, eyes shining. "And that would have made all the difference because I wouldn't have let them leave no matter what Nate said."

Evangeline smiles sadly as she realizes that she and Destiny have reached the same destination after walking very different paths to get there. She wonders why finding your way to your truest self, and then fully embracing and accepting it, is always the most difficult journey of all.

They're quiet for a moment, allowing the sun's warmth to burrow into their bones.

Eventually, Destiny stands and brushes the sand off the hand not cradling the urn. "When I came here, I thought maybe Mordecai could be my father, which would make you my half sister."

There's so much hope shining in Destiny's eyes that Evangeline can't look away.

"It was silly, I know," Destiny quickly adds, flushing.

Evangeline shakes her head. "It's not silly at all. Considering everything with Dominus…who knows? Just because you didn't get to hear it from the horse's mouth doesn't mean it isn't true." Despite all the nasty surprises of late, Evangeline finds that she quite likes the thought of being related to Destiny, and how lovely it would be to have a half sister who isn't Minx or Angel.

Destiny nods, looking encouraged, which breaks Evangeline's heart. Imagine needing connection so desperately that you're disappointed that a mass murderer didn't claim you.

"Do you know where Darius is?" Destiny asks, looking around the beach. "Your mom thought he might be down here with you."

Evangeline is instantly on her guard, feeling especially protective of her brother after their discussion this morning. She was hoping he'd open up to her during their walk to the beach, but he said what he needed more than talking was to have a strong drink.

"He *was* here," she replies cautiously, "but he left for the inn just before you arrived. Why?"

"There's just something I need to clear up," Destiny says, trying but failing to tame her wild curls in the wind. "I'll head there now."

For a moment, Evangeline wants to insist that Destiny take her with her, but then she thinks of all the times she's been a shield, protecting Darius and making excuses for him. Perhaps who he is today is the unintended consequence of her actions since he was never forced to step up and take accountability for himself.

Perhaps it's time for Evangeline to let go and stop trying to control everything.

But she isn't the only one who needs to let go. Nodding at Destiny's urn, Evangeline says, "The dead struggle to move on when we cling to them so fiercely. We think we're doing it for their sake, to keep them alive in our world, but we're actually selfishly doing it for ourselves. Sometimes the kindest thing we could do is set them free."

Destiny pales. Instead of looking down at the urn, she gazes off to the left, focusing on something Evangeline cannot see. "You're absolutely right," she murmurs, nodding as though reaching a decision.

CHAPTER 65

Darius

Tuesday—2:44 p.m.

As Darius nears the inn ahead of the meeting with his contact, he swings the satchel off his shoulder and gazes up at the silhouette in the attic window. After banging on the door, he has to wait more than two minutes for a flustered Madigan to finally open up.

"Well, someone had a wild night," Darius says dryly, taking in Madigan's rumpled appearance. "Is she still upstairs?"

"Who?" Madigan asks, wide-eyed with innocence as he runs a large hand through his mussed-up hair.

"Whoever's stopping you from doing your job. You realize that's what I'm paying you for, right? To work."

"Sorry," Madigan says, looking sheepish. "With there bein' no guests at the moment, I thought..." And then, remembering himself, he says, "I heard about yeh father, Silver. I'm so sorry."

"No, you're not," Darius says, waving it off. "He was a complete and utter bastard, and we all hated him. How did you hear about it?" Darius asks, thinking of how Hexabus put the castle on lockdown not only to figure out what happened to Morty, but also to avoid the news spreading.

"Everyone knows," Madigan says, shrugging.

"Of course they do." *Small villages*, Darius thinks. *You can't*

*fart in the morning without everyone knowing what you had for din-
ner the night before.* "Do you mind getting out of my way so I
can enter my own inn?" Darius says.

Madigan flushes and apologizes, stepping aside to allow Darius to pass.

The two have known each other for fourteen years, ever since
Madigan arrived on the island looking for a job at the Grimshaw, though that was long before Darius bought the inn on
a whim. Darius doesn't believe in friendships. The more you
confide in people, dropping your guard to reveal your truest
self, the more ammunition they have against you.

But as Darius's employee, Madigan isn't his equal, which
is something the innkeeper is all too aware of because Darius
won't let him forget it. What works about the relationship's imbalance is that Madigan desperately needs Darius and this job,
which means he's incentivized to keep his mouth shut about
anything Darius might have let slip on the nights when he's
had a little too much to drink.

Not that Darius relies solely on Madigan's discretion.

He's been using Madigan as a guinea pig for the past two
years, practicing his newly acquired powers on him and then
promptly erasing his memory so he wouldn't recall all the humiliation and torture.

"Yeh come for a drink?" Madigan asks now, trailing Darius
through the lobby to the bar.

"No," Darius replies, thinking how he's come for something
Madigan can't give him. "I've come for ten."

Madigan laughs. "That's quite a bump yeh have on yer noggin. Yeh quite alright?"

"Never better!" Darius lies, thinking he might very well
have a concussion, but who has time to deal with such incon-
veniences?

As Madigan pours Darius a full glass of neat whiskey, there's
a squeak overhead, footsteps against floorboards.

Darius shakes his head, annoyed. "Go back upstairs to whoever's waiting for you. I'll pour my own damn drinks."

Madigan's eyes dart up at the ceiling. "Nah, she can wait. I'm happy to—"

"Didn't you hear me?" Darius growls, his mood souring. "I don't feel like your shitty company, so piss off."

Madigan blinks in surprise and then nods, backing away. "Of course. Sorry."

Once Madigan has made his way back up the groaning staircase, Darius takes his glass and sits next to the hearth, which is still full of ash, Madigan not having cleaned it out recently. He didn't use to be quite so useless and forgetful, neglecting such basic tasks. Darius wonders if all the memory-erasing spells have had a cumulative effect. If so, he's going to have to find a new innkeeper.

Setting the satchel down at his feet, Darius waves his hand to conjure a roaring fire. He downs half his glass and scoffs at this pathetic use of his newfound power. All those months of training, all that sacrifice, and for what? So he doesn't have to instruct Madigan to carry wood inside and set it alight manually?

No, he refuses to accept that.

Darius is owed the throne. It should have been his two years ago and it's his even more so now. He's paid his dues, endured years of psychological and emotional abuse at his father's hands, all so he could be king one day. To have Dominus step in and swipe the crown when he hasn't earned it, or suffered for it, is not an acceptable outcome.

Once his contact shows up and Darius pays for the Eye of Gormodeus, instead of handing the artifact over to his father— as was the original plan—he's going to use it for himself. Let the challengers come for the crown; there can be only one victor.

After draining the first glass of whiskey, Darius goes back to the bar for another. And then another. He foolishly got here too early and the waiting is making him jittery.

As he stares into the flames, a memory resurfaces. It's one that he's buried so deeply it only ever rises from the well of a glass that he's drinking particularly deeply from. It's what he witnessed the night Bramble died.

While spying on Eva and Bramble from behind the rocks, burning with jealousy as he watched his younger brother's incredible display of power in the surf, Darius spotted Morty and Lurk making their way down to the beach. At first, Darius thrilled at the sight, thinking Morty was there to punish Bramble for sneaking out. But when Darius saw his father raise a hand and point at Eva, making her slump to the sand, Darius's stomach twisted in knots, the ache so bad that he turned tail and ran all the way home.

And yet, even after Bramble's body washed ashore, Darius never told his mother or sister what he'd witnessed.

This morning, when his mother and Eva told him about Morty being the island's serial killer, Darius acted shocked, as if he couldn't believe it. But the truth is that after what he witnessed with Bramble, Darius figured it all out. He honestly believed, though, that if he could keep Morty's secrets—protecting his father from everyone discovering the truth—that he would somehow become worthy of his father's love and respect.

Thanks to Morty, Darius learned how to split himself in two. There's the person everyone sees, so perfectly wrapped up in appealing and charming packaging, and then the shadow self he keeps hidden. He'll never be complete, or truly grow into his powers, unless he acts now to shed that pathetic coward of the past.

Aware he's becoming ridiculously maudlin, Darius tries to harness his anger from earlier. But it's gone, consumed by his melancholy. He feels spent and sad, mired in self-hatred. Damn the whiskey for always doing this to him, for holding up a mirror when what Darius seeks is a mask.

He's so immersed in his dark thoughts that he doesn't register the tapping until it becomes an insistent knocking. As he looks up, his heartbeat quickens. He's about to get what his father so desperately desired. He just wishes Morty were here to see it.

But instead of his contact, Darius spots Destiny with a hand cupped around her face, nose pressed up against the bar window.

When she points at the door, he groans. Making his way to the lobby, he mutters, "For god's sake. Can't a man just get some fresh air and a few drinks without being harassed?" Upon opening the door, Darius says, "Tell my mother I'll be back when I'm good and ready." It's difficult speaking for some reason. His lips don't appear to want to obey his brain.

"Actually, I just wanted to talk with you," Destiny replies, looking windswept and sun-kissed.

Darius sighs. "Now's not a good time. I'm waiting for someone."

"I'll be really quick," Destiny promises.

Casting his gaze down the street and not seeing anyone making their way to the inn, Darius huffs. "Fine. I'll give you five minutes."

She follows him back to the fire and sits down across from him.

"So, what's up?" Darius asks.

"I wanted to discuss how you blackmailed Minx and Angel," Destiny says, firing the bullet of a statement at point-blank range.

CHAPTER 66

Destiny

Tuesday—3:25 p.m.

Darius startles, sloshing his whiskey over the lip of his glass as he regards Destiny with steely, unfocused eyes. The cuts and scrapes on his face look painful, as do the bruises, which have a purplish tinge. He's more than a little drunk, making her wonder if confronting him this way is a good idea.

Because Destiny is now completely and utterly alone after severing her connection to Bex as she left the beach filled with so much shame.

Until Evangeline's remark, Destiny hadn't considered how disrespectful it's been dragging her best friend around to use as a ghostly mop to help clean up her messes. Especially when Bex surely has better things to do in the afterlife than act as Destiny's babysitter.

At least she knows Madigan is around in case she might need him to save her a second time. Though, judging by the weird dynamic she's witnessed between Madigan and Darius, Destiny can't be certain he'll stand up to his boss. The thought makes her queasy, and she tenses as she waits for Darius to respond, unsure whether he'll issue a flurry of denials or explode with fury.

He does neither.

Instead, Darius takes a measured sip of his drink, assessing her. "How did you figure it out?" he asks, voice flat.

"Your spelling," Destiny admits. "I noticed it when you were writing up Madigan's to-do list two nights ago. You made the same spelling and grammatical mistakes in the email." As Darius reddens at the criticism, Destiny quickly adds, "To be fair, there were only a limited number of suspects considering that Angel would have been disfigured had she confessed to a Peasant—" Destiny stops to correct herself. "A nonmagical person. Plus, it occurred to me that Angel must have known the person she was speaking with in the video."

She thinks of what Angel said in the clip.

…because we're magical and have actual magical powers…like fantasy characters who can work all kinds of cool spells… Most people wouldn't believe us… They'd ask me to prove it…but not—

"The 'we' she was speaking of wasn't her and Minx," Destiny continues, prattling on because his blistering silence is making her nervous. "She was including the person she was speaking to. And she didn't need to prove anything to *you* to convince you of her powers, because you already knew."

There's a muffled bang and Darius startles, looking behind Destiny to the arched entranceway. When no one materializes, he turns his gaze back to her. "Carry on."

"At first, I thought you were blackmailing them to pay for your magical lessons with Balzanon, the wizard tutor your mother told me about."

Darius flinches at the word *tutor*, his bloodshot eyes narrowing, and Destiny realizes too late that she's used the wrong word, making Darius sound like a teenager in need of afterschool instruction. Infantilizing him is the last thing she should be doing to a man who clearly feels like the world owes him for not recognizing and celebrating his genius.

As Darius clenches his fists until his knuckles go white, Destiny understands that her approach here needs to be the exact opposite of what it was with Hexabus last night. No waving her arms around, making herself large while owning her many achievements. Here, with this man, who might very well be her half brother, Destiny needs to make herself small so that he can feel so very big in comparison.

"Your father was after a magical relic called the Eye of Gormodeus," Destiny says, taking note of how Darius twitches in response to the name. "It's supposed to grant its owner unimaginable power. But Mordecai didn't know where it was. He'd had Lumina researching it, and he still couldn't figure it out even with the additional help. But you were smarter than your father," Destiny adds. "And you found it. You just needed the money to purchase it."

Her efforts are rewarded as Darius smiles, tipping his head in acknowledgment of the praise.

"When I saw you down in the dungeons last night," Destiny continues, "I assumed you were leaving Tempest's room. But on the walk over here, I realized my assumption had been incorrect. You hadn't seen Tempest at all, because if you were leaving her room, you would have been walking toward the stairs. Instead, you were coming from the direction of the secret passageway *toward* our rooms. Also," Destiny says, "when I asked Tempest later if you'd led her up there from the dungeons, she looked very bewildered at the mention of your name. That's because she didn't know you as Darius yet. She still knew you as Silver from the night before. She was shocked to see you in the ceremonial room."

"So, where was I coming from, then, if not her chambers?" Darius asks. There's an edge to his voice, like he's tiring of this game and the degree of Destiny's insight.

Her instincts tell her to tread carefully. It's time to wrap this up and get out of here. "The vault," she says. "After it was broken in to two nights ago, you wanted to see if someone else might have gotten clues to the Eye of Gormodeus's whereabouts."

"Yes, that," Darius says, waving off her reductive reasoning as though it were nothing, needing to point out the one thing Destiny hasn't figured out. "But I was mainly trying to look for Morty's will, wanting to make sure there wouldn't be any surprise reveals during the gathering." He laughs, a harsh sound. "So much for that."

Destiny wonders if it's even occurred to Darius that it was his blackmail attempt that put a target on his father. Had the twins not been blackmailed—with the threat of Mordecai disfiguring them in punishment for what Angel did—Minx wouldn't have tried to poison her father. Perhaps he's grateful to Minx for it.

When Destiny came to the island hoping to find family, she wasn't expecting to find two siblings capable of murder.

It feels like more than a coincidence that two murders have bookended Destiny's life thus far. First Liz's and now Mordecai's. The more time she spends with the Scruffmores, the more convinced Destiny is that the two deaths are linked.

"Thank you for your time," she says, preparing to leave and spotting the satchel tucked away at Darius's feet. "I know you have an appointment and don't want to get in your way."

Darius is clearly here to meet with the person who has the Eye of Gormodeus, which is incredibly worrying. The medallion is still missing even though the sigil has been retrieved. If Darius has the medallion, instead of the raccoon being in possession of it, and he then also acquires the relic, he'll have way more power than a man of his nature should be allowed to wield. Destiny will need to warn his mother immediately. She can only hope Hexabus won't be blinded by love for her son when it comes to realizing how potentially dangerous he might be.

As Destiny stands, Darius rasps, "Wait!" He clears his throat, swallowing deeply as his shoulders sag. His pinched expression dissolves into something resigned. Tears gather in the corners of his eyes, and he brushes them away. "I know what you think of me and you're right about a lot of it. I'm not a good man. I've done some really shitty things that I'm not proud of." Pushing his drink away, he sniffs. "But the only reason I went after the Eye of Gormodeus in the first place was to gift it to my father."

Something in the fire pops and fizzles, startling Destiny and Darius.

When he looks up at her again, his eyes glisten. "I'm about to hand over the money I took from Minx for the relic, and as soon as I have it, I'm planning to pass it on to my mother so that we have some kind of weapon to wield as we fight back against whoever killed Morty and stole his talismans."

This admission surprises Destiny, as does the gruffness in his voice, the sound of deep emotion weighing him down.

"All I ask is that you let me be the one to tell my mother about the blackmail. I need to account for my actions, of course, but I'm also hoping hearing it from me will allow her to forgive me."

Studying him, Destiny is relieved not to see any of the telltale signs of lying. He looks contrite, defeated, which means there might be hope for Darius, after all.

Taking a deep breath, Destiny forces herself to say, "I'll give you until eight this evening to confess to the blackmail. After that, I'm afraid I'll have to tell her myself."

"Thank you," he whispers, his voice scraped raw with sorrow.

CHAPTER 67

Hexabus

Tuesday—5:07 p.m.

As they make their way down the stairs to Morty's office, Hexabus updates Destiny on Minx. "She's in the dungeons for now until we get this all figured out. Don't worry, no visitors are allowed."

Hexabus wouldn't put it past Newton to help her daughter escape despite how badly Minx has backstabbed her. After all, this is what it means to be a mother. You'll kill for your children even as they rip your heart out.

Besides, if Minx were able to retrieve the sigil Hexabus confiscated, she could stage a coup against Dominus. If successful, that would put Minx on the throne, promoting Newton to being mother of a queen. For a social climber of epic proportions, that would be a powerful incentive.

"How secure are the dungeons?" Destiny asks, sounding nervous. "Isn't there a chance she could use magic to escape?"

"Her powers have been muted so she can't hurt herself or the guards," Hexabus replies.

The air suddenly turns thick as clotted cream, static making it hard to breathe. The flames crackle in their sconces, molecules of air popping all around them. Hexabus stiffens in alarm.

"What's happening?" Destiny asks, wide-eyed. Strands of her red hair rise as though she's being electrocuted.

"The castle's warning us," Hexabus says, trying to maintain a measured tone so as not to scare Destiny. While Hexabus has been expecting this, it doesn't make it any less terrifying.

"About what?"

"It's picking up signs of dark magic on the island, which means we need to hurry if we're going to stop whoever's coming to claim the throne." Hexabus picks up her pace, jogging down the next few steps, wiping her clammy palms on her cloak. "They have to make an attempt while Dominus is still here to defend it, you see, and they only have until morning when the lockdown ends and the first ferry arrives."

"You didn't find the medallion in Minx's quarters?" Destiny asks, keeping up.

"No, it's not anywhere in the castle," Hexabus replies, annoyed that Minx has outsmarted her. "We've worked summoning charms everywhere."

"Where's Mordecai's sigil now?"

"Killian has it for safekeeping."

Destiny stops and frowns. "How certain are you that you can trust him? After all, he was Mordecai's right-hand man, his most loyal servant—"

"The allegiance spell I worked, and whose conditions he accepted, means he can't betray us," Hexabus says impatiently. They don't have time for this kind of second-guessing. "You must learn to trust the magic, Destiny, even if you don't trust the magician."

Coming to a stop outside Morty's office, Hexabus hovers her hand over the handle just as Darius instructed. But something's wrong. There's none of the prickling in her fingertips that she'd expect, a sensation alerting her to the presence of resistant energy. Reaching out, Hexabus turns the handle, surprised when it yields.

"What?" Destiny asks, seeing Hexabus's confusion.

"The door doesn't have a protective spell on it like there was when Darius snuck in here, which means anyone could have been in here in the meantime."

"Like the raccoon," Destiny muses. "Only this time, it wouldn't need me to bypass any security. It could just walk right in." She's silent for a moment, biting her lip as though mulling something over. "You don't think Maximus and Dominus might have anything to do with the raccoon, do you?" she asks.

Hexabus recalls her meeting with Dominus two nights ago and the almost impossible task she set for him. Maximus wasn't happy about it, of course, insisting that Hexabus was asking too much of his son. But Dominus readily agreed to help once he understood what was at stake, immediately setting out to communicate with the island's cats as her intermediary.

Powers like his take an enormous physical toll on a sorcerer. Plus, Dominus is still processing the shocking news about Mordecai being his father. Hexabus doesn't want Destiny draining his powers even further by asking him pesky questions, not when time is running out. Besides, Hexabus can't entertain the possibility that Dominus might be a double agent. Not when he's her only hope to find the person she's so desperately looking for.

"No." Hexabus is emphatic. "They're definitely not involved. Why would they be? Dominus has already been granted the throne, so what's to gain from it?"

"Maybe the throne isn't all they're after," Destiny says, looking like she wants to push the matter further. She begins to speak, but upon seeing Hexabus's annoyed expression, seems to decide against it.

Opening the door and stepping into the room, Hexabus changes the subject. "Did you find out anything more about the blackmailer?"

It's Destiny's turn to be cagey, which is worrying since

Hexabus doesn't want the young woman keeping secrets at this point. Destiny mutters something about still looking into it, and Hexabus decides to circle back to this later.

Destiny gasps when catching sight of the desk.

"It really is something, isn't it?" Hexabus muses, running her hand along its smooth surface as they skirt around it. "This opening didn't use to be here." She indicates the entryway into the middle of the desk where the throne-like chair sits. "You had to use magic to part the wood so you could get to the center. This is where Morty did all his research and spellcrafting," she says. "Lumina would bring him whatever he requested from the vault so he could work from the source materials here."

As Destiny takes a seat on the throne, Hexabus shivers thinking how much the young woman—with her air of complete concentration as she sets about sharpening her mind like the well-used tool it is—reminds her of Morty.

For the first time, Hexabus thinks it's more than just a possibility that Destiny could be his daughter.

CHAPTER 68

Destiny

Tuesday—5:27 p.m.

After reaching for one of Mordecai's notebooks, Destiny begins paging through it. They're hoping to find something useful to help them deactivate the power of Mordecai's medallion. If the thief can no longer harness its substantial powers, they might not be able to make a successful attempt at the throne. Especially since they don't have the sigil to act as a booster.

Noticing something interesting, Destiny asks, "What are these calculations?"

Hexabus examines a few of the pages. "Morty would study ancient tomes for clues for his spellwork. Many of them needed to be deciphered or translated, requiring multiple attempts at solving them."

"Spellwork?" Destiny asks.

"Yes, any sorcerer can just replicate a spell, merely doing what many have done for centuries before them. But it takes a truly talented one to invent spells of their own, tapping into ancient magical lore to create opportunities to use our powers in all-new ways. He was famous for the elegance and brilliance of his spellwork." Hexabus shakes her head, muttering, "The quintessential evil genius."

Destiny flips through the notebook, seeing variations of the first calculation, though none of these appear to lead to any conclusive answers until the ones right at the back. Not wanting to get distracted, she sets the notebook aside and reaches for one of the leather-bound volumes. "This looks interesting," Destiny says, holding up *Occult Magick for the Darkest Practitioners of the Blackest of Arts*.

"Yes, a bit of light reading before bed," Hexabus retorts.

As Destiny looks through it, she notices a few pages of illustrations. They're compass stars like those tattooed on Morty's face. Turning from them to the strange text, she asks, "What is this written in?"

"Fungellian," Hexabus replies. "It's an ancient occult language."

There isn't time for Destiny to decipher it. Pointing to the only part of the text in the whole volume that's been underlined, Destiny asks, "Are you able to read that?"

Hexabus squints, pulling the book closer. She reaches for an enormous magnifying glass and holds its brass handle up to the page as she begins translating.

"For he who strives for invincibility,
forget mere mortal crimes.
The killing curse will point the way,
if performed the right number of times."

Destiny goes cold, reaching for Morty's notebook again. "How many pieces is the medallion made up of?" she asks. "Eight sigils?"

Hexabus counts them off on her fingers. "Ones for Morty, myself, Mr. Lurcock, Evangeline, Darius, Bramble, Minx, and Angel."

Remembering her dream vision and how the medallion was broken apart, Destiny asks, "Can you do a drawing of it for me so I can see how the sigils all fit together?"

Hexabus reaches for a blank piece of parchment as Destiny hands her a pen. She starts drawing two outer circles, one tucked into the other. Then she does a squiggle in the middle, adding fractured lines radiating out from there. "Kind of like this," she says, regarding her work. "Sorry, I'm not the best artist."

Destiny stares at the illustration, feeling like she's getting close to understanding. "You and Mordecai are the two outer rings, correct?" When Hexabus nods, Destiny continues, "So, with Bramble's sigil being at the center of the medallion, he was the connector, the one who could join all the inner sigils together, right? Meaning that all of Mordecai's children could use their combined powers against him if they banded together?"

"Yes," Hexabus tentatively agrees, "but only if they also managed to turn Killian against Morty because his sigil is in the middle as well."

"And with your own sigil surrounding all of theirs, if you worked with them, you'd be even more powerful with all of them touching and linked?"

"Yes, exactly. Which is why Morty killed Bramble. Without that connector link, even if the rest of us joined forces against him, we couldn't kill him."

Destiny nods, looking back to the very first calculation in Mordecai's notebook.

$$\text{⚥} + \text{⚥} + \text{⚥} = 30$$

$$\text{⊕} + \text{⊕} \times \text{⚥} = 55$$

$$\text{⚥}^{\ominus} \div \text{⚥} = 1000$$

$$\text{⚥} \times \text{∈} + \frac{\text{⊕⊕}}{\text{⊕⊕}} \div \text{⊕} = \text{?}$$

"Mordecai had twenty-four compass stars tattooed on his forehead, right?" Destiny asks.

"Yes," Hexabus replies thickly. "One for each of the victims he claimed, including Bramble."

"You didn't think at the time that his having the tattoos done was strange?" Destiny asks.

"By the time he started getting them," Hexabus says, "our marriage was over in every way that mattered. I considered them proof of Morty's unraveling, which I'd long suspected. They never appeared one by one, straight after each victim was claimed, or I'd like to think I would have put two and two together. He was careful, getting them in batches at seemingly random dates not linked to the last killings."

Destiny turns again to the last calculation that Morty did.

$$\text{☿} + \text{☿} + \text{☿} = 30$$

$$\text{㊐} + \text{㊐} \times \text{☿} = 66$$

$$\text{㊐} \div \text{∈} = 3$$

$$\text{☿} \times \text{∈} + \text{㊐} + \text{㊐} = ?$$

★★[13]

---

13. You now have all the information you require to work out this equation. If you need a clue to assist you, email DestinyWhipClue@gmail.com using the subject line Clue Thirteen. Once you've solved the equation, turn to page 474 to check your answer.

★ ★ ★

"Holy shit," Destiny murmurs as she scribbles the answer.

"What?" Hexabus prompts. "What is it?"

"He was wrong the first time." Destiny pages back to the original calculation and taps it. "When Mordecai did the initial calculation, the magical number answer that he got was twenty-four." She looks up at Hexabus. "But after he killed the twenty-four victims, he still wasn't invincible. He realized he'd made an error, used the wrong calculation."

"Okaaaay," Hexabus says, drawing the word out so that it becomes a question.

"So Mordecai started again, scouring the source material to see where he might have gone wrong." Destiny points to the answer she just solved. "He needed to kill more people," Destiny prompts. When Hexabus still shakes her head, not understanding, Destiny says, "How many of you were at the family gathering?"

Hexabus murmurs each name as she counts on her fingers. "Myself, Mr. Lurcock, Evangeline, Darius, Minx, and Angel. That's six." And then she sees it. "Plus Maximus and Dominus. Oh my god."

Destiny remembers her visions on the night of the gathering when she fell against Mordecai, her hand connecting with his chest. She saw a succession of faces all staring back in horror, their arms raised in self-defense, as well as the birth of two dozen compass stars. But she also saw the family members in the room beginning to drop, one by one.

What she was witnessing was both the past *and* the intended future.

"His aim was to kill as many birds with one stone as possible," Destiny says. "One, stop the rest of his children uniting with you to work against him in any capacity. Two, kill The Player who, according to the prophecy, was thwarting him at every turn. Three, eliminate the child whose power was surpassing his. And four, reach the magical number to make himself invincible."

It's as they're sitting there in stunned silence, grappling with the magnitude of Mordecai's evil, that the door creaks open and a shadow oozes inside.

Dragged behind it is Mordecai's henchman, who's dressed in a three-piece suit paired with his usual white gloves. He stops just inside the doorway, standing with his spine ramrod straight like a soldier reporting for duty.

Destiny's chest tightens. She doesn't care about the binding spell Hexabus has cast on him. Anyone who could enable their master to work the kind of dark magic Mordecai performed has to be truly evil themselves. What Hexabus has done is make the butler a puppet performing acts of servitude because the magic forces him to. But without that—if he had free will to behave however he wanted—how long ago might he have sunk a dagger into their backs to avenge his master?

He studies Destiny, eyebrows raised as though reading her thoughts. And then his stern features soften when his scrutiny moves from hers, concern replacing his customary stoicism.

Following his gaze, Destiny sees that he's studying Hexabus, taking in her stricken expression.

"Mrs. Scruffmore," he says in that gruff voice of his. "Are you quite alright?"

Hexabus shakes her head, her face crumpling as she dissolves into tears. "Oh, Killian," she says. "It's so awful."

Displaying the kind of reflexes Destiny suspected him capable of upon their first meeting, Mr. Lurcock springs into action. Within three strides, he's at Hexabus's side.

She stands and turns to him, melting into his open arms.

What the hell? After a few startled seconds, Destiny finally understands. *Ah. So, not Maximus Scruffmore, after all.*

CHAPTER 69

Hexabus

Tuesday—6:02 p.m.

With her cheek pressed against her lover's chest, Hexabus allows each thud of his heartbeat to tug a little more at the knot of her. It was terrifying enough to believe Morty was about to take the life of another of her children, but to now know that he planned to kill them all is almost more than she can take.

It's been a struggle keeping it together the past few weeks, trying so hard to figure out what Morty was planning so they could stop him. And to realize that even after everything they still had no clue is enough to undo her completely.

She begins to cry in Killian's arms, her body racked with sobs.

He doesn't say anything in response, only makes that low grumbling noise that she finds so soothing because she doesn't just hear it, but feels it reverberating through her like waves of consolation. When the worst of it has passed, she pulls away from him, dabbing at her eyes. He withdraws his handkerchief from his pocket and hands it to her.

She wipes her nose. "Morty thought his original calculation of the twenty-four was wrong," Hexabus says. "He thought he needed more souls and he was planning to reap them at the gathering while eliminating all the threats that the prophecy foretold."

Shock irons out Killian's perplexed features as he clearly realizes, along with Hexabus, that what they experienced—as they raced against time to anticipate what Morty had planned—was a complete failure of imagination regarding how far he would go to get what he wanted.

Looking to Destiny, Hexabus expects the young woman to be staring at them, scandalized. Instead, she's averted her gaze to give them some privacy, which Hexabus appreciates.

She sits and Killian pulls up a chair next to her. "So, I guess this is where I tell you that Killian and I are... Well, it's complicated," Hexabus says, laughing self-consciously as she sniffs. She swats at the black smudge her mascara has left on Killian's white shirt. "I'm sure this is quite the surprise."

"Yes. I was convinced it was Maximus." Destiny's words shock Hexabus.

"Max?" Hexabus laughs.

Killian stiffens beside her.

Oh, dear. He's always been ornery around Maximus, who's so very charismatic and such a terrible flirt. It didn't help that Morty suspected his brother of having a romantic interest in her.

It must have been insecurity that made Killian keep pace with Max two nights ago when she first arrived at the castle, him wanting to welcome Hexabus before Max could. But no matter how handsome and charming Max is, Hexabus has never been attracted to him. It was Killian's presence that unsettled her so much upon her arrival; she wanted to escape the kitchen to be alone with *him.*

"Definitely not Max," Hexabus says. Turning to Killian, she affectionately studies the firm line of his jaw and the wrinkles around his eyes. "I've been in love with Killian for a really, really long time."

Destiny looks skeptical. "I have a lot of questions," she says.

"Let's answer them for you as quickly as possible," Hexabus replies, all too aware that time is running out.

CHAPTER 70

Choose Your Own Conundrum
Killian

Forty-Two Years Earlier

You're twenty-three-year-old Killian Lurcock and you're attending a Sorcerer's Guild event at the Griswolds' mansion in the hope of making useful connections you can leverage once you've graduated. But while everyone else orbits you—coming together in pairs or in clusters of three or four before splitting apart and then forming again—you mostly stand alone, a tranquil island in a sea of frenetic personalities. While you know you should be making small talk and engaging, you wear your solitude like a custom-made suit, quite comfortable with sipping on your tepid wine while studying the family's eclectic art collection.

You notice her before she notices you, a beautiful young woman who makes heads turn in her wake. She looks restless and slightly disappointed, as though she were hoping for something this soiree is not able to deliver. But when she spots you, her frown clears, and she makes her way over.

"Mind if I join you?" she asks, turning to examine the same painting you're studying.

"By all means," you reply.

She startles at the sound of your voice as so many people do when hearing you speak for the first time.

"Reminiscent of boulders shifting deep within the earth?" you ask. "Almost like giants gargling with rocks?"

"I beg your pardon?"

"My voice," you clarify. "That's what I've been told it sounds like."

She laughs and nods. "Now that you mention it, yes." She reaches out a hand to shake yours. "I'm Hexabus Dwellhorn," she says.

Pretending not to see her outstretched hand, you turn back to the painting. "Killian Lurcock," you reply.

To your relief, she doesn't appear offended, and you're able to quickly gloss over the awkward moment as you begin discussing whether a wall-sized painting called *Orgy in Hell* really should be hung in a dining room where people are likely to be nibbling on canapés while examining the obscene goings-on conducted by the demons above them.

"It's obviously not pornography if it's painted by a Renaissance master," Hexabus says, making you laugh.

That is the genesis of your friendship. Though, if you were being entirely honest with yourself, you'd admit that you fell in love with her within an hour of meeting. You suspect she has feelings for you too when she begins making a point of touching you every time you get together, sometimes placing a teasing hand on your arm or reaching out to flick a lock of hair from your eyes.

While there's a part of you that thrills each time she begins reaching out, you don't experience any enjoyment in the actual contact. For, each time her fingers connect with you, you are seared by visions you know you shouldn't be privy to. Like clods of sand being shoveled over her father's grave. And her mother's face, staring up, pleading, desperate for the cancer gnawing away at her insides to stop using such sharp teeth.

Besides the invasion of privacy being so troubling that you struggle to look Hexabus in the eye, the sorrow that accompanies the visions takes your breath away. With your special gift, you feel her emotions at their most fresh and fierce, not the faded way she experiences them in the moment while standing there with you.

This is what makes you an island. This gift. This curse.

And while you would do anything to be rid of it, it isn't one that allows itself to be declined.

When Hexabus confesses her feelings for you one day while you're walking in the botanical gardens, you have two options.

You can either admit how you've been invading the privacy of her soul for weeks on end, and will continue to do so for the rest of your lives if you marry, predicting that her feelings will end up drowning you.

Or you can spare her that torment by pretending not to feel the same way in return.

What do you do?

A. Confess—go to page 331.

B. Spare her the torment—go to page 333.

OPTION A:
CONFESS

You confess your feelings to Hexabus and explain the curse and how it works. At first, she's upset that you didn't confide in her before, embarrassed by all the things she's revealed to you without ever meaning to. As you suspected, she feels as though you've x-rayed every inch of her without permission, almost like you've read her journals, only so much worse.

But she forgives you and ends up blaming herself instead for forcing those interactions on you, understanding them for the form of assault they are.

You tell her that being together will require enormous sacrifices on her part, that despite her being such an affectionate person, one who never hesitates before she reaches out to another, she will have to learn how to stifle any impulse to touch you, loving you with a barrier forever between you.

Even worse, she will have to starve that part of herself that craves affection in return. You cannot ever hold her hand or stroke her face. You cannot kiss her passionately or make love to her. You will never be able to give her children, and so if she has any dreams of being a mother, she will need to suffocate them.

All that you have to offer in return is a lifetime of living as if cloistered in a cult of sensory deprivation. That, and your love.

And because she loves you in return, she accepts your offer-

ing, though it's worse than just being meager—it's like present-
ing someone with fruit that's riddled with maggots.

At first, it's fine. You find ways to make it work. She never
complains because that's the kind of woman she is. But as time
goes by, you see the toll it takes on her, how the sacrifice erodes
her until what remains is just the husk of the vibrant woman
you met all those years ago.

You suspect there's a part of her that hates you for it, wishing you'd done the merciful thing and broken her heart quickly
and cleanly, rather than in increments, day by day.

And so, one night while she's asleep in the single bed that's
positioned next to yours, you arise quietly so as not to awaken
her, and you leave so that you might give her some chance of
happiness.

She ends up marrying Mordecai Scruffmore a year later.
Your honesty did nothing but delay the inevitable.

Go to page 336.

OPTION B:
SPARE HER THE TORMENT

Lying to Hexabus, and seeing the terrible hurt in her eyes, is more painful than you could ever have imagined. But you tell yourself every minute, then every hour, that you've done the right thing. Because allowing her to love you is to either make her the front-row spectator to your rapid descent into madness, or to condemn her to a sterile existence in which she'd be starved of any affection as you try to save yourself from drowning in her.

She deserves better.

You run into your friend Prince Mordecai Scruffmore while you and Hexabus are at another event, and you can immediately see how besotted he is with her. It's like standing outside yourself and being a witness to the exact moment you met her and how completely she captivated you.

Morty doesn't play games; he makes it clear how infatuated he is. His interest makes you uncomfortable. While the future king is charming and charismatic, there are moments when you've seen his guard drop to reveal a darkness glistening just below the surface, almost as though you were staring into the desolate blackness of a bottomless pit.

Hexabus, tired of the games you've been playing with her—selfishly keeping her close when you should have cut her free—responds to him. At first, she's just trying to make you jealous, but soon enough she caves to Morty's aggressive wooing. And why not, since she is the object of every young woman's envy, the one who's been singled out to be future queen.

You allow yourself one night to fall apart and rage over how desperately unfair it all is. The next day, you vow to get out of their way so they can fall in love without your being an impediment. You convince yourself that Hexabus will make Morty a better man.

A year later, on Valentine's Day, you stand there as his best man while your friend marries the woman you love. You tell yourself that you'll get over it, that there are worse things to endure.

You're still struggling to find gainful employment that doesn't require you to be around others too much. Hell would be working in an office, dozens of people accidentally brushing up against you in the elevator each day or wanting to shake your hand during social functions.

So when Morty reaches out, saying he needs someone he can trust as he prepares to take over the throne from his father, you leap at the chance to work with him at the remote castle. You tell yourself it's because Morty knows about your gift and will create an environment in which you can work around it, but you know it's mostly because it means you'll get to see Hexabus each day.

A year after you begin working for Morty, he returns from a trip brandishing a package he's excited to show you. Upon opening it, you discover a bundle of neatly folded white cloth. Seeing your nonplussed expression, Morty bursts into laughter. He explains that it isn't just any old cloth, but in fact a magical fabric that, when made into a pair of gloves, will act as a shield, preventing you from experiencing the full force of the psychic assaults you've thought would be your burden for the rest of your life.

Six months after that, he returns from another journey with two talismans that, when worn, offer even further protection.

And three months after that, he acquires the eye-wateringly expensive source materials that enable him to invent the kind of spellwork that will allow you to be intimate with someone for the first time without the experience being so traumatizing.

You are grateful beyond measure to your friend who has made an almost-normal life possible for you. You try not to wish this had all happened in time for you to make his wife your own.

Go to page 336.

CHAPTER 71

Hexabus

Tuesday—6:28 p.m.

Once they've filled Destiny in on how they met, Hexabus is tempted to cut off this avenue of discussion and insist they all return their attention to Morty's source materials. Time is marching on and they're not any closer to figuring out how to deactivate the medallion. But for them to work effectively as a team, Destiny needs to trust Killian as much as Hexabus does. Which, for Destiny, means asking all of her questions so she can reach her own conclusions about him.

"Is there a name for your special powers?" Destiny asks.

"I'm an empathician. A sorcerer who's able to see a person's entire library of memories, and feel a lifetime of their emotions, just upon touching them."

"That's why you wear gloves all the time," Destiny says. "And why you won't shake hands."

"Yes, exactly," Hexabus replies on Killian's behalf, hoping to hurry things along. "He's since learned how to control it, but when we first met, it was a constant struggle."

Destiny's brow puckers. "Forgive me for asking," she says to Killian. "You referred to Morty as your 'best friend,' but that implies a relationship based on an equal footing. Two people who have mutual respect and affection for one another. And yet…" She trails off.

"I became his servant," Killian finishes for her. "You're wondering how that happened?"

Destiny nods.

"It began," he says, "as any abuse of power generally does. So slowly and insidiously that you don't even notice it at first." He looks to Hexabus here, silently asking her to explain something that has always been terribly painful for him.

"Morty did so much for Killian that completely changed his life," Hexabus says, "and he was immensely grateful for all of it. What he didn't realize, though, was that none of those actions were gifts of friendship, but would rather come at an extreme cost, because Morty knew exactly how to weaponize gratitude. At first," she continues, "he asked Killian to come work for him in an assistant capacity, saying he needed the help of a contemporary he could trust. Soon enough, though, as Morty began to walk the dark path, he began to wield that power in cruel and unsettling ways, setting all kinds of trials for Killian to test his loyalty."

Hexabus explains about all the times she watched Morty degrade Killian, how she couldn't understand why her friend didn't walk away. She will always feel responsible for his appalling treatment because it turned out that Killian was staying on, allowing himself to be humiliated by Morty, purely so he could keep an eye on Hexabus and offer whatever protection he could.

Six years after marrying Morty, when his father stepped down from the throne, Hexabus was heavily pregnant with Evangeline at his coronation as the Sorcerer King. She had been queen for barely a month when she finally confronted him about one of his many affairs. Morty took great pleasure in informing her that he'd only pursued her because he knew Killian was in love with her. Plus, Hexabus had a circular birthmark that matched his own, a sign if ever there was one that she had genetic material he wanted his children to share.

He'd warned her not to even think of leaving; that he'd let her know when he was done with her. Morty was so certain of her obedience, and so assured of his power, that it never occurred to him that Hexabus and Killian might find their way back to each other, both seeking shelter from the storm of Mordecai.

"So, Bramble was actually *your* son?" Destiny asks Killian in the way of a nurse dressing a wound, taking care not to cause unnecessary pain while performing an essential task.

"Yes," he says. "But that's not why I tried to save him." Looking back to Hexabus, he shakes his head so sadly that it breaks her heart all over again. "I tried to save them all."

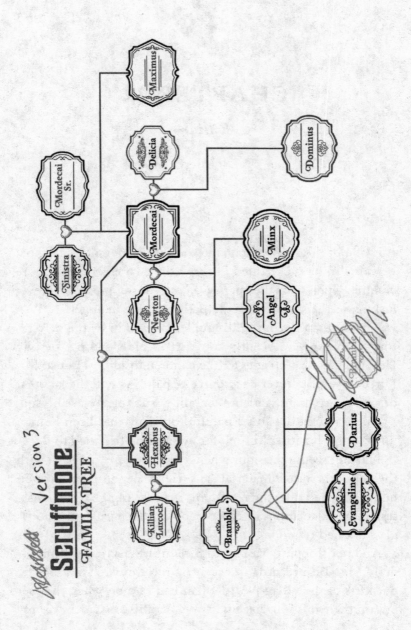

CHAPTER 72

Killian

Tuesday—6:51 p.m.

It is one of the smaller tragedies of Killian Lurcock's life that
he came to be nicknamed Lurk by the two elder Scruffmore
children when what they perceived as a sinister presence forever
lurking in the shadows was actually a guardian angel.

That Killian's own son, Bramble, knew him by the deroga-
tory moniker—innocently copying his older siblings despite
Hexabus's many entreaties for the children to address him as Mr.
Lurcock—will forever be a source of pain. As will the fact that
despite the constant vigilance, he still wasn't able to save his son.

These regrets are just a handful of many that keep Killian
up at night, berating himself for everything he failed to do.

Like not seeing the signs when Morty became obsessed with
the dark-arts source materials, his friend spending hours upon
hours hunched over them with his magnifying glass, furiously
scribbling calculations in his notebook as the Scruffmore hourglass drained of sand.

And not stopping Morty from claiming his first victim, el-
derly Miss Beauregard, an eccentric recluse who lived on the
outskirts of the village. All Killian had known when they set
out on their mission that night was that his assistance was re-

quired as Mordecai harnessed the power of the moonless hours to conduct particularly complicated spellwork.

It was only after Morty opened the woman's rickety back gate and then led them through the darkness to the unlocked door that Killian began to feel deeply uneasy.

"Though I wasn't consciously aware of it at the time," he says, explaining it all to Destiny now just as he explained it to Hexabus a few weeks ago, "it was probably seeing her cat that gave me the idea. The ginger-and-white creature was sitting on the bedroom windowsill, its orange eyes trained on me."

Killian wasn't sure what they were doing at the cottage, but he can still recall the horror he felt when Morty cocked his hand with the thumb, index, and middle fingers in the killing spell position, like he was pointing a gun but holding its barrel at a 180-degree angle.

"There was no way I could stop Morty without it being viewed as treason. Besides, I simply didn't have enough magical power to do so. All I could do was react with a protective spell."

It was silent and completely lacking in the showmanship of Morty's flashy kind of magic. When the old woman gasped and went rigid before slumping back against her pillows, Killian thought he'd failed completely, that he'd done nothing at all.

Upon satisfying himself that he'd acquired his first soul, Morty turned and left the room.

That's when Killian took off his gloves to lay his hands upon Miss Beauregard's still-warm body, not quite believing that she was dead. What he saw, as all the images flashed through him like a movie projected against the white screen of his mind, was someone belittled by a tyrannical father and then jilted at the altar, a woman who'd been beaten down so relentlessly by other people undervaluing her that she'd given up on relationships a long time ago, preferring the company of a lifetime of pets.

Her cat mewled then, as though wanting to confide a secret. Killian walked over and examined its name tag, which read

Wombat. Reaching out to stroke the creature's velvety fur, he was accosted with the exact same images as he'd experienced while touching the dead woman moments before. That's when he realized his protective spell had actually worked, allowing Miss Beauregard's soul to enter the cat's body as she died.

It gave Killian some measure of solace that the old woman would now be close to the creature she had loved so dearly in life, having spent hours with it upon her lap as she stroked it like a security blanket. He was thinking how he might bring the creature back to the castle when the cat yowled, scampering off into the night.

In the weeks that followed, Morty confided to Killian the magical number of souls he needed to reap in order to attain invincibility. Killian tried everything he could to figure out who Mordecai's next victims would be so he could either convince them to leave the island for a short time or shield them in some other way. All he could ever be sure of, however, was that the killings would happen on the darkest nights; there appeared to be no logic as to how Morty picked those he chose for death.

"At first," Killian says, "when he still appeared to have some semblance of a conscience, he targeted older people, like Billy Hastings, who ran the laundromat, and Mr. Carmichael, the village grouch. But then," he says, lifting his gaze from his hands so he can look Destiny in the eyes, "he began to target children. And that…was entirely my fault." Anguish and guilt gnaw at him. "As was the fact that Morty thought he had to claim another eight lives at the family gathering when his original calculation was actually correct."

"What do you mean?" Destiny asks, head cocked.

"My protective spells meant Morty wasn't collecting any souls at all toward his tally," Killian explains. "Each person he killed, instead of fueling Morty's strength, had their soul redirected into one of the island's many feral cats with the hope that I might figure out how to revive them one day. When

Morty didn't begin to feel more powerful, he first assumed it was because he was taking the life force of older people. Surely younger victims, with more vitality, would make him feel stronger."

"These are all unintended outcomes to good deeds," Destiny says, her voice hushed, sounding much older and wiser than her years. "You were doing your best to save as many lives as possible. There was no way you could anticipate what the fallout would be, not with the limited information you had at the time."

Killian's breath hitches at the possibility that she might be right. He wants so much to believe it, to find absolution where forgiveness has refused to tread.

"You were the one who arranged the bodies so lovingly, weren't you?" Destiny asks, surprising him. There's such empathy in her gaze that Killian struggles to look at her. "You took off your gloves for each of them so that you could stage them in a way that paid tribute to who they were."

Killian swallows the lump rising in his throat. He nods. "Giving them that small dignity was the least I could do considering I couldn't save them."

CHAPTER 73

Destiny

Tuesday—7:14 p.m.

Studying Mr. Lurcock's immeasurably sad expression, Destiny is reminded once again of how dubious one's judgment can be rendered by preconceptions. There's nothing remotely sinister about the man. He's just someone who, like her, has been grossly misunderstood.

"Mr. Lurcock—" she says.

"Please," he replies, "call me Killian."

Destiny nods, accepting his graciousness with gratitude. "Killian, do you think that's why Mordecai...targeted Bramble? Because he knew Bramble was your son?"

Both Hexabus and Killian shake their heads emphatically. "No, definitely not," Killian replies. "Believe me, that's not something he would have been able to hide. We wouldn't be alive today talking to you had he even suspected it."

Hexabus reaches for a bottle of whiskey along with three crystal glasses. She holds one up to Destiny, who shakes her head. After pouring drinks for Killian and herself, Hexabus conjures ice, magically wringing it out of the damp air so that each jagged clump of it plops into the amber liquid with an ecstatic sigh.

Passing a glass to Killian, Hexabus says, "Morty was born with a birthmark of a perfect circle on his chest, directly over his heart. He viewed it as a stamp of approval from the magical gods, like a bull's-eye target, proof that he was the chosen one. I also have a circle birthmark, but mine is on my shoulder. He took that as the sign that we were meant to be together. Straight after each of our children were born, he checked them for similar birthmarks. Evangeline's and Darius's were both abstract, nothing definitive. That's why Morty was so disappointed, refusing to bestow his name upon Darius. He was keeping that for a more worthy candidate he was certain would eventually come along."

"Ah," Destiny says, realizing something. "That's how you knew who the twins' father was. They were also born with magical birthmarks."

"Yes, exactly," Hexabus says. "Though theirs were very faint, I recognized them for what they were."

Destiny suddenly thinks of her own distinctive hourglass birthmark on her wrist and how that might be further proof that Mordecai was, indeed, her father.

"When Bramble was born," Killian continues, "he coincidentally had a distinctive mark on his chest in the same place as Morty's. It was a keyhole shape rather than a circle, but Morty still took that as a positive sign of his power."

"Why not give Bramble his own name, then?" Destiny asks. "Why not call him Mordecai?"

"Because there was always a chance that he could produce a more worthy heir down the line, which is what he was trying to do with Minx and Angel."

"So, it came down to the prophecy, then," Destiny muses. "That, and the power of the medallion, which he belatedly realized could be used against him. That's why he killed Bramble?"

Killian nods. "I think so. Though I never completely understood the power of the sigils and how they worked together, I suspect that he put Bramble's in the middle of the medallion when he forged it so he could leverage that power since all signs pointed to Bramble being his most powerful child."

Hexabus sounds brittle when she adds, "That's probably why

the force of Morty's magic completely obliterated Bramble, the only victim to die in that way. He wanted to be a hundred percent sure that he'd completely eliminated the threat." She squeezes Killian's hand, and he squeezes it back, the couple united in their shared pain.

"And you two…" Destiny tentatively begins, not wanting to be indelicate but needing every answer that might somehow help her.

"We ended things after Bramble died," Hexabus says. "Both of us were too heartbroken to continue the relationship. We weren't strong enough to see one another's pain reflected back at us. It would have been like living in a hall of haunted mirrors." And then she smiles. "We recently found our way back to each other, though."

"Can I ask why you continued to work for Mordecai even after he and Hexabus divorced?" Destiny asks Killian.

"Because I knew what Morty was capable of. And I knew how frustrated he was that the killings hadn't empowered him. He was never going to be satisfied until he'd found a way to gain that degree of power, and it terrified me what he would do with it. I needed to stay close so I could keep an eye on him."

"And thank god he did," Hexabus adds, "otherwise Killian wouldn't have seen Morty going into that same frenzied mode recently, recognizing the signs."

"So, Killian was your informant, Hexabus?" Destiny asks. "The one you told me about?"

"He was *one* of them," she clarifies. "I got an anonymous letter telling me about the power of the medallion and how we might join forces with our sigils to incapacitate Morty." In response to Destiny's unspoken question, she says, "I still don't know who sent that."

That's the part that bothers Destiny. Whoever tipped off Hexabus saved the entire family from being murdered. What was their motivation if not to prevent a travesty? Their actions ensured that the entire Scruffmore family will forever be indebted to them, so why haven't they stepped up and claimed responsibility along with everyone's gratitude?

Oblivious to Destiny's agitated thoughts, Hexabus continues, "Killian reached out to me a few weeks ago, telling me about Morty's killing spree and what really happened to Bramble. He only did it so that I'd understand the magnitude of the danger, and so I'd work with him to stop Morty." She sighs. "I just wish he'd told me everything before."

"I was trying to protect you," Killian protests, his voice strained.

"I didn't need your protection, Killian!" Hexabus snaps, withdrawing her hand and turning her body away from his as she crosses her arms over her chest.

Destiny sighs. "Why didn't you tell me all this before?"

Hexabus tasked Destiny with building a jigsaw puzzle but then withheld more than half the pieces, thereby setting her up for failure.

"I'm sorry," Hexabus says, clearly uncomfortable being the one now having to defend her decisions, "but I couldn't be honest without opening up a whole can of worms about Killian and me. Also, I couldn't take the chance that you might let any of it slip to Evangeline. If she heard about the cats, she'd get her hopes up that her brother might be out there, only to potentially have them dashed all over again."

Hexabus's eyes fill with tears. She takes a thoughtful sip of her drink, crunching the ice, which Destiny imagines must taste like melancholy. Killian automatically tops up her glass. Whether the act is out of chivalry or a lifetime of service, Destiny can't say.

"That's why I reached out to Maximus before we all came to the island for the gathering," Hexabus says once she's centered herself. "I wanted to see if Dominus could use his gift with animals to help us find Bramble, so we could be certain he was still out there before telling anyone. So many of those cats were granted unusually long lives, but that doesn't mean… something hasn't happened to him in the intervening years."

Destiny is awash with guilt, remembering how her umbrella knocked into that poor cat when she first arrived on the island.

Rubbing her temples, she feels a headache taking root as she learns of yet another thing that's been kept from her. She's frustrated beyond measure at how much brainpower and energy she's wasted trying to figure out answers that Hexabus could have immediately provided. All this time she's been suspicious of Maximus and Dominus when they have, in fact, been allies.

"So, Dominus has been working with you this whole time?" Destiny asks, needing to be certain of her facts.

"Yes," Hexabus says. "He's been trying to have conversations with the cats to find out if Bramble is...still alive."

Another thought occurs to Destiny. "You lied to me about the number of sigils working against Mordecai on the night he died," Destiny says.

Hexabus startles, looking guilty.

"It wasn't just yours and Evangeline's. Killian's was used too. So that makes three as you all laid hands on him."

"Our plan," Hexabus begins cautiously, "mine and Killian's, was to use the combined forces of our sigils to incapacitate Morty at the gathering. We weren't sure if it would be enough, but I was reluctant to get Darius involved, as I worried that telling him about the threat would set him off, making him an unpredictable variable. And I didn't want to ask Eva for help because she tends to overthink everything. But then," Hexabus continues, "when she got that message and went to dig up Bramble's grave, I had to tell her. Though, of course, I left out the parts about Killian and me, and anything to do with the cats. Once she knew, Eva was determined to help me stop Morty."

"Three sigils still wouldn't have been enough to kill him," Killian insists, "because they weren't connected, which is exactly why Morty ensured Bramble's sigil could never be used against him."

And then, as if conjured by their earlier conversation, Maximus suddenly appears like a specter at the room's threshold, chest heaving from exertion.

Destiny sits frozen, staring at him, not sure what he's doing here but certain it can't be anything good.

Following her gaze, Hexabus spins around. "What is it, Max? What's wrong?"

Maximus takes a moment to catch his breath before declaring, "Minx escaped."

"What?" Hexabus yelps. "How?"

Maximus glares at Killian. "Your *boyfriend* over here clearly didn't work a strong enough spell to mute her powers."

Killian is immediately on his feet. "There was nothing wrong with my spell, Maximus! Someone must have helped her."

Hexabus and Destiny reach the conclusion at the same time. "Angel!"

"No," Maximus says. "She and Newton have been in the great hall the whole time. If Minx had help, it wasn't from her sister." He rubs the peppered stubble on his jaw. "Dominus is out speaking with the cats, so I'm going to head out and look for her on my own."

"I'll come with you," Killian says, scraping his chair back.

"No." Maximus holds up a hand. "Stay here and protect the castle. I'll send word if I find anything." With that, he reaches forward, grabs Killian's drink, and downs it in one swallow before turning, his cloak flapping in his wake.

"Shit," Hexabus says, groaning as Killian slams a hand against the desk in frustration.

"Is this why the air crackled earlier?" Destiny asks. "Because Minx escaped and was working dark magic?"

"Could be," Hexabus says grimly.

So much for trusting the magic. Destiny automatically reaches up to stroke her amulet.

Killian's gaze is drawn first to the amulet and then to the birthmark on Destiny's wrist.

His intensity as he studies her sparks a realization. If she wants an answer from him, she senses now's the moment to push for it. "When you first saw me," Destiny says, "you did a double take, like you couldn't believe I was here at the castle. Which can only mean one thing." She holds her breath for a moment, terrified to speak the words because so much hinges on the answer they will elicit. "You recognized me, didn't you?"

Killian goes pale. He's quiet for a few excruciating seconds, and then he nods.

"Mordecai had you keeping tabs on me," Destiny says, "because I was his daughter. I thought you looked familiar when I first met you, and that explains why. So, you knew who I was. You just didn't know what I was doing at the castle because neither of you had invited me."

When Killian doesn't correct her, only stares at her sadly, Destiny has all the answer she needs.

As Hexabus erupts at Killian, saying she knew he was keeping something from her despite his many assurances that wasn't the case, Destiny tunes them both out.

Mordecai Scruffmore was my father, she thinks. Destiny doesn't know why she's so stunned. After all, it's what she suspected all along. Perhaps it's knowing what she now does about him that makes it feel so surreal.

She came here searching for family and connection. What she discovered instead is that she is the daughter of a man whose god complex made him murder dozens of innocent people in the name of his so-called genius.

But Destiny too is a genius. And it's Nate who called it during his last hours on this earth. She too is unhinged.

It's terrifying that Destiny is her father's daughter in more ways than she could ever have imagined.

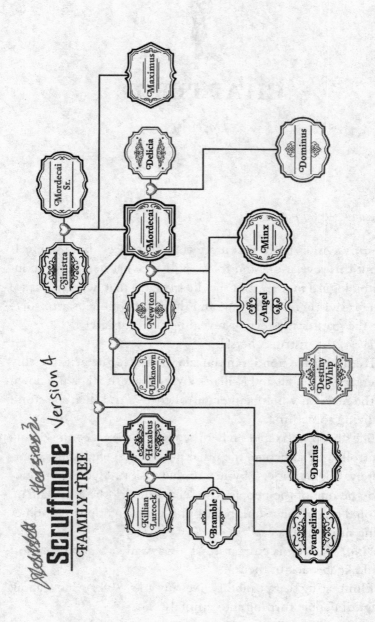

Scruffmore Version 4 FAMILY TREE

Maximus

Delicia

Dominus

Mordecai Sr.

Mordecai

Sinistra

Minx

Newton

Angel

Unknown

Destiny Whip

Hexabus

Darius

Killian Lurcock

Bramble

Evangeline

CHAPTER 74

Destiny

Tuesday—8:05 p.m.

Destiny wishes there was more time to process how she feels about this revelation, and to ask Killian what he knows about her biological mother. But she doesn't have that luxury because time is swiftly running out, and they're still no closer to solving the greater mystery or revealing the murderer.

Focus, she instructs herself.

Recalling the nonogram puzzle she left for herself, Destiny interrupts Hexabus and Killian's lovers' spat. "It all comes down to the raccoon who's being controlled—" And then she stops, realizing something.

She's been so fixated on her theory that the raccoon is being controlled by someone, the other possibilities eluded her completely. She's annoyed by her tunnel vision. "Could the raccoon be one of the people Mordecai killed?" she asks Killian. "Could one of their souls perhaps have gotten trapped in something other than a cat?"

"No." Killian is emphatic. "I always, always used cats so I could keep track of them."

Eliminating that possibility, Destiny asks, "Okay. How about magical people turning into animals?"

"That's possible," Killian replies, "though no one in the family has that particular ability. At least not that I'm aware of."

"Is it a gift they'd need to be born with?" Destiny asks.

"Yes, like I was born an empathician," Killian offers. "And how you were born a seer."

"No, wait," Hexabus ventures, "it would also be possible, theoretically, that with the right spellwork, you could acquire and develop an ability even if you weren't born with it."

"Okay, let's say a sorcerer developed it," Destiny posits. "Would they have to be either fully human *or* fully raccoon at any given time?"

Hexabus's eyes widen as she realizes that Destiny means someone splitting themselves in two so they can be part-human, in a room full of other people, and also part-raccoon elsewhere. "It would take some very complicated spellcasting."

"But it's not impossible?" Destiny asks.

"Not if you figured out the right spell," Hexabus says, then quickly adds, "*and* if your psyche allows for that kind of fracturing. Few sorcerers could achieve it without going mad."

Destiny immediately thinks of Darius, how rapidly he oscillates between sunshine and darkness. Would he be capable of performing that warped kind of magic?

Checking the time, Destiny realizes it's now past the deadline she gave him for confessing to his mother about the blackmail. They need the Eye of Gormodeus if they stand any chance at all of stopping Minx, especially since they haven't found anything helpful in terms of deactivating the medallion's powers.

And yet Darius is nowhere to be seen.

Destiny recalls the tears glistening in his eyes at the inn, how contrite he appeared to be. Did she misread his sincerity? Has she been conned, effectively giving Darius more time to prepare for his fight for the throne?

Dread settles over her like a seeping mist as it becomes clear that that's exactly what she's done. All this time Destiny suspected Hexabus of flawed judgment—losing objectivity about Dominus because of her affair with Maximus—but here Destiny is, guilty of the same crime.

"Killian." Destiny's voice jars in the quiet office. "Where's the sigil?"

"I have it here," he says, patting his chest. "I didn't want to leave it unprotected in my quarters." He reaches into his jacket and unbuttons the pocket. Dipping his hand inside, he freezes, the color draining from his face.

"What is it?" Hexabus asks.

Killian frantically searches his pocket before delving into another and then another. "It's...it's gone," he stammers, disbelief slackening his features.

"What do you mean?" Hexabus demands. "Did you lose it?"

"No!" he exclaims. "It was buttoned closed." He shuts his eyes to remember. "I took the jacket off briefly in my chambers. But only for a few minutes. I've worn it the rest of the time."

Picturing a raccoon's hand deftly slipping inside a pocket, Destiny groans. "Hexabus," she says. "I think I know who took it!" And then she fills them in on the details of her meeting with Darius and how foolish she was to trust him. "I think he's the raccoon and that he snuck into Killian's room to steal the sigil to add to his collection of artifacts."

"No," Hexabus says, blanching. "There's no way!"

"How can you be sure?" Destiny presses. "He had all those magical lessons with Balzanon. Who knows what he was taught in terms of transformation magic? And if Darius didn't intend to use the Eye of Gormodeus for himself, why hasn't he come to deliver it to you?"

"He might still be on his way," Hexabus replies, optimism buoying her voice. "It's barely after eight, and you said yourself he was drunk when you saw him." Turning to Killian, she says, "Can you—"

"I'll go look for him," Killian says. He's out the door in a few short strides.

"He's probably passed out," Hexabus says, clearly in denial. "Killian will find him and bring the Eye to us."

Unable to sit and wait for Killian to return with the bad news that Darius cannot be found—not without berating herself endlessly for being so gullible—Destiny stands. Reaching a decision, she says, "I need to see Lumina Le Roux's chambers."

Hexabus startles. "Why?"

"We've been acting like Mordecai's death was the first crime," Destiny says. "But it wasn't. It was the second, after Lumina's kidnapping, which means the two must be related. She disappeared from her quarters within the castle, right?"

Hexabus nods.

"Then we need to visit the scene of the crime."

CHAPTER 75

Hexabus

Tuesday—8:32 p.m.

As they approach Lumina's quarters on the first floor, Hexabus grapples with the awful possibility that Darius might be their villain. On the night of Morty's murder, Destiny suggested that Darius's attack might have killed Morty, but Hexabus waved it off, insisting her son's magic wasn't strong enough. But what if she was wrong and he'd gained dark powers beyond anything she could have imagined?

She could understand his killing Morty in self-defense or even in a fit of rage. But if that were the case, Darius would have owned up to it and then made his interest in the crown known. If Destiny's right and he has been scheming and black-mailing, it certainly suggests more nefarious intentions.

No, she can't believe that of her son, who isn't capable of anything that terrible. The likeliest culprit is Minx.

Far easier for Hexabus to focus on right now, rather than the possibility Darius has committed patricide, is Killian's treachery.

She thinks back to when Killian left her room two nights ago, how certain she was that he was withholding something. She was right, but try as she might, she can't figure out how Destiny factors into it. Why keep that kind of secret for Morty?

Unless there's more to it, with Destiny just being the tip of the iceberg in terms of what Killian's been hiding.

And just when Hexabus thought they might actually have a shot at happiness. What a fool she's been.

As she opens Lumina's door and they step into the historian's quarters, Hexabus waits for guidance from Destiny, who takes in the clutter. The space hasn't been properly cleaned since Lumina disappeared, Morty insisting the rooms remain exactly as they were just in case there was a clue to be found. Becoming aware of an unpleasant odor, she asks, "Do you smell that? It's...musky."

"Like wet dog," Destiny says. "My chambers smelled the same this morning. I assumed it's from the damp in the walls."

"No," Hexabus says. "That smells more like chalk. This is something different." Gazing around the space, she says archly, "So, this is the den of debauchery where Morty and Lumina conducted much of their affair." At Destiny's shocked expression, Hexabus shrugs. "Lumina was one of many," she says, only realizing belatedly how insensitive the comment is since it diminishes the experience of Destiny's own biological mother.

Destiny, thankfully, either doesn't pick up on it or chooses not to comment. Instead, she digs through some boxes, asking, "Was Lumina already working here when Maximus still lived in the castle?"

"Yes." Hexabus is relieved to be moving on to safer ground. She sinks into a chair and says, "Dominus was very fond of her because she used to allow him into the vault whenever Morty was traveling. He was such an introvert, that boy. Nose always buried in a book. A lot like Evangeline, actually. I think they would have been quite close if it weren't for the age difference."

Giving up on the boxes, Destiny shuffles over to look under a couch before opening a large trunk, her upper body disappearing inside. "How long did Lumina work for the family?" she asks, her voice muffled.

"Let me see..." Hexabus says, trying to work it out. "She

was already employed when Darius was born, although she was away for half the year when I gave birth, finishing some historian qualification in Edinburgh. She must have arrived a year before that? So...about thirty-four years."

"And how old was she when she started?"

"A bit younger than you are now, I'd say," Hexabus says, remembering the baby-faced girl Lumina used to be.

After a few moments, Destiny stands and brushes off her jeans. Her oversize gray T-shirt, which bears the slogan *I like big books, and I cannot lie*, is now covered with streaks of dirt. She looks around the room, heading for a row of bookshelves.

"Can you check those?" Destiny asks, pointing at another row lining the wall on the opposite side.

Feeling every one of her sixty-five years and then some as she stands, Hexabus asks, "What am I looking for?"

"Anything that might point toward what Lumina was working on just before she disappeared." Destiny knocks against a few books with her knuckle to make sure they aren't just hollow facades.

The two work in silence, Hexabus flipping through the pages of each volume, as well as checking the spaces behind them on the shelves. Lumina's quarters might be a mess, but it's clear she had a lot more respect for books than Morty did. There isn't one page turned down or any hint of marginalia that Hexabus can find.

When Hexabus finishes scouring the shelves, she follows Destiny into Lumina's bedroom, which is as much of a mess as the living quarters are. The bedding is disheveled, cascading onto the floor. Even more clothing is either flung over chairs and screens or puddled on the ground. The wardrobe, unsurprisingly, is mostly empty. Enough books are piled up under a wall sconce in the corner that Hexabus is amazed Lumina didn't torch the whole place by accident.

There are sketches and paintings framed and hung on the walls, all of them bearing the flourish of Lumina's signature. She appeared as fond of calculations as Morty was, though hers are rendered in a kind of abstract art.

Two paintings appear to be missing, one's enormous outline forming a yellowed rectangle against the wall.

"Hmm," Destiny says, hands on her thighs as she leans over to examine the side of the bed.

"What is it?" Hexabus goes over to join her.

"Look at these marks." Destiny points out the many scratches. "Don't those look like claw marks to you? As though a pet was scrambling to pull itself up on the bed?" Before Hexabus can answer, Destiny pulls back the comforter and gets up on the bed, crawling over it. She picks up a tuft of something gray and black and shows it to Hexabus.

"Raccoon fur?" Hexabus guesses.

"The raccoon has definitely been here," Destiny says. "Quite often, I'd say, judging by the damage it's done to the furniture." She examines the scratches again, pointing out how some are clearly quite old, having been oiled over by whomever maintained the castle's furniture.

"You're thinking Darius regularly visited in raccoon form?" Hexabus says wryly, hoping Destiny will see how ridiculous her theory is.

"It's possible," Destiny replies, making her way over to Lumina's desk, which is piled with even more books than Morty's was. "Interesting," she murmurs.

Hexabus can't see what she might be alluding to. "What is?"

Destiny juts out her chin at an uncapped silver fountain pen on the desk's blotter. "It looks like she was in the middle of writing something that she suddenly abandoned, but there isn't a notebook or letter lying open here like you'd expect."

Hexabus studies the neatly stacked planners sandwiched between two bookends. Their spines are all embossed with the year, going back a decade. She reaches out for this year's and pages through it, marveling at how orderly the woman's mind was despite the chaos of her environment.

Each hour of Lumina's days was accounted for. Breakfast at 8:00 a.m., lunch at 1:00 p.m., and dinner at 6:00 p.m. Research was conducted in the mornings, restoration and filing took place in the afternoons, with transcribing and decoding happening in the evenings. She didn't appear to have any kind of social life, as there weren't any lunches or dinners with friends ever scheduled.

"Huh," Hexabus says, flipping through the pages. "There's one symbol repeated over and over in some kind of code."

It appears at least four times a week, sometimes more, always scheduled at 1:00 a.m.

"Quite the night owl." Hexabus reaches for last year's planner. "Same symbol at the same time in this one too. And in the year before's," she says, checking that one as well. "Do you have any idea what the symbol means?" Hexabus asks, pointing it out.

Destiny examines it, her face suddenly lighting up. "I've seen this before!"

"Where?"

"In a painting at the Grimshaw Inn and Tavern." She closes her eyes. "I just need to visualize it so I can figure out what it means."

★★[14]

14. You now have all the information you require to solve this word puzzle. For a clue, email DestinyWhipClue@gmail.com with the subject line Clue Fourteen. Once you've solved it, turn to page 475 to check your answer.

★ ★ ★

Staring over Destiny's shoulder as she writes down the word, Hexabus says, "How very strange."

"Do you think it might be a name?" Destiny asks.

"Like for a pet, you mean?" Hexabus asks, thinking that makes sense. "Maybe Lumina wasn't kidnapped," Hexabus muses. "Maybe she made a run for it along with her pet raccoon, sending it back to the castle to do her bidding. Lumina could have been masterminding all this from the start."

The thought is encouraging as it means Darius definitely can't be the raccoon since, beyond living in the same castle, he has no ties at all to Lumina.

But Dominus does. He and Lumina were always very close.

It's a startling thought, one Hexabus wonders if she should articulate considering she's the one who vouched for Dominus. Her stomach roils at the possibility that he could have helped Minx escape, only pretending to set out to find her to throw everyone off the scent.

"You're right. It's possible Lumina's behind everything," Destiny says, walking back to the desk. "Though I don't know anyone who schedules a time in their planner like this specifically for their pet, unless it's for a vet's appointment or an outing, which seems unlikely at that time of night. Seems more like a meeting time." Destiny begins tugging at the desk.

"What are you doing?"

"Can you help me move this?" Destiny asks.

Hexabus grips one side of the heavy desk and pulls at it so they can maneuver it away from the wall.

"Aha!" Destiny shouts, darting at something black that's revealed once the desk is free. "As I suspected! It fell between the wall and the desk." Standing and studying the space, she adds, "Although the distance from the chair to the wall would indicate this didn't just slip down accidentally. It was flung there on purpose."

"What is it?"

"Looks like a journal." Destiny begins riffling through the book. She stops at the most recent page, where she points out a long squiggle trailing the last word, suggesting Lumina was interrupted as she was writing. She reads the entry and then begins flipping backward.

Watching her changing expressions is like being taken on a wild ride of shock, confusion, suspense, and anger. Hexabus wants to know what Destiny is discovering but doesn't want to break her stride.

Excruciatingly aware of each minute that's passing without Killian returning with Darius, Hexabus begins pacing.

When Destiny finally looks up, her eyes burn as though she's caught a fever. She fires off a barrage of questions, which Hexabus struggles to keep up with. After processing the answers for a few moments, Destiny says, "I know who the killer is, and I have a plan to capture them. But for it to work, you have to promise to do exactly as I say."

Hexabus winces, suspecting she isn't going to like it one bit.

CHAPTER 76

Tuesday—9:15 p.m.

As the raccoon darts through the secret passageways, unimpeded by those bothersome security codes, it smiles at how close it is to attaining everything it ever dreamed of thanks to both the artifact *and* Destiny Whip. And to think she was under Morty's nose the whole time and the old bastard didn't even know it.

Now it's just a case of finding her and putting her to use.

She's not in her chambers, but that's to be expected. With just a few hours remaining until everyone leaves the island, Destiny will be working furiously to figure it all out. The raccoon can't wait to see her crestfallen expression when it has to explain everything because Destiny couldn't solve it on her own. It takes a genius to outwit one. The raccoon just hopes Destiny isn't a sore loser.

Reaching a crossroads in the corridor, the creature needs to decide which way to turn. Stroking the pouch strapped around its neck, it considers its options.

Hexabus, it thinks.

Turning left, the raccoon races toward Hexabus's quarters and is rewarded with the sound of voices it recognizes as hers and Lurk's. Ha! Yet another thing happening under Morty's watch that he had absolutely no clue about.

When the raccoon comes into power and claims the Scruff-more throne as the true heir ascendant, it won't make the same mistake of allowing an inflated sense of dominion to render it oblivious to the many acts of treason its underlings are likely to commit, especially when they think their master isn't paying attention. The raccoon will be an omnipotent and merciless ruler, ensuring everyone lives in constant terror, which is the only way to keep them all in line.

"Slow down and take a breath," Lurk says in a tone likely meant to be calming.

Hexabus howls in frustration, like an animal caught with its leg in a trap. "Just listen to me! We don't have much time!"

"I'm trying, Hex, but you aren't making any sense. What's happened?"

"Destiny's lost her damn mind, that's what's happened," Hexabus yells. "We have to stop her."

"Why?"

"She's convinced that Darius is the raccoon," Hexabus says. "And absolutely nothing I say can change her mind."

The raccoon startles as though caught in the headlights of an oncoming eighteen-wheeler.

"She wants us to set a trap for him in the vault. The plan is to lure Darius there and she wants us to use our magic to force him into an unbreakable cage to detain him."

"We've been trying to find Morty's killer," Lurk says, "and if it's Darius—"

"If it's Darius," Hexabus exclaims, "then I'll take care of it. I'm not letting her cage him like he's some kind of animal."

"If he's responsible for Morty's death, he *is* guilty," Lurk says, clearly taking great care to sound measured, not wanting to set Hexabus off. "Why bring Destiny into all of this if you weren't prepared to face the possibility that one of your children might turn out to be the suspect?"

"Because I didn't think it *was* one of them," Hexabus snaps. "Obviously." There's the sound of drawers opening and closing. "We need to pack and get Darius off the island just as soon as we can find him. I've already arranged for a private boat…"

As the two continue to discuss their plans, the raccoon turns and heads for the passageway that leads to the vault, where it will transform into human form and don its treasures.

CHAPTER 77

Darius

Tuesday—9:23 p.m.

Approaching the vault, Darius runs a hand through his disheveled hair.

The enormous round door stands wide open like a portal to another dimension, an invitation if ever there was one.

Rubbing at his bloodshot eyes gives him no relief. But this, finally stepping up and taking action instead of being so damn reactionary, will bring him enormous satisfaction. He doesn't have much time, so he needs to get a move on.

As he steps across the threshold, he tells himself he's ready to do whatever it takes to claim what is rightfully his. And now that he finally has the Eye of Gormodeus, nothing can stop him.

CHAPTER 78

Dominus

Tuesday—9:25 p.m.

Dominus makes his way to the vault, brushing at the fur cling-ing to his gray woolen sweater, wrinkling his nose as he real-izes how much he smells like a wet dog.

God, he can't wait for this to be over.

Dominus hasn't worked this hard, achieved as much as he has, just for it all to have led to this. He's going to ensure that everyone will remember him in his own right and not just for being Mordecai Scruffmore's bastard son.

Destiny waits for no man, he thinks, making himself smile, *except for me.*

CHAPTER 79

Minx

Tuesday evening

As Minx stalks through the secret passageways, she has only one thing on her mind: to take care of Destiny once and for all.

Ever since that redheaded fashion disaster's unexpected arrival on the island, she's done nothing but turn up in the unlikeliest of places to stick her freckled nose in everyone's business.

No one would have known about the poison Minx slipped into Morty's whiskey—or about the blackmail money she extorted from him—were it not for Destiny's meddling.

And it's not like Minx had the opportunity to explain herself to her mother before being thrown into the dungeons. She's sure Newton would have forgiven her if only she'd heard why Minx used those staged pictures of Madigan and how her ingenious plan was supposed to serve multiple noble purposes.

The first was to procure the money for the blackmailer in the event the poison wasn't strong enough to kill Morty. Both of those tasks, the extortion *and* the murder, were highly unpleasant, obviously, but also wholly necessary thanks to Angel's carelessness and the fact that Newton has always expected Minx to protect her twin. That's what happens when you're born a Capricorn eighteen minutes after your twin is born a Sagittarius. You're always the one left juggling the grenades, forced to deal with the fallout of your sister's impressive résumé of gigantic fuckups.

Minx's second purpose was to put a target on Madigan's back, revenge for first love bombing and then ghosting her. As a woman who's been scorned herself, Newton would undoubtedly understand Minx's desire for vengeance.

And the third was to set Newton free from a cruel man whom Minx thought her mother would never leave, regardless of how many blatant affairs he had. That Newton only told her about the prenup—and about using Tempest as bait to invoke the infidelity clause—once Minx was being dragged to the dungeons isn't Minx's fault; that's on Newton entirely. Minx was only trying to help free her mother from her father's evil clutches.

But now, thanks to Destiny, neither Angel nor Newton is speaking to Minx. Plus, she's lost the sigil, *and* someone stole her bag full of money. Even worse, it turns out she didn't kill Morty and none of his powers have been transferred to her.

Had the gods not been smiling down on her, Minx would have only her cunning and rage at her disposal to seize the throne from Dominus. Though neither is enough to fuel a revolution.

Luckily, in this, the final hour, she's been gifted an even more powerful weapon than anything she had before.

But first, she needs to take care of that meddling bitch, Destiny.

CHAPTER 80

Darius

Tuesday—9:26 p.m.

"Come out, come out, wherever you are," Darius calls into the recesses of the vault.

Giggling, he remembers how he, Eva, and Bramble used to play this game as children. Though not in the vault, of course, since Morty never allowed children in there. Correction, he didn't allow children who weren't Dominus to be in there. *He* was always the exception, which Darius never understood. Until now.

But Morty is dead, and Darius can go wherever he pleases.

"Destiny," he calls in a singsong voice. "Where are you?"

"I'm over here," she calls back, her voice muffled by all the paper stacked up, scrolls atop scrolls, parchments next to books.

Following the sound, he's released from the maze when he steps into a side room that used to be Lumina's office.

Destiny looks up, startled.

"Why so surprised," Darius says, "when you were clearly expecting me?"

CHAPTER 81

Dominus

Tuesday—9:32 p.m.

Dominus is surprised by voices drifting out from deeper within the vault.

This ruins his plan for a private chat without any witnesses.

Not wanting to alert them to his presence, he takes care to proceed quietly, following the thread of the conversation through the stacks. He knows he's near once he can begin to make out the faint words.

"We have a problem," a man's voice says. "Surely you can see that."

"What do you mean?"

Dominus is intimately familiar with the vault's layout after all the time Lumina allowed him to spend in here both as a child and then as a teenager. The voices filter from her office and so he veers off to the right, taking an indirect route that will keep him mostly hidden.

"You made a big mistake and now it's up to me to correct it." It's Darius speaking, but his words are slurred.

"What mistake?" Destiny asks, a wary edge to her voice.

"You said you'd tell everyone about the blackmail if I didn't confess to it, but you know why I can't let you do that, right?"

"It's too late," Destiny replies. "I already told your mother when you didn't show up by 8:00 p.m. And I told her what you bought with the money you stole from Minx, that you have the Eye of Gormodeus."

Dominus freezes at the mention of this new development. This is most fortuitous. The Eye can greatly help him boost the reach of his powers. And it won't be difficult to relieve Darius of it, not when he's so utterly wasted.

"Your mother sent Killian to find you when you didn't show up as promised," Destiny adds. "He's looking for you as we speak."

"You bitch," Darius spits.

"How did you know where I was?" Destiny's clearly trying to buy time. She must be hoping for reinforcements.

Dominus will have to hurry if he doesn't want a rescue party to contend with.

"I set an alarm spell in case the intruder came back to the vault," Darius replies. "And you set it off fifteen minutes ago."

"Don't try anything reckless." The high pitch of Destiny's voice betrays her anxiety. "Your mother's on her way here right now so—"

"Shut up!" Darius shouts. "Just shut up so I can think." He's quiet for a moment and then mutters, "I didn't want to do it. But you forced my hand. And now I'm going to have to make you disappear. If it looks like you ran off with the Eye of Gormodeus to use for yourself, she'll believe that you lied—"

"I don't think so," Dominus says as he steps into the room, having heard more than enough from this blathering fool.

Darius almost topples over as he spins around. He tries to shoot off a spell, but it's a feeble attempt that misses Dominus completely. After reaching into his pocket, Darius removes something silver, holding it up as though wielding a shield. It's a metal pyramid with intricately carved symbols surrounding a giant eyeball embedded in its center. A blue pupil gleams un-blinking back at Dominus.

"Stand back," Darius commands. "Stand back or I'll—"

Dominus snaps his fingers, and the relic is wrenched from Darius's grip.

Darius lets out an anguished cry as the corner of the pyramid slices his palm before rocketing into Dominus's outstretched hand.

"Thank you, brother," Dominus sneers. "This is going to be most helpful, indeed." He freezes Darius in place before turning to Destiny.

Her eyes are wide and she's clutching the desk so tightly that the freckles on her hands stand out in stark relief. "Relax," Dominus says. "I'm actually one of the good guys."

Destiny looks dubious, but he can hardly blame her.

"I finally got some information from the cats that I thought you should know," Dominus says. "The rats told me where to find you." He walks up to Destiny and leans down close to her ear, whispering the real identity of the raccoon.

When he pulls away, he expects Destiny to look surprised. But it's clear she's already figured it out and that he's just confirming what she already knows.

Tired and cold from spending most of the night outside with the island's animals, Dominus now wishes he'd headed straight for his claw-foot tub instead of stopping here. But had he done that, he never would have arrived in time to confiscate the Eye of Gormodeus from Darius.

Holding the relic up to Destiny, Dominus says, "This should help amplify my powers with the cats, which will help with my search for Bramble."

"Bramble?" Darius squawks, still frozen to the spot.

Ignoring him, Destiny reaches out and clasps Dominus's hand. "Thank you. For everything." Squeezing it, she says, "You aren't condemned by your father's DNA, you know. Those were the bricks you were handed, but you get to decide what you build with them."

The sentiment closes Dominus's windpipe, making it difficult to speak. Instead, he nods his thanks before casting a spell that will allow him to drag Darius behind him like the deadwood he is.

He's about to offer Destiny help with dealing with the raccoon but realizes she doesn't need it. It looks like she has everything under control.

CHAPTER 82

Destiny

Tuesday—10:05 p.m.

If Destiny's calculations are correct, the raccoon should appear any minute. Time is running out. It needs to make its move. Unless it was early, in which case Darius and Dominus sent it into hiding.

And yet still she waits.

And waits.

She wishes Bex were here even as she recognizes the selfishness of it, how constantly dragging Bex alongside her meant holding Bex back from moving on.

Destiny's thoughts are interrupted by a shadow darkening the doorway. Acting the part, she pretends to look surprised when Madigan finally steps inside.

The first thing she notices, besides his height, is the dark circles under his eyes, which, when she first met him, made him look severely sleep-deprived. Now she sees them for the clues they were. Same goes for his wet hair.

It must be raining again.

"Madigan?" Destiny exclaims, forcing herself to look incredulous. "Oh my god, it's you!"

Madigan bows theatrically. "The one and only. Apologies I couldn't arrive as Sarcophagus and then turn into myself in

375

front of you," he says. "But then I'd be naked, and that would be terribly awkward. So, instead, I did the transformation near one of the stashes of clothing I keep stored around here." He smiles, gesturing down at his red flannel shirt and black jeans. "Excuse the bare feet. It's impossible to hide boots that size from a bloodhound like Mrs. Scuggs."

"Where's your Scottish brogue?" Destiny asks. This is a development she *wasn't* anticipating.

"An affectation put on purely because people find it so charming," he says with the slightest burr, his real accent. "Plus, the ladies love it." He winks.

Destiny recalls a study conducted by sociolinguists in which they determined that we place more value on things that are less common. An unusual accent can therefore be a shortcut to getting people on your side, assigning you value without you having to prove you're worthy of it.

"Smart," Destiny says. "You're so smart. I had no idea you were the raccoon—"

"Cut the crap," Madigan snaps, making her spirits sink as he takes a few steps forward, blocking the only escape route. "I know you got Hexabus and Lurk to put on a really good performance so that I would believe you *thought* the raccoon was Darius."

Destiny's stomach twists into a knot. "Why would I—"

"So that I'd race here," Madigan says, "all cocksure, thinking they were leaving the island with Darius, when they were actually planning to overpower me while you kept me talking."

That's it. That was the extent of what Destiny considered a genius plan to lure Madigan out to reveal himself. She can't help it. Her eyes flit to the door, hoping to spot Hexabus and Killian about to incapacitate Madigan.

"They're not coming." Madigan rolls up his sleeves. "They're all a bit tied up right now," he adds, barking a laugh. "It's just you and me, prodigy."

His words shatter what little hope Destiny was still clinging to.

CHAPTER 83

Destiny

"How did you figure out their conversation was a decoy?" Destiny tries to buy more time so that she can come up with a plan B, something she foolishly didn't consider might be necessary at this juncture.

"I almost didn't," Madigan admits. "I'd already turned around to head straight here when it occurred to me that it had all been just a tad *too* easy. They were talking loudly, enunciating properly, and taking great care to explain their motivations. Overhearing their conversation was either a gift from the gods—and let's be honest, those are rare—or it was a trap."

Destiny's plan had seemed so elegant in its simplicity.

Considering the risk of a hostage situation at the inn, going there to confront Madigan was out of the question. Ambushing and overpowering him at the castle, where they had backup, was their best bet. After they'd neutralized his powers and tied him up, the plan was to demand the medallion back.

Destiny had entertained the possibility he wouldn't show up. Even that he might not overhear the contrived conversation between Hexabus and Killian. But she hadn't conceived of an option where he'd be the one to neutralize her entire arsenal before her first shot could even be fired.

"What did you do to everyone?" She dreads the answer but needs to know.

"I incapacitated Hexabus and Lurk first. Then I let the staff and the guards think they had permission to leave the castle before I went to round up everyone else. It took me a while to find Dominus because, as it turns out, he'd taken Darius down to the prison cells. That's why I was so late. Forgive my tardiness."

Hearing the faintest crunch coming from behind Madigan, Destiny risks a glance at the doorway again.

Oblivious to it, Madigan sighs and ambles around the desk to where Destiny's seated. "I'm not going to make the mistake of underestimating you." He rests his huge palms on each of her shoulders, his powerful fingers pressing into her collarbones.

It would be easy for him to strangle her in this position, his hands so close to her throat.

Destiny gulps, listening for the sound outside again, certain she didn't imagine it. But all she can hear is Madigan's breathing.

"Tell me how you figured it out," he commands. "Where did I slip up?"

It's as though a swarm of hornets is smashing against Destiny's breastbone, frantic to escape the smoky prison of her chest. Madigan must feel her pulse in her neck tapping out its SOS distress signal.

Taking deep breaths, Destiny tries to steady herself. She focuses on the facts to calm herself. "In Lumina's journal," Destiny says, "she referred to—"

"Journal?" Madigan startles, tightening his grip. "Lumina didn't keep a journal."

"She did, though she took great care to hide it from you. She was actually busy writing in it the night you arrived to kidnap her. Since it wasn't yet 1:00 a.m.—your usual time to visit after calling last round at the tavern—she must have considered it a safe time to do so. When you materialized unexpectedly, she hid the journal between the desk and the wall, which is where I found it."

"She's going to be punished for that." Madigan squeezes Destiny's shoulders before his grasp eases.

She senses the rippling muscles of his forearms, how easily he could snap her neck.

"Carry on," he instructs.

Intent on ignoring the tremor in her voice, Destiny says, "Lumina referred to a child in her journal, one she didn't name. While Hexabus was emphatic Lumina never had a child, I recalled those six months when she returned to Edinburgh to finish her qualification. Of course, there was no qualification. Morty sent her away to have the baby with instructions to return without it if it didn't have the birthmark he was looking for."

When Destiny asked Hexabus about it earlier, she said Madigan appeared on the island fourteen years before, which further aligned with Destiny's theory that Madigan was Lumina's son. Whoever adopted or took care of him would have fulfilled their duties by the time he was eighteen, freeing him to go in search of his birth parents.

Once Madigan found Lumina, it must have been difficult to visit her considering that she lived and worked in the castle. But with his mother having full access to the Scruffmore vault, she was privy to advanced spellwork, the kind that would enable a determined young sorcerer to play around with metamorphosis magic. While a strapping young man would draw attention, a raccoon would not. And what better animal to learn how to transform into considering a raccoon's dexterity and intelligence.

Destiny takes Madigan through the rest of her reasoning once she figured out who the raccoon was. He'd have to slip out of his clothes each time he transformed. That explains why, when Destiny first met him, Madigan's hair was wet while his clothes weren't. The dripping raincoat and umbrella she'd noticed in the foyer had belonged to Darius, for if they'd belonged to Madigan, his hair would have been kept dry by them.

"When heading out into the storm to check on my progress," Destiny says, "you left your clothes just inside the inn's doorway. That was the bundle that Darius was complaining about having to step over upon his arrival at the inn."

Madigan is no do-gooder. He's just made everyone believe it so that no one ever questions the mysterious puddles of clothing found around the inn.

"Also, the towel you handed me to dry myself off with was damp because you'd already used it on yourself before quickly getting dressed. You were following me as I made my way to the inn," Destiny says. "I even saw you in the street when I held up my cell phone flashlight, only I didn't know it at the time. Raccoons' eyes mostly commonly reflect a bright yellow." Destiny pauses as she realizes something else she hadn't quite put together yet. "The sparks I saw coming from that alleyway? They were caused by you, weren't they, when you worked the spell to send Evangeline that secret message in the book?"

"Yes," Madigan grumbles, and Destiny can feel the vibration of his chest against the back of her skull. "My alarm spell rather inconveniently alerted me to Evangeline's presence in the library just as I was having to chase you down. I'd sent a buggy for you and Tempest, you see, not anticipating what an absolute bitch Tempest is, and how she'd abandon you at the harbor in that foul weather, leaving you to fend for yourself."

Madigan finally releases his hold and walks around the desk to sit in front of Destiny. As he moves, she swears she can make out the faintest creak and shuffle issuing from farther inside the vault.

Has someone managed to free themselves to make their stealthy way here to help her? She can only hope so.

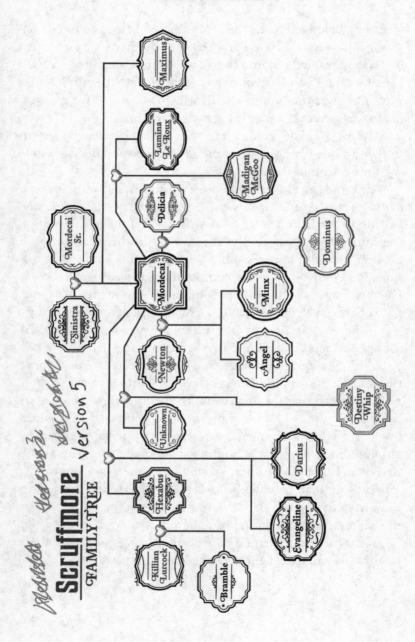

CHAPTER 84

Destiny

Trying not to make her distraction obvious, Destiny continues with the thread of their conversation. "You put a tracking spell on me as I made my way to the inn. That's what alerted you to my arrival, allowing you to save me in the nick of time despite not being able to see me from the bar."

"Good thing I did too," Madigan says, "or everything would have been for naught. Those damn carriages are a menace."

"What I couldn't understand at first was that, besides the hidden message," Destiny continues, "what differed between the versions of the letters Newton sent and the ones Tempest and I received was the instruction to come to the inn the night before. I wondered who had something to gain from making that change. And not just in *my* letter, but in Tempest's as well."

It was seeing the enormous blank space on Lumina's wall that helped Destiny figure it out. The painting missing from the historian's quarters was the exact same size as the one that had supposedly mysteriously appeared on the Grimshaw's tavern wall. Only it hadn't been hung up by an unknown bene-factor as Madigan claimed; he'd just said that in case anyone from the castle came by and recognized it.

He'd actually stolen it from Lumina's room and put it up in the bar in time for Destiny and Tempest's arrival, because he needed Tempest's art knowledge and Destiny's cipher expertise to make sense of it.

"I know you swapped the interview letters out when you purposefully ran into Newton on the day she was in Gwillumbury to get them posted," Destiny says. "I just don't know how you came to figure out what Newton had done with regard to planting her sister as a candidate for the position."

Madigan explains how he befriended Newton through trickery. Because of how long she'd spend each day gazing at her own reflection, he bewitched her mirror. As Dolos, the friend in the looking glass, Madigan listened to Newton's anguish over Morty cheating on her, as well as her concerns about aging and becoming less attractive.

"She told me all about her sister, Tempest, who was an art appraiser specializing in occultist paintings, and how much Tempest would have *loved* all the art at the castle. And how terribly sad it was that Morty wouldn't let her visit." Madigan makes an exaggerated *boo-hoo* face. "That got me thinking about the painting hung in my mother's quarters that she'd stolen from the vault to prevent Morty from getting his hands on it."

"But," Destiny protests, "they were lovers… Why would she—"

"She hated his guts," Madigan says emphatically. "She worked against him at every opportunity."

"But wasn't he often in her chambers? Wouldn't he have seen the painting there?"

"He only visited her when she was young and beautiful. When she got older, all he cared about were her brilliant research methods and how they'd aid his quest for immortality."

"If Lumina hated Mordecai so much, why didn't she just work with you to usurp him?"

"You'd think she owed me that, at the very least, wouldn't you?" Madigan's face is contorted with resentment. "But no. Apparently she'd seen firsthand how power could corrupt a person and said she didn't want that kind of life for her son." Madigan scoffs before continuing. "She wouldn't tell me the painting's significance at first, but considering she'd hidden it from Morty, I knew it had to be an important clue."

Destiny nods. "So, as Dolos, you concocted a plan for Newton to invite Tempest in the guise of one of the historians to set a trap for Morty, but your plan was actually to pick Tempest's brain about the painting." Here's the part Destiny isn't clear on. "How did you find out about *me*, though?"

"You mean my prodigy half sister?"

"Did you overhear Mordecai speaking with Killian about me?" Destiny presses, ignoring the barb.

Madigan shakes his head. "Contrary to what you might think, I had an inn to run and couldn't spend every minute eavesdropping from secret passageways. I took time off when Darius wasn't on the island to follow Lurk, curious to see what he might be up to. He attended two of the conferences where you gave keynote presentations. That's how I first discovered how very useful you could be to me."

"Because my area of expertise could help you decipher the painting's glyphs?" Destiny asks.

"Among other things," Madigan says. "Give me your hand." He indicates her left one.

She reluctantly reaches out so he can clasp it.

Madigan ignores Destiny's proffered palm and grabs her wrist instead. "See that?"

"My birthmark?" she asks, certain now it's proof that she's Mordecai's daughter. It singled her out, just as the twins' birthmarks did to Hexabus.

"I saw it during one of your presentations when you gestured at a slide. And then I confirmed it by zooming in on a photo taken for the *Washington Post* article. Do you know what that birthmark is?"

"Some kind of weird hourglass?" That's how it always looked to her.

"No," Madigan says. "It's a magical keyhole." He drops Destiny's arm and withdraws a pouch from where it hangs beneath his shirt. Taking it off, he removes Mordecai's medallion and places it on the table so she can view it close-up for the first time.

Waving a hand over it, he breaks the medallion apart from its ornate frame into eight separate sigils.

Madigan explains how when Darius was drunk one night a few years back, he let slip that he saw Morty and Lurk on the beach the night Bramble was killed. Putting two and two together from what Madigan had already gleaned about the medallion's powers from Lumina, he realized Morty had killed his own son to stop him from ever harnessing the power of the sigils against him.

While Morty could use the medallion for various feats of magic, his children couldn't unite against him using its powers, because without Bramble's functioning connector sigil in the middle, the magic would be fractured and erratic.

"But," Madigan continues, "your birthmark is also a connector like Bramble's, meaning I could harness its magic just as the prophecy foretold."

Destiny thinks back to what Hexabus showed her in the vault. There was nothing in the prophecy about Destiny beyond a warning about the coming of The Seer. "I don't understand," she says. And then it occurs to her, sweat dampening her armpits. "You found the rest of the prophecy, didn't you?"

"Yes! My mother ripped it out of the volume when she found it, wanting to torture Morty by withholding that essential information. And then I found where she hid it." Madigan clears his throat and recites it.

"Take heed, the thirteenth Mordecai,
born under a blood moon.
You'll breathe as darkness stains the sky,
your birth come all too soon.

Be warned, you known as The Slayer.
As your sixty-sixth year dawns,
you'll be challenged by The Player,
who'll turn your Kings to Pawns.

For the sands are running faster
with every passing day.
You command them as their master
but cannot hold them at bay.

With power that's beyond compare,
there will soon come a time
when your very own child will dare
to summit while you climb.

Fear the coming of The Seer
with her wild hair aflame,
whose secrets fuel her quest to hear,
and fate writ in her name.

Be wary of the family tree,
whose deep roots you'll strive to burn.
You might, for good, have lost The Key,
but The Keyhole...she will return." ★★[15]

---

15. You now have all the information you require to solve the puzzle of how the sigils connect and how this enabled the killer to murder Mordecai Scruffmore. For a clue, email DestinyWhipClue@gmail.com using the subject line Clue Fifteen. To check your answer, continue reading for Madigan's explanation.

Destiny's breath catches to hear herself described in this way. And suddenly, the answers all fall into place, aligning perfectly. But there's no time to react because Madigan's tapping the sigils, demanding her attention.

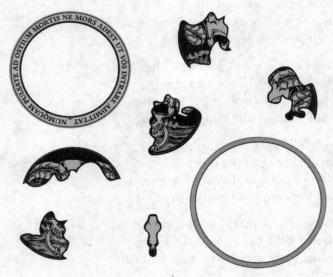

"The thin outer ring is Morty's, and the thicker inner one belongs to Hexabus. The top right part that looks like a puzzle piece is Angel's. The sigil containing the rest of the Scruffmore crest's horn is Evangeline's. Minx's is the one that looks like the blindfolded horse. Darius's looks like a blue whale opening its mouth, and Lurk's is the one that has the waves in the corner."

Destiny thinks of how each of them has a physical manifestation of their birthmark. Morty's circle was his monocle; Hexabus's is her ring; Angel uses hers as a cell phone charm; Evangeline's is hung as a pendant from her neck; Minx's is a tattoo on her forearm; Darius's is a signet on a ring; and Killian's is his tiepin.

Madigan begins to arrange all the sigils on the table, making sure Destiny's paying careful attention.

She nods for him to continue.

"All I needed was for two of the inner sigils that touch Hexabus's to be linked by a connector that would act as a conduit through which the magic would flow. If their owners touched Morty at the same time I was casting a deathspell, they would amplify it." Once he puts the rearranged pieces in place, he says, "The night Morty died, Evangeline's and Lurk's sigils both touched Hexabus's like this when they all laid hands on him."

Looking up at Destiny, he says, "The medallion is trained to recognize everyone's birthmark shapes rather than the individuals themselves." Madigan smiles like a child who's particularly proud of himself. He slips the keyhole-shaped sigil into place.

"Bramble was The Key and you're The Keyhole as referenced by the prophecy. His sigil was the key to unlocking the
medallion's powers, and you're The Keyhole who would return to replace him. You're both connectors with the same
shaped birthmarks, and the medallion recognized you as such
when you laid hands on Morty. You were my secret weapon,
the only person without a motive. And yet you helped me kill
the great Mordecai Scruffmore." He throws his head back and
laughs. "The two ironies here are that Mordecai never needed
to kill Bramble. Had he seen the rest of the prophecy, he would
have known how futile it would be. And also that you've been
searching for the killer all this time when all you had to do was
look in the mirror to find her."

CHAPTER 85

Madigan

Tuesday—11:21 p.m.

Destiny is so horrified that Madigan chuckles. "What? Morty was a psychotic despot who was about to kill his entire family," he says. "We did a good thing, you and me. You should be proud."

But Destiny doesn't look proud. She regards Madigan as though *he's* the psycho. So much for her genius, for her being the child born with the powerful birthmark, the one Morty would have salivated over if only he'd known about her, if Lurk hadn't betrayed his master by protecting her from him.

Madigan shrugs at how small-minded Destiny is. He wishes they had more time together so he could reframe this all for her, get her to see it more objectively. "Well, I for one sleep better knowing that I eradicated that kind of evil," he says philosophically. "It wasn't easy, you know. Just because I made it look effortless doesn't mean it was."

"There was obviously a lot of planning involved," Destiny says, as though the words are boulders that she's pushing uphill with her tongue. "You first had to send Hexabus the anonymous note about the sigils and medallion so that she'd figure out how they all work together. And then you sent Evangeline the secret message about Bramble to get her on board when it became clear Hexabus wasn't going to involve her." Destiny takes a beat and then cocks her head, asking, "How did you know about Hexabus and Killian's relationship?"

"She was summoned to the castle from time to time," he says, "supposedly for business with Morty, but she came because of Lurk. I overheard them on one of those visits."

Destiny studies him, as if waiting for more. She's so strangely curious about such an inconsequential detail that it makes Madigan wonder what he's missing.

But Destiny moves on, saying, "You also had to get *me* here."

"I actually thought that would prove a lot more challenging considering how you hadn't left your apartment in a year," Madigan admits.

Destiny's eyes suddenly widen. "Oh my god," she whispers. "Did you... Did you have something to do with Nate and Bex's accident?"

Madigan scoffs. "Not everything is about you, prodigy. And not all tragedy is related to some kind of mastermind plan. Sometimes shit just happens." He sighs, thinking of all the terrible hands he's been dealt, none of which he ever deserved. She needs to grow up, get tougher so that life doesn't knock her around so easily. "Luckily for me, getting you to come wasn't difficult because of how desperate you were to meet your father. Man, what a disappointment *that* must have been." He chuckles.

Destiny's gaze suddenly shifts behind him. Madigan turns to see what's caught her attention. "What is it?" he asks.

"Nothing," she says, her eyes snapping back to meet his.

He listens but can't hear anything. His auditory perception is best when he's in raccoon form. Finally satisfied that there's no one there—that Destiny, true to her nature, is being wildly optimistic that someone is going to save her—he turns back again.

"The trickiest part was ensuring the timing of it all," he continues. "I knew that Hexabus, Lurk, and Evangeline would be ready to pounce on Morty at some point during that meeting to incapacitate him, but I had to make sure that you and I also laid hands on him at the exact same time. That's why the wall disappeared and you were shoved onto him just as they reached him."

"The flash when we all touched him?" Destiny says. "That was you working the deathspell?"

"I thought it was quite cinematic, don't you?" He doesn't wait for her answer. "The most dramatic flourish of all, though, was how Morty recognized you as his daughter just before he died." Madigan bugs out his eyes and flails about, imitating Morty's death throes. "'You! You!'" He pantomimes while gasping, dissolving into fits of laughter.

"You've come to use the medallion for a last spell," Destiny says, surprising him. "That's why you had to get here before everyone left, so you could harness their collective powers before you seize the throne."

"Yes," Madigan concedes, ever so slightly annoyed that she's constantly a step ahead of him.

"That, *and* you've got Mordecai's sigil, which you stole from Lurk earlier."

Madigan smiles, pulling the sigil from his neck pouch. "Indeed." But then he sighs. "Unfortunately, neither is quite as powerful as I'd hoped, which shouldn't surprise me since they're our father's creations." He stands and stretches, needing to work off some of his energy, which is always so much easier to do in raccoon form. Returning the relics to the pouch, he says, "Much more valuable was the spellwork you and Tempest helped me unlock by solving the painting's glyph and then pointing me in the direction of the artist's shaman." Pausing his pacing, he recites, "'The key to eternal life lies at the end of the banshee's scream.'"

Destiny nods, clearly regretting the part she played in helping him translate the glyphs. "It didn't make much sense, though."

"On the contrary, it made a *lot* of sense," Madigan says. "You see, *The Banshee's Scream* is a memoir of sorts that the shaman Carlos Estrava wrote."

"Estrava," Destiny murmurs. "Why does that name ring a bell?"

"Because Tempest told us about him."

"No," Destiny says, closing her eyes. "I saw it somewhere else." She's quiet for a moment and then nods, her eyes snapping open. "'Axenite. Binglebottom. Dramworth. Estrava. Funkel. Gwellington. Hearkens.'"

Madigan chuckles at the gibberish. "Are those supposed to be some kind of magical incantations?"

"No, those are the names I read on the spines of the books when Hexabus brought me here to show me the prophecy," Destiny replies. "You were the one to break in to the vault that night while we were sleeping at the inn," Destiny says, "so you could get access to Estrava's book straight after we helped you figure it out."

"Yes, I tore out what I needed and left the book behind so Morty wouldn't figure out what was taken during the break-in."

"What was in it that you needed so badly?"

That's when Madigan hears it. An unmistakable footfall.

He spins around to find Minx in the doorway, her face like a thundercloud.

CHAPTER 86

Minx

Tuesday—11:44 p.m.

Disgusted by everything she overheard while creeping up on the room, Minx spits, "You bastard!" Conjuring a shield to stop Madigan from hexing her, she says, "You came on to me even though you knew I was your half sister?"

Destiny gasps. Her hand flies to her mouth as though she might throw up.

"It's sickening, isn't it?" Minx advances upon the desk. "Madigan started love bombing me a few months ago during one of my visits to the island. I wasn't interested at first, naturally, because of how old he is," she says, scoffing, "but then I actually fell for the bullshit Scottish accent and the fake aw-shucks charm. But just as soon as I showed interest in return, he ghosted me, making me feel like I'd imagined it all. And now," Minx spits, "it turns out we're related."

"Come now, Minx," Madigan says amiably. He sits and leans back in his chair, so much at ease he's not even bothering to try to stage a counterattack. "Don't be that way. It was all purely strategic. Nothing personal." Turning to Destiny, Madigan says, "There was a chance I'd need Minx's sigil, and I wanted to make sure I was best positioned to use it when an opportunity arose." Facing Minx, he adds, "But then I decided against it. It's not that I'm anti-incest, per se. You just put me off with those psycho-killer vibes."

Furious, Minx pulls her secret weapon from her pocket. "You made a huge mistake when you tied everyone up in the ceremonial room earlier. You didn't frisk Dominus for weapons." She holds the relic up to the light. "I was pretty pissed when Hexabus confiscated Morty's sigil. But its power is nothing compared to this. Recognize it?"

"The Eye of Gormodeus," Madigan says, eyeing it, finally giving her a reaction she wants.

"Dominus confiscated it from Darius earlier." Minx twirls the pyramid like a fidget spinner, its corners satisfyingly sharp against her fingertips. "Darius offered me all manner of riches if I'd just free him and hand this over. He even said I could have the throne," Minx says, laughing. "As though the crown were his to give."

"Did you release everyone?" Destiny asks warily, her mismatched eyes filled with concern.

"Why would I do that?" Minx retorts. "Thanks to Madigan here, they're all exactly where I want them. And just as soon as I deal with you two, I'm going back to teach them a lesson they'll never forget." Now that Minx has the Eye of Gormodeus, she doesn't need Morty's medallion or his sigil. With everyone captive and at her mercy, seizing the throne will be a relatively quick affair.

It will probably be painless too, but what fun would that be?

"You won't use the Eye on me," Madigan says, smirking. That he's still so relaxed is infuriating. Minx expected him to be on his knees begging by now, much like Darius was earlier. "You couldn't wield that kind of magic even if you tried," Madigan adds, goading her.

"Madigan," Destiny hisses, her eyes widened. "What are you doing?"

"I think she's full of shit." Madigan shrugs, smiling widely in a challenge. "All sound and fury, signifying nothing."

Minx grips the Eye of Gormodeus so tightly she can feel its corners slicing her flesh. How dare he make fun of her. How dare he belittle her in this way.

To harness the artifact's powers against Madigan, she first needs to break her shield so the magic doesn't bounce back at her. Squaring her shoulders, Minx stands with her legs apart, knees bent, as she braces for the magnitude of the spell she's about to work. Dissolving her shield, Minx taps into the relic, expecting an onslaught of power to detonate through her with the force of a nuclear explosion.

But nothing happens. There isn't even the faintest trickle of magic responding to her summons.

By the time Minx realizes that she's been tricked, Madigan has risen with one hand outstretched, shooting off a hex that knocks Minx sideways into the desk before she crumples to the floor.

She groans in agony as he looms over her, a blood moon rising.

CHAPTER 87

Madigan

Wednesday—12:01 a.m.

Madigan glares at Minx, who winces while clutching her side. He shoots off another hex for good measure, making her writhe in pain, teeth gritted to stop herself from screaming.

Destiny leaps up, rushing to Minx's side.

"Don't touch her," Madigan says as Destiny crouches next to her. "Get back to your chair. We're not done here."

Destiny pauses, considering Minx, who's curled up in a ball whimpering.

"There's nothing you can do for her," Madigan snaps. "The magic needs to work its way out of her system like a fever."

When Destiny still doesn't move, Madigan uses his powers to pick her up and thrust her back into her chair. She lands with a thwack, the air knocked out of her.

"Now," Madigan says, "had Minx eavesdropped just a fraction longer, she would have spared herself that embarrassing display." He tuts at Minx's lack of patience, her stupid reckless-ness. "We were talking about Estrava's memoir, *The Banshee's Scream*, and how the key to eternal life lay at the end of it."

Destiny stares at him, looking wounded.

God, she has no clue what it's been like for him, having to pretend to be a lowly barkeep and general dogsbody—bowing and scraping to Darius, even as his half brother used him as a guinea pig for his burgeoning magical powers—so that Madigan could hide his real identity to fly under the radar. All this while Destiny has been allowed to realize her full potential, collecting accolades and acclaim at every turn.

He resents her for it, for all the media coverage and the awards, for the way her mind was polished to a shine by the brightest professors in the best institutions, while his was left to tarnish.

"What is the key to eternal life?" Destiny asks.

This is Madigan's favorite part. "The Eye of Gormodeus, of course. Only," he says, throwing the pyramid up and then catching it, "it's not an artifact, after all. It's actually a spell."

"Then what's that?" Destiny asks, nodding at the relic Madigan is playing with.

"It's a fake." Madigan smiles and bows, accepting the imaginary standing ovation he's due. "Both Morty and Darius *thought* the Eye of Gormodeus was an artifact to be acquired and harnessed rather than a spell to be conducted. Idiots. Darius blackmailed Minx to pay for a fake." Madigan laughs, amused beyond measure.

"And I assume you were the one who arranged to sell him the fake he acquired today?" Destiny asks, her voice dripping with judgment.

"Yes, and why not?" Madigan replies defensively. "A fool and his money are soon parted. It's just basic economics."

Minx emits a sound that is half groan, half growl.

"It can't bode well that you're telling us this." Destiny has gone pale, her freckles like flakes of cinnamon floating on milk.

"Yeah," Madigan says. He's sad that their time is coming to an end. This meeting of the minds has been a gift he didn't anticipate unwrapping. "But to be fair, you're not the only one who's going to have a bad day. It isn't going to end well for anyone except me." With that, Madigan sighs, wanting Destiny to understand his burden. "You see, I'm The Player *and* the child foretold by the prophecy, so it's not like I have any choice. I need to fulfill my destiny."

CHAPTER 88

Destiny

Wednesday—3:33 a.m.

Destiny's throat constricts as Madigan's palm lands between her shoulder blades. His shove sends her stumbling into the ceremonial room, where everyone, minus Minx, is seated in a circle, ropes of fire binding their arms behind their backs. Two empty chairs remain.

Newton's and Tempest's complexions are even ghostlier than usual. When Madigan snaps his fingers and Minx marches into the room like an uncoordinated puppet from a B-grade horror movie, Newton moans an ungodly sound that sets Destiny's nerves on edge.

Held in place by the force of Madigan's spell, Destiny waits as he gets Minx seated and restrained next to Angel. Newton squirms as Madigan leads Destiny between her and Tempest's chairs to an empty one at the far side of the room. Destiny takes care as she steps over the huge crack in the floor, not wanting to trip and fall.

Hexabus catches Destiny's eye as she passes, the force of her gaze conveying her impotent rage. It looks like she wants to mouth something, an apology perhaps, but her lips stay frozen. Darius, seated to his mother's right, is passed out, his head lolling to the side. Evangeline, on Hexabus's left, sits ramrod straight, her eyes blazing with indignation.

Maximus struggles against his magical restraints, jaw bulging as he grunts in protest. Dominus, in contrast, sits completely still, a storm holding its breath. Blood trickles down the side of his face from a gash at his temple.

Destiny's gaze shifts to Killian, but he refuses to look up at her. The slump of his shoulders is proof that he can feel the weight of her stare.

Once Madigan has pushed Destiny into her chair and bound her hands, the fiery restraint searing her wrists, he walks to the center of the room to the ceremonial fire's gray flames. "Isn't this lovely?" He turns slowly as he speaks. "The whole extended family together again. Such a pity, though, that Morty can't be here with us to enjoy this fire he spent so long conjuring for the family gathering, and which I've now revived."

Newton tries to speak, but the words that fall from her mouth sound like they've been hammered to a pulp by a meat cleaver. Madigan has clearly cast some kind of garbling spell on everyone. Still, Newton tries again, a guttural moan escaping her lips.

"Yes, absolutely," Madigan says, clapping. "Just as eloquent as always, Newton."

Darius hunches forward, heaving once and then twice, before throwing up all over himself.

Angel squeals as the stench of whiskey and bile permeates the room. Hexabus looks like she either wants to smack Darius or clean him up, probably both, in that order. Considering what Darius did earlier—how he came to find Destiny with the express intent of making her disappear—she struggles to find any sympathy for him.

When Darius is done, Madigan waves his hand to make the vomit disappear. A second flick of his wrist restores everyone's voices.

"How could you do this, Madigan?" Darius whines, a string of spittle dangling from his chin. "After everything I did for you, giving you a job, treating you like—"

"Dirt," Madigan finishes. "Like your personal punching bag. When what you should have been treating me like was a brother, since that's what I am."

The room erupts with echoing exclamations of surprise and disbelief. Darius's unfocused gaze becomes even glassier.

With that, Madigan smiles. "So, just to catch everyone up... I'm Madigan McGoo, bastard love child of Mordecai Scruffmore and Lumina Le Roux. Which makes six of you lucky buggers my half siblings."

"Actually," Evangeline says through gritted teeth, "there are five of us, not six."

"Good to know you're paying attention, but I'm afraid you're wrong," Madigan scoffs. "There *were* four of you, but then you all found out about Dominus, which makes five. Now, allow me to introduce you to yet another of your half siblings." He motions at Destiny, declaring, "Ta-da!"

All eyes turn to Destiny. She can feel herself flushing under the force of their scrutiny. Obviously, this is not how she wanted everyone to find out.

"I'm particularly excited about these newfound family bonds," Madigan continues, "because the spell I'm about to work calls for the sacrificial blood of siblings. The more siblings, the stronger the magic. And wouldn't you know it? I've suddenly hit the jackpot, going from being an only child to having this embarrassment of riches."

"But we're half siblings," Evangeline says, clearly hoping to find some kind of magical loophole. "The spell won't work with—"

"While this is a *very* finicky spell," Madigan agrees, "as long as we all share genetic material from the paternal line, the Eye of Gormodeus spell absolutely *will* work. I can promise you that."

"Spell?" Darius startles, his unfocused gaze struggling to latch on to Madigan.

"Yes, brother," Madigan says. "I know you thought you got your slimy little hands on the Eye after blackmailing Minx and

Angel so you could acquire it..." Madigan trails off, allowing Angel and Newton to express their outrage at this reveal. "But," he continues, "you and Morty weren't even close considering you were both looking for an artifact rather than a spell." He laughs. "Sorry to say, but that villager you met with earlier at the inn sold you a fake trinket, one I found at a Peasant novelty shop."

Darius groans as Madigan strides over to an ominous-looking cabinet that's hunkered down in the shadows. Madigan returns a moment later with a ceremonial dagger that's entirely black, its hilt made up of an ornate rendering of the Scruffmore family crest.

Destiny shivers as she spots the skull with ram horns, a knocker embedded in its mouth. How many more times must the Scruffmores knock on Death's door before they'll be satisfied?

Killian finally looks up from his examination of the floor. "You know with this kind of spellwork, one miscalculation could completely obliterate you, Madigan. Are you certain you're able to wield that much power?"

"Don't you worry about me, Lurk," Madigan replies, mocking Killian by mimicking his deep voice. "Unlike your old boss, *I* know exactly what I'm doing." With that, he spins the dagger like it's a baton, the blade glinting in the firelight. "Right, let's get this party started."

When Madigan turns his back to them, Killian's gaze flits over to Destiny, just as she expected it would. He raises an eyebrow, inviting an answer.

But considering everything she's feeling, she can't bring herself to give it just yet.

CHAPTER 89

Madigan

Wednesday—3:59 a.m.

"Dominus," Madigan calls, releasing the fiery bonds wrapped around his wrists, "we'll begin with the eldest. Get up."

When Dominus remains seated, arms crossed, Madigan experiences a twinge of annoyance. Does Dominus really think acting like an obstinate child will deter him? Especially when he's magic-proofed the room so only his own powers will work?

Nothing Dominus or anyone else can do will stop Madigan at this point. He thought his earlier violence when getting Dominus bound and moved to this room would've made him more compliant. But no. Some people apparently aren't all that smart.

With a sweep of his hand, Madigan shoots a spell that knocks his half brother off the chair. Dominus pitches forward, grunting as his knees slam into the stone floor. Madigan twitches his index finger and Dominus is instantly yanked to a standing position like a marionette whose strings have all been tugged at once.

When Maximus cries out in protest, Madigan says, "The more of a fuss you make, Maximus, the more I'll hurt him. We can either do this the easy way or the excruciating way. You decide." Maximus shuts up immediately and Madigan nods. "Good choice." And this is one of the reasons Madigan hates

Dominus, for having two fathers who would fight over him. One out of love, and one out of a sense of pride and entitlement. No one has ever fought for Madigan.

Turning back to Dominus, he says, "Any further insubordination from you, and your *father* will bear the consequences. I'm not messing around here."

Dominus hangs his head, limping to the fire while trying to keep his weight off his injured knee.

When he reaches it, Madigan throws the knife, sending it somersaulting across the room. Dominus flinches, but the dagger stops just short of him, hovering between his eyes.

"Life essence," the fire demands.

"Hold out your hand," Madigan instructs.

Dominus obeys and the dagger makes a small, precise incision intersecting the heart and life lines of his palm.

"Now make your blood sacrifice," Madigan commands.

Dominus holds his hand up over the fire, letting the blood drip into it.

The flames crackle, rising up to meet his arm, consuming it so that it appears as though he's been set alight. Dominus groans as searing pain must be shooting through his nerve endings.

"Now for your *other* sacrifice," Madigan says, delighting in the murmurs of alarm that ripple through the room.

"What other—"

Before Dominus can finish the question, four tentacles of blinding light erupt from the dagger, snaking out. One attaches itself to his chest, another to the center of his forehead. The other two make landfall, one on each of his temples.

"No!" Dominus shouts, but it's already too late.

The tentacles begin pulsating, creating enormous suction as they wrest from him what he isn't prepared to voluntarily give. He screams and then groans, thrashing wildly as he tries to rip the magical appendages free. The harder he pulls at them, the more fiercely they cling. It takes less than a minute until Dominus goes limp, his eyes rolling back.

It's over. Madigan has what he needs. "You may return to your seat."

Dominus staggers back to where he was sitting; he looks so bereft that Madigan has to smile. The offering must have been a strong one.

"Evangeline, you're next," he says. When she hesitates, her gaze affixed to Dominus's pale and clammy face, Madigan snaps, "Don't make me have to hurt your mother to encourage good behavior."

She does as she's told, though her eyes glisten with more fury than fear. *Ah, the suppressed rage is intense in this one*, Madigan thinks.

Evangeline's reaction to the unnatural probes isn't as strong as Dominus's, which is disappointing. The bleaker the victims appear to be afterward, the more they've sacrificed, meaning that Madigan has more power to work with.

After Evangeline returns to her seat, Madigan calls on Darius.

While he might have thrown up earlier, Darius is still so drunk that it's comical to watch him stagger to the fire. He makes his blood sacrifice and doesn't even protest when the tentacles attach themselves to him. He is a husk, a shell, with very little left to give. But he surprises Madigan with how haunted he appears once the leeches have done their work. Despite everything, Darius's childhood apparently harbored a few happy memories. More reason for Madigan to despise him.

"Angel and Minx," Madigan calls once Darius has stumbled back to his chair with his bleeding hand tucked into the opposite armpit. "Make your sacrifices together."

Angel stands, but Minx looks as though she's considering resisting him. Madigan nods at Newton to let Minx know what the punishment for her disobedience will be. He expects her to capitulate, just as Dominus and Evangeline did, but he's given her too much credit. Minx hesitates a moment too long, making it clear she's weighing up her options, not overly perturbed with the thought of her mother being tortured on her behalf.

Madigan flicks his middle finger with his thumb. Minx screeches, her hands flying up to cover her ears. What he's sent her is a sound so high-pitched that it's like a cyclone ripping through her eardrums. She screams for him to stop, and while he'd like to make her suffer indefinitely, he wants to hurry this up. He plans to have them all dead within the hour.

Silencing her shrieking, Madigan doesn't bother speaking to Minx since he knows she won't be able to hear him, not with her eardrums still ringing. He glares at her and it is enough to get her moving.

She places her trembling hand next to her sister's. The dagger draws a continuous line down both of their palms, blood rising to the surface of the surgical cut to kiss the air.

This time, when Madigan calls on the dagger, eight tentacles shoot out from it. The twins make their second sacrifice together, both shuddering and resistant. And why wouldn't they be? Their childhoods were the equivalent of fairy tales, at least the ones with happy endings. They grew up as princesses in a castle, their every need met, their every whim indulged. This, while Madigan grew up in Dickensian orphanages, wearing hand-me-down clothing, and going to bed hungry.

And all because *they* were born with the right birthmarks while he wasn't born with one at all. They owe him this and so much more.

Once the twins' sacrifices are complete, Madigan turns to Destiny. "Sorry to keep you waiting, but isn't that usually the way of the bastards? Always last in line, meekly waiting our turn with cupped palms outstretched."

He and Destiny are so much alike. Both outsiders who will never fit into the gentility and polish of this wealthy, refined world. Both looked down upon by the Scruffmores.

Destiny rises and begins walking to the fire, but then she comes to a halt and turns back to him. "You said you had no choice, because this was your destiny, but that's not true. You don't have to do this. You can choose to be a better man than our father was."

Madigan snorts, more amused than angry. "Okay, Oprah. Thanks for the pep talk."

"I'm serious." Destiny brushes red tendrils from her full moon of a face.

The shade of her hair is so violently offensive that Madigan can't help but wonder what her mother looked like. Try as he might, he was never able to determine the woman's identity because she covered her tracks thoroughly, ensuring that her mutt of a daughter never hunted her down and showed up on her doorstep.

Even Lumina, for all her faults, didn't go to that extreme.

There's a part of Madigan that feels sorry for Destiny and just how thoroughly she was severed from her mother upon the cutting of the umbilical cord. He wishes now that he'd asked Morty who his mistress was so Destiny could have some degree of closure. Considering her imminent death, though, he's not sure it would have mattered very much.

"You said our father deserved to die," Destiny continues. "You said you sleep better knowing you eradicated that kind of evil. But if you do this now, if you kill all of us like he was planning to do, what does that make you?"

"Smarter *and* more powerful than he was," Madigan crows. "It makes me triumphant in the one thing he yearned for but could never accomplish." As Destiny starts to speak again, he holds up a hand. "Save your breath. I don't want to hear the 'winning isn't everything' speech. Look around at these people, whose lives you're trying to save," he says, gesturing at them. "Do you think they give a damn about you? You think Minx wouldn't shank you just as soon as look at you?"

Destiny opens her mouth to protest but then, to her credit, closes it again. At least she's not completely deluded.

"They might not care about you, but I know you weirdly care about them." Madigan indicates Hexabus and Evangeline with the dip of his head. "I don't have to tell you what I'll do to them if you don't make your sacrifice."

"He's going to kill us all anyway," Hexabus cries out, her voice strangled. "Don't do it, Destiny."

Madigan is annoyed by Destiny's indecision as she considers the veracity of Hexabus's logic. He shuts them all up again with a flick of his wrist.

"Hexabus has a point," Destiny says. "We'll all be dead soon either way. I'd rather not help you become a murdering megalomaniac if I can help it."

Madigan sighs, amused by her goodness. "I didn't tell you this earlier," he says, softening his voice to match his expression, "because I didn't think it would make a difference, but I know who your mother is."

Destiny gasps, the sound amplified in the quiet room.

"Help me with this spell, and I'll not only reveal her identity, I'll also set you free so you can find her."

Destiny blinks. Tears begin to gather, making her mismatched eyes sparkle. "What about everyone else?" she asks cautiously, clearly torn. "Can't you use their sacrifices for the spell without killing them?"

God, her naivete almost hurts. There's believing the best in people, and then there's just plain stupidity. How she's managed to live this long, while being this gullible, is beyond him. Had they grown up together as real siblings, Madigan likes to think he would have helped Destiny toughen up and develop some street smarts.

"The spell will really work better if they're all dead," he says, pretending to mull it over.

"But you're such a powerful sorcerer," Destiny counters.

"Surely there's a way you can still make it work without them having to die?" Her eyes sparkle as she imagines a future in which she gets to meet her mother guilt-free. The desperation emanates from her, stinking up the place.

He once felt that too, needing so much to meet his birth parents. Life is full of disappointments even when your dreams come true. Especially then. But maybe he doesn't need to be the one who teaches her that lesson. Not yet anyway.

"You're right," he says, as though conceding the point. "I could."

Evangeline and Hexabus both protest, but the sounds come out like soft grunts, as if they're punching bags that are being pummeled.

"So, to be clear," Destiny hedges, "if I give my sacrifices, you'll let everyone go *and* you'll tell me who my mother is?"

The twins protest now, squawking like baby vultures. If anyone can spot deception, they can because it takes a soulless liar to recognize one. He won't have them raining on Destiny's parade.

"You drive a mean bargain, Destiny Whip," Madigan says, shaking his head ruefully as he rocks on his heels. "To be honest, it's tough to say no to you. So…okay, you've got a deal."

Destiny smiles shyly. "You promise?"

"I do," he says. He makes sure to maintain eye contact with her the whole time.

Destiny nods and then extends her palm as though to shake hands, making a target of herself for the dagger. When it slices her hand, she dutifully transfers it to the flames so none of her blood will be wasted. Pausing for a second, she casts Madigan an indecipherable look. And then she makes her sacrifice.

CHAPTER 90

Destiny

Wednesday—4:21 a.m.

There are all the exact same tells that gave Madigan away as a liar when I first met him, Destiny thinks with a sinking sensation.

She wishes that she'd listened to her instincts without talking herself out of mistrusting him. She wonders how many women do the same to their own detriment, telling themselves that they're imagining things, or being overly critical, or are just too sensitive.

Her own subconscious tried to warn her that Madigan was a threat, someone to pay attention to, and yet Destiny didn't believe or trust herself. Same went for Darius, whom she sensed had a darkness in him within mere minutes of their meeting. And yet she wanted so much to believe that he was better than he'd ever shown her to be that she foolishly gave him the benefit of the doubt only to have him weaponize it against her.

Finally, what she's doing now, is placing complete and utter faith in herself. She's all in, her chips all bet on herself. It's utterly terrifying, but it's the most powerful step she's ever taken.

Her palm stings, but that's to be expected considering the nerve endings of the epidermis have been sliced. Destiny doesn't think the knife administered any kind of poison while cutting her. That would be too subtle an approach, since poison is usually a woman's weapon of choice.

Madigan has proven that, just like his father, he prefers grand gestures and big flourishes rather than anything silent or invisible, no matter how deadly. When he kills them all, she's certain that his plan will be for everyone to go out with a bang *and* a whimper.

Destiny's so distracted by her thoughts that she forgets to brace for what's coming next. When the enormous tentacles of light flail out from the dagger, she reflexively steps back, but there's no escaping. Each one firmly attaches like a giant leech trying to burrow under her skin. It was scary enough witnessing them being unleashed on everyone else; being on the receiving end is terrifying.

They pulse and writhe, sucking with all their might. Destiny's mind tries to shut down to block them out, but they bulldoze their way in. She gets a sense that the tentacles are giant parasites hunting for something, as though their hunger can only be satiated by one very particular morsel of food. The three at her head tug and tug at her memories, while the one at her heart opens a floodgate of emotions.

As the memory blooms into vivid color, Destiny feels untethered and lightheaded. There she is, eight years old, sitting at the table in her living room with her mother, and Annie, and Nate. The four of them are huddled together over a Clue board. When Destiny announces that she's ready to solve the murder, everyone groans, complaining that they haven't even eliminated a single suspect yet.

This is Destiny's last completely happy memory of her childhood.

In it, she feels safe and loved, but also smart and confident. She's surrounded by her unusual little family. While putting on a big show protesting her declaration of victory, they are all so incredibly proud of her, never missing an opportunity to tell her as much.

In just three days after this moment, her mother will be dead, and nothing will ever be the same again.

The warmth that usually accompanies this memory ignites melancholy. The cohesive image explodes into a billion individual pixels that begin to get siphoned off one by one. At first, only the edges disappear, as though gnawed on by a pack of rats. *It's fine*, Destiny tells herself to fight off the panic. *I don't need the edges.*

But then Annie's face disappears, followed swiftly by Nate's and Liz's.

Destiny screams, trying desperately to cling to her security blanket of the memory. But this time, it's her mental fingers that don't have sufficient ridges to provide a firm enough grip. Like the umbrella plucked from her hand on the night she arrived on the island, this recollection is snatched away along with all the happiness it's cocooned in. What remains is the same gray mist that enveloped Destiny on the ferry.

She pants, licking her dry lips. What Madigan has been doing is stealing all their happiest childhood memories for himself, harnessing them because he has none of his own.

The familiar darkness hovers, ready to swoop in. She's about to stagger back to the refuge of her seat when Madigan grabs her wrist, apparently not done with her.

"Why don't you stand here while I make my sacrifice?" he says. "That way, you can supervise me to be sure I keep my promise."

What he means is that he plans to use her as a human shield just in case something goes wrong with the very finicky spell. This could be it, the end for everyone in this room. Destiny's surprised to discover that she doesn't care all that much.

As Madigan drops her wrist and busies himself with the dagger—running it through the fire as though to sterilize it—

Destiny looks back to Killian. The usually unflappable butler is perspiring now, beads of sweat running from his temples. If he could speak, she suspects he would, but Madigan has silenced everyone again.

Instead, Killian widens his eyes as he nods at Destiny's chest. She looks down, expecting to see blood seeping from where the tentacle attached itself. But there isn't any.

Is it her heart that he means? Something he's trying to tell her about courage?

No, that's not it.

The last of the puzzle pieces fall into place as Destiny finally understands.

Madigan turns to face her, and Destiny tears her gaze away from Killian, careful not to alert Madigan to their interaction.

Looking down, she notices that Madigan is still barefoot, his feet dirty from when he was scampering through the castle as Sarcophagus. The sight of his toes feels somehow obscene and so she looks at his hands, remembering how she thought his calluses were proof of a man who did manual labor when, in fact, they were a clue to Madigan's nocturnal habits in raccoon form.

"Thank you, dear siblings, for your selfless offerings," Madigan says once he's satisfied that the blade is clean. "You should be grateful to Destiny for sparing your lives. I would have happily killed you all."

No one believes he'll keep his promise. They're all squirming in their seats, issuing muffled entreaties or cries for help. Minx glares at Destiny like she can't believe what a fool she is for falling for Madigan's lies.

"Let's do Christmas together this year." Madigan chuckles, removing the medallion and Mordecai's sigil from the pouch around his neck. "I make a mean Yorkshire pudding. You're all going to love it." He winks at Minx. "Though probably not you, considering how you feel about the evils of carbs."

Minx growls.

Madigan drops the sigil into the fire, which groans appreciatively. He then tosses the medallion up, and the fire snakes a tentacle out to snatch it. The groan deepens into something repugnant.

Madigan holds up his palm to cut it, and blood rushes to embrace the blade. Closing his eyes, he begins to center himself for the Eye of Gormodeus spell. Taking a few deep breaths, he starts by uttering a guttural lament, producing noises that are half reminiscent of language and partially like the howling of wolves. The sound makes goose bumps prickle her flesh.

The howls give way to hissing, which then builds into a kind of gasping, before Madigan reaches to hold his hand over the flames.

A few crimson droplets gather themselves in slow motion, becoming bottom heavy with potential. As they begin to plummet into the flames below, Destiny reaches up and snatches her amulet out from under her T-shirt.

Her mother's voice whispers to her across the chasm of death, an echo from the past. *Hold on to the amulet. Don't let go, okay?*

Destiny holds on just as she did the night Liz was murdered, holding on as she has every single time that life became too much, when fear and anxiety and dread threatened to overwhelm her, sucking her into the bottomless pit of darkness. Or when grief rose like a tide that would never recede. Or when regret became a siren call, luring her to existential rocks that promised to batter her to pieces.

She holds on because sometimes that's all you can do when the abyss calls to you.

And then the ground shakes and shudders as though the castle were built on the back of a dragon that's trying to buck them all off. Destiny is knocked sideways as the stones ripple beneath her, the amulet still clutched in her hand.

There's an explosion as the firepit erupts, gray flames snatching wildly at any fuel they can feed themselves with.

Wind whips through the vaulted room as though summoned by the gods. It whirls and whooshes, a twister that has been unleashed. It shrieks and sighs, whoops and hollers. Just when it feels like its attack will never end, the wind abruptly dies down, completely spent.

The ensuing silence is almost worse than the fury.

Destiny opens her eyes as a bolt of lightning tears through one of the windows. The glass is obliterated, shards exploding into billions of tiny filaments of glitter, which swirl from the sky, a blizzard of sparkling snow.

Madigan roars as the bolt hits him. He shudders, the electric storm tearing through him, refusing to release its grip. His howling builds and builds, never quite reaching its crescendo.

Destiny shields her eyes so that she can look up at him, a human lightning rod.

She blinks and when she opens her eyes again, Madigan is gone. All that remains is the glitter and the dust, the air crackling with static.

Destiny doesn't know how long she lies there before she hears movement, crunching footsteps getting louder. Killian suddenly comes into view, bent over her, covered in debris, and looking somehow both terrified and hopeful all at once.

"Dad?" Destiny croaks.

Her father nods and kneels to wrap her trembling body in his arms.

CHAPTER 91

Killian

Wednesday—9:00 a.m.

Killian pauses outside his bedroom door, hesitant to cross the threshold. He's had Mrs. Scuggs move Destiny into his quarters to convalesce, knowing she'll be more comfortable here than in the damp dungeons, where he never wanted her in the first place.

He's utterly spent after returning from Hexabus's chambers. They say confession is good for the soul, but it's hell on the adrenal glands. She always maintained that he was withholding information, and she was right, though not in the way she suspected. It wasn't out of any sense of loyalty to Morty that he didn't tell her everything.

All along, Killian was just trying to protect Destiny.

His hand automatically rises to straighten his tie, a ridiculously futile gesture considering how disheveled he is. *Quit stalling*, he tells himself, and then knocks.

"Come in," Destiny calls, her voice faint.

Killian first hopes he hasn't woken her but then quickly wishes he has since that would mean she's gotten some rest, at least. Opening the door, he steps inside and is immediately struck anew by how much Destiny looks like her mother. The same beautiful flaming hair and mismatched eyes, the same tentative smile and disarming gaze.

"Are you up for a visit?" Killian asks, breaking eye contact. Looking down, he notices how dirty his gloves are and tucks his hands behind his back.

"Yes," Destiny says. "Thank you for giving me your room. It really wasn't necessary."

A lump begins to rise in Killian's throat, cutting off the torrent of protests about how wrong she is. He approaches her tentatively, and finally comes to a stop at the foot of the bed. She has his quilt pulled up to her chin, and her emotional-support urn is tucked into her arm like a stuffed toy. From close-up, the bruises and scrapes on her face are startling.

He winces. "You warm enough?"

She nods.

"Has the elixir Hexabus mixed helped with the pain?"

Destiny nods again. "Did someone release Lumina?" she asks.

"Yes! We found her restrained in the inn's attic. She's dehydrated and a bit worse for wear, but we've brought her back to the castle, where she'll be taken care of."

"That's good," Destiny says, and then comes to his rescue by taking control of the situation. "Pull up a seat." She nods at a chair next to the bed. "There's a lot we need to discuss."

Oh, thank god, Killian thinks. He's never been very good at small talk. Not that he's much better at big talk or deep talk, but he'll take them over the former any day.

Sitting, Killian says, "I know you figured a lot of it out yourself, but I'd like to tell you everything. And then I'd like to ask you a few questions, if I may?"

"Go ahead," Destiny replies, nodding.

Killian begins speaking, explaining that, when Destiny first arrived at the castle, he immediately recognized her as his daughter from the conferences he'd attended to see her in action. What completely flummoxed him, though, was how she'd come to be there, insisting that she'd been invited. He wanted her gone, as far away from Morty as possible, and yet he also needed to know who'd sent for her so he could understand the extent of the danger she was in.

"After I failed to save Bramble," Killian says, "I was wild with grief. I wanted to kill Morty, but I didn't have the power. I wanted to leave and never come back but couldn't because too much was at stake. My hands were tied in so many ways, and yet the one thing I knew was in my control was that I could prevent the eradication of more seers."

He describes that, just after Bramble died, Morty heard whispers about a seer who'd managed to slip through the cracks, one who might have a lead on the prophecy about him. Killian offered to go and kill the seer himself to spare Morty the trip. After all, Morty's son had just died, and the appearance of bereavement needed to be maintained.

"That's when you met my mother," Destiny ventures.

"Yes," Killian replies. He explains the shop of curiosities she was running and how he only intended to discover what records she might have about the prophecy. "But we had an instant connection. She saw right into the heart of me," he says, patting his chest, "and how very broken I was." It takes him a moment to compose himself before he can speak again. "She saw my grief and invited me to stay. And so I did."

Killian sent missives to Morty saying the hunt was proving more challenging than expected, and that he was following various trails to find the seer as well as others he'd been tipped off about. "None of which was true. I stayed with her because, for the first time in my life, I wasn't being drained by being with another person. To the contrary, she was healing me and fueling me in a way I'd never experienced before."

Killian smiles as he thinks of his surprise at discovering he could be touched without a galaxy of pain being transferred to him, how very freeing it was to experience that without all the usual amulets and protective spells he'd been using as a kind of psychic prophylaxis.

"One thing led to another, as they do," he says, coughing as he blushes. "It's important for you to know that I had feelings for her, ones that could have developed with time had I not been as emotionally wrecked as I was, and had I not needed to return to keep watch over Morty. She was an incredibly special woman, your mother."

Destiny smiles through the tears that glisten twin trails down her cheeks.

Killian pulls out a handkerchief that's less white and starched than he would like and hands it to her. "I found the prophecy there just as Morty's intelligence said I would. It was in her attic. Tomes and tomes of scrying records that had been kept through the generations. It was actually her great-great-grandmother who made the original prophecy about Morty. A copy of it ended up in his vault, which is where Lumina found it."

"You thought the redheaded Seer as foretold by the prophecy was my mother," Destiny says, "and so you knew she was in terrible danger. You memorized it and then destroyed the original to protect her, returning to Mordecai empty-handed, saying it was a dead end after all."

"Yes, exactly. Though I told him I still took care of her, one less seer to worry about."

"How long after I was born did Morty find out the truth about my mother, returning to kill her?" Destiny asks. She's trying to sound matter-of-fact, but her voice is raw with pain. "I'm assuming it was soon afterward, while I was still a baby, which is how I ended up adopted by Liz."

Killian startles, taken aback. "No, he didn't find out about her for a long time, not until you were eight."

"Wait…" Destiny says, brows furrowing. "I don't understand…"

Killian tries to say it as gently as he can. "Destiny, Liz *was* your biological mother. She was the seer I went to see, though I knew her by another name, her real one, before she legally changed it."

16. You now have all the information you require to solve these two word puzzles, which will reveal the real name of Destiny's mother. Each name must use all seven letters at least once. The name could be more than seven letters, using some of the letters twice. For a clue, email DestinyWhipClue@gmail. com with the subject line Clue Sixteen. Once you've solved them, turn to page 476 to check your answer.

CHAPTER 92

Destiny

Wednesday—9:30 a.m.

There must be some mistake, Destiny thinks as she shakes her head. "No, Liz adopted me as a baby."

Killian sighs, running a hand over his forehead, looking exhausted and gray. "After I returned to the castle," he says, "I suspected that Morty didn't believe that I'd killed the seer. I immediately sent a message telling her she needed to go into hiding for her own safety. That's when she told me she was pregnant." Killian shakes his head as if the action might rid him of a lifetime of shame and regret. "I wanted so much to go to her, to meet you, but I couldn't. I was terrified that in doing so, I'd lead Morty straight to you both. And so I helped her disappear and become Liz. She had a home birth, so there would be no record of it, and we forged documents saying you were adopted. No one asked any questions in her new town."

It seems impossible and yet...

What Destiny recalls so vividly when she was locked inside that closet is hearing her mother's muffled voice pleading, *She doesn't have it, I swear.* And then, after opening and closing drawers, her declaring, *Here, I have proof!*

Destiny had clutched the amulet as she hid, thinking *that's* what her mother was lying about, though she wasn't sure what Liz might have offered as proof. A decoy amulet, perhaps?

But now she understands.

Liz changed her name, pretending to be Destiny's nonmagical adoptive mother. So if Mordecai ever came for Liz—believing her to be The Seer mentioned in the prophecy—and then discovered she had a daughter, she could show him the adoption papers. They would prove Destiny couldn't have inherited the gift from Liz since it could only be passed down from mother to biological daughter. In that way, he wouldn't view Destiny as a threat after he'd already eliminated The Seer.

Destiny marvels at the lengths her mother went to, to protect her: selling her family's business, switching her occupation, and then moving away. Liz legally changed her name, wore colored contact lenses to hide her heterochromia, dyed her hair black, touched up her red roots on a weekly basis, and obsessively straightened her curls each day.

She also cultivated a deep friendship with her neighbor, Annie Carter, so that in the event anything might happen to her, Annie would step in to take care of Destiny.

One of the last conversations Destiny had with her mother comes back to her now.

What have I always told you about dreams?

That they're nonsense, just figments of the imagination that are not to be taken seriously.

And why is that?

Because the only things that hold value are facts and logic, rationality and reason.

And what did I say about intuition?

It's never to be trusted.

Good. Why not?

Because feelings are like the weather—they change every day. The only constant is knowledge and the pursuit thereof. It is the bedrock upon which civilization is built.

Her mother's almost tyrannical insistence that Destiny ignore her strange dreams and strong intuition was because allowing her daughter to indulge them meant that she could unwittingly expose herself to Mordecai. All along, she was trying to save Destiny's life.

And in that, she'd succeeded.

No wonder Destiny found nothing but dead ends every time she tried searching for her birth records. Liz and Killian did everything they could to ensure that Mordecai would never be able to find Destiny.

And yet he'd found Liz somehow. "Is that why you sent my mom the letter when you did? The one you signed 'Yours, Kye,' her nickname for you? Was it to warn her that Mordecai was coming?"

Killian hangs his head sorrowfully. "No. Had I known, I would have made sure to move her to another place of safety. She'd actually communicated with me just prior to that—"

"Via letter?" Destiny asks.

Killian laughs softly. "No. She'd send me messages through my dreams."

Destiny gasps, thinking of all the times she was feeling down because the kids at school teased her for being a nerd or a weirdo, and how these bouts of the blues would be followed by a fiery guardian angel who visited her dreams, telling Destiny how incredibly smart and capable she was, and that she was going to change the world, so it didn't matter what those bullies had to say. The dreams ended abruptly after Liz died, only to be replaced by terrifying nightmares. Now she knows why.

"Your mother said you were a very bright and sensitive child," Killian continues. "And on top of the seer's gift you'd inherited from her, she was worried you might have inherited my own gift and that you might become an empathician."

"The amulet," Destiny says, looking down at it. "I figured out earlier that you'd been the one to send it, which is why I knew it would help against Madigan's spell, but I thought you'd sent it to my adoptive mother."

They sit in silence for a while, Killian giving her time to process everything.

Finally, Destiny says, "What did you want to ask me?"

"How did you figure out that I was your father?" Killian rests his chin on his steepled fingers, his elbows balanced on his knees. He's a tall man and looks quite awkward sitting in this position.

"Madigan didn't realize Bramble was your son, though he knew you and Hexabus were romantically involved. And so he made three incorrect assumptions." Destiny holds up a finger each time she points one out. "One, he thought Bramble's birthmark was inherited from Mordecai. Two, he followed you a few times when you left the castle to watch me speak at events, assuming you were keeping an eye on me for your boss. Three, on one of those occasions, he saw my birthmark and thought that because it was a keyhole connector sigil just like Bramble's, I had to be Mordecai's daughter."

Killian nods but remains quiet, gesturing for Destiny to continue.

"I knew Bramble wasn't Mordecai's son, though I did think I was his daughter. But I quickly realized that you never confirmed that theory. When I made my own foolish assumption, you didn't correct me, which isn't the same as confirming something."

Killian swallows deeply, his Adam's apple bobbing. "I'm so sorry, Destiny. I wanted to tell you, and I was planning to. I'd always imagined how it might be if I ever got to have that conversation with you, but I didn't want it to be like that, not with Hexabus sitting there, so angry with me. And not when I couldn't do it properly because we were running out of time."

"I understand," Destiny says, and she really does. "Everything fell into place quickly after that," she continues. "If Bramble was your son, and he and I shared the same birthmark, then we had to share the same father. I realized why you were so alarmed to see me at the castle and why you were so eager for me to leave. Also, that the Kye from my mother's letter was a nickname for you, short for Killian. And you'd sent the amulet, which has always helped me in times of deep distress."

"And so, when Madigan spoke of the Eye of Gormodeus..." Killian prompts.

"You and I both realized that using my blood would backfire on him because he and I didn't share genetic material. I didn't know I needed to hold on to the amulet until you nodded at it. I never understood that it had magical powers."

"The only protection I could give you was a black opal amulet guarding against dark forces and the darkness within us," Killian says. "When I loathed myself so much for not saving Bramble and all those villagers, the amulet helped keep the self-hatred at bay so I could continue to function. In the same way, it helped you deal with grief and depression. It wasn't nearly enough, but it's all I had." Killian clears his throat, a sound akin to earthmoving equipment trying to disassemble a mountain. "Your mother and I knew we could never tell you who I was as long as Morty was looking for The Seer. I dared not hope that one day, if the threat ever went away, we might have a relationship. I wouldn't blame you if you wanted nothing to do with me."

Destiny thinks how she came here looking for family. And how she found it.

Discovering that Killian is her biological father doesn't detract from anything her two mothers gave her. If anything, it makes her appreciate Liz and Annie even more, understanding all they gave up to keep her safe.

She wishes so much that motherhood wasn't so closely entwined with sacrifice, and that it were possible to either give someone life, like Liz did, or love them unconditionally despite not birthing them, like Annie did, without it meaning a life sentence of giving and giving and giving.

A child should not be the knife that whittles away at its mother bit by bit, leaving nothing but a meager pile of shavings.

A mother should be the one doing the carving, turning that block of wood into something essential and useful so the world will be made better by it. And she should be able to work on her own block as well, turning herself into as much of a beautiful creation as her children are.

Thinking of mothers brings Hexabus to mind.

Destiny looks up at Killian. "I think I know where Bramble is."

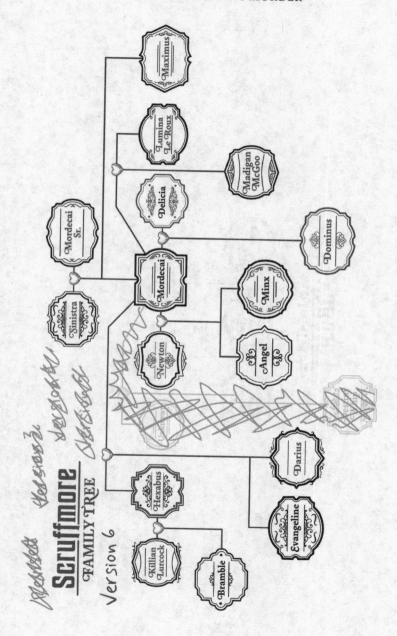

Scruffmore
FAMILY TREE

Version 6

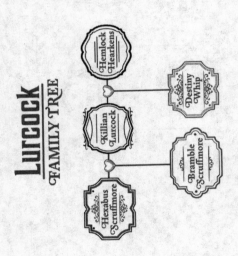

Lurcock
FAMILY TREE

Hemlock Hearkens

Destiny Whip

Killian Lurcock

Bramble Scruffmore

Hexabus Scruffmore

CHAPTER 93

Destiny

Wednesday—11:30 a.m.

Destiny winces as the pain in her hip flares with each step down the cobbled side street. She wishes she'd accepted Killian's offer of a cane but knows forgoing it was the right choice. She doesn't want to take the chance that if she spots Bramble, he might view it as a weapon.

That's also why she insisted she come by herself.

The only person Bramble has revealed himself to is Destiny, and that was on the night she arrived on the island.

She remembers how, after her umbrella tumbled away, she spotted the cat's glowing eyes in the recesses of a storefront doorway. The creature was almost completely jet-black except for a white patch between its eyes that reminded Destiny of the hourglass-shaped birthmark on her wrist.

After the cat had warned her to leave, Destiny held up her hands and backed away. That's when its hackles lowered and it stepped forward, threading its way between her legs as it began to purr.

She understands now that Bramble was reacting to Destiny's birthmark. He might have let her pet him, perhaps even followed her, had she not ruined it by asking him if he wanted to go to the Scruffmore castle so they could be besties with Mordecai together.

That's when he scratched her nose, clearly considering her an enemy since she was aligned with Mordecai, the father who'd killed him.

There's a chance that if Bramble came to her once, he might trust her again. And a mob of people accompanying her would just frighten him away.

Following the same route she took that night, albeit much more slowly because of her injury, Destiny spots a few cats lounging about, though not as many as she'd expect. None is the one she's looking for. She can't help but wonder if any of them are Mordecai's victims or their offspring. If she manages to find Bramble, there's still a lot of work in figuring out whether they might be able to restore him and the other cats to some semblance of their human form.

They have more questions than answers at this point. Still, it's worth trying.

Destiny finds the overhang where Bramble was taking shelter the night she arrived, but it's not raining today, so he'd have no reason to be here. There are a lot more people milling about too, islanders who're taking advantage of both the sunshine and their improved circumstances. A motorbike whizzed past Destiny earlier, charging up the hill to the castle, and there are workers who appear to be installing electric lights in the streets.

So if he's not taking cover here, and likely to be wary of all the villagers, where might Bramble be?

As she walks along, Destiny thinks of the list Hexabus gave her of places where Bramble used to love exploring. She has a feeling she won't find him in any of them since she can't imagine how difficult it would be for him to watch other children enjoying the very experiences that he can no longer partake in.

She stops, realizing that she could walk the island for weeks on end and never stumble upon him. She needs to be intentional, really think it through. Might he go to the beach, the last place he was alive and vital as a little boy, where he made the churning ocean do his bidding? Destiny doesn't think so, as that would also be associated with his ensuing death.

Have the cats noticed the changes on the island? she wonders. *Do they know that Mordecai is dead?*

Animals are extremely smart and incredibly intuitive, so it's highly likely. And if Bramble wanted to be found now that his father has been vanquished, where might he expect his family to look for him?

It comes to Destiny in a flash. She groans as she turns and begins her ascent up the hill, back the way she came.

★ ★ ★

The cemetery gate squeaks as Destiny opens it, though it sounds more like a welcome than a warning. Turning around after closing the gate behind her, Destiny gasps.

More than a dozen cats sit alert throughout the graveyard, all of them perched atop tombstones. As she passes each one, they regard her with interest, their gemstone-colored eyes following her progress. When she holds out a tentative hand, some greet her with a gentle meow, allowing her to stroke them. Others retreat, wary.

A black cat farther along catches Destiny's eye, and her heart begins to race.

She wants to run to it and sweep it up, but she's also terrified of scaring it off. Instead, Destiny murmurs words of comfort as she makes her way over to a tombstone that depicts an angel slumped over a grave. It's only when Destiny's up close that she sees, to her disappointment, that the cat's face is completely black; the white hourglass mark Destiny remembers is missing.

Still, the cat is friendly, and it leans into Destiny's palm, purring loudly as she rubs her hand along its arched spine. Looking down at the tombstone, Destiny sees the name *Dawn Montgomery* chiseled into it.

"Oh!" Destiny exclaims, her hands flying to her mouth. "You're Evangeline's friend." The cat meows plaintively and Destiny gently reaches out to pick her up. Remembering the damage Bramble did to her nose, she's wary of the cat's claws. But she needn't be. As Destiny cradles the creature in her arms, it nuzzles into her neck, rubbing its velvety head back and forth against her skin.

Destiny thinks of everything she now knows. How Dawn was discovered lovingly laid out on the beach, a flower threaded through her black hair. And how it was Destiny's father who did that, her father who reached out and put his bare hands on Dawn after Mordecai murdered her, and who—despite the huge emotional toll it took on him—saturated himself with her memories so he could pay tribute to her in her death.

Destiny aches for Dawn. And for Killian. And for Dawn's parents. And for every one of these souls whose light was snatched by a man who was nothing but a bottomless pit of darkness. It enrages her that Mordecai felt entitled to Dawn's future, that he tried to feed and empower himself with it simply because he could.

She is so proud of her father for ensuring that didn't happen, for refusing to allow Dawn's pure soul to be tainted by Mordecai's evil.

The cat, perhaps sensing her inner turmoil, disentangles itself to hop down, and Destiny casts her gaze around until she spots the towering headstone.

Bramble Mordecai Scruffmore
28 February 1992–28 February 2000
"It's never too late to be what you might have been."

She's chilled by the epitaph, understanding it to mean Bramble was meant for greatness in life, but he only achieved it by dying, thus ensuring Mordecai wouldn't have an Achilles' heel. Of course, Mordecai judged Bramble's greatness only in terms of how well the boy was able to serve his father. That is, after all, the way of narcissists.

Drawing close, Destiny's disappointed not to find a cat seated on the black marble. All the others appear to be waiting at their own headstones, sensing their loved ones will come and visit soon enough. She walks around the grave that was so recently dug up, double-checking that a cat isn't hiding behind it.

But there's nothing.

Destiny thinks back to what Hexabus said. *So many of those cats were granted unusually long lives, but that doesn't mean…something didn't happen to him in the intervening years.*

While Destiny's certain she saw Bramble three nights ago, something might have happened to him since then. She thinks of the awful weather, the lightning strikes and fallen branches, the racing carriages, and the unruly umbrellas.

Would life be so singularly unfair as to keep Bramble alive for this long only to take him hours before he could be reunited with his family?

It's a silly question and Destiny already knows the answer. *Yes, of course it would.*

She doesn't want to cry, but she was so hopeful. Finding a father seemed like an impossibility, and yet the impossible came true, which allowed Destiny to foolishly believe that it just might happen for her half brother, that they could find and restore Bramble in some way.

She sacrificed an essential childhood memory to Madigan, and while she can't remember what it was, she feels its loss like a broken rib, the ache punctuating each breath. Though she can't ever retrieve it, there was a part of Destiny that was hopeful the formation of new memories could help heal the break, making it easier to breathe.

She sniffs and swats away a tear, telling herself she's being ridiculous. This loss is not hers. It's Hexabus's and Killian's. It's Evangeline's and even Darius's. And now she has to break their hearts after getting their hopes up, exactly what Hexabus asked her not to do.

Destiny turns to address the other cats, about to tell them to stay here because help is coming. That's when something springs down from an overhanging branch and lands on Bramble's tombstone. The creature is as black as the marble, and when it turns to gaze at Destiny, she feels as though fireworks have been set off inside her.

This one has the white keyhole marking on its face.

"Bramble," Destiny whispers. "It's you. It's really you."

If she was expecting her brother to jump into her outstretched arms, it's only because she hasn't had a lot of experience with cats. Instead, he turns and makes a show of majestically flashing her his butt. Which, though Destiny doesn't know it yet, is the highest compliment a cat can bestow.

Destiny's heart swells and she thinks back to four days ago when she sat in her darkened bedroom, her pills all positioned on her bedside table, standing up like mini headstones. And here she is now in a real graveyard. But instead of burying her hopes and dreams, she's finally digging herself free.

As Bramble turns and nudges Destiny's hip, she whispers, "Family."

If that isn't the most powerful magical word ever spoken, then Destiny doesn't know what is.

CHAPTER 94

Destiny

One Year Later

Destiny waves goodbye to Stanley, who honks his horn twice in farewell before turning the taxi around to head back over the drawbridge. It's a beautiful day, the air crisp, and the sky a dazzling blue, like a celestial field of forget-me-nots.

Seagulls glide overhead, squawking their greetings as Destiny reaches down to pick up the cat carrier that, due to its transparent viewing bubble, looks more like a space helmet than a backpack. It's this feature that appeals to Bramble, who enjoys being ferried around like a feline prince.

"We're here," Destiny trills, adjusting the straps over her shoulders.

In response, Bramble issues a protracted meow, one she recognizes as expressing excitement.

As she navigates the path, she's careful not to jostle him since travel sickness is unfortunately a trait the half siblings share. Once at the castle's entrance, Destiny's about to lift the enormous iron door knocker when the door swings open.

"Dezzie!" Zephyr exclaims. "Welcome back!"

Destiny smiles at the nickname, which is no less thrilling despite her having become accustomed to it. It's not as if she's developed a crush on Dominus's royal adviser. Not at all. That would be incredibly foolish considering how closely they've been working together, not to mention that Zephyr—with his astonishing mind, his immense talent, and his dark auburn hair and deep violet eyes—is highly unlikely to return her feelings.

But still… As Zephyr pulls her into a bear hug, Destiny allows herself a frisson of something that isn't entirely platonic regardless of how inadvisable it is.

"We've missed you," Zephyr exclaims, making Destiny blush. And then he reads her T-shirt's slogan aloud. "'A well-read woman is a dangerous creature.'" His eyes shine with amusement. "She is, indeed. I'm so glad to see the T-shirts are back. I missed them."

That makes Destiny flush even hotter. The last time she was here, she tried dressing up in ill-fitting flouncy blouses, feminine skirts, and strappy high-heeled sandals thinking they would make more of an impression on Zephyr. They didn't. If anything, he just asked whether it was laundry day.

Plus, she felt ridiculously self-conscious, unable to bend to properly play with the cats in case her boobs spilled over the low-cut neckline, and nervous she might flash someone while sitting down. Also, those heels were killer on the ankles.

As difficult as it sometimes is being herself, she still finds it so much easier than trying to be anyone else.

"Destiny!" Dominus calls as he jogs down the stairs to welcome her.

"Dom, hello." Destiny hugs him in greeting. "Thanks for hosting all these sessions!"

"Of course. It's the least I can do."

But that's not true. It was Dominus who most firmly sided with Destiny originally, insisting that the human islanders be told the truth about what had happened to their loved ones all those years ago. And he's spearheaded the project of reconciling the families, hiring Zephyr as their chief translator and adviser while they've been rolling out the program Destiny devised.

Dominus has gone above and beyond to make reparations for all the destruction his father wrought. Each day, in every choice he makes, Dominus proves that we are not just the clay;

we are the sculptors' hands as we mold and form ourselves into the people we want to be.

Zephyr reaches for Bramble's carrier, carefully unclipping it from Destiny's back. "Where's your luggage?"

"Oh, I'm staying at the inn this time around," Destiny replies. "I stopped there on the way to drop off my suitcase and to collect Bramble."

"I take it that means the renovations are complete." Dominus ushers Destiny into the foyer. "How's the place looking?"

"Beautiful. Dad and Hexabus did such an amazing job." Destiny no longer superstitiously hesitates before using the word *Dad*, as though the act of speaking it aloud might tempt any vengeful gods who happen to be eavesdropping. "They'll be following along shortly. They're just making the finishing touches ahead of tomorrow's grand reopening."

Zephyr sets the carrier down and opens it. Bramble hops out and stretches before making his way between Dominus's legs.

Looking around the entrance hall, Destiny says, "I see they haven't been the only busy ones."

She notes the changes made since she was last here a month ago, before she left for her consultancy in Istanbul. The magical black substance that covered the walls has been scoured off completely, revealing a warm red stone underneath, and a gleaming wooden banister has replaced the staircase's deadly swords. The portrait of Mordecai with Newton, Minx, and Angel has also disappeared. In its place is a beautiful tapestry of the island, the castle perched atop rock, nestled between cerulean sky and azure sea.

Since Dominus officially accepted the crown and moved in to the castle ten months ago, the island has transformed completely. Many of the islanders have left now that the restraining magic is no longer in effect, but new inhabitants have also arrived, eager to start businesses in a burgeoning tourist destination.

For, while the daylight hours are filled with glorious sunshine and ample opportunity to swim and sunbathe, the evenings are known for swirling mist and spectacular thunderstorms. The island is the best of both worlds, a portal to another realm that attracts those on a pilgrimage to connect with the supernatural.

Or, at least, that's what the website and glossy brochures say.

The marketing campaign's success has been as much of a surprise as the person who stepped up with the vision to spearhead it.

After they recovered the bag of blackmail cash from where Madigan had stashed it at the inn, it was Hexabus who suggested the money be given to Newton because no one could find Mordecai's last will and testament, and settling the estate could take decades. Instead of taking the money and running as everyone expected, Newton invested it in a tourism firm, leveraging Angel's influencer status to literally put Eerie Island on the map.

While Newton and Angel do a wonderful job attracting a constant flux of tourists, they don't visit very often, citing a host of social engagements that keep them away. Minx has another five years of her sentence to serve for the crimes of extortion and attempted murder, though there's talk of her getting out of the magical prison in Romania early due to good behavior. Destiny can't imagine that the bar for said behavior can be set very high, but she remains hopeful that Minx has been changed by her incarceration, perhaps even become a better person in the process.

"Everyone's waiting for you," Zephyr says as Bramble dashes off to meet his friends in the great hall. "I have a few documents to assist Dominus with, but I'll join you as soon as I can to help out."

"Perfect," Destiny says. "Thank you."

"I have a feeling the islanders won't be needing my translation services for much longer, though, thanks to you."

Zephyr dips his head and Destiny mentally begs her nervous system not to prompt the blood vessels in her face to expand and send color rushing to her cheeks. She's firmly come to believe that the blushing curse of the redhead is far, far worse than the curse of being a seer.

Dominus smothers a smirk as he looks between Zephyr and Destiny, adding that he'll see her later as well.

As Destiny follows Bramble, the sound of yowling and hissing, meowing and mewling, grows ever louder. She smiles, quickening her step, eager to see how much everyone has progressed since her last visit.

Upon entering the great hall, the uninitiated might be forgiven for mistaking all the carefully coordinated activity for absolute chaos. Dozens of people are scattered about the room, sprawled out in chairs, crawling under tables, perched on tabletops or window ledges, or craning their necks to listen to what the various button devices are saying.

Interspersed between all the humans are cats of every color, breed, and size. Some are fast asleep, completely disinterested in all the busyness, while others are fully engaged with their humans.

Destiny spots Evangeline, who's standing just inside the entranceway, kneading the small of her back with one hand. "Eva!" she hollers.

Eva turns, beaming a megawatt smile. "Please, please don't tell me I look ready to pop," she pleads, laughing. "If one more person tells me that..." She tries bending to pick up Bramble, but her pregnant belly makes it difficult.

She doesn't need to worry, though. Gabe is at her side in an instant, scooping Bramble into his arms before handing him to her. Eva's lovely husband has the dazed air of a man who's won the lottery every single day over the past year and who still can't believe that he continues to pick all the winning numbers.

"I look like a beach ball, don't I?" Eva says, laughing.

"You look radiant," Destiny replies, and she means it.

Eva may as well be orbited by a personal sun whose sole function is to shine light and warmth onto her. Destiny didn't think she'd see Eva happier than she was on her wedding day, but in hindsight she realizes that Eva's joy had an ephemeral quality to it that day, as though she was trying to wring every drop of pleasure from each precious second because she didn't quite trust that it would last.

This new happiness is more permanent; she wears her contentment like a favorite cozy sweater that can be relied upon to keep her warm through many more winters to come.

As it's turned out, Destiny and Eva aren't related by blood— they're not the half sisters that Destiny was hoping for—but that little technicality hasn't mattered.

Let's choose each other is what Eva so earnestly proclaimed before Destiny left the island for the first time, a week after they'd vanquished Madigan. *Family is messy and random and painful, especially since you come into it without any actual say in the matter. So, to hell with that. Let's make that choice for ourselves!*

And Destiny has learned that once Eva chooses you, you will forever remain chosen. While Darius has been in and out of rehab facilities over the past year, struggling with the demons he's inherited from his father, Eva's support for him has not wavered. Nor did she stay angry with Hexabus for long about keeping her relationship with Killian a secret for so many years. Not to mention that ever since her youngest brother came back from the dead, a Lazarus in cat form, Eva's been putting in months of work to connect with him in every conceivable way, trying everything to rekindle their childhood relationship.

What Destiny often thinks about is the scratches she spotted ingrained in Lumina Le Roux's bedpost when she and Hexabus were searching the historian's quarters for clues. And of the truths those claw marks revealed about Madigan. As an orphaned boy raised in an institution, he must have yearned for an alternate reality in which his mother got to tuck him in, reading him a bedtime story.

It breaks Destiny's heart thinking of how the little boy in the adult Madigan would wait for Lumina to fall asleep before he clambered up the side of her bed, in his raccoon form, to snuggle next to her each night.

And how the seed of abandonment that was planted in him all those years ago grew into a strapping tree that dripped with poisoned fruit. She's learned that how we nurture our wounds will determine what they will either blossom or fester into.

"What did we miss?" Hexabus asks as she arrives alongside Destiny's father. "How's my grandbaby?" Hexabus rushes to place her hands on Eva's belly.

As she and Eva discuss the baby's due date and how likely it is to arrive early, Killian comes to stand next to Destiny. Though they embraced less than an hour ago at the inn, he unselfconsciously wraps his arm around her shoulders and pulls her close so he can plant a kiss on her temple.

Destiny, just like her mother, does not activate Killian's powers. Her father does not need amulets or magic to receive Destiny's affection. And she is learning to lower her defenses so she can accept his.

Not all fortresses are curses we are born with; some are self-built, like the moat that surrounds the castle. Sometimes you need to lower the drawbridge and let others in, even when you're already anticipating the hurt you will experience when they will no longer be in your life. Especially then.

At least, this is what Dr. Shepherd reminds Destiny regularly. "Just because loss is what life has always dealt you doesn't mean it's the only lesson it has to teach you. You of all people should know our enormous capacity to learn and grow, to expand the horizons of everything we ever thought we knew."

Destiny's smart, but Dr. Shepherd is wise. Destiny hopes to achieve that same distinction one day.

She and her father chat for a few minutes about the Grimshaw Inn and Tavern's grand reopening, how many guests they're expecting, and how much Killian is looking forward to the new challenge. While he loathed serving a despot, he enjoyed being needed by the castle's extensive staff. The service industry suits his generous temperament.

A shout interrupts their conversation, and they both spin

around to seek its source. Ian and Jill Montgomery sit on the floor in the corner with their daughter, Dawn, the beautiful black cat Destiny met at the cemetery. As they all watch, Dawn reaches out a paw to swat first one talking button. And then another and another.

The devices squawk words in response that make her parents' faces light up with wonder.

"She did it," Jill Montgomery cries out. "Oh my god. She just spoke to us!"

Evangeline rushes over to join the family and hear what her childhood friend has finally said. The room erupts into applause, everyone celebrating this incredible breakthrough, for they all know how hard the Montgomerys have worked, how much frustration they've had to endure, to achieve this milestone.

Destiny joins the chorus, clapping until her palms sting. Turning to Killian, she's surprised to see tears wending down his cheeks.

"*You* did that," he says, beaming at Destiny. "You made it possible."

She knows they're thinking the same thing: what a devastating blow it was when, after five months of frantically searching for the spellwork to restore the cats to human form, they realized it might not be possible. While Killian's protective spells allowed each of the cats' bodies to accommodate two souls, the host cat's *and* the murder victim's, the human spirits had no physical bodies to return to. They had all been buried or cremated decades ago, and only the darkest and most unnatural magic could resurrect them.

But as long as the cats continued to be gracious hosts, allowing their uninvited guests to live rent-free in their feline bodies, that wasn't the problem. The real issue was bridging the gap between the human souls and their living family members to enable some kind of meaningful connection.

In the beginning, all of that communication fell to Dominus. And then to Zephyr, a sorcerer Dominus hired as his assistant because Zephyr had the exact same gift with animals, allowing him to act as the translator between the two species.

But this wasn't an efficient process. There were just too many cats and too many missing decades, all stacked up against each other. The burden weighed far too heavily on Zephyr, leading to near burnout.

So when magic let them down, Destiny turned to science.

Diving into research, Destiny discovered the work of a speech-language pathologist named Christina Hunger, who was combining modeling behavior with operant conditioning, using speech buttons to communicate with her dog, Stella. The pathologist programmed the buttons to speak in her voice when Stella pressed them with her paw. When the individual talking buttons were combined, an entire storyboard could be created, allowing Stella to communicate her needs and, even, her feelings.

As Destiny quickly discovered, the same training could be applied to cats, especially ones whose bodies so generously hosted human spirits. The victims who died as adults took to the speech buttons faster. But those, like Dawn, who died as children struggled to adjust. There were even a handful who refused to participate at all, feeling so betrayed by humans that they chose to remain feral, never setting foot within the castle grounds.

To the Scruffmores' relief, Bramble mastered the buttons quickly, having as much of an aptitude for them as he'd once had for magic.

He's content, though, to remain in feline form if they don't discover the magic that will transform him back into a human. Bramble has lived so long as a cat that he now identifies as feline. While he loves being back in the heart of his human family, he'll never turn away from the community that accepted him as their own, protecting him all this while even when his humans couldn't.

And he isn't the only one who feels this way, which alleviates some of Killian's guilt for the part he played in what he views as their eternal imprisonment.

The plan is for Destiny, along with the help of Lumina Le Roux, to continue scouring the vaults for the spellcasting that might grant the cats a choice in how they live. In the meantime, they have the speech buttons, and they have Zephyr as their translator. Which means, at least, that they have hope.

As the Montgomerys nuzzle Dawn, who purrs loudly, Eva joins Destiny, Hexabus, and Killian. They huddle together, not needing words to express the many thoughts and feelings that thrum between. It's been this way ever since they discovered that Madigan used the four of them as superconductors to kill the Sorcerer King.

But Mordecai's death wasn't the only consequence of Madigan's plan. Just as Destiny's keyhole birthmark made her the medallion's epicenter and connector, she has now been slotted firmly into the heart of the unit, no longer a lone puzzle piece, but an integral part of a greater whole.

Without ever meaning to, by making them unwitting weapons, Madigan has also made them a family, an unintended result he could never have foreseen. What Madigan wanted to inherit was power, but what he inherited instead was trauma.

Destiny inherited trauma too. But with the help of Dr. Shepherd and her new family, she's realized it doesn't have to define her. Something in Destiny broke after what happened to Liz, but that's not what caused the prophetic dreams, despite what Nate believed. Instead, Destiny now knows she was born with the seer's gift already there in her DNA long before life took a baseball bat to her childhood.

It reminds her of the ceramic bowl she once bought, its broken shards joined by gold lacquer through the Japanese art of kintsugi. She is that bowl, rarer and more beautiful, but also stronger, *because* of her broken pieces and how hard she's worked to make herself whole once more.

CHAPTER 95

Destiny

The Next Day

When Destiny slips out of the inn before the sun has announced its intention to rise, she has the amulet clasped around her neck and the emotional-support urn tucked into the crook of her arm. Bramble, only now returning from his nocturnal escapades, rubs against her leg, his tail bent into a question mark.

"Thanks for the offer," Destiny says, reaching down to stroke his damp fur, "but this is something I need to do alone."

Bramble mewls his understanding.

As Destiny heads down the winding cobblestoned footpath, the chilly air puckers the bare flesh of her arms. The island is still shrouded in mist, as though hundreds of white sheets have been hung out to dry on laundry lines throughout the village.

Besides the crashing of the surf, and the muffled thunk of her footfalls echoing between the damp walls, the air is hushed.

This is where Bex would usually have jumped in to fill the silence, but Bex has been quiet ever since Destiny severed their connection over a year ago. Despite Destiny's opening it up again a month afterward so she could talk to her friend about setting her free, Bex has remained obstinately silent. Destiny can feel her hovering nearby, though, an opinionated ghost keeping her own counsel.

Once Destiny's freed herself of the alleyways, the ocean reveals itself in the manner of a party guest jumping out from behind a couch to yell "Surprise!" The horizon buckles into an orange hill as the sun begins to raise its head. Seagulls and crabs, never ones to slack off when there's work to be done, are already foraging the quicksilver sand for whatever gifts the waves saw fit to bestow overnight.

Destiny heads for a smoldering fire next to a gleaming hunk of driftwood, nature's elaborately carved artwork. Sitting on it, she's annoyed to see a few beer cans scattered about when a garbage can isn't more then ten steps away. As she returns from discarding them, she snatches a cigarette butt away from the seagull about to grab it, apologizing when he squawks his displeasure.

Why can't tourists leave only their footprints behind like the birds and animals do? Why must there always be this detritus in their wake?

Shrugging off her irritation, Destiny wipes the condensation from the urn before setting it down. It glows in pinks and purples, reflecting the breaking dawn, lending it an otherworldly quality.

"Bex?" Destiny asks, sensing she's nearby though not certain she'll get an answer.

"Dezzie," Bex replies teasingly, making Destiny flush. "Looking a bit pink there, aren't we?"

"Oh, shut up," Destiny grumbles, trying not to laugh.

Bex sits next to her on the driftwood, her chestnut hair billowing like a sail struggling to catch the breeze.

Destiny's gathering the words to tell her friend how much she's missed her when Bex breaks the silence. "I know you're about to say goodbye, but here's the thing—you're absolutely going to suck at it because you've never said one before."

Destiny realizes Bex is right. Destiny never even said goodbye to Annie, who insisted, after her cancer diagnosis, that she was fine and that Destiny not miss any classes to come see her. She said there would be plenty of time for that later, but there wasn't. By the time a frantic Nate called and Destiny was on her way, it was already too late.

"So, I'm going to make this easy for you," Bex continues. "You're going to open that urn and sprinkle Nate's ashes, forgiving him what he said, because he didn't mean a word of it. He was just freaked out and scared, regretting the words almost as soon as he'd spoken them."

Destiny nods, finally believing the truth of this at her very core. It's like she's been walking around with a fishhook embedded in her heel for the last two years, and now Bex has gently extracted it.

After removing her shoes and socks, Destiny stands and rolls her jeans to her knees. She picks up the urn and unscrews its lid, gazing ambivalently at the water.

"We'll do it together," Bex says simply, leading the way, though she leaves no prints on the wet sand.

Destiny wades into the surf, feeling fully grounded even as the retreating water snatches greedily at the sand beneath her feet. She reaches into the urn and withdraws a fistful of ashes. In movies, people fling them majestically into the air, but there's enough wind that Destiny doesn't consider this advisable.

As she sprinkles them gingerly into each incoming wave, she thinks of Nate. Not of that last day, but of all the days that came before.

The ones in which Nate stepped up and showed up, a young man barely out of childhood who suddenly found himself counseling and cajoling, nurturing and bolstering a teenage girl so emotionally wrecked that it became a full-time job.

She's been so hurt by that one thing he said in a moment of utter panic that she's allowed herself to forget the Nate who lies buried beneath the rubble, a fallout of Destiny's sense of betrayal. The true Nate, her real brother, is the one who gave up his dreams so that she could pursue hers, the man who loved Destiny's best friend so much that not being able to put her back together almost broke him.

The one who, with his very last breaths, called Destiny to speak words of apology and love.

As the waves collect Nate, gently gathering him up into their folds, Destiny finally answers her brother's last voicemail, whispering her own apologies and appreciation that in a life full of darkness, the universe gifted him as her lamp to guide the way.

She's not sure how much time passes, but finally, there are no more ashes left to scatter.

When Destiny turns to Bex, her best friend smiles sadly. "We're not doing a protracted goodbye," she says, nodding at Destiny's face. "You're already covered in more snot than a two-year-old being dragged away empty-handed from an ice cream truck."

Destiny snorts, just as Bex knew she would. Then she feels it, her best friend's love like a shot of adrenaline injected directly into her heart, Bex's goodbye.

Destiny waves, but there's no one to wave to. Bex is gone. She feels terribly sad but not bereft. This is a weight she can carry.

Once she makes her way back to the beach, Destiny sets the urn down and sits with her back against the driftwood, warmed by the rising sun and the last embers of the fire. Reaching up, she clutches her amulet, preparing herself.

Hexabus has been teaching Destiny how to control her seer's gift, instructing her to spend time each day trying to tap into it instead of letting the dreams lie in wait, ready to pounce when Destiny is feeling particularly exhausted or run-down.

She closes her eyes, shutting out the world, which is slowly waking around her. Destiny pictures herself cupping ice blocks in her palms, allowing the sensation of numbness to seep through her entire body until she feels nothing at all. Her mind is a blank canvas, inviting a vision, rather than a helpless victim unprepared for an attack.

Shadows begin to form and gather, rising from the canvas to walk around, colors blossoming from their depths. A vision begins to reveal itself.

CHAPTER 96

Choose Your Own Conundrum

A. If you're drawn to Eerie Island by the blue skies and gorgeous sunsets, on a pilgrimage to find inner peace, turn to page 452 for your ending.

B. If you're drawn to Eerie Island by the thunderstorms and mist, on a quest to discover a realm of magic and adventure, turn to page 454 for your ending.

OPTION A:
YOU'RE DRAWN TO EERIE ISLAND BY THE BLUE SKIES AND GORGEOUS SUNSETS, ON A PILGRIMAGE TO FIND INNER PEACE

The first thing Destiny sees in the vision is an enormous pile of leather-bound books stacked nearby. And then Zephyr's face comes into focus, his brow furrowed in concentration as he studies a blank piece of parchment laid out before him.

The image blurs and then shifts, Dawn Montgomery slinking along the table between them like a shadow that's been brought to life. She reaches out a paw and swats at a bottle filled with what looks like mercury, tipping it over so that the silvery ink begins to run like a river toward the estuary of the parchment.

The vision is punctuated by a scream and the sound of glass shattering.

"No," Destiny says, shaking her head firmly. "No."

After a moment, the horrifying sounds die down. Destiny waits for her wildly pounding heart to find its natural rhythm before she can return to the vision.

It takes a few seconds and then…

Silvery paw prints track over the parchment, from which hidden words rise to the surface like bubbles.

And there it is, the spell they've been desperately searching for.

Zephyr whoops and draws Destiny into his arms. When they pull apart, his violet eyes glow with something Destiny can't interpret. Longing, perhaps. As he dips his head, brushing his lips against Destiny's, Dawn hops down from the table to give them a moment of privacy.

This, Destiny's very first kiss, is a revelation. Judging by the tingling sensation that spreads throughout her entire body, either she's just unlocked all the mysteries of the universe, or she might be falling in love.

She isn't sure which, exactly. But for the first time in her life, she doesn't mind not having all the answers.

The End.

OPTION B: YOU'RE DRAWN TO EERIE ISLAND BY THE THUNDERSTORMS AND MIST, ON A QUEST TO DISCOVER A REALM OF MAGIC AND ADVENTURE

In Destiny's vision, she's looking across the dining room table at Hexabus, Killian, Eva, Gabe, Dominus, and Zephyr. Bramble is curled up in a seat between his mother and Eva, hind leg extended as he meticulously grooms himself.

Judging by what Destiny's wearing, this must be taking place at the dinner they're planning at the castle tonight.

They're laughing at something Zephyr has just said when suddenly the air turns thick as mud, static making it hard to breathe. The flames crackle in their sconces, molecules of air exploding all around them.

This time Destiny knows exactly what it means. The castle is warning them.

The image writhes and morphs, jumping beyond the confines of the dining room as Destiny experiences a vision within the vision.

What she sees is lightning flashing, casting a spotlight on Minx as she marches up the island's steep main roads. Her magenta hair glows like a flame in the darkness, a maniacal gleam in her eyes. She's not alone. Behind her are Angel and Newton, and trailing them are a few dozen villagers.

Destiny realizes the truth with a jolt of alarm.

Many of the newcomers were never really transplants to the island, ones attracted by all the opportunity. What's been happening this past year, right under their very noses, is that Minx has been assembling an army that's patiently been waiting for her escape from prison.

And now here they are, about to storm the castle so Minx can challenge Dominus for the throne.

After Destiny informs the family of the group's advance, Dominus stands first, followed swiftly by Hexabus and Killian. Gabe scoops up Bramble in one arm while wrapping the other protectively around Eva. Zephyr reaches out and takes Destiny's hand as they both rise.

Everyone Destiny loves is in this room. All of her new friends, both human and feline, are on this island, their safety now threatened by Minx's arrival. There was a time, not too long ago, when Destiny was prepared to give up on herself without a fight. But that was before everyone here brought her back from the precipice.

And she'll be damned if she'll allow Minx to take this, her new life, away from her.

"Ready?" Dominus asks, his expression grave as he prepares to issue instructions for the battle.

Destiny is the first to respond as she squeezes Zephyr's hand. "Ready!"

The End.

ANSWERS

PUZZLE ONE
The Hidden Message

The ticket numbers in the postscript provide the key to unlocking the hidden message contained in the letter. *L* stands for "line number" and *W* stands for "word number."

The hidden message in Destiny's letter of invitation

Dearest Ms. Whip,

I hereby acknowledge receipt of your application to replace Ms. Le Roux as the Scruffmore family historian. I'm sure you know how coveted the position is—it's no secret that ours is a most illustrious and mysterious lineage—and so I congratulate you on your compelling application and for making the short list of two approved applicants.

Our family history has been a rather fascinating one with most of the information required to unlocking it hidden within the Scruffmore vault, safe from prying eyes. Were you to be successful, you would be one of the rare outsiders granted access to those thousands of records that have come from all over the world, wherever a Scruffmore has lived in the past two thousand years.

Come via the last ferry on the 27th of February and then make your way to the Grimshaw Inn and Tavern for the night. Tell them arrangements have been made and all expenses will be taken care of. Be at the castle on the morning of the 28th ahead of your interview at 12 p.m. Should you be awarded the position, the secrets of the vault will be yours to be revealed.

Until then,

Mordecai Scruffmore

Scruffmore Castle
Eerie Island

P.S. Your ferry tickets have been purchased. The ticket number for the 27th is L2-3-3-4-5-7-7-8-8-9-12-12-14-14-16-13-4-7 and that of the return is W1-7-10-2-4-2-4-5-11-2-1-11-2-4-5-9-8-1-9.

I know the secret your family has hidden from you. Come and all will be revealed. Tell no one.

PUZZLE TWO

Mordecai's Calculation

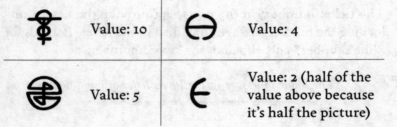

☿ Value: 10   ⊖ Value: 4

⊕ Value: 5   ∈ Value: 2 (half of the value above because it's half the picture)

PEMDAS/BODMAS Calculation:

$$☿ + ☿ + ☿ = 30$$

10 + 10 + 10 = 30

$$⊕ + ⊕ × ☿ = 55$$

5 + (5 x 10) = 55

$$☿^{⊖} ÷ ☿ = 1000$$

10 (to the power of 4) is: 10 x 10 x 10 x 10 = 10,000
Then:
10,000/10 = 1,000

☿ × Ɛ + 🪙🪙 ÷ 🪙 = ?
🪙🪙

(10 x 2) + [(5 x 4)/5] = ?
20 + 20/5 = ?
20 + 4 = 24

PUZZLE THREE

Word Scramble Answer

Bramble's
death
wasn't
your
fault
Check
his
grave

Bramble's death wasn't your fault. Check his grave.

PUZZLE FOUR

Glyphs Answer

Sounding the glyphs out aloud gives you the answer:

Thuh—The
Kee—key
Too—to
Ee + Ter + Nil—eternal
Lyf—life
Lie + Zzz—lies
At—at
Thuh—the
End—end
Ov—of
Thuh—the
Ban + Shee + Zzz—banshee's
Ssk + Reem—scream

The key to eternal life lies at the end of the banshee's scream.

PUZZLE FIVE

The First Rule of Crossword Club Answer

The first rule of crossword club is:
You do not talk about crossword club.

PUZZLE FIVE POINT ONE

The Anagram Answer

To unlock an important bonus scene, email DestinyWhipClue@
gmail.com either of these seven-letter word possibilities that can
be made up from the word *crossword*:

Sorrows
Sordors

Remember to use the word in the subject line.

PUZZLE SIX

Riddle Answer

It's the question to ask for the reason—Why
And it's the pronoun that means me and you—we
Plus your payment to stay for a season—rent (we + rent
= weren't)
And the possessive first name of McGoo—Madigan's

Items you choose from your closet each day—clothes
What you are when you are not dry instead—wet
The word for similar to, in a way—like
And two words: what should grow on a man's head—
his hair

Why weren't Madigan's clothes wet like his hair?

PUZZLE SEVEN

The Five-Digit Code

The clue here was in "Time is of the essence."
Each symbol indicates the time on a clock showing the
hour and minute hands.

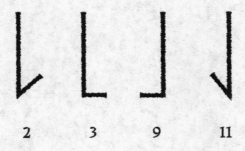

2   3   9   11

PUZZLE SEVEN POINT ONE

Adding Up the Five-Digit Code

2 + 3 + 9 + 11 = 25

Email DestinyWhipClue@gmail.com using 25 as the subject line to get a bonus scene that will give you additional clues to solve the mystery.

PUZZLE EIGHT

How to Open the Lock

Clue 1: 804—One digit is correct and in the correct place.

Clue 2: 836—The 8 is in the same place, so it can't be a number in the combination, which leaves the 3 and 6.

Clue 3: 428—The 8 is already eliminated, so the 4 and 2 *are* in the combination, but they're in in different places.

Clue 4: 950—9, 5, and 0 can all be eliminated.

Clue 5: 502—One digit is correct, but in the incorrect place, so 2 must be in the first position.

Also, in the first clue, one number is in the correct place, and we have learned that 8 and 0 are not part of the combination, so 4 is in the third spot.

From the second clue, we learned that one number is correct but in the wrong spot.

We only have the middle spot left, so it must be 6.

Answer: 264

PUZZLE EIGHT POINT ONE

Emailing Destiny for Bonus Content

Email DestinyWhipClue@gmail.com using the subject line 264 to get access to bonus information that will help you solve the mystery.

PUZZLE NINE

Who Should Destiny Be Focusing On?

Draw up a table with the following headings for the rows:
- Angel
- Minx
- Evangeline
- Newton
- Tempest

Then, for the column names, use all the categories as mentioned in the Einstein's Riddle/Zebra Puzzle:
- Destination
- Item of Clothing
- Carrying
- Late-Night Mission Reason

Using deductive reasoning, assign the known categories to the table to eliminate options.

For example, we know that Evangeline does not have a cell phone, so someone else has the cell phone. We also know that the person carrying a purse is also wearing a cloak. And so on and so forth until you establish, through a process of elimination, who is wearing the slippers.

Who is wearing the slippers?
Tempest

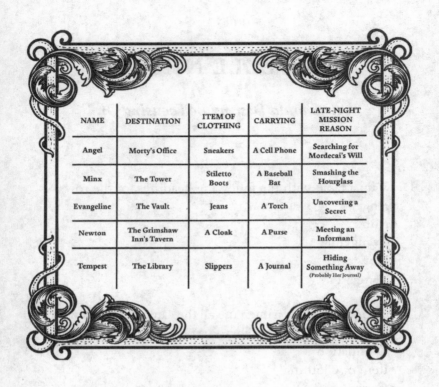

NAME	DESTINATION	ITEM OF CLOTHING	CARRYING	LATE-NIGHT MISSION REASON
Angel	Morty's Office	Sneakers	A Cell Phone	Searching for Mordecai's Will
Minx	The Tower	Stiletto Boots	A Baseball Bat	Smashing the Hourglass
Evangeline	The Vault	Jeans	A Torch	Uncovering a Secret
Newton	The Grimshaw Inn's Tavern	A Cloak	A Purse	Meeting an Informant
Tempest	The Library	Slippers	A Journal	Hiding Something Away (Probably Her Journal)

PUZZLE TEN

What Is Hexabus Hiding?

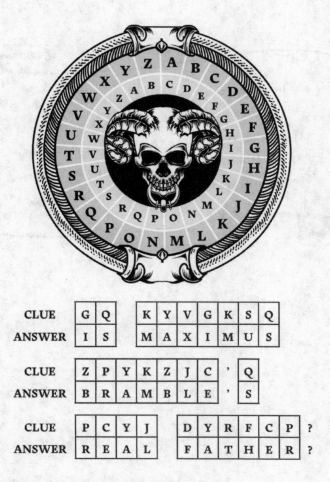

CLUE	G	Q		K	Y	V	G	K	S	Q
ANSWER	I	S		M	A	X	I	M	U	S

CLUE	Z	P	Y	K	Z	J	C	'	Q
ANSWER	B	R	A	M	B	L	E	'	S

CLUE	P	C	Y	J		D	Y	R	F	C	P	?
ANSWER	R	E	A	L		F	A	T	H	E	R	?

Is Maximus Bramble's real father?

PUZZLE ELEVEN

Note Slipped Under the Door

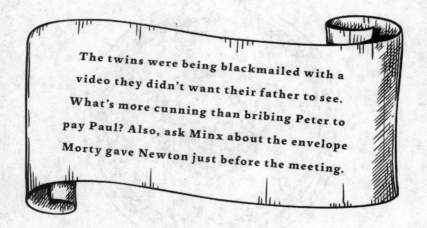

The twins were being blackmailed with a video they didn't want their father to see. What's more cunning than bribing Peter to pay Paul? Also, ask Minx about the envelope Morty gave Newton just before the meeting.

PUZZLE TWELVE

Nonogram

The Answer to Everything Is...

		4 1	2 1 3	2 4	6	2 1 1	4 1	1 2 1	1 2 1	4 1	2 1 1	6	2 4	2 1 3	4 1	
		1 1														
		2 2														
		3 3														
1 1	1 1															
		1 1														
		2 2														
		8														
3 1	1 3															
		6 6														
		3 3														
	2	2 2														
	1	2 1														
		1 1														
		4														

The raccoon

473

PUZZLE THIRTEEN

Mordecai's Adjusted Calculation

 Value: 10

 Value: 4

 Value: 6

 Value: 2 (half of the value above because it's half the picture)

PEMDAS/BODMAS:

 + + = 30

10 + 10 + 10 = 30

 + × = 66

6 + (6 x 10) = 66

 ÷ = 3

6/2 = 3

 × + + = ?

(10 x 2) + 6 + 6 = 32

PUZZLE FOURTEEN

Symbol Word Puzzle

( -T) +

(Star - T) = (Sar) +

( -IN) + A +

(Coffin - in) = (Coff) + A = coffa +

G + (⬜ -B&T) = ⚙

G + (Bust - B&T) = G + (us) = gus
Sar + coffa + gus = Sarcophagus

PUZZLE SIXTEEN

The Real Name of Destiny's Mother

Hemlock

Hearkens

ACKNOWLEDGMENTS

I'm not going to lie; writing this book almost broke my brain! I've always been a pantser (an author who flies by the seat of their pants instead of plotting out a novel), and so writing a closed-room murder mystery when you don't know who's going to die, who's killed them—or why—is extremely difficult. But not impossible, as I discovered, if you have more than just a little help from your friends!

A huge thank-you goes to my long-suffering agent, CeCe Lyra, who continues to roll with the punches and whose eyelid only twitches a tiny bit every time I announce a genre change. CeCe, I know I make your job so much harder than it needs to be, but I couldn't imagine being on this journey without you. I'm in awe of your fiery ass-kickery and all-round fabulousness.

Thanks as well to the incredible Kade Dishmon, who continues to work magic on all my messy first drafts, and to the P.S. Literary team for your ongoing support.

To my editor, Nicole Brebner... It was an absolute honor and a privilege working with such an icon. Thank you for being so wonderfully you! To Evan Yeong... Thank you for leaping into the breach, and for being such an incredibly lovely human being. It's been such a pleasure working with you. Thanks as well to Margaret O'Neill Marbury and the rest of the MIRA team who worked so tirelessly to bring this book baby into the world. I appreciate all the efforts of Alice Tibbets, Ashley MacDonald, Brenann Francis, Tara Scarcello, Bora Tekogul, Emer Flounders, Stephanie Van de Vooren, Kirsten Clawson, and Victoria Hulzinga. It was a particularly difficult book to birth, and there were a lot of labor pains. I'm beyond grateful to each and every one of you for all the time and hard work you've put into it.

Poodle, thank you for lending me that enormous noggin of yours and for spending so many hours helping me create all the puzzles. Thanks as well for mopping my brow and keeping the coffee coming. I couldn't do any of this without you.

Lisa Rivers, thank you so much for your amazing notes and for always making my work so much better. I can't express how grateful I am that we ended up in that U of T SCS class together. Thanks as well to Stephen Want and family for test-driving all the puzzles! Suzy Dugard, thank you for reading an early draft and for cheering me on. Writing friends truly are the best friends!

Brendan Fisher, thanks for doing so many graphics for me and for always being an enthusiastic reader. Thanks as well for allowing me to flex so many creative muscles at the cabin, which is as much of a safe space as you are.

Charmaine Shepherd, thank you for making me well enough that I could finish writing this book without being in a constant brain fog, and for reading every single draft of it. You're my oldest, most faithful reader, and my biggest champion. I love you stukkend, bok.

Special thanks to Margy Stratton, Mike Barefield, Alan Golding, and Lizzy for helping with the Latin translations. Thanks as well to Gus Silber, whose Facebook post first introduced me to Knorozov and Aspid.

As always, an enormous thank-you goes out to the true rock stars of the literary world: the booksellers, librarians, and Bookstagrammers. I can't express how much I appreciate everything you do to get the right books into the right hands and for making my career possible!

Thanks as well to the amazing authors who so generously

took time out of their busy schedules to read and blurb this book. I am enormously indebted to them for their extraordinary literary citizenship.

Thank you to all my marvelous friends and family for bolstering me as I brought this book to life—your support and love make all the difference in the world.

Finally, my biggest thanks go to Wombat and Muggle, who kept me company for so many years as I sat typing away furiously while making shit up. Wombat, you always asked me why there were no cats in any of my books, which is why I decided this would be the cat book to end all cat books. I miss you and Muggle more than words can possibly express. It's not the same without you. I carry you both in my own emotional-support urn.